# WAR GAMES

DIA General Eugene Kuster arrived at the Pentagon's Electronic Situation Room shortly after noon. The first thing he detected was the strong undercurrent of nervous tension.

A Navy lieutenant was on the phone to National Security Council members. Several enlisted personnel huddled around the telex machines waiting for information. Officers of less than field grade gave orders in loud voices, looking for the attention of their superiors. The chatter level was high.

Jack Coriolanus of the CIA was in the corner with the assistant to the chairman of the Joint Chiefs of Staff. He pointed to the large electronic map of Nicaragua on the far wall highlighted a Contra military base near the north border with the designation: 2 fat/16 cas/.5 destr.

It didn't look good.

"Gentlemen," the national security advisor said loudly, and the room was silent, "it's been confirmed. Early this morning, Contra Camp Rogers was attacked by a new Sandinista force of helicopters of Soviet design and manufacture, probably flown by Cuban pilots. Two Americans have been killed. The State Department is now delivering an official note of protest to the Nicaraguan government. The President has issued orders that all area forces be put on twenty-four-hour-alert status until the intent of the enemy attack is known."

Kuster's throat tightened. His information put the reason closer to home. And it was time to blow the whistle before America was pushed into war.

Other books by Hank Bostrom

GABRIEL'S FLIGHT

# PRESSURE POINT

## HANK BOSTROM

**LYNX BOOKS**
New York

PRESSURE POINT

ISBN: 1-55802-086-1

First Printing/December 1988

This book is published by Lynx Books, a division of Lynx Communications, Inc., 41 Madison Avenue, New York, New York, 10010. The name "Lynx" together with the logotype consisting of a stylized head of a lynx is a trademark of Lynx Communications, Inc.

Printed in the United States of America

0 9 8 7 6 5 4 3 2 1

This one is for Jodi and Dave

# PRESSURE POINT

# RECRUITMENT

# ONE

"**Y**ou dumb son of a bitch."

Steve Hamm did not respond. He sat in the leather straight-backed chair and waited for his boss to cool off. As an army colonel and intelligence officer, he had often faced irate generals, even Kuster on occasion. He looked at the surrealistic rendering of the Golden Gate Bridge on the wall behind the desk. It was done in oranges against a peppermint sunset.

"You hear me?"

"I heard you, sir." This would pass.

"I didn't say *stupid*. I said *dumb*. You went way the hell beyond your orders on this one. And you've done it for the last time."

Lieutenant General Eugene Kuster sat tall behind his

oak parquet desk with the scribbled green blotter, his long
face tinged in ire, and his eyes hot. His bass voice echoed
in the closed office, several decibels above the necessary
level. The heavy door to the deputy director's outer office
seemed to tremble.

Hamm waited out the storm. He had worked under Gene
Kuster on and off for sixteen years. Kuster was one of a
few general officers who still knew what the objectives
were and had managed to keep them in perspective. Paper
war-games for power didn't interest him.

"What did you do in Prague?" Kuster demanded.

Hamm had spent eleven days in Prague on his last undercover assignment. He raised his eyebrows in query.
"Prague? I got the Czech dissident file for you. Aren't
you happy with it?"

"Shit, happy! You put a bullet in a Soviet political officer, goddamn it!"

"Nine millimeter," Hamm agreed. "But what the hell,
Gene? He got in the way, but I got the job done."

Hamm's reputation for accomplishing tasks had kept him
active in the Defense Intelligence Agency for a long time,
except for a two-year purgatory in the audit division of the
Inspector General when the chairman of the Joint Chiefs,
Admiral Joseph Dilman, wanted him out of the public eye.
His reputation happened to include a penchant for completing his assignments in ways that did not necessarily
follow his orders to the letter. A tendency he had of crit-
icizing the establishment in a public arena did not help,
either.

"I don't give a good goddamn about the job. One single
bullet has everybody running for cover. The CIA is bitching about exposed networks."

"The CIA? Coriolanus? He's blowing smoke?"

"The Director raised hell at the Pentagon. You've exceeded the authority of your orders for the last time, Steve. I can't risk your fucking up any more political balances." Kuster's volume was not diminishing. Hamm figured people on the next floor down would be gathering in the stairwells.

Hamm let his puzzlement show on his face by raising one eyebrow. "Christ, Gene. The bastard was a tiny, egotistical, sadist in a rotten regime. I probably did more for the Kremlin than I did for us."

"Not with the bright-and-shiny new climate Moscow is bringing in."

Hamm was getting mad now. "You're not falling for that crap?"

Kuster ignored the attempt at diversion. "That's not the goddamn issue. The issue is your twenty years of ignoring orders. That shit stops now."

Hamm shrugged.

"You're big, and you're ugly, but you can't take on every star in the Pentagon, Hamm."

Hamm was a large man at six two and 200 pounds, and he was in good shape, if he did not count the broken bones and the scars. The worst of the scars ran along the underside of his left jaw—the result of a skin-burrowing 7.62-millimeter slug. Most people missed it because they tended to focus on his gunmetal blue eyes. His eyes were a counterpoint to his easy smile. Other than the mementos of battles—both public and private—the rest of his face was just rugged, showing a few lines around the eyes and at the corners of his mouth.

Hamm tried to keep his temper in check. "I guess I'm moving on?"

"Damned right you are. Again." Kuster looked straight

at him, unaware of the doodles he was drawing on the green blotter on his desk. The doodles looked like missiles to Hamm. Army generals doodled missiles. Admirals doodled flattops.

Hamm shrugged again. "I guess you've been talking to Joe Dilman?"

"Dilman's been talking to me. He wasn't interested in a response."

"Back to the Inspector General?" he asked. The job had been a paper hell, chasing overpriced hammers, trying to figure out how the civilians were ripping off Uncle.

"No." The general picked a sheet of paper off the pile in his in-basket and flipped it across the desk. "Second Infantry Division."

"Shit," Hamm said, both his anger and his tone rising by several degrees. "It's cold in Korea."

"Not as cold for you as the Pentagon is at the moment. Goddamn it! Why can't you follow a simple damned order? It's not that difficult."

Hamm read these particular orders, picking his way through the abbreviated militarese. It was not even a command located in Seoul. He was to be adjutant in some damned detached intelligence unit south of Pusan. "You know who the commander is?"

"Roger Ulmann. He just got his first star."

"Jesus Christ! Another case of incompetence being promoted out of the way. And he only likes ass-kissers on his staff. He wants prestige, not intelligence. I can't work for the son of a bitch."

Kuster and Ulmann belonged to the same brotherhood of epaulet insignia, and Kuster was not a back stabber. He would not comment on Ulmann's capabilities. "You'll damned well learn to do as you're told."

"Not for Ulmann, I won't."

The mercury in Kuster's thermometer lowered about a quarter inch. "We've been working together long enough that you know I've backed you where I could. I can't help you this time."

"That means Prague is only the excuse," Hamm said. "Beyond that, it's good old, all-around, shitty politics."

"You want to tell me about Martinson?"

"Martinson? He's an undersecretary at Defense. What about him?"

"He had a long talk with Dilman."

"I'll bet I was the star of the moment," Hamm said.

"Goddamn it! What the hell happened?"

"I got carried away and described his face as brown at one of Milly Tilitson's shindigs. That's from having his head stuck up his ass."

"Jesus Christ, Steve! Those eagles on your shoulders don't give you that right."

"Purely a personal opinion. I wasn't speaking for the military . . . or maybe I was?"

Kuster slapped the flat of his hand against the desktop. "You son of a bitch! You're trying to shrug this off. Try it in Korea."

"Maybe not. I've got twenty-four years in."

"Sure," Kuster said, "it figures. Ask you to act like a damned professional soldier for once, and you decide to slink off."

Hamm stood up abruptly, nearly knocking over the chair. "Fuck that. I'll match my professionalism against any of the goddamned generals and admirals hanging around this town." There were 450 of them.

"And lose," Kuster shouted.

Hamm estimated that at least a quarter of the people in

that particular wing of the building were aware of the shouting match in Kuster's office by now. He did not give a damn about the other people in the building. "I don't lose, General. I'll just go out on top. I'll send you the paperwork. Sir!"

"You know this is what Dilman is hoping for, don't you? Why don't you just do it, and get it over with? A year in Korea isn't going to kill you."

Hamm shook his head. "No. I'm tired of fighting with political assholes like Martinson and bureaucratic assholes like Jack Coriolanus. I'll let them win the battle, if not the war. It's not worth the effort anymore, Gene."

Kuster rose to his feet and came around the big desk. His face was red with his anger. "Take the discipline, damn it, and turn yourself around."

"I took the discipline once before, remember? I didn't like it then, and I don't like it now. Not when I accomplished what I was told to accomplish. What I need is a few years in the sun, away from this town."

Steve Hamm came to attention crisply, saluted Kuster very properly, turned to open the door, and walked out.

So much for a career.

# TWO

Jackson Coriolanus was on the telephone, but when Harry Downs appeared in his doorway, he waved him in and pointed to one of the two black chairs in front of his desk. Downs entered the office in his particular weaving walk, rounded the chair, and flopped into it. He was carrying a file folder with a black band across its front.

Coriolanus considered himself one of the few remaining essences of the Central Intelligence Agency, and his officious nature grated on many of his subordinates like a rusty, dull rasp. He had overcome a Greek heritage and a less-than-average stature in order to succeed quickly in the CIA. After Wild Bill Donovan, naturally, Allen Dulles was one of his idols. Coriolanus had survived the John McCone and Richard Helms administrations, and had come through the purges after Nixon, which was an indication of his perceptive accumulation of friends and influence both inside and outside the Agency. As special assistant to the deputy director of operations, Coriolanus had a fairly free hand beyond the specific assignments provided by the DDO.

Harry Downs was a specific assignment.

On the other end of the line, Colonel Winfield Storch, aide to Admiral Joseph Dilman, was jubilant.

"I'm not sure I caught that, Winnie. Or maybe I can't believe it."

"Hamm resigned his commission. Retired, actually." Storch's elated tone ran counter to any mental picture of the man that Coriolanus could dredge up. He was normally a serious and sober individual, wrapped up in both himself and his paperwork. "He's finished with embarrassing anyone in your service or mine."

"I was right. I can't believe it." Coriolanus had first met Hamm when he was recruited out of an Army aviation company to work for Coriolanus's Special Operations Group in Saigon. Coriolanus did not often reflect on the years behind him until someone mentioned the retirement or death of some person he knew. Retirements seemed to pop up more frequently lately, but it was not a label he would have attached to Hamm. He did not see the man teaching military history in some backwater college: Colonel Steven Hamm, U.S.A. (retired), assistant professor of history. The world Coriolanus knew was deteriorating quickly, and even the people he did not like were dropping out.

"After his latest fuck-up, we reassigned the son of a bitch to Korea. He opted for retirement, instead. Dilman was pretty damned certain he would."

Coriolanus was less elated by the news than Storch was. "Korea wasn't such a hot idea, Winnie."

"Why the hell not? It got rid of him."

"While he was in uniform, like when you stuck him in IG, you had some control over him. This way, you've gone overboard and forced his hand, and now that he's a civilian, you have no control. Shit, Defense, and probably the Agency, too, would have been better off if he'd died an old soldier. I'd expect him to be talking to all those friends he has in the media. Maybe he'll write a book. How do you think you'll be characterized, Winnie?''

Storch was not quite as happy when ·Coriolanus hung up. The CIA special assistant had a penchant for bursting people's balloons. He turned his attention to Downs. ''So, what's up, Harry?''

''Not a hell of a lot. What was that about?''

''You know Steve Hamm?''

''We've shared a drink or two.''

''He retired.''

''No shit? Forced into it, no doubt. What's he going to be doing, you know?''

''Probably running around with his mouth open, bitching about Washington.''

''Maybe he'll become a consultant. They all do. I'm going to miss the headlines he made.''

Coriolanus did not want to talk about headlines, especially the kind Hamm made. ''You said there's not much happening in your arena?''

''No. I talked to Clark this morning, and he figured it's so hot this time of year, the Latinos are thinking more about *siesta* than anything else. Status quo down there, at the moment. Bobby has an uneasy feeling, though, as if something spectacular might be shaping up.''

Bobby Clark was the liaison officer for Central America and reported to Downs, who headed the Western Hemisphere Division in the Directorate of Operations. Since the Iran-Contra foul-up, however, Coriolanus had been charged by the Director of Central Intelligence, through the DDO, with monitoring the whole area, staying sensitive to potential cracks in the Agency's image. ''He can't pin it down?''

"No. Just a feeling. He's going to do some deep digging."

"All right. What else?" Coriolanus leaned forward in his chair, planted his elbows on the desk, and pointed a well-manicured forefinger at Downs's file.

"I'm not sure it's anything, just yet. Maybe just more paperwork. Create another file." Harry Downs did not care for administrative detail. He was, however, quite good at it. Having been recognized in the ranks early, based upon his talents in intrigue, network creation, and production of intelligence, Downs had found himself in a succession of supervisory posts, and finally named to the Western Hemisphere Office without really having targeted the position for himself. In two years in that chair, he had assumed the aura of a bureaucrat—slightly overweight, sometimes overwrought, favoring wrinkled brown suits, the appearance of being harried. Part of that was the result of being forced to protect himself from some of the overkill that had taken place in his sphere of influence in recent years. Downs had been kept in the dark during the Iran-Contra operation, and although that saved his job, it did not keep him from being suspect. He was doing his best to correct that impression since he did not want to join the people in his area who had gotten the ax as soon as the new DCI had taken over.

Coriolanus accepted the folder, opened it, and withdrew a single sheet of paper and a single photograph.

"The photo's from an SR-71 overflight," Downs explained. "What you see is an area about forty miles south of the Cape of Good Hope. That's the South Africa coastline in the top of the shot. The report gives the details."

The picture had been taken on a clear day, and four

oceangoing craft were vividly visible, one of them circled. "Four ships? Tell me about them."

"The one we're interested in is circled in red. She's a Panamanian-registered freighter called the *Southern Merchant*. The registry is a front for a Cuban company."

"So?"

"We didn't pick up on her until she was coming out of the Persian Gulf, but we'll track her for the rest of her voyage, now."

"I still don't get it, Harry. What's this bucket got to do with your desk? Beyond the registry?"

"She's a regular caller in Nicaragua, Jack. Usually, she puts into Laguna de Perlas, after making round-trips to Havana."

Coriolanus rested back in his chair, elbows on the padded arms, and the fingertips of his left hand pressed against those of the right. "Cargoes?" he asked.

"The normal for Havana runs. Small arms, ammo, medical supplies. Maybe a box of cigars for the guys in charge. Our people in crateology have analyzed pictures of the crates, of course, and determined Eastern Bloc origins from the wood and metal fittings. Nothing surprising there."

"So, you think this voyage is out of the norm?"

"That's what I'm guessing. We're backtracking photos, now, to see if we can spot what, and where, she loaded. Maybe Iran." Harry Downs did not look happy at that prospect.

Coriolanus dropped the photograph on his desk. "You're thinking she's carrying heavier weapons?"

"I don't really know. There's nothing visible on deck. But there aren't a hell of a lot of other reasons for this particular ship to be in that part of the world."

"Okay," the special assistant told him, "I'll pass it on to the DDO. Keep me informed."

Downs pushed up out of the deep chair. "I'll do that, Jack."

One of the advantages of Clark's position in the Central Intelligence Agency was his access to most of the Langley computer files. Those files, and the sophisticated gaming programs, proved quite useful in the special operations for which Clark held responsibility.

Bobby Lee Clark ripped the hardcopy from the printer and returned down the long corridor to his office, the reception area of which bore the legend, "Supervisor, Offshore Drilling Operations." In his job, like every other person in every other job in the Sunstream Oil Building, Clark had never been within a mile of a drilling rig; or if he had been, he was not aware of it. Sunstream was a CIA front located on Hialeah Drive in Miami, close to Miami International. It was a place where he could regroup between his many trips to Mexico and Central America where he collected more than the deep tan of his face and the gray beginning to spread through the umber at his temples.

Bobby Clark's hair was cut short, in line with Agency standards for mid-level management. His eyes were pale aqua, appearing bright against the skin of his face. He leaned toward straight-cut suits to enhance the length of his six-foot frame. Active in tennis, golf, and hiking jungle trails, he had not added any flab to a stomach as flat as it had been in Vietnam in the early seventies. He had been present at the fall of Saigon, catching one of the last choppers to rise off the embassy grounds.

Spreading the printout on his desk and easing into the

tweedy cushion of his swivel chair, Bobby picked up the secure phone and tapped out a number.

"H'lo." Soothing baritone.

"Peter, it's Bobby."

"Hello, big guy."

"You want to meet for dinner, or do you have a playmate aboard?"

"How's five o'clock?"

"Usual place, " Clark said and hung up.

Bobby did not reach his apartment much before five. Once inside, he tossed his beige suit jacket on a chair, rummaged in the freezer for four pork chops, shoved them in the microwave, and punched in a defrost cycle.

After mixing himself a screwdriver, Clark picked up his suit coat and went into the bedroom to hang it up. He changed into soft Levi's, a polo shirt, and Reebok running shoes, then hung up his suit pants and dumped the rest into a clothes hamper. Clark was meticulous about maintaining order in his life, though he did not care much about superficial appearances. His apartment was a collection of rented furniture and accessories. If pressed, he could not have remembered the subject of the sofa-sized painting hanging in the living room.

Peter de Veres arrived on time—he was always on time for appointments—and he brought two tall bottles with him. "Chablis or burgundy, Bobby? I wasn't sure of your menu."

"Hell, open both of them. I'm just zapping a couple of pork chops."

De Veres was dressed against the Miami heat in light gray slacks, a pale blue blazer, and an open-throated blue sport shirt that revealed a black mat of chest hair. A perfectionist about his appearance, he devoted a lot of health club time to jogging and working with weights. He was perpetually tan, and his curly black hair was always in place, three careful locks haphazardly falling on his forehead and partially obscuring the ragged four-inch scar that ran diagonally across it.

On paper, he made his living as a consultant to large corporations regarding their business travel efficiency. In reality, he preferred living off his inherited trust fund, consorting with the peers of his fast-moving set, and pursuing creatures with long legs and hourglass figures. His eyes were dark and intense, though lately, a bit of yellow was showing in the whites. Clark kept telling him to slow down before his health went bad on him.

While the pork chops absorbed microwaves, the two men sat out on the lanai in wrought-iron chairs, watched the bikinied girls sunning around the pool thirty yards away, and drank the white wine.

"Have you talked to Sean?" Clark asked.

"Not for a couple of days. He was in New York last time he called."

"After we eat, we'll see if we can't run him down. I've got another possible."

Clark pulled the folded computer printout from his hip pocket and passed it to De Veres, who spent five minutes scanning the biographical data.

"Not bad."

"Not bad, my ass. There's talent there, in addition to the competencies we want. When I ran him against the profile, he matched on sixteen of the twenty points."

"You run the model on him?"

"Uh-huh." The gaming model was a complex computer program on the CIA supercomputers that projected probabilities for mission success based on the data provided in various scenarios. The value of the gaming model was dependent on the value of the detailed variables entered into the program, of course, but Bobby Clark was confident of his ability to cover any contingency. For six months, Clark had continually updated his data base each time he obtained more detailed and more factual information about the various players and run it against the program. "Currently, we're showing a fifty-seven percent chance of success."

"And with him?"

"Jumps to sixty-eight percent."

"Jesus Christ! He can't be that good."

"Part of the jump is the increase from eleven to twelve members of the team and from five to six birds."

"And you know this guy?" De Veres asked.

"I know him."

"And you think he's available?"

"The way I got it, when Downs mentioned it, he was just forced into retirement. He won't be a happy man."

"Which meets the profile on one point."

"Yes," Clark agreed. "Either way, though, with him or without him, we're running short of time. We've got to get under way."

"No shit," De Veres said. "The clock is already running."

Clark laughed. "Ticking down. And we sure as hell don't want the alarm to go off before we've even gotten into bed."

# THREE

The sound of a big V-8 engine groaning on the side of the scrub- and tree-covered hill that sloped up behind his cabin was out of place in the torpid air. Few vehicles besides Hamm's black Trans Am or battered Jeep made the trek.

With the exception of Elena, who came in to clean and occasionally cook a meal for him, no one appeared at the estate whom he did not bring himself. And his invited guests had rarely included men.

On that Tuesday afternoon, the Maryland sun burned healthily, baking Hamm's naked torso evenly. He half dozed, as content as he could be. His sun time interrupted by the distant engine, he levered his frame up from the white beach. Carrying his towel up to the veranda, he tossed it on one of the yellow-cushioned chairs. He pulled on dark blue swim trunks and looked out toward the bay.

A dozen yards off the beach, the *Mariposa* rode at anchor. His twenty-two-foot day cruiser had a metal-flake–gray finish, and it shimmered under the beating sun, awaiting its twilight cruise into Allen's Fresh where he berthed it in the protected harbor.

He pulled open the screen door and went inside where

the thick walls and small windows made the day instantly cooler.

Hamm referred to the two rooms and kitchenette of the cabin, with its rock-and-mortar foundation gripping thirty-eight acres of beach, untamed grass, wildflowers, and rocky slopes as his "estate." It was the only real estate he intended to own after selling the town house in Georgetown. The cabin had existed as a shack until Hamm bought it and devoted a few months' effort to plumbing, electrical, roofing, flooring, and cabinetry work. He enjoyed the labor, and he liked the result. While he had been rebuilding it, he had not thought of it as a retirement home, but he was not dissatisfied with that thought, either.

He padded across his oak floor scattered with Mexican rugs, skirting the big round oak table, to the kitchenette and retrieved an icy Dos Equis from the refrigerator. Popping the cap from the bottle, he carried it out the back door. The shadows of the pine trees fringing the beach were beginning to move away from the trunks, and in a few hours, the breeze off Wicomico Bay would rise, keeping the mosquito population at bay.

Hamm listened to the engine and waited to see what might come down the hill. In the four days since he had handed in his letter of resignation to Kuster, several people whose opinions he respected had called and asked him to reconsider. He wondered if this visitor was someone on a similar mission.

Hamm leaned against the dusty Trans Am and watched as the Chevy Blazer struggled down the two rutted trails, guided by a driver with a pale face under a tan slouch hat. Almost familiar, but then many faces were almost familiar to him.

The truck slid to a stop in the loose gravel behind the

cabin, and the door opened. "Goddamn, Hamm. That is you, isn't it?"

The face was rugged from many years in the sun, and clear bright blue eyes shone through the pilot's squint. He took off the hat and rubbed at the perspiration on his forehead with a thick forearm. The hair was a thinning blond, the mouth a wide line chopped on each end by deep vertical wrinkles. When he emerged from the Blazer and rose to his full six feet, six inches, Hamm knew the wide and muscular shoulders. He grinned. "Sean. I'll be damned!"

Sean McDonough paced across the hard, parched earth to grip his hand in a solid and remembered handshake. "You're a tough mother to find, you know?"

Hamm had not advertised his address. "How did you manage it?"

McDonough tilted his large head to one side, as if listening to the wind. "I still know a few people."

His visitor waved a beefy arm at the terrain. "You like your privacy, I guess?"

"That's right. Hey, come on in." Hamm led the way through the back door, found another bottle of beer, and opened it for McDonough.

The big man tipped the bottle back and drained it with three movements of his prominent Adam's apple. "Damn, that hits the spot. You got hot country here, my friend." He looked around. "And a nice place."

Hamm opened another bottle for him, and they sat at the table. The screen doors at front and back allowed a slight breeze to ventilate the interior. "Open your own from now on, will you? Plenty there." He sipped from his dark bottle and asked, "Been what, almost twenty years? What have you been doing?"

"I got me a little flying service outside Bakersfield.

Couple light-twins and a couple aerial spraying bipes. One JetRanger. All hocked to the hilt.'' McDonough dug a large cigar from his khaki shirt pocket. "Mind?"

"No. Ashtray over there on the counter. You like your private enterprise?"

Leaning back in his chair to retrieve the ceramic ashtray, McDonough said, "Yeah, I do. Damned sight better going after potato bugs and grasshoppers than what we used to go after. The bugs don't shoot back.''

"Seems to agree with you. You're looking fit.''

"You only say that because I'm still bigger than you.'' McDonough ran a hand through his hair. "This is starting to go, though.''

"You married?'' Hamm asked.

"Once upon a time. Didn't mix with airplanes. But I got a boy going to college over at Fresno. Fine kid. How about you?''

"Once. Gave it up." Barbara did not mix well with intelligence work.

"Too bad. Maybe we both had the wrong training?''

"As I remember it,'' Hamm told him, "a lot of our training took place around tables in disreputable night spots.''

"Lot of *bau me bau* went under the bridge. Or into the gutter,'' McDonough agreed. "You remember that night in Nha Trang I saved your ass from the MPs?''

"*You* saved my ass? The way I remember it, I was the one who stole the getaway Jeep.''

"Yeah, but I decked the three cops.''

"And the four sailors.''

McDonough laughed. "Forgot about them. Good times, though.''

"For kids. You grown up, yet?''

"Maybe. Hated it, though."

"So what are you doing on this side of the country? Hustling business?"

"In a way, I guess I am. I've been on the road for ten, eleven days now."

"Big question, Sean. What brought you down here?"

The big man's grin spread wide. "You don't think it was for old time's sake, buddy?"

Hamm shook his head.

"Well, no, I guess not. One thing first, though. I've got to know what you've been doing since we last saw each other."

The first time had been at Ton Son Nhut in 1963, both of them with brand-new second lieutenant's bars, and both assigned as chopper pilots in the 155th Aviation Company. That was before the war got under way in earnest, and that was before Charles Black, stationed at the Saigon Embassy, recruited Hamm to assist in the frustrating and hopeless task of determining just where the Diem administration was going. That was the reason he had been recruited, but later it turned into some special missions.

"Let's see, last time we ran into each other was at Ton Son Nhut again, wasn't it? Sixty-nine?"

"Right. I was on my third tour, flying with the 1st Air Cav." McDonough exhaled a gigantic blue cloud.

"I must have been pulling my third tour, then, too," Hamm said. Or fourth or fifth. It blended together: Burma, Thailand, India, Afghanistan, Germany, Africa, and the Caribbean.

"You still fly?" McDonough asked.

"Anything with wings. I've got an old Cherokee hangared over at Fredericksburg." He missed his former access to the DIA's Lear jets.

"Rotary?"

"I can get them on the ground in ten pieces or less."

McDonough pursed his lips, nodded, then got up to get himself another beer, bringing one for Hamm. For all his mass, and for all the years that had gone by, Hamm noted that his movements were still fluid, controlled. He said, "Back to my question. You been sticking to aviation?"

"Not as a job, no."

"What, then?"

"I signed a statement about that, Sean."

"Spook. I won't push it, but it still works for me. What I heard, Steve, I heard you just retired. What'd you retire at?"

"Bird colonel."

"Decent. I only got to major, but then you stuck it out for a lot longer. Still, the pension keeps me in beer while the flying service goes under. How about you? You happy?"

Hamm turned his palms up. "I've only had a few days to get used to it. Ask me next year."

McDonough stared hard at him a moment, then shook his head affirmatively. "Let me recap it, then, Steve. You're retired from the service, no close ties, still up on your flying, living here, maybe not very well, on your pension. Maybe you're a little pissed at life, at the way some things turned out, like Vietnam. Not rare, though, my friend. Just like a few others I've been talking to lately."

Hamm grinned and did not change the picture McDonough wanted to paint for him. "That's what you've been doing, chasing down old 'Nam vets? You're getting the good ol' boys together? To form a club? To create a political-action committee?"

"Ah, hell no! We've got a little project we want to talk about."

Hamm asked, "Who's 'we'?"

"I think you remember Hank Bellows?"

He remembered Bellows as an Army chief warrant officer, a hell of a mechanical genius who had gone on to rotary-winged school. He nodded. "What's Hank doing now?"

"Teaches aircraft mechanics in L.A. How about Clay Harper and Peachy Keen?"

"Both good men. Clay got me out of some trouble one time." Both of them were helicopter pilots, too. Hamm wondered where this was going.

McDonough dipped his cigar against the ashtray. "You ever meet Bobby Clark?"

"Air Force brat—Daddy was a general. Opinionated. Loud. Brassy voice. That the one?"

McDonough grimaced. "I don't remember all that brass."

"Depends on your perspective," Hamm told him.

"Bet you didn't know he was CIA?"

"He was an Air Force operations planner, I think, when I first met him in Bangkok." And he had become an Agency operative sometime during the Vietnam era, though Hamm had never worked directly with him.

"Well, he's been a spook for years," McDonough confided. "Right now, he heads up some section having to do with Central America. Based in Miami."

"And Bobby's one of your good ol' boys?"

"One of 'em. With you, we got twelve." McDonough paused to drink from his bottle, keeping his eyes trained on Hamm.

"So what's the project?"

"Let me go get something out of the truck. I've got some pieces of paper to show you."

McDonough went out the back door, letting the screen door slam, and Hamm got up to check the weather. Still hot and clear, though the sun was sinking fast now. He decided the *Mariposa* was not threatened by afternoon squalls, and could ride out the night at her current anchorage. From the upright freezer next to the refrigerator he extracted two two-inch-thick sirloins, stripping off the white freezer paper and setting them on the counter to thaw.

The screen door slammed again, and McDonough came in to bend over and examine the steaks. "Damn, those're the best-looking pieces of meat I've seen in a long time."

"As I recall, Sean, there wasn't an officers' mess in Southeast Asia that you hadn't cleaned out. One going to be enough?"

"One of those will do the job nicely. I do like your Maryland hospitality."

Hamm wrapped two large potatoes in foil, set the oven, and shoved them in. "It's going to get hot in here. We'll go out on the veranda."

Outside on the veranda, Hamm wheeled his gas barbecue grill to the corner of the deck and checked the weight of the propane bottle by shaking it. "With luck, Sean, there'll be enough gas left to do the job."

"Won't take much. I go for rare."

With two new, iced bottles of Dos Equis, they took chairs with their backs to the bay and the descending sun. McDonough laid a manila envelope on the glass-topped table between their chairs and took his shirt off. A mild zephyr carried the fragrance of pine from the copse of shrubs to the south of the porch.

"Jesus. This's a hell of a lot better than running a flying service."

"Tell me why I'd want to leave it," Hamm said. He was already formulating a plan of action for checking out McDonough, Clark, Bellows, Keen, and Harper. McDonough had been the epitome of reliability in Saigon, but then, twenty years had gone by. If Clark was still an active Company agent—one Hamm had never taken too seriously, he would want to know more about his reputation and connections. And he had lost track of the others a long time before.

"There's a scenario for that, Steve, but I can't go into it until we've talked for a little while longer."

"Until you've got a commitment, you mean."

"Let's call it a half-assed commitment. One that says you'll keep your mouth shut if you don't want to play in our yard."

Hamm smiled at that. "How many tactical operations you think I've given away in my career?"

"I don't read the Washington papers, buddy, but Bobby tells me you've made a few headlines from time to time."

"Purely on the philosophical end," Hamm told him. "Give me a general idea of your project."

"It's kind of a PR thing."

"Public relations? Doesn't strike me as being your field, Sean. Or mine."

"There's a little action involved."

"How little?" Hamm asked.

"Have to deal with that later. There's a nice paycheck involved, though. No withholding and no Social Security."

"Clark's still CIA, right? The Agency backing this?"

"Privately funded," McDonough assured him.

"It seems like I've heard that line somewhere before. A congressional hearing maybe?"

"This is covered, Steve. Well covered." The pilot watched for his reaction, then added, "No shit."

"How is it covered?"

"If you're interested, you'll find out. You get a briefing."

"What kind of money we talking?"

"Your pension a little thin?" McDonough asked.

"I'll get by all right. But, hell, I could always use a newer airplane."

"Would a quarter million do it?"

Hamm sat up straight. "Shit. What's the catch?"

"You hear me say there wasn't some risk attached to this?" McDonough asked. "The way it's planned, the risk could be a little higher than usual. The money end does two things: It rewards the risk, and it gets us guys who wouldn't normally get involved. You understand that?"

"Nobody responding to ads in *Soldier of Fortune*?"

"That's right. No ads, no mercenaries. We want guys that will keep their mouths shut after it's over."

"How long is 'over'?"

"Couple months."

"Tell me about it."

The big man shook his head negatively and handed Hamm the manila envelope.

Peeling the flap open, Hamm saw green and spent a minute counting twenty-one hundred-dollar bills. "It's not even Christmas, Sean."

"That's expense money, if you want to come out to Las Vegas and listen. You decide against it, you keep the cash and keep quiet. Put it on the roulette wheel, whatever.

You go with us, and you get some more of those, deposited anywhere you want them.''

Hamm shoved the bills back in the envelope and laid it on the glass-topped table beside him. "Why you, Sean?"

"I told you I was in debt. I'd like to shed that load. Then, when it comes down to it, Steve, I'd just like to feel good about myself, like I'd done something the politicians couldn't fuck up, for a change. You going to listen to the pitch?"

Hamm tapped the envelope with his forefinger. "Doesn't cost me anything to listen, does it?"

# FOUR

Friday night, Bobby Clark did not sleep well. He got out of bed frequently to drink a glass of water and look down on the neon of the Strip. The revelers were still crisscrossing from one casino to another at three in the morning.

By three, he decided he was less nervous about the presentation than he was about Steve Hamm.

All his analysis indicated that Hamm could be an essential element of the project, but subconsciously Clark was worried. He had not even seen Hamm in three or four years, since the hospital in Frankfurt, just after Hamm had been evacuated from Pakistan. All he remembered was that he had been blunt and uncooperative at his debriefing.

In the last couple of days, Clark had learned something else that bothered him. He prided himself on knowing everything about the people he was involved with, but when Hamm's name had come up, and he had gone into the computer files, he had met a large chunk of brick wall. First of all, his DIA file was secured by an access code used only by people at the director level. That suggested that Hamm performed some rather special operations for the DIA. It also indicated a couple of possibilities that he had never before considered as far as Hamm was concerned: Someone in the hierarchy thought him valuable, and Hamm was probably on that select list of agents utilized for executive actions, for assassinations.

He had not seemed the type. Of those on his list, Patrick Canton was the type. Canton and maybe Pickett. Hamm was the kind who bitched to reporters about bureaucratic foul-ups—a whistle-blower on overpaid people, rather than on overpriced toilets.

Clark had had to build his profile of Hamm from peripheral data, available partially in operations reports, in medical reports, and from the secret list of decorations awarded to operatives—finding that Hamm had twenty-one decorations, most of them of the highest order. There were a couple of Bronze Stars, three Silver Stars, a Distinguished Service Medal, a Distinguished Service Cross, a Distinguished Flying Cross. And multiple Purple Hearts. Surprisingly, there was a Distinguished Intelligence Cross, the highest award issued by the Central Intelligence Agency. Clark did not have one of those, and Hamm was not even Agency. And still, based on skimpy data from the operations reports that were not classified above Clark's access level, Hamm's Success Ratio had come out high.

At 4 A.M., knowing he would not be able to sleep, Clark

dressed in his best geologist-on-assignment uniform of charcoal-vested suit, white silk shirt, and "power red" tie. As far as the world might know, they were attending a convention of the American Management Association in Las Vegas. Peter de Veres actually belonged to the AMA, one of his professional associations as a result of his work as a consultant.

He picked up his black calfskin briefcase, left his room, and descended to the lobby. He headed directly for the coffee shop and found De Veres already planted in a back booth. De Veres wore his customary blazer and gray slacks, and he was tieless. He hated ties, and had probably not worn one since his military days.

"Don't you ever sleep, Peter?"

Looking up from his copy of the *Deseret*, De Veres grinned. "Sit down, Bobby. Who could sleep with an enchanting young thing like Gwen Jackson around?"

"Who's Gwen Jackson?"

"The blond stew on our flight?"

"Oh, yeah. You order yet?"

"Just coffee."

Clark got the attention of a sleepy-eyed waitress, and they both ordered steak and eggs. After eating in silence for a while, De Veres signaled the waitress for more coffee, then said, "Seems to me, Bobby, that your task this weekend is going to be highly charged with persuasion strategies. Do I assume correctly?"

Clark was halfway offended. "It's worked out to the nth degree. I don't expect any resistance at all."

"This is one of the danger points. If one of these guys backs out and yaps in the wrong place, it all goes to hell."

"Nobody will back out. It doesn't fit their profiles."

Peter de Veres curled his lip in a half sneer. "Remember that you're going to be talking to a bunch of guys who've been there. There's a built-in distrust of administrators. And one more thing. Some of the people on that list left military service before retirement. Have we got some bad apples in the basket?''

''I don't think so. From what I could reconstruct of their reasons, they got out because they were fed up with the political situation. The bad taste after Vietnam. That works in our favor.''

''Any of them do mercenary work?''

''Canton, maybe. There's a couple of blank spots in his history, and I'll have to hit him up about those. But the rest are on the list specifically because they *haven't* been identified with mercenary operations. We want a clean roster, so no one can make connections later. Hell, we set our profile qualifications so high, it's a wonder we found ten men to fit them.''

''We managed to make ourselves fit them.'' De Veres grinned, lifting his cup in toast.

''Yeah, maybe. I've never been enticed by quick dollars.''

''If these guys feel the same way, it's all the more reason you're going to have a tough time recruiting them, Bobby.''

''They've never come face-to-face with two hundred fifty thousand quick bucks.'' Realistically, Clark knew he was going to run into some resistance, and he suspected it would come from Hamm. It was instinctual, that feeling, but he thought the son of a bitch would try to ruin the stated objectives. Hamm had a reputation for screwing up his orders. With that feeling, though, had come the necessity for preparation, and Clark had written copious notes to himself, outlining rationales against any objection raised by anyone in the group.

"Speaking of quickies, Bobby, my new friend Gwen has a friend."

"We don't have time for this, Peter."

"Bobby, I think that straitlaced general who happened to be your father got your priorities all screwed up."

Steve Hamm had flown in the night before the "convention," checked into the MGM Grand, had a superb beef Wellington for dinner—he was never afraid to spend his money on classy hotels or food—and lost four hundred dollars of his expense money at a blackjack table.

He had taken the elevator up to his room shortly after midnight, gone directly to bed, and automatically awakened at 5 A.M. He donned shorts, T-shirt, and running shoes, then took the elevator to the Grand's lobby and marched through it, glancing idly at the diehards still in the casino. The hotel's coffeeshops were packed with weekend gamblers reenergizing before heading back to the tables. He did not see anyone with an inordinate interest in his routine, and that made him wonder why he was even looking over his shoulder. Some habits died slow deaths.

Five miles of running along the nearly deserted Strip helped him think. Ollie North's operations might have been misconceived, but North at least had some decent experience on his resumé. While Bobby Clark had a little combat experience from his Air Force and early CIA days, he had been primarily a paper pusher for most of his career. Hamm had known Clark's father when the man was an Air Force brigadier in Bangkok, a rigid and uncompromising dictator. He had always figured that Bobby's career had hinged on trying to emulate the old man, and that was close to impossible. Besides, why would anyone want to try?

After his run, he took hot and cold showers before dressing in blue slacks and a light blue sport shirt, and heading down to the chrome-and-red-leather coffeeshop for breakfast.

Finally, it was time, and he went out to the parking lot, climbed into his rented Buick, and drove down the Strip to the Riviera, another old favorite in his personal inventory of hotels of the world. Among the entertainment names on the marquee was a welcoming word or two for the American Management Association.

The suite was on the ninth floor of the Riviera, and Clark opened the door at his knock. He looked about the same as the last time Hamm had seen him, in Frankfurt, except for a touch of gray at the temples. He wore the good-times tan well, and his aqua eyes were clear.

Hamm grinned, and gave a lot of heart to saying, "Fellow conventioneer! You're looking terrific. Better than last year!"

Clark frowned at him and maintained his serious, bureaucratic demeanor. "Hello, Hamm. Come on in."

It was a spacious suite, with two doors giving off to separate bedrooms, but it was crowded now. Peter de Veres was there, was introduced, and Hamm wondered about his origins. He looked a bit too much of a pretty boy, an aristocrat of idle means, to have the background necessary for a serious covert operation. The scar across his forehead did not seem to be the kind to inspire confidence.

Hamm turned to the giant.

"Made it, huh, big fella?"

"Hello, Sean." Hamm shook hands with McDonough, who was sporting an unlit cigar and his felt-brimmed slouch hat, then surveyed the room. There were six others. "I'll be damned. Peachy. Hank." He knew Keen and Bellows, and their responsive handshakes were warm, their greetings lively and heartfelt. Hamm reciprocated.

"Shit," Keen said, "if I'd known you were coming to this party, Steve, I wouldn't have held out on Sean for so long."

"All of fifteen minutes," McDonough said.

"Hank," Hamm said, "I thought you'd always be freckles and red hair."

Bellows grinned. "The gray was contributed by some of my students. These kids don't know how to think today, especially around aircraft engines."

Hamm was introduced to Jerry Pickett, Hal Cherry, Rick Talbot, and Pat Canton. They were all reserved, perhaps because they didn't know him. The friendships of earlier years were random, and the men with shared pasts tended to stick together.

By nine-fifteen, Harvey Ketchum and Clay Harper had arrived, and they were an even dozen, milling about, re-meeting, or discussing old times. They dipped into the boxes of donuts and splashed coffee from a large urn. This was a party, not a planning session for a clandestine mission.

Harper said, "I never expected to run into you in a place like this, Steve."

"Hell, Clay, I wouldn't be here if you hadn't been there."

"I think we're even on that," Harper said.

"What's this about?" McDonough asked, finally lighting his cigar.

"Steve had a patrol up in the DMZ, and got pinned down by a battalion of NV regulars. . . ."

"I don't think it was that many," Hamm said, "even though it seemed like it at the time. Clay had an unarmed slick in the area, and he popped in to pick us up. Didn't have to do it."

"Yeah, but that's not the half of it," Harper said. "They scrambled aboard with these two prisoners, NVA majors, both of them, and I climbed out of there, trailing fuel from a few holes. Hell, we weren't ten klicks down the road before one of the majors jumps up and gets an armlock around my neck. He was going to put us down before he ended up in some ARVN interrogation cell. I flashed through about twenty-two of my twenty-four years, and we were maybe ten feet off the deck, when Steve rammed a K-Bar to the hilt in the guy's kidney."

McDonough's eyes sprouted instant suspicion. "What the hell were you doing on the ground in the DMZ, Steve? I though you flew all your tours."

"Got drafted for some extra duty," Hamm explained.

"I remember one time, when I was still in the One Fifty-fifth," Keen said, "Davey Conners was my number two, and we were doing an insertion in a hot LZ east of Ban Me Thout. Steve was the first ship in, and I was about four behind. I get my skids on grass, dump the squad, and all hell breaks loose. AK-47s everywhere. Davey took five slugs, but he lived to tell about it—got the slugs on a necklace. Anyway, I've got Plexiglas shattering all over me, and I'm packing a flak jacket around my balls, just in case I live through it, and boom! Here's Loo-ten-hut Hamm damned near plowing ground in front of me, his door gunners chewing ass with those M-60s. I bet they blew up twenty Cong."

The stories went on for a while, and Hamm began to

get bored with the whole thing. There were not a lot of episodes in his history that he wanted to relive.

Clark let them get the old news out of the way first. At a moment when he stood by himself, near the window, Hamm approached him. "Bobby, what have you said about me?"

Clark had a direct, clear gaze. He kept his voice low. "Nothing. Your file's sealed and marked 'Directors' Eyes Only—Top Crypto,' even though you're retired. I'm aware of what that means, and I haven't given anyone much more detail than has been in the newspapers."

"All right." Hamm shrugged, filled a Styrofoam cup, and went back to his group, learning that Keen, who had once been a very capable communications man before going on to rotary-winged flight school at Fort Polk, had left the army as a chief warrant officer after fifteen years to take over a family business that dealt in personal and business radios and telephone systems. Keen had been prematurely bald—one of the reasons for his nickname—and so did not look much different to Hamm. The rosy glow of his skin suggested good meat and whiskey; he must be doing well in the communications business.

Hank Bellows, too, had been a chief warrant, though in aircraft mechanics, before undergoing pilot training in the warrant officer program. He had retired after twenty-five years' service and was currently an instructor in aircraft mechanics for McDonnell Douglas in L.A. He lived in Long Beach. "Where do you get a tan like that, Steve?"

"Laying in the sun, Hank."

"Well, you look damned near like you did twenty years ago. Look at Peachy, though. More forehead than ever." Bellows laughed, slapping the shorter Keen on the shoulder.

Keen's eyes were vibrant and his constant grin good-humored. "You know, of course, Hank, that a smooth pate is the manifestation of extreme intelligence. Keeps the mind from getting too fuzzy."

"Hey, everybody!" Clark called out. "Can we get under way?"

Hamm leaned back against the built-in bar, resting his elbows on the padded edge, and watched as seats were taken on the scattered folding and cushioned chairs. Some instinct suggested that these men had appeared in Las Vegas more as a result of curiosity and as a favor to old friends McDonough or De Veres than as reverence for Bobby Clark.

Or maybe it was the money.

Clark was not as nervous now as he had appeared to be earlier.

"You've all heard very little about what we've been calling my 'project.' What you've heard about is some quick and big dollars, and maybe that's why you're here. Let me make one thing clear: You're also here because I know a hell of a lot about each of you and thought it worthwhile to invite you. One thing I know is that you can be trusted not to mention anything said today to anyone else in the world. Not to a wife, not to a girl friend. If that's not true, take off now and spend your money in the casino."

Clark waited, but no one moved.

"All right, before we get into operational details, are there any general questions?"

No one else seemed to have an immediate query, so Hamm asked, "This going to be a little foray into Nicaragua, Bobby?"

Clark's eyes widened in minor surprise. "What gave you that idea?"

"I know your current position with the Company. I suppose you have some expertise in Central America.'' Hamm had called on some old contacts for information about the names he had gotten from McDonough.

''That's right. Nicaragua.'' Clark scanned the faces watching him. ''Anyone have a problem with that? Anyone sympathize with the communist position?''

There were a few chuckles.

Hamm had another question. ''Sean said it's a public-relations enterprise. In what way?''

''The first goal of the operation is to alter public and congressional opinion in the U.S. in favor of the Contra position in Nicaragua. Get them some military support.''

''Why?'' Peachy Keen asked.

''Because we don't need more Soviet puppets in the hemisphere.''

''And the other goals?'' Hamm asked.

''One other goal: a strong military punch that will hurt the Sandinistas.''

Clark let them brood over that much for a few minutes before asking, ''Anybody disagree with those goals?''

There was a chorus of negatives. Hamm did not say anything, but he did not disagree, either. He had never admired Castro clones.

Hank Bellows went right to the core. ''What's *your* motive, Clark?''

By the flicker of shock that passed across Clark's face, Hamm was certain he had never considered the question. If he were to guess, Hamm would say that Clark had developed the whole thing as a personal exercise in administration, playing with the personnel and the logistics.

''I think I have the same motives as most of you, though perhaps not in the same order. For me, the cash reward is in last place. I'm primarily interested in changing the positions of certain legislators in regard to Contra aid. I'm secondarily interested in inflicting some damage on Nicaraguan Communists and, indirectly, on Soviet egos. And I guess I'd like to prove that politicians can't fight wars as well as trained military men can." He smiled. "The people in this room can do all that."

A few minute nods of agreement.

"Anything else?"

Hamm had a whole bag of questions, and he proposed another one. "Bobby, before we get to anything operational, I want to know about the funding."

"In what way?"

"Americans have learned that it's not impossible to trace the source and the flow of covert cash. Where did it come from, where is it, and how are you accounting for it?" Hamm kept his voice level. He noticed a few of the men raising eyebrows in anticipation of the answer. Hal Cherry's chin rose, and he watched Clark with deadly seriousness.

Clark's face demonstrated his anger in a tiny way; the ends of his mouth dropped a fraction. "You've got to believe me on that end, Steve. It's covered."

"I'm glad to hear that," Hamm said. He pushed off the bar and stood straight. "Tell me how."

"You don't need to know."

"Fuck the old 'need to know' shit. This isn't the goddamned Agency."

Clark held his stare, but Hamm could see the cords tightening in his neck. "It's not government dollars. The entire fund came out of private contributions—Americans with overseas cash. There has not been, and will not be, cash flow through any U.S.-controlled bank."

"How were the contacts with the contributors made?"

''Through Peter.''

''How much?'' Hamm asked.

''Slightly over twenty million dollars.'' Clark tapped his briefcase. ''You want the exact figure, I can give it to you.''

''I'm sure you can,'' Hamm said.

Pat Canton, who had not said much until that point, whistled. ''Twenty million! For one fucking operation?''

Peter de Veres appeared a trifle disdainful. ''Wars are expensive these days, Canton.''

Hamm asked the next of his questions. ''Where's the money located?''

''We spread it. There's a couple of Cayman Island accounts and several in Hong Kong and Singapore. Deposits and withdrawals go through a complicated chain.''

''And how are you accounting for it?'' Hamm continued. ''I don't suppose you're using the back of an envelope.''

Clark shook his head. ''No. I'm using a computer system.''

''Not your home computer?''

''The Agency's.''

''That's keeping it covered,'' Hamm exclaimed.

''Now, listen, goddamn it! I've got the file blocked with six access codes that only I know. No one but me. And it's not only the accounting. Hell, that much is simple. We need the major computer and program resources available through the Agency. That's critical.''

''Why so?'' Hal Cherry asked.

''This whole operation was designed on a gaming model. From personnel to equipment to supply. Shit, you want to win a war, or even a battle, you use the resources available so you can do the best possible job.''

Clark was getting a little rattled, Hamm thought. The light blue-green eyes shifted around the room defensively. ''All right, Bobby. I'll think about that for a while, but I guess I can buy it. I'll listen to how your computer is going to win this one.''

Clark went to the coffee urn and filled his cup, recomposing himself. ''Okay, let me start by showing you why we picked on the present personnel.'' He stopped by his briefcase on the coffee table to pick up a sheaf of paper, then passed out single sheets to everyone.

Hamm looked at his copy, assigning the names to the faces in the room, and guessing that the SR stood for ''Success Ratio.'' He had never played with the DIA's computer programs, preferring to let planners plan while he went out and did the job. On his own list of priorities, computers were one step above paper, and paper was at the bottom of the list.

''In Agency practice,'' Clark continued, ''any person or project with a Success Ratio of point-seven-five or better is considered highly desirable. Rarely do we find ratios exceeding eighty percent. Everyone here, however, has an eighty or better and has a record which suggests that future endeavors, on an individual basis, will meet with favorable ends. When your individual ratios are combined into a team ratio, the chance for success is extremely good. Part of the team result is based on the fact that none of you is a known mercenary, and part of the team result is based on the fact that we will be using state-of-the-art equipment, all brand-new.''

''Where the hell is the team result on this page?'' Harper asked.

"It's not on there, but it came out sixty-eight percent for the entire operation."

"How the fuck do all these eighties and nineties add up to sixty-eight?"

"What you're looking at are just the individual ratings. The gaming model inputs those, but it also considers the weapons systems, the equipment, the difficulty of each of the three missions. It's still hazardous."

Looking around, Hamm suspected each of them was evaluating his particular SR ranking against the others, and he could not help interrupting. "The final team ratio depends, doesn't it, Bobby, on just what other variables are introduced into the scenario? The objective, the timing, the time on-site, the geography, the defensive security—radar, guards, whatever."

"Of course, and I've got that one, too." He passed each man a thin stack of computer paper stapled together. "On the second page are listed the variables Steve mentioned, plus many more. You can see that, in every case, the variable was fed into the program at the low end of its scale, on a worst-case basis. On the first page is the scenario, the sequence of events—step one, step two, step three, right down the line. The third page is a summary of the potential success, given the plan, the variable ratings, and the participation of the twelve of us. The bottom line, gentlemen, is a sixty-eight percent chance of a favorable outcome. Fifty-five percent is considered sufficient in most Defense Department operations."

That was for extremely high priority projects, where the desired end made acceptable much higher risk. Clark did not mention that, Hamm noted.

Hank Bellows looked up from his green-and-white-striped sheets. "This shows three missions?"

"Correct," Clark said. "There are two minor attacks intended to focus media attention on the area and prepare the international community for the big blow."

"It just says 'missions.' What are the targets?" Harper asked.

"They'll be identified later."

Pat Canton, who had been introduced as a free-lance pilot for construction firms, said, "Uh, Peter, you want to explain this Line Fourteen on the third page?"

Clark was immediately aware of the slight. Canton was seeking his information from De Veres, the man he had flown with in Vietnam. Clark ignored the addressee and responded, "I'm responsible for the program and the figures. Line Fourteen is the potential mortality rate."

"That's what I thought it was," Canton said.

"Sixteen percent is not high," Clark told him.

"Not when it's a number," Canton agreed. "When it's people, it means that two of the twelve of us don't come back."

"There's always a risk. The number is there because I'm not hiding anything from you. Is the reward worth the risk to you?"

"Let's hear the reward again," Pickett suggested. He was a sallow-faced, slightly acned man with thinning brown hair. The last two fingers on his left hand were missing.

De Veres replied, "Quarter million dollars. You pick a place offshore for it, and we expect you to launder it as you bring it into the country. We don't want splashy displays of wealth to raise questions. You get a third of it after training and the balance after the operation. Or realistically, your beneficiary possibly gets it."

The big man, Sean McDonough, asked, "How about

borrowing against it? If I'm going to desert my business for a couple of months, I need to pay my bills ahead.''

"We can make some special arrangements," Clark told him. "Come and talk to me after we're done."

Hank Bellows said, "We're going to be here for a couple of days, right? Let's let everyone have a chance to read all the goddamned paper you have here, then come back to the tactical bit later."

Harper was as tall and skinny now as he had been in Vietnam, with fine black hair and shaven cheeks blue-black from his thick whiskers. Hamm remembered him as normally supercautious. "Everybody here is a pilot, so I'm assuming we're supposed to fly these missions. What about the aircraft? Just to give me an idea."

"Choppers," Clark said. "All new, with the latest in weapons and electronics."

"That's the part I like," Peachy Keen interjected.

"We want to humiliate Managua and Moscow," Clark said. "We don't want to blow it by using half-assed, half-shot equipment."

"Cobras?" Canton asked.

"I'll bet they're Sikorsky Eagles," Rick Talbot said.

Hamm was accustomed to the enthusiasm of pilots for new aircraft. He liked a new thrill as well as anyone there.

"Let's follow up on what Hank suggested first," Clark said. "We'll break for lunch and you can read the printouts, and we'll get into the detail later."

They were all dressed casually, but that did not matter in Las Vegas, and they went down to the posh restaurant in four elevator loads. Hamm hung back and managed to get himself and Clark alone on the last car.

He leaned against the wall farthest from him.

"Going like you thought it would?" he asked.

Clark's mouth was a tight, straight line, suggesting buried anger. "You know it's not. I'm about two hours off my agenda."

That was the problem with agendas, Hamm thought. They assumed everybody had the same goals. "Look, Bobby. You and I have a commonality the others don't have. Let's not bullshit each other."

"I'm not trying to bullshit anyone."

"Then your goddamned computer is. These guys flew shit missions in 'Nam. They'll recognize leadership, and they'll follow it. They won't follow some voice speaking for a computer."

Clark went quiet until the elevator doors opened and they stepped out into the hushed excitement of the casino. "I guess we'll find out, won't we?"

"Just a suggestion, Bobby."

Hamm did not know why he was trying to help out Bobby Clark. He did not even like the son of a bitch.

# FIVE

They split up into two groups at lunch. Clark sat with one, De Veres with the other. They had planned it that way, knowing it was important for the leadership to integrate with the team and be available to allay any fears.

From the beginning, Clark had known he would be in

command. De Veres filled the role of executive officer chiefly because it was De Veres who had come to Clark as an emissary of concerned Americans who had a potful of excess cash. And De Veres was handling most of the materiel logistics through his contacts. For the six months of planning that had already taken place, Clark had handled the intelligence end, involving just the right people in just the right Washington positions. Their little exercise had support in extremely influential regions. And now it felt to Clark as if it were all falling apart. Goddamn Hamm and his questions.

Just before they were seated, De Veres had whispered, "If we went back up to the room and voted right now, I think we'd be going into Nicaragua with four holy terrors. Counting ourselves, of course."

"We didn't come here to vote," Clark had told him, then followed the hostess to his table.

Around his table, he had Cherry, Pickett, Bellows, Talbot, and Ketchum. Clark ordered a club sandwich and a bottle of St. Pauli Girl and, after the waitress left them, said, "Go light on the booze. We've still got a lot of ground to cover."

"Bobby, how hard is it to get twenty . . . uh, this kind of funding?" Hal Cherry asked after his drink was served. "I mean, who comes up with it?"

Looking at the people at nearby tables, Clark said, "We really shouldn't discuss business here, Hal. But to answer your question, I don't think I could have done it. Peter knows sympathetic people who have the resources."

"He's from Florida, right? De Veres?" Pickett asked.

"That's right."

"All these rich people his neighbors?"

"No, I don't think so. It comes from all over the nation,

but I don't know the names. I don't want to know them. Tell me, Rick, what do you do? Teaching, isn't it?''

"In Iowa," Talbot said, and the conversation diverted to current events. By the end of the meal, each of them knew more about the others, and Clark thought that was helpful.

When he saw De Veres get up and head for the men's room, Clark excused himself, followed, and pushed through the door into the rest room. Except for the two of them, it was vacant, and he went to the adjoining urinal, unzipping. "We shouldn't have asked Hamm in."

"You're the one that was impressed with his credentials. And hell, Bobby, the points are valid. He's asking the questions the others might not. It's okay. You're handling them all right."

"Maybe I thought he'd be hungrier. Angrier. The way I heard it from Harry Downs, he was forced out of his job."

"You can't blame any of them for being cautious," De Veres said. "I don't want to find myself testifying before some damned congressional committee, either. You know David Conners or Harley Havechuk on that Senate committee?"

"I've met them. Liberal assholes."

"They'd be less interested in our mission than in the headlines it would generate. You won't find me sitting at their witness table," De Veres said.

Clark went back to the immediate. "The only thing they got excited about was the aircraft."

"They're pilots."

"Should I jump right into detail after lunch?"

"Might as well. It might draw some enthusiasm, and I think your computer profiles are right. I'm getting a feel for them now, and none of these guys will blow the caper, even if they don't go along with it.''

"I guess I'll try that," Clark said.

"You see another alternative?"

"Not at the moment."

The group went back up to the room at one-thirty, and Sean McDonough went directly to the phone on the bar, tossing his slouch hat to one side. The receiver disappeared in his huge hand. "Room Service? I want two cases of Heineken sent up to nine-two-four. Cold as you can get it."

If they started drinking, Clark thought, it could only deteriorate from this point on. He hated making decisions under pressure, without time to evaluate all the consequences, but his deadline was coming up soon, and he could not afford to delay, to have another meeting in two or three weeks, before reaching agreement in the group. When he had started the clock on the operation, he had not anticipated reluctance on the part of the recruits, not at a quarter million dollars apiece.

He also hated compromises, though most of his career had been a result of them. He interrupted the several good-natured squabbles that were taking place. "Gentlemen. It's time to take stock."

They leaned back in their chairs, attentive, but somehow, in the same attitude that had prevailed in the morning, not really taking him seriously.

Peachy Keen's short and wiry frame was tilted against the wall, as if he were holding it up. "How long before that beer gets here, Sean?"

"Soon, my friend."

Clark held up his hand and achieved a begrudging silence. "All right. We've got some practical considerations to discuss. Let me see if I'm reading you right. In terms of the general objectives, I think everyone here could find himself in agreement with a mission directed against Nicaragua and Soviet public esteem. And I think everyone, after going through the documentation, feels there is adequate evidence to suggest that the likelihood of a successful mission is high enough to make the effort, given the reward."

Harvey Ketchum was an introspective type, with hooded dark eyes and a shaggy mane of black hair. His teeth were prominent, large and white. He tossed his copy of the model on the table and interrupted: "I don't recall coming to any conclusion like that. I can't even wade through that shit."

"If that's the way you're reading me," Talbot added, "there's something wrong with your eyes, Bobby. I've got a personal war going against computers. What makes your computer better than the one that sends me fucked-up electric bills?"

"You disagree with what I've said?"

Talbot, like Ketchum, had been an Army captain, but now taught engineering courses in a midwestern college. He was a trifle overweight, with a belly that fought a cinched-up, hand-carved Western belt. He, too, suspected the data. "I haven't heard enough, yet. All I've got are these goddamned pieces of paper."

Clark sighed and continued. "I've lived and worked in the real world long enough to know that, especially in a military endeavor, there is always a suspicion of what the planners propose."

"Fucking-A!" Peachy said.

"And yet, every successful operation hinges on a well-conceived and thought-out plan. You want to at least discuss it before turning your thumbs down?''

Sean McDonough, the first one recruited by De Veres, and supportive throughout, spoke up. "Come on, guys. Give it that much."

Peachy Keen scratched his chin. "Okay, Clark. Tell us how easy it is to get killed."

The bellman and the beer arrived before Clark could get under way.

While McDonough passed through the room, handing out icy bottles of beer, Hamm asked, "How deep into the operational details are we going to get, Bobby?"

"Obviously, I don't want to reveal certain specifics until I have a commitment from each of you. No sense in taking chances that there will be a leak before the mission takes place. The actual mission objectives, weaponry, and the like, won't be discussed until we have a group in the training camp."

"What kind of training?" Jerry Pickett asked. While he had the look of a cocky youngster, he had pretty much kept his opinions to himself. He was blond, with a cowlick at the back of his short-cropped hair, and his green eyes held a suggestion of mischief. He had performed CIA operations of some kind in Vietnam, according to the roster sheet, and he was currently running a security business. Hamm wondered if some guard dog had taken off with the two fingers of his left hand.

Hamm was restudying each of the men in the room, making his own evaluations, admittedly more subjective than Clark's computer.

"There will be three phases: training, staging, and mission. I'm hoping to accomplish the training in three weeks, staging in two days, and the mission exercises in three days. The training will take place at a site within CONUS and will emphasize familiarity with the equipment and ordnance. Some of you men are a little rusty with military equipment, naturally, and some of you won't have had experience with the flight, weapons, and electronic systems we've got lined up.''

"How rigid is the timetable?" Hamm asked. "I wouldn't want to jump off before we're ready."

"The timetable is in place," Clark said. "There are . . . other aspects to the operation that are already under way. The crucial date is June seventeenth, when we have to be in the staging area. The only way to extend the training period is to start it earlier."

Hamm checked the calendar readout on his watch. May 12. Not a hell of a lot of time to shape up a new military unit. The roster had a hell of a lot of experience on it, but it was dated.

"What kind of birds?" Harper asked.

"You won't know that until you reach the training site. But you'll be surprised. And I think you'll be pleased."

"How about the area we'll be operating in?" Hamm asked. "You have a rundown on the defenses?"

"The country is peppered with radar, especially along both coasts. The inland borders have a great many blind spots, however, because of the mountainous terrain. Practically all the equipment is of Soviet origin. Some of it is American, though twenty years old, or older. The bulk— and I do have the latest surveillance maps of the radar locations—is of Soviet manufacture that is obsolete by at least one generation of development. They weren't about to move their best equipment in."

"No look-down radar?" Keen asked. He was probably

the most knowledgeable man in the group as far as electronics were concerned.

"They have a couple of aircraft, based in Managua, that are AWACS look-alikes, Soviet hand-me-downs. One has look-down capability, but intelligence indicates it is averaging less than fifteen hours a week of utilization."

"If that's the case," Bellows said, "then we're fairly invisible at about five hundred feet or less, over land." Bellows would not be invisible anywhere. He was six three, with orangey hair going gray, and a long face made longer by a sagging jaw. Ill-fitted dentures kept him working his mouth.

"That's what I've figured," Clark told him.

"What about Managua's communications with Moscow?" Hamm asked. "Are they going to have access to spy satellite information? Lacking radar contacts, they could go for photo or infrared tracking."

Clark scowled. "I'll check that."

Jesus Christ!, Hamm thought. He had already located a hole in the planning. He looked at the few sheets of paper Clark had given to each of them, then eyed the full stacks of folders in Clark's briefcase. Obviously, they had been given summaries, and Clark had the full computer model.

Hal Cherry chewed on his lower lip, ruminating. "I haven't been following the situation in Nicaragua very closely. What have they got for air defense?"

Hamm watched while Clark dug through his briefcase, thinking, "Everything you ever wanted to know about the country is here, right here, in this little box."

Clark leafed through more paper, then said, "The primary military aid comes from the Cubans, but naturally, it's being underwritten by Moscow. Besides a couple of squadrons of training craft, they have a squadron of Sukhoi Su-17s for ground attack, two squadrons of MiG-23s as all-purpose fighters, and a bunch of cast-off MiG-19s. There's three squadrons composed of odd bits of older MiGs and some prop-driven planes, used mostly as a stepped-up training schedule. These are all based in Managua and flown by Nicaraguans. The instructors and advisors are generally Cuban, though we understand a few Soviets are on hand, too.''

"I suppose you've got the lineup on choppers?'' Cherry asked.

Clark flipped to another page. ''Mil Mi-24, NATO designation "Hind.'' There are four units, composed of four helicopters each. They are the prime squadrons, and they get spread around the country, supporting ground units. Agency intelligence says the level of pilot training in these birds is not high. There are a few older Mi-4s around Managua, in addition to some Bell and Hughes models. The American aircraft are short of repair parts. There are two aviation companies using Mi-8 and Mi-14 choppers in combat-support roles.''

The men in the suite sat quietly, digesting that information. Hamm visualized himself in Huey UH-1H, the center of attention for half a dozen Hinds and a whole air force of MiG's. The Hinds alone were bad news.

''What about AA?'' McDonough asked, stripping cellophane from another cigar.

Clark had a page on that also. ''There's a variety. In more or less permanent emplacements, they're using the ZU-23 twin anti-aircraft gun. It's not radar controlled. There are several mobile units using the ZSU-23-4 Quad. That one's got radar tracking, but the units they have are normally spotted along the coasts.'' Clark went on to another page. ''Some ground troops have the SA-7 Quail surface-to-air missile, and that's the one that will be the chief concern in our theater of operations.''

Hamm thought that Clark wanted to say more, but he did not. Now he was taking a different tactic, letting the group get involved, and interested, by asking questions, talking it up. With his palms, Clark shook his papers back into alignment, then dropped them in the attaché case.

''You're using designations I'm not even aware of,'' Talbot said. ''I've been out of it for a long time. Probably too long.''

''That's what the training's all about,'' De Veres told him.

''It's not a pretty picture,'' Harper offered. ''What little I've read about new weapons technologies scares the shit out of me. Super high tech. I haven't flown combat in fourteen years.''

''But you have been flying,'' McDonough said.

''Not looking over my shoulder for SAMs.''

''Me, either,'' Cherry agreed. ''I don't know what you've got set up for us, Bobby, but the odds are a little out of whack.''

''How many birds on our team? We set on having two pilots per chopper?'' Keen asked.

''That's the idea,'' Clark said. ''At the staging area, we take delivery of nine helicopters and hold three in reserve.''

''I'd say fuck the reserves and use them all,'' Canton observed. ''I'm better solo, anyway.''

''The weapons systems require a gunner who is also the backup pilot,'' Clark told him.

''These choppers will be fully prepped?'' Sean asked.

''Glad you brought that up, Sean. They'll be crated, and you'll have to put them together. It's one of the reasons

you men were selected. Besides the obvious flight qualifications, you each have competencies that are also necessary to the operation, from engineering to electronics to
ordnance."

Clark's buddy, De Veres, checked his watch and broke
in, "Nobody's afraid of a little manual labor, I hope? The
paycheck is better than minimum wage, after all."

Hamm walked to the end of the bar and dug another
bottle of Heineken out of the plastic chest. He twisted the
cap off. "You're just shooting us facts now, Bobby. What
does your computer say about the odds?"

"You have to keep in mind that the Sandinistas haven't
yet engaged in an air war beyond ground support. Every
man here has experience the Nicaraguan defensive forces
have only read about. Their opposition does not have aircraft, other than a few supply planes and some baling-wire
JetRangers and Cayuses."

"Some of which have been shot down," Ketchum
noted. "Ask that guy Hasenfus what he thinks about Nicaraguan AA fire."

"They lack experience," Clark insisted. "The Cuban
and Soviet advisors are doing the training, but the trainees
would rather drink *cerveza* and chase pussy."

Hamm took a long pull on the bottle. "That's one aspect, Bobby. But you've got something else up your sleeve.
What is it?"

"It's not something I'm going into, just yet. You'll have
to take my word on it."

"Get to your word, then," Hamm told him. "What's
the general idea?"

Once again, Clark was pushed into revealing data he
did not yet want to discuss. "The way the missions are

set up, the Nicaraguan air defenses are all but neutralized.''

''What if,'' Canton asked, ''we got to this training camp of yours, learned all the details, and decided to back out?''

Hamm did not know about the others, but if he decided later that Clark's estimates were too optimistic, he would just fly his bird to friendly territory.

Clark was regaining some of his old confidence. ''You won't back out.''

''We need to vote to get it over with, Bobby?''

''It's too early to vote, Sean,'' Hamm said. ''Unless you want to. I know how my vote would go, based on what I know so far.''

Hamm could tell from the look on his face that Clark had not planned on any vote. And he had not planned on waiting.

''Shit, let's vote now,'' Peachy Keen said, ''so I can go home.''

''I'll second that,'' Bellows said, grinning at Clark's discomfort.

Bobby Clark held up both hands. ''Now, hang on a . . .''

''Goddamn it!'' Sean McDonough roared. ''Let me have the floor for a damned minute.''

Half-stunned by the shout, the men sat back in their chairs. A few eyed the levels in their bottles.

''We've been sitting around here for hours listening to a long list of shit from Bobby. . . .''

''And reading a bunch of shit from a computer, '' Canton interjected.

''I don't know about you guys,'' McDonough went on, ''but in all the combat briefings I ever got, they only told me about the objectives, the ordnance requirements, and the weather. Sometimes they got the weather right. Maybe it was different for the guys at Commander Cherry's and Colonel Hamm's ranks. Nobody ever told me what jackass, or what computer, planned it. They just told me to do it, and I did it. Why in the hell are we worrying about that now?''

Bellows had an answer. "Because, Sean, back then, we couldn't talk back. These days, I want to make my decisions on more information.''

"Bullshit! We did the things we did because we felt something. You pull the trigger because a computer told you to do it, or because you hated the son of a bitch in the sights?''

"Sometimes we just buried it, Sean. Kinda cold.''

"You guys feel anything at all for those poor bastards fighting Moscow with sticks and Molotov cocktails? Just because they'd like their country back?'' McDonough glared at the whole group.

Hamm could feel the heat in the big man's stare. Everyone else maintained an uneasy silence. "I've got a question for Peter.''

De Veres glanced up at him from the deep chair he was seated in. "Shoot.''

"I get the impression you're doing all right. Enough money, you can play around.''

Smiling, De Veres said, "I'm not hurting.''

"What the hell are you doing here? You need the bucks?''

"I don't need the money,'' he said, looking around at the faces studying him. "You want true confessions? Okay. I'm not looking for any suicide missions. Hell, my biggest challenge in a month was a blond stewardess yesterday, and that didn't take long. I haven't felt on the edge for a long time. I want to feel alive again, feel like I was doing something worthwhile. Like Sean said, doing something the bureaucrats don't fuck up. That answer your question?''

"That answers it," Hamm said.

Maybe it was an answer for the others, too. It was quiet in the room for a long moment.

Finally, McDonough turned to Clark. "You know the only thing we need to make this go, Bobby?"

Clark's tone was reserved after De Veres's little lecture. "What's that, Sean?"

"We need a leader. You want a consolidated unit, put Hamm in tactical command of the mission."

Canton objected immediately. "Fuck that! Why Hamm?"

Hamm did not bother to react. He could see the flush creeping up Clark's throat. Peter de Veres sat mulling it over, running a forefinger along the scar on his brow.

McDonough responded to Canton. "Experience, primarily. You got out after twenty years, didn't you, Pat? As a captain. And that was five years ago. Hamm outranks all of us; he's only a couple weeks out of active service; and he knows what has been going on in the Pentagon. He's been based in Washington for the past eight years."

"Shit. I spent nine years in enlisted ranks, or I'd have retired in a higher grade."

"But you didn't," McDonough told him.

"Give it to Cherry," Hamm said. With his elbows resting on the padded rail of the bar again, he appeared at ease, but his eyes roamed the room steadily, watching the reactions. He could not tell whether or not Clark was buying any of this.

Hal Cherry, having retired as a Navy commander, was

the next ranking man in the group. In appearance, he could have been the trustworthy captain of the airliner—thick face carefully shaved, dark hair graying along the sides, steady brown eyes. He was almost six feet tall, with a thick torso.

"Not me. My background is water, and so far, I don't see any."

Hamm knew from the roster sheet that Cherry had spent three tours in Vietnam working the Mekong Delta area as a SEAL.

Finally, Clark said, "Maybe that would work, Hamm as tactical commander, myself in the planning role."

"I flew Hamm's wing in 'Nam. I'd fly it again, anywhere," Sean added.

"So would I," Harper said.

Peachy Keen pushed himself off the wall. Like a bantam rooster looking for a fight, he locked eyes with Clark. "Final authority for Steve?"

"Not on goals or objectives. On operational methodology, he gets final authority," Clark agreed reluctantly.

"Hell, I'd go along with that," Keen said.

"That's fine with me," said De Veres.

Hamm counted seven of eleven in agreement. The others, who had not known Hamm before, ruminated, then inclined heads in affirmation. Canton shrugged.

Hamm stood at the bar, somewhat bemused by the change in course. "This all assumes I'm going somewhere. I've thought about the odds, and I've thought about what else I could be doing, and I guess I'd just as soon take a poke at the bastards myself. Sean said something in Maryland that intrigued me, that Peter repeated, something about fighting a battle without the politicians getting in the way. I've had politicians up to my ass. And maybe that's enough for me.''

Hamm went over and started digging through Clark's briefcase.

''What the hell are you doing?'' Clark asked.

Hamm held up the printouts. ''I've got some homework to do, Bobby. I want to be sure you and I are using the same textbook.'' He went back and climbed up on a stool at the bar, spreading the printouts in front of him. ''Why don't you guys go down to the casino for about an hour, lose your money and grab some ass, while I do a little reading.''

''Damned right,'' McDonough said. ''I need the break.''

They all trooped out, except for Clark, who went behind the bar and mixed himself a Scotch and water. Hamm accepted one when Clark offered it.

It took him nearly an hour, while Clark nursed his drink and sulked in one corner. The detailed gaming model did not give him full details. The targets, the helicopters involved, the deployments were all listed under code names. But he did gain a hell of a lot from reading the specifications listed under the ''Variables Input'' section of the model. Not only had Clark entered the psychological characteristics of major figures in Nicaragua—names not coded—as well as the KGB resident named Zhukov, he had also entered the detailed operating specifications for every piece of equipment with potential utilization. He studied the range, payload, turbine shaft output, and similar data for the aircraft for several minutes. When he finally caught on to the gimmick, he was surprised. Sure as hell, Clark had neutralized the Nicaraguan Defense Forces.

Hamm spun around on his stool and spoke: "Bobby, that's a stroke of genius. And a hell of a lot of work."

Clark looked up, pleased at the compliment. "You found it?"

"I found it."

"Don't give it away just yet, please."

"No, I see your point. I'll hold on to it for now." Hamm picked up his glass from the bar, dumped in more ice cubes, and poured freely from the Chivas Regal bottle. He said, "How did you get the machines?"

"Peter's work. He's damned good at it."

"I'd say."

"You're in, then?" Clark watched him closely.

"Why not? This just might work. If you can go along with the command structure."

"Sure. Shit, I've always been more of a planner, anyway."

Twenty minutes passed before everyone returned, all of them in a pretty fair mood, Hamm thought. They spread around the room, looking expectantly at him.

"Hell, if I'm going to be part of some conspiracy, this one's as good as any other, I guess."

"You're buying in, Steve?" McDonough asked.

Hamm rotated the bar stool back and forth and studied every man. "I'm in, if each one of you is in. I need every one of you."

"That's all I need to hear," Peachy Keen said. The others nodded, slapping one another on the back.

Clark looked relieved. "Okay, guys. Here's the drill. . . ."

# SIX

Diego Contrarez arrived in his rented 55OSL at the airport Holiday Inn early, to have a look around the parking lot and the lobby before entering the restaurant. He liked to be aware of his environs before important events took place. All he found were a collection of garish-looking tourists, a lot of Cubans, several Drug Enforcement Agency agents watching everyone else, and perhaps two dozen representatives of Contra and El Salvador organizations holding meetings among themselves and with sleazy characters in expensive suits. The motel was a favorite of freedom fighters from all over Central America.

Inside the restaurant, a twenty-dollar bill got him a table in a back corner, shielded by a long planter full of dwarf palm trees and elephant-eared greenery. He ordered a rum and Coca-Cola to pass the time while he waited.

Bobby Clark arrived fifteen minutes later. Contrarez did not like Clark, nor did he like Clark's insistence upon endless details of logistics and planning. The CIA agent did not understand that the war for independence was something that arose out of the heart and the soul, and could not be relegated to paper. Yet, with Clark, he was required to be attentive. Ostensibly, the man was his and Maldonado's control officer, a relationship that assured that their thirty-six-thousand- and fifty-thousand-dollar salaries were deposited to their accounts with regularity. Clark had once explained the fine distinction to him. As controlled agents of the CIA, Contrarez and Maldonado were considered as any other such agents in the world. It had nothing to do with a banned support of the Contra effort.

As Clark took the chair opposite him, Contrarez noticed a change in the American agent. His eyes seemed more intense. His shoulders were stiff with a new resolve. And he ignored a somewhat traditional rite of casual foretalk.

"I don't have time to eat, Diego. I only have time to tell you about what's going to happen in the next couple of months."

Contrarez offered one of his rare smiles. "I will be happy to pass your suggestions on to Colonel Maldonado, naturally."

"Let's not start off on the wrong foot, Diego. These are not suggestions."

Contrarez was almost offended, but let it pass for the moment. "It is often a difficult task to obtain obedience from the leadership."

Clark rummaged in his briefcase, then handed him a stack of paper. It was just what he had expected, of course, and just what he detested.

"That is a list of troop movements and attack objectives for your freedom fighters. It is to be accomplished in the last weeks of June."

Contrarez smiled again. What else could he do in the face of such an impossibility?

"There is also a list of some four million dollars in arms and munitions that will begin to arrive at various resupply encampments in the second week of June. The funds are from concerned Americans."

"Certainly, that is welcome news. But do I sense that these concerned Americans bind their gift to a set of actions on the part of the FDN?"

"That is correct."

"An impossible task. The bickering on tactics and strategy among the leadership is getting worse."

"That is Maldonado's and your problem. You will get Bermudez, Calera, and Matamoros to follow the outline of that plan. We are looking for a major success that will reverse the tide of American opinion."

"Ah, yes . . ."

"And if you are successful, on July first, there will be three hundred thousand dollars for Esteban and two hundred thousand for yourself."

Contrarez sucked on his teeth, then hefted the weight of paper. "Perhaps a down payment would convince Esteban."

"No down payments. You get it afterwards."

"I will read this and see what can be done." Contrarez sighed.

"I know what can be done, Diego. You just see that it gets done."

"Where may I contact you?"

"You can't. I'm going to be out of touch, so it's up to you."

Such intensity, Contrarez thought, as Clark disappeared through the wide portal into the lobby. He looked with distaste at the paper, but then decided that the reward perhaps justified the effort.

On the morning of May 16, Jack Coriolanus sat at the big worktable in his office, finalizing his portion of the briefing papers that the Director of Central Intelligence would carry with him to the afternoon meeting of the National Security Council. At noon, over lunch, he, the DDO, and several others were to brief the DCI in preparation for the meeting. It was a planned monthly meeting, but frequently, he was required to make similar preparations for similar meetings in times of perceived crises.

Coriolanus had eleven projects ongoing, and he kept track of them on a magnetic board that was small enough to fit in his desk drawer. The projects were listed in the left-hand column in grease pencil, and the specific deadlines for the accomplishment of various objectives were printed across the top row. Blue magnets in the grid below the heading kept him aware of progress.

In the left-hand column, below his assigned projects, in parentheses, were listed the odd topics that came up from time to time and that he tracked for as long as they seemed important.

The special assistant checked off the projects as he assembled his brief. He always tried to keep the progress report on each activity to one page. His bosses did not have time to read more.

Shuffling through the eleven pages, he arranged them in a priority order, then called to his secretary through the open doorway. "Toni!"

She came to the door, a trim and attractive redhead just admitting to forty years of age. "Yes, Mr. Coriolanus?"

Handing her the thin sheaf of paper, he said, "Two more copies, then type a cover sheet. 'Eyes Only—DCI, DDO, SA to DDO.' "

"Yes, sir."

"And you want to check and see what's holding up my suit?" Coriolanus had sent one of his office suits out for pressing. He liked to appear at his best for upper-level meetings.

"Yes, sir." Toni trotted out of his office, and Coriolanus went back to his planning board to consider the fifteen items in parentheses, making certain he had in mind the latest information on each, in case he was asked about them.

When he reached the item "SM," he had to think a minute before recalling what it was. He picked up the worktable phone and dialed Downs. "Harry? Coriolanus."

"What do you need, Jack?"

"Where's your *Southern Merchant*?"

"Hold on. I'll get the file."

A minute later, Downs came back on the line, "As of yesterday, she was moored in the harbor at Luanda."

"Why Angola?"

"I don't know. Yesterday's photo is from Big Bird. I've got a Key-Hole Eight pass due for the area at three o'clock, and we'll get another shot."

Big Bird was the best-known surveillance satellite in American inventories. Its multispectral scanners could identify objects as small as a foot across.

Coriolanus asked, "You get any deck detail in the photo?"

"Lot of rust. This baby's on her last legs. But no, no cargo visible."

"Maybe she was just making a run from the Gulf to Angola. Maybe she's off-loading in Luanda?" The old freighter was something of an irritant to Coriolanus. He would like to get her off his magnetic board.

"It's possible Angola was her destination, Jack. But we've backtracked her only as far as the Arabian Sea. I

don't think she was ever in the gulf. The people at NPIC''—
the National Photographic Interpretation Center—''think
she rendezvoused at night with another freighter. We believe that one is the *Riga Star*, and we're trying to backtrack her now.''

"Shit," Coriolanus said. "It's all backward. We're re-
gressing more than progressing, and all on a hunch."

"I can drop it if you want," Downs told him.

Coriolanus thought about it. With old hands like Downs,
hunches were only one level down from fact. "No. Let's
watch her for a couple of more days."

# TRAINING

# SEVEN

When he was fifteen or sixteen years old, and reading a lot of espionage thrillers, Hamm's vision of a dirty, dangerous, spy-ridden, international city had been labeled Hong Kong, or sometimes, Istanbul.

Now it was Miami.

The prevalent language of Miami was Spanish. The Casablanca section was home to the homeless political manipulators of Cuba, Nicaragua, El Salvador, Colombia, and practically every other Latin American country. The political arm of the Nicaraguan Contra movement was centered in Miami. If intrigue flowed like molasses throughout southern Florida, then arms and drug money flowed like water. Helpless retirees from the North struggled on fixed incomes in 1950s pastel-colored bungalows while cocaine subsidized the brand-new multimillion-dollar condos and office buildings along Brickell Avenue and drove up the cost of living. Million-dollar deals for arms, conducted at curbside, were paltry in comparison to the billions of dollars being laundered through offshore banks, then transferred to the solid, long-standing financial institutions of Miami.

Illicit drugs, weapons, and currency were like a tidal wave washing over, and drowning, the Drug Enforcement Agency, the Treasury Department, the Justice Department, and law enforcement agencies from local to state levels. Steve Hamm could not think of a better place for the personnel of Bobby Clark's expedition to meet.

He took an Eastern Airlines flight into Miami International Airport from Washington D.C.'s National Airport on the morning of May 17. As the DC-9 touched down in a squeal of rubber on hot pavement, he studied the area situated far off the main runways, a collection of dated hangars, tarnished offices, and row upon row of unmarked aircraft, mostly of the transport variety. The clandestine and semiclandestine air carriers—Southern Air Transport and Vortex among others—called Corrosion Corner headquarters.

It was also a good place to buy a used airplane cheap. Some of the aircraft available were obtained from DEA auctions of confiscated drug runners.

His DC-9 worked its way up to the terminal, and Hamm relaxed in his first-class seat while the tourists and businessmen who thought they were in a rush crowded the aisle. After the mob thinned out, he rose, retrieved his carry-on from the overhead compartment, and deplaned. The terminal was chilled nicely, a strong contrast to the sun glancing off hot windshields lined up in the parking lots.

The only concern Hamm had as he followed the flow of humanity along the concourse and through the terminal was for the airport watchers. The CIA and the FBI would have a large force spread about, and Hamm's face was known to many. He saw several possible watchers, but they appeared to pass him over. Near the main doors, Hal Cherry rose from a settee and joined him. They passed through the automatic doors together. The heat was a slap in the face after two hours of refrigeration.

"Thought I'd hang around until I saw a familiar face," Cherry said.

"Have you seen any of the others?"

"Canton. I should have said, 'familiar *and* friendly face.' I let him find his way by himself."

Cherry carried a suitcase similar to his own, supposedly packed as ordered by Clark's computer, and the two of them slid the bags into the first cab in line, then followed them. The driver, a Cuban with slick black hair, peered back at them from the front seat, the back of which was almost taller than he was.

Hamm told him, "Let's go around to general aviation."

"Shit, man! You coulda walked it."

"You might get a tip if you make it."

The cab pulled out into traffic, and Hamm rotated in his seat to scan the doors, people, and cars behind. Cherry noticed. "You always travel with your head backward?"

"Habit," Hamm said. No one appeared interested enough to follow them.

The cabbie let them out ten minutes later in front of a small passenger waiting room, and Hamm gave him enough to keep him happy, but not enough to be memorable. He and Cherry went inside, found a cafeteria, bought coffee with a Cuban bite, then sat together at a window-side table.

Six others of the team were already present, reading newspapers or books, or watching fellow travelers from eight different tables. Hamm and Cherry got to know each other a little better for an hour, then rose and carried their suitcases out to the tarmac.

"Herc and a Buffalo, right?"

"That's the way I got it, Hal." Hamm scanned the rows of airplanes, most of which had had company markings sandblasted from their fuselages. There were some vintage planes—DC-3s, DC-9s, an old PBY Catalina, some Twin Otters—in the lineup. In the second row, he spotted the tall tail of a C-130, and they walked out to it. Peter de Veres was there, walking around the plane on an inspection tour. He looked up as they approached, then checked his watch.

"Hello, Peter." Hamm had earlier decided De Veres was the kind who would not like to be called Pete.

"Right on time. Your buggy's next door, Steve."

"Okay. Hal, you want to check with Operations, get the weather, and file a plan?"

"On my way." Cherry handed his carry-on to Hamm, then walked away.

Hamm crossed under the wing of the Hercules and went to inspect the De Haviland Canada Buffalo. He toured the perimeter, examining the working surfaces and looking for oil, fuel, or hydraulic leaks. There were a few, but nothing to be alarmed about. The airplane had seen its share of hard times. Dings, dents, and scratches were profuse, and the gray paint was faded and peeling away from the aluminum skin in spots. The only marking was the tail number.

Undogging the side hatchway, Hamm tossed the bags inside, then clambered after them. A sizable stack of wooden crates and cardboard boxes had been lashed to the center of the steel-mesh floor. The canvas sling seats along both sides had been let down. He did not bother checking the cargo, but pulled his previously prepared charts from a side pocket of his bag, then walked forward and pulled himself up into the flight compartment. Settling into the left-hand seat, Hamm rummaged in the pouch next to the center console, came up with the log, and studied it. The DHC-5 had been built in 1965, so it was one of the early models. More reassuring, both of the GE CT64-820-1 turboprops had had major overhauls less than a hundred hours before. Some of the instrumentation had been recently recalibrated. There were three notations of erratic behavior with the weather radar, then a final note that it had quit working.

Sliding open the side cockpit window in search of ventilation, Hamm spent some time familiarizing himself with the instrument and control locations; he had flown a Buffalo only once before. It was his since none of the others had flown one at all.

Cherry came back, climbed aboard, then found his way to the right-hand seat. "Jesus! If it won't start, we'll be in luck."

He handed Cherry the log.

Hamm saw some of the others starting to leave the building and cross the apron toward them. "You think De Veres was bargain shopping, Hal?"

"He only had twenty million dollars, Steve. You don't want him to blow it all on one airplane, do you?"

"Yes," Hamm said, and Cherry grinned.

He felt the fuselage dip slightly as somebody climbed aboard. Looking across at the Hercules, he saw that Clark and De Veres were both seated in its cockpit. With its 42,000-pound payload capacity, the C-130 was carrying the two helicopters and some of the supplies, primarily fuel for the choppers. Hamm's Buffalo was to transport the rest of the supplies and the remaining ten members of the team.

The number-one engine of the Hercules snorted blue smoke, then fired.

Cherry got up and stood in the flight-deck doorway and counted heads. "We got eight, Steve. Door's secured."

Hamm buckled up while Cherry returned to his seat, then went through the start procedure with Cherry reading from the checklist. Both engines cranked easily and settled quickly into a steady, purring idle.

"I feel better," Cherry said.

"Give me a couple of hours, then I'll tell you how I feel." Hamm called Ground Control and received permission to follow the Hercules onto the taxiway. Both aircraft trundled along, heading for Runway 27, and fell into line behind a Pan Am 747.

"I can't believe we're getting off without a Customs check," Cherry said.

"That's a CIA arrangement."

"The bastards break the law all the time."

"Only in the interest of the country, Hal."

Hamm kept testing the engines, running them up while watching RPM, manifold pressure, and temperature. As the 747 took to the air, Cherry signed off with Ground Control, dialed in new frequencies on the NAV radios, and contacted Miami Air Control.

The Hercules pivoted onto the runway ahead of them, and Clark, who was in the pilot's seat, shoved his throttles in. The four engines belched blue smoke, and the transport rushed down the runway like an obese goose.

Cherry kept up the dialogue with the air controller, receiving wind velocity, barometric pressure, and other data. Hamm listened on his headset, moving out onto the runway and applying left brake to line up on the center stripe. "Flaps?" he double-checked.

"Forty degrees."

The air controller told them, "De Haviland two six, you are cleared for takeoff."

"Roger, Miami, two six cleared for takeoff," Cherry replied.

Hamm shoved the throttles forward and the elderly airplane began to roll, picking up speed quickly.

Cherry called off the numbers. "Seventy knots . . . eighty knots . . . one hundred knots . . . hundred ten . . . hundred twenty. Rotate."

Hamm eased the yoke back, and the nose lifted. The rumbling of the main wheels suddenly ceased. "What do you know," he said, "the son of a bitch flies. Gear up."

Cherry reached out for the landing-gear lever. After three satisfying thumps, three green lights appeared on the instrument panel. Hamm adjusted fuel mixtures and prop pitch, ordered the flaps retracted, and then trimmed for climb. The old fuselage structure moaned and creaked. The Hercules was a distant speck ahead of them.

His co-pilot signed off with Air Control and reset the radios for the Tampa signal, to give them a navigational fix. When he was done, Cherry asked, "Where's that damned stewardess?"

"I'll bet she's taking care of the passengers ahead of the crew. No sense of priority."

Cherry stripped off his seat and shoulder harness, then went back to the cargo bay. By the time he returned with a Thermos and two plastic cups, Hamm had leveled off at sixteen thousand feet and the Gulf of Mexico was dead ahead, the coastline about to pass under them. The city of Naples was below to the right. Tall cumulus clouds were stacked high on the left horizon, their undersides blue with the threat of rain.

Hamm locked in the autopilot and took his coffee. "You know much about weather radar?"

"Inside or outside the black box?"

"Inside. The log says ours works part of the time."

"It's probably something that has to be fixed on the ground, but I'll get Peachy up here."

For the next three hours, the three of them talked easily, if loudly, to overcome the drone of the engines, while Keen sat on the flight-deck floor and disassembled the accessible components of the weather radar. He had an aluminum case of specialized tools and instruments and looked entirely happy to have a project to pass the time.

At three-thirty, Hamm spread his chart out on his lap and checked the notations and course he had plotted earlier. They were almost directly 225 miles south of New Orleans. The Gulf of Mexico was on every horizon except for the southern, where the cloud banks had built up even more. He could see several dark areas where the rain was pouring into the gulf.

Cherry eyed the storm clouds. "How far off, you think?"

"Maybe seventy miles?" Hamm guessed.

"Your eyes have gone bad," Keen said. "Ninety-three miles."

They all looked to the radar scope mounted in front of Cherry and saw the sweep moving steadily. The three-hundred-mile scan clearly indicated the line of weather. "Smartass," Cherry told Keen.

Keen packed his tools, then levered himself off the floor. "Give me a ring if anything else breaks down."

"Leave your business card, will you?" Hamm asked.

"I'm in the book."

At five o'clock, with Houston as their navigation fix, Hamm told Cherry, "All right, Hal, it's time."

"Gotcha. I'll call in."

Fort Worth-Dallas had been their air control for the past fifty minutes, and Cherry radioed them and let them know that De Haviland two six was transferring to Monterrey, Mexico, air control. Ciudad Victoria was the destination listed on their flight plan. Fort Worth–Dallas acknowledged, but Cherry did not bother calling Monterrey. That was not part of the plan.

Hamm adjusted the autopilot for a slow descent, and wondered where Clark and De Veres were. The Hercules had a ninety-mile-per-hour edge on them and was probably already close to the destination.

At seven o'clock, the radar scan showed storm clouds thirty miles off their left flank. They were going to beat the weather, which would pass behind them.

At seven-ten, the Buffalo crossed Padre Island fifty miles south of Kingsville, Texas, at an altitude of five hundred feet. The Intracoastal Waterway flashed under quickly, then the tan desert was below. Cacti and sagebrush cast long shadows from a sun low in the west and directly in Hamm's face. He had donned sunglasses and pulled down his dark plastic window visor.

He wanted to stay below radar attention on the run inland, but he planned to leapfrog Highways 77 and 281 so as not to alarm travelers. They might not be alarmed, anyway, since all kinds of strange aircraft flew out of the Confederate Air Force's headquarters at Harlingen, sixty miles to the south, but crossing highways at treetop level, if there were any trees around, was not good for drivers' hearts. After ten minutes, he climbed to twelve hundred feet.

Highway 77, with very little traffic, slipped under them, then he dove back to five hundred feet for a few minutes before climbing again for the next highway.

"Looks good to me," Cherry said. He pulled a map light down and opened the chart. Their signal landmarks were indicated on the chart, and they both started searching for them as the co-pilot called them out.

"Highway Seven Fifty-five on the left," Cherry said.

Hamm banked to the right, got the sun out of his eyes, and settled on a 350 heading. Seven minutes later, the low and small, box-shaped butte went by on his left.

"Off to the right!"

Hamm saw the small stand of cottonwoods that surrounded the spring and rolled the plane again to the right to pass directly overhead.

"There she is," Cherry said.

The Hercules was on the ground, nosed up to the trees. He could see its landing tracks in the undulating ground to the north of the spring. "Looks soft as hell," he told Cherry.

"The Herc made it."

Hamm made a wide circle after clearing the landing area, then came back to the south, ordering landing gear and flaps lowered. He bled off power, trying to focus his eyes in the bad light of twilight Texas.

"We've got a hundred and ten knots."

He eased back the throttles another fraction. The cottonwoods were coming up fast.

"Ninety knots."

The wheels touched down, bounced three small hops, and Hamm pulled the throttles back to their detents, reversed pitch, then ran up the engines again. The Buffalo slowed quickly, her nose dropping, plowing through soft dirt that was hub high on the wheels. Changing prop pitch again, he taxied up alongside the Hercules and cut the power off.

It seemed awfully quiet.

Cherry stood up first, threw his arms back, and stretched. "First thing I'm going to do, I'm going to piss for a couple of hours."

"Leave the lid up for me," Hamm told him.

The team scrambled out of the side door to find Clark and De Veres waiting. The hot engines of the aircraft pinged as they began to cool. Clark was beaming. "Welcome to Brooks County, Texas."

Peachy Keen asked, "Where are the girls you promised, Bobby?"

Clark was in a good mood. "Due in on the next plane, Peachy. First thing, though, we've got to get the camouflage nets spread over these planes."

Pat Canton pushed himself to the head of the group. "That can wait a minute. I want to see those choppers while it's still light."

The loading ramp of the Hercules was already lowered, and the team scrambled up it into the cavernous cargo bay to find the two helicopters shrouded in khaki canvas. They took up most of the room available, and stacked fifty-five-gallon drums and the dismounted rotors took up the rest. It took five minutes to peel the covering away from both aircraft.

"I'll be a son of a bitch!" Sean McDonough exclaimed.

He was not the only one. "Motherfucker!" the normally taciturn Jerry Pickett echoed.

It was about what Hamm had expected when he had read the aircraft specifications in the "Input" section of Clark's gaming model. He certainly had not recognized the specifications as those of U.S. helicopters.

Standing tall in the cargo bay, the largest of the two craft was an Mi-24 Hind, manufactured by Mil in the Soviet Union. Angled in alongside it, rotor to nose, was an Mi-28 Havoc.

Both of them looked strange, painted in Air Force blue.

## EIGHT

**B**oth helicopters had USAF insignia painted on the fuselage sides, but the aircraft numbers were "X" numbers, designating experimental airframes. While the training camp site selected by Clark was desolate, and a long way from maintained roads, there were still a few gravel roads and single-strip airports around. If some rancher in an old

Piper or Cessna 140 flew over the area, and happened to see an odd and menacing silhouette, he was expected to believe the Air Force was testing new helicopters.

As part of that cover, all the team members were to wear Air Force fatigues during training, though no rank insignia was to be worn. Clark finally ushered everyone away from the Soviet helicopters and back to the Buffalo to dig out the cardboard boxes of clothing and boots. While they donned uniforms, which fit fairly well, except for Keen's which was too large, the men talked excitedly: "Bet those suckers outrun any Huey I ever flew . . . Thirty-mike-mike cannon, can you fucking believe it? . . . How in hell we supposed to read instruments with Cyrillic characters? . . . You see that son of a bitch has a missile-guidance pack?"

"The birds we pick up in Nicaragua," Keen asked, "they going to be painted for Nicaragua, Bobby?"

"That's right," Clark told him. "The ruling council of the Sandinista government is going to wonder where they got the firepower."

Even Harvey Ketchum did not have to brood over the topic for long. "Damned good trick, Bobby. Those people ain't going to shoot down their own choppers."

Clark was enjoying the praise, Hamm thought. He fitted the brass buckle to his belt, then sat in a sling seat while he laced his boots. The interior of the Buffalo was warming up, even as the sun disappeared.

"I get first shot at the Havoc," Canton said.

Hamm did not think so since he had already composed a training schedule, based on his guess regarding Clark's aircraft, but he planned on waiting until morning to bring it up.

"Okay," Clark said, "let's get the camouflage netting up."

"Fuck that," Canton told him. "We'll off-load the choppers first."

Hamm ignored the remark. "Peachy, you want to drop the ramp on this thing, and unlash the Jeep and trailer, first? Then, we'll want power."

"Yo, Steve." They had one CJ-7 Jeep with them, a civilian model with Texas license plates and a gas-powered generator in tow.

"Then, Clay, Jerry, and Rick, grab some machetes and go cut down some of that long grass and sage. We'll lace it into the netting."

The three men dug through several equipment crates, found the right one, came up with the machetes, and stepped off the ramp as it hit the ground.

"The rest of us will haul netting."

"Ah, shit!" Canton grunted, but joined the others in uncrating the camouflage netting, dragging it out behind both planes, then hoisting it up and over each craft. By nine o'clock, neither the Hercules nor the Buffalo would have been spotted from a half mile away in daylight. The tan-and-brown netting, flat areas broken up with scrub and sagebrush, draped off the wings and provided a shaded area in which to park the Jeep and get out of the hot sun occasionally. Keen parked the generator trailer in the trees and got it running, with cables trailing across the ground to power lights inside both planes and a massive refrigerator aboard the Buffalo.

They shoved the helicopters out of the C-130 and tossed netting over them, then rolled the fuel drums down the ramp and set up a fuel depot thirty yards away, under the cottonwood trees. The larger plane was where they'd sleep, and Hamm put McDonough and Bellows to work stringing hammocks up inside the cargo bay, while the rest of the team went back to the Buffalo to unpack food, tools, and equipment and set up the DHC-5 as a supply and maintenance facility.

It was eleven o'clock, a black night under a star-strewn sky, before Hamm thought they were organized enough for the first day. He called a halt, and everyone gathered around the Buffalo's ramp, in the light spilling from the cargo bay. Several of them peeled off fatigue blouses sopped with sweat. Hamm guessed the temperature at about 80, humidity close to the same number.

McDonough lit up one of his stogies and asked, "Okay if we pop a beer, Chief?"

"Sure enough, Sean."

While McDonough passed bottles of Michelob around, Bellows doled out cartons of C-rations. Bellows's ash-red hair was plastered against his skull with sweat.

Hamm sat on the slanted edge of the loading ramp and took a long pull at his beer. It was not very cold. He ripped the top off his food kit and spilled out the contents on the ramp. How many times had he been faced with the same olive drab can of beans and franks in his career? He kept the M&M's, probably packaged in 1950, and tossed the mini-pack of Lucky Strikes to Rick Talbot.

Both Clark and De Veres had worked without pause and without questioning one of Hamm's few orders to them. He was halfway surprised; he had expected Clark to drag his feet when it came down to accepting Hamm's authority, and he had wondered how the playboy would take to work. He looked over the stacked boxes of canned goods, the complete tool sets in castered cabinets, the delicate instrument calibration gear, and the unopened crates of specialized equipment that lined the fuselage sides. "Bobby, I'm damned impressed with your logistics."

"Thanks, Hamm," Clark said. "I came up with a list of what we needed, but Peter went out and got it. Arranged all the loading and transshipping, too."

"Cold green cash has miracle qualities," De Veres explained.

"How the hell do you locate Soviet choppers?" Hal Cherry asked. "They don't have them in my San Diego supermarkets."

"All it takes is a little *baksheesh* in the right palm," De Veres explained. "I don't know how much it costs Moscow to produce these things, but I'd guess it's the equivalent of two million bucks a copy. I bought six Mi-24s and five Havocs from a very accommodating deputy defense minister in Angola. I don't suppose he paid for them, but I gave him a Swiss account with ten million U.S. in it. He insisted on American dollars."

"That cover the ordnance, too?" Ketchum asked. He was the weapons man.

"That covered the chopper ordnance—machine-gun ammo, rockets, and missiles. I just went through an Armenian arms dealer's catalog for the assault rifles and sidearms, which came out of a Czech warehouse, complete with end users certificate."

"Jesus, I wish I could go on a ten-million-dollar shopping spree," McDonough said. "Buy me a Cessna Citation, couple cases of beer."

"You transport all the helicopters out of Angola by air freight?" Hamm asked.

"Just the two we needed for training, by way of Rome. The others are coming by ship."

Cherry asked, "How the hell do you bring that kind of weapon into Miami without landing in the federal prison at Atlanta, Peter?"

"That's Bobby's department."

Clark explained, "The CIA has an arrangement with U.S. Customs. All it takes is a phone call, if we don't want a shipment inspected."

"Some of the other stuff—the Jeep, the soft goods, the fuel—was purchased and loaded in Miami," De Veres went on. "No big deal, really."

Hamm finished his beans and franks, and while the others had another beer, gathered his other sets of fatigues, a sleeping bag, and his carry-on, then carted them across to the larger plane. He chose a hammock closest to the port-side doorway, stashed his gear underneath it, and sat on the hammock with the rosters he had developed in Maryland.

Bobby Clark came up the ramp, went forward to retrieve his briefcase, and then sat on the hammock next to Hamm's. "I'm glad you approve of the arrangements, Steve."

"Seems well thought out," Hamm told him, preparing for the coming debate with a mild compliment.

Clark rummaged in his case, then handed Hamm several sheets of paper. "Here's the training schedule."

Hamm looked it over. Clark had himself, De Veres, Talbot, and Hamm training only in the Havoc. The rest would take turns learning the flight characteristics of the Hind. Very little time was devoted to airframe and mechanical education. Clark had compressed everything into an eight-hour day. He asked, "How did you make your selections, Bobby?"

"Number of hours and variety of aircraft on the record of each man. Rick and Peter racked up quite a bit of time in the Cobra."

"But you used only military records, right? Records that are dated?"

"Well, that's what I had available."

Hamm found the twelve photocopied pages he had obtained from the Federal Aviation Administration and handed them to Clark.

"Shit. How did you get this?"

"Friend of a friend. But it gives a more recent picture of everyone's ratings and aircraft qualifications. You might want to note Canton's record. He had his instructor's certificate lifted, along with his commercial ticket."

Clark looked up at him. "Why?"

"I guess he got a thrill out of scaring his students and passengers with ground-level aerobatics. He's the show-off type."

"I'll keep an eye on him," Clark promised.

"That'll be two of us." Hamm handed him the schedule he had made up. "This is the way I'm going to do it."

"But . . ."

"It's not open to discussion."

Clark shut up and read through the chart. "Damn it, Hamm, they're not going to put up with ten- and eleven-hour days."

"They'll put up with it. Or hit the road."

"And you've got as much book time here as flying time."

"That's right."

"You're going to have us all qualify for both aircraft? That's a hell of a waste."

"No. It's not. When that sixteen percent mortality rate of yours hits us, we don't want to be caught maybe losing a Havoc capability. And there's one more thing I'm doing

with that schedule. The best pilots end up as A/Cs"—
aircraft commanders—"and the rest are backups."

"Damn it! Count me out of that, Hamm. Peter and I
will each be flying a Havoc, and . . ."

"Not until you both outfly me and about half of everyone else."

Clark sat, gently swinging in the hammock, and glared
at him. The aqua eyes were not happy, but the man apparently decided against an argument which was likely to
prove futile.

That was all right with Hamm. He did not mind having
people mad at him if it made them try harder. And he
thought Clark would have to try harder. Of all the pilots
present, Clark had spent the least time in the air in recent
years. Less time in control of the aircraft, anyway.

"One thing, Bobby."

"What's that?" Clark's voice squeaked a bit, as it always had in the past when he was irritated.

"What's De Veres doing here?"

"I don't know what you mean."

"My sources tell me he's making nearly two hundred
fifty thousand a year, after taxes, from some trust fund.
He doesn't have to screw around with this."

Clark's eyes narrowed. "You've got good sources. I
didn't know how much it was."

"He's a playboy with all the right toys and a showcase
full of women. Why should he risk his ass for what he's
got coming in annually?"

"I believe what he told us in Vegas, Hamm. You should,
too."

Clark's tone was confident enough, and Hamm decided
not to press any further for the time being. He eased out
of the hammock, stuffed the papers in the side pocket of

his bag, spread the bedroll on top of the hammock, and started unlacing his boots. His feet ached a little from breaking in the new boots.

"You hitting the sack?" Clark asked.

"Damned right. Four o'clock comes early."

"Four o'clock! In the morning?"

"That's the one."

Ham actually rolled out of his hammock at three-thirty and dressed quietly in the chilled dark of the cargo bay. The ramp was still down and the night air was crisp, though it carried the smell of dust. The breathing of sleeping men was a dull cacophony, highlighted by one snoring soloist. He had not slept in the same space with this many men in quite a few years, and he did not feel sentimental about the experience.

He crossed the open space to the DHC-5, ducked under the camouflage webbing, and found one of the lights hanging from an engine nacelle that Keen had rigged the night before. He turned it on, and the battery pack hooked in with the now-silent generator gave him light. Under this wing were two long folding tables with twelve camp stools and a small preparation table next to an oversize, propane-fired field range. After igniting the grill, he climbed into the Buffalo and began to fill a cardboard box from the refrigerator—four pounds of link sausage, three dozen eggs, butter. He found three loaves of bread, a couple of dozen doughnuts, and the supply of plastic plates and dinnerware. Hauling everything outside, he started the sausage on the grill, then filled a fifty-five-cup coffeepot with water from a five-gallon jug. It took him a few minutes to find the coffee with which to fill the basket.

By five minutes after four, he had some decent aromas

mingling with the smell of Texas dust. He went out and hit the electric starter on the generator, got it whining, then went back aboard the Hercules and walked down the center of the bay, carrying a mug of coffee and turning on lights.

"All right, you clods! Up and at 'em!"

"Jesus Christ! Can it!" McDonough yelled at him from under the slouch hat pulled over his face.

Hamm kicked McDonough's butt as it hung in the hammock. "You too, Sean! Bright eyes now!"

There were moans and groans. Clark rolled out of his hammock, bleary-eyed.

Hamm sipped his coffee. "In five minutes, I'm dumping breakfast in the ditch, and we'll go without."

"Go to hell," somebody called out, but without much conviction.

"You're a sadist," Cherry told him. "I haven't done this shit in years."

"No time like the one you're in," Hamm said. "C'mon! Everybody out."

Slowly, the team came alive and trudged over to the mess tables, dressed in everything from boxer shorts to fatigue pants. Eyes began to open as coffee mugs were filled. They stood in line to scoop scrambled eggs, sausage, and toast off the grill, then found seats at the tables.

"Damned if you aren't a fair cook," Peachy Keen said, his mouth stuffed with eggs.

"I wanted to set a good example for the rest of you," Hamm said.

Cherry caught on right away. "Uh-oh. What kind of example?"

"For the next twenty-six days, everyone draws KP.

We'll rotate by meals. I was first, and I'll post the roster inside the Buffalo.''

"Shit!"

"That's right, Pat. No enlisted men around to take the shit details, so we do the best we can. Listen up, now." Hamm dug his duty roster out of his breast pocket and stood under the light to read while the others ate. "We have two sets of aircraft and flight manuals, translated into English, so we're going to shift time on those. Everyone will read them thoroughly because it's the only way I know for you to become familiar with the aircraft and, especially, the translation from the Cyrillic alphabet. Pickett, you and Harper start reading aircraft manuals right after breakfast. Tomorrow, you will go on to the flight manuals.''

The two nodded.

"McDonough, Bellows, Keen, and De Veres. This morning, you put the Hind together, quality-check it, fuel it, and crank it up . . ."

"All right!" McDonough yelled.

". . . then take it apart again."

"What!"

"So somebody else can learn to assemble it. In the afternoon, you do the same thing to the Havoc. This morning, Clark, Ketchum, Cherry, and Talbot are to assemble the Havoc, then break it down. In the afternoon, you switch to the Hind. I've got a list for tonight, too. Keen starts on electronics, with Ketchum as his backup. Bellows, McDonough, and Talbot on hydraulics and mechanics. I want Canton, Cherry, Clark, and Pickett to learn everything possible about those Swatter missiles. Harper, De Veres, and I start on instrumentation. Any questions?''

"That all we're going to do, play mechanic?" Ketchum asked.

"For the first few days, that's all we're going to do. We want everyone to know these birds inside out, as well as the written documentation for them, before we put them in the air." Hamm gave them a lopsided grin. "And we'll be switching the teams around, so everyone learns to work with everyone else. I will, by the way, be giving an oral test every now and then."

"No shit?" Keen asked.

"No shit, Peachy."

Canton spoke up. "You forgot me for this morning, Hamm."

"No, I didn't. You and I are maids-for-a-day. We're going to build a shower, dig a latrine, wash the pots and pans, and prepare the laundry. Problems?"

No one had a problem, and if Canton did, he was not going to talk about it.

By five o'clock, everyone had set to their tasks.

Hamm tried to involve Canton in any kind of a dialogue as they cleaned up from breakfast, but the man did not seem proficient at give-and-take conversation. He was difficult to read as it was, and he was not going to make it any easier.

It took them three hours to dig the latrine with undersized field shovels, thirty yards south of the cottonwood stand, and they were both soaking wet by the time they finished. The temperature and the humidity had climbed steadily throughout the morning, making a bank of clouds in the southwest look desirable. Hamm was sure any rainstorm would pass them by, as had the storm of yesterday.

Erecting a shower did not take long. The copse of cottonwood trees, some so old they were rotted through, contained about thirty trees. In the middle of the stand, ten feet off the ground, they suspended ten fifteen-gallon lister bags, attached nylon pull cords to the spigots, then interconnected each of the bags with half-inch plastic tubing. Tying the tubing to tree trunks, they ran it down to the small spring-fed pool. With an electric pump hooked into the generator, Hamm began pumping water into the overhead bags. The sound of a spurting drip into the first lister bag was refreshing.

Canton worked his shoulders out of his wringing wet fatigue shirt. ''Hot damn. We'll have showers tonight.''

Hamm peeled off his own shirt. ''Hot-water showers, too, in this heat.''

Canton looked at his watch. ''Jesus. It's noon already. What're we having for lunch?''

''You'll have to check Bobby's menu, Pat. The only thing I remember is chocolate-chip cookies.''

''You've got to be shitting me. Every meal is on some printout?''

Hamm grinned at him. ''What did you expect? Makes it easy for the cook, though.''

''Who's the cook?''

''Your turn.''

''Ah, fuck! This thing's no fun at all,'' Canton complained.

''You thought killing a few people in Central America was going to be fun?''

''Hell, yes.''

Hamm mulled that over a bit, then said, ''Well, things are looking up. This afternoon, it's our turn to read operations manuals.''

''It's a goddamned waste of time, Hamm. I can fly anything invented.''

"Maybe that's right, Pat, but can you fix it after you break it?"

The man thought that statement unworthy of reply. While Canton went to prepare lunch, Hamm checked with everyone and collected their carry-on luggage, now only packed with the clothing they would need after the operation.

As he stacked the bags in the back of the Jeep, he wondered which two bags would not again meet up with their owners.

# NINE

Jackson Coriolanus's driver double-parked the limousine at the River Entrance to the Pentagon. Coriolanus opened the door on his own and got out. Leaning back inside, he said, "Be back here at eleven-thirty, Dean."

"Right you are, Mr. Coriolanus."

The Chrysler pulled away, and Coriolanus stood for a moment, studying the white monuments to democracy shining in the sun on the other side of the Potomac. It was a sight he loved, though not particularly from the vantage point of the Department of Defense.

He turned around to look at the monolith that obscured the landscape to the west. Imposing and ponderous, the building represented to him many of the characteristics he found to be true of the military: overweighted, slow to react, ultraconservative. Behind the uniform, bemedaled facade lurked a roiling, tumultuous clamor—Marines, Air Force, Navy, and Army, all fighting for prominence. The civilian side—the service secretaries and their staffs—were no better than the military component. None of them could agree on a course of action in an emergency. It required a strong-willed person to obtain the support of even a subordinate.

Directly above him, on the second of the five floors, the SecDef's office windows looked out on the river. It was located on E-Ring, the outer of the five rings of the building. Looking upward at the monstrous structure, one of the largest office buildings in the world, made him conscious of his diminutive stature.

Juggling the leather envelope he carried, so he could smooth the cuffs of his Savile Row, charcoal suit jacket, Coriolanus joined the flow of people pressing the River Entrance. Twenty-five thousand people worked in the building, and thousands of tourists, emerging from the Metro station below the Concourse or from the neighboring Arlington Cemetery, added to the population.

Inside, he ignored the shops and cafeterias and headed toward the stairway leading to the second floor. His credentials allowed him past the checkpoint, and he climbed the steps, then made his way to the meeting room Winnie Storch had designated, the Gold Room opposite the secretary of defense's office suite.

Storch was already there, dripping coffee into a mug from an urn on a side table.

"This is impressive, Winnie. You must be damned close to your first star if you get to use the SecDef's side of the house."

Storch looked up at him. An ex-helicopter combat pilot in Vietnam, with lingering rumors about his effectiveness in that role—founded or unfounded—Storch was a competent administrator. The fruit salad adorning the left breast of his summer khaki uniform was a reflection of efficiency, rather than valor.

"It was available, Jack. The service chiefs are holding staff meetings in most of the conference rooms this morning."

Despite the Pentagon's massive size, the number of people working in it caused space to be at a premium. Some of the higher-echelon people, military and civilian, had large offices, but most of the staff worked out of tiny cubicles. "I feel like we should have about thirty more people joining us in this cavern," Coriolanus said.

He filled a mug of his own, then sat across from Storch at the end of the large conference table. He was about to ask a courtesy question regarding Storch's family when General Kuster arrived.

From his longtime association with the man, Coriolanus knew that the Deputy Director of the DIA was generally in a good mood in the early part of the day. Kuster bobbed his head and smiled in confirmation of that observation and told them, "Good morning, gentlemen."

"Hello, Gene," Coriolanus said.

Within the twin services, Kuster held a position about equal to that of Coriolanus's boss, but that had never intimidated Coriolanus. Generally, he felt that DIA often traipsed on ground that belonged to the CIA, and he and Kuster were not above heated arguments over jurisdiction. Kuster was military clear to his brass core, but Coriolanus also knew that the general quite often disapproved of public military policy.

Kuster filled a coffee cup, then found a seat next to Storch, leaving Coriolanus by himself on the opposite side of the table. The maneuver was probably supposed to make the CIA operative feel outnumbered by the military, but he knew that Kuster did not have a great deal of admiration for Storch. Thinking about that, he wondered who did.

"What's this all about, Jack?" the general asked.

Coriolanus opened his leather portfolio, extracted two sets of photographs, and handed them to each of the men. "The DDO asked me to update you on a scenario we've been following for several weeks. He's planning on raising it as a potential major issue in next week's National Security Council meeting, and he doesn't want anyone at Defense to be surprised by the information."

"Out of character for the CIA, isn't it, Jack?" Winfield Storch asked. "The DCI usually likes to spring an intelligence coup on us now and then."

"What have you got here?" Kuster asked.

The photos were numbered in the top right corner, and Coriolanus started with number 1, and worked his way through the rest. "The freighter is *Riga Star*. She loaded small arms, heavy machine guns, ammunition, grenades, SA-7 SAMs, food, and clothing out of Rostov, on the Black Sea. For the next several weeks, she steamed through the Suez, then made stops off Pakistan, Sri Lanka, and Cambodia. Check pictures two through eight."

"The milk run," Storch said.

"She linked up with a freighter named the *Southern Merchant* in the Arabian Sea during this journey. It was a night rendezvous, and we didn't have infrared working for us, but we suspect that there was a transfer of cargo. The *Southern Merchant* normally works a run into Nicaragua."

"The Sandinistas may not know it," Kuster said, "but this might be one of the last major resupply efforts. The data we've got coming in now suggests that the Soviets are trimming back their expenditures. They're beginning to think milk and cheese are more important."

Coriolanus knew that, but figured Kuster was offering a tidbit. Usually, the intelligence services saved their good stuff for trading among themselves.

"That's what we're sensing, too, Gene," Coriolanus confirmed. "But even if that's true, this shipment may be worth following. In the next shots, you see that the *Merchant* put into Luanda, Angola. She was there for seven days, and she loaded nine crated aircraft, two of which are secured to her foredeck."

"What do your crateologists say about them?" Kuster asked.

The CIA had made a science out of studying crates. Surveillance photographs yielded much information from the grainage of the wood used—helping to define the region of its origin, the metal fittings, the construction techniques. Craftsmen left their trademarks, whether it was on a violin or on a wooden box. If there were gaps between boards, the eye of the camera peered within.

"There are five Hinds and four Havocs aboard that ship," Coriolanus said.

"Havocs!" Storch exclaimed.

Kuster thought that one over before saying, "The Kremlin doesn't normally loan out, or give away, their latest technology. Hell, we don't even have a good picture of a Havoc."

"All I can show you is that little peek there. But we used some of our sources in Soviet military logistics and backtracked that one, too, Gene. Angola has . . . or rather, had, eight Mi-28s on hand, shipped in last January. Now they have four, and those four are still in their crates. It looks like the Russkies might be spreading around a few of their knockout punches."

"You suppose some defense minister has made his Swiss banker very happy?"

"Undoubtedly," Coriolanus agreed.

"Where's your ship now?"

"Looks to be en route to Nicaragua. We estimate her arrival there on June eighteenth."

"Nicaragua has a minor air force already, based on hand-me-down Soviet aircraft," Kuster said. "Not very effective because of the level of pilot competence, but a presence. What you're suggesting, though, is that they're going to boost the air war, even while they're talking peace."

"And I'm saying one more thing, Gene."

"Yeah, I know. In the past, they've used the sham of Cuba supporting the Sandinistas. Now it's Angola. Or maybe even more directly, straight Soviet support."

"Abandoning the pretense is an important change," Storch managed to contribute.

"Exactly," Kuster agreed.

"It's worth both of our agencies keeping an eye on," Coriolanus suggested.

"And that's what this meeting is about?" the DIA director asked.

"Certainly. We don't want to keep secrets from each other."

Kuster's horsey face was normally implacable and did not make for easy reading. For a split second, Coriolanus thought he saw a strange expression in the general's eyes and eyebrows. But he just said, "I agree, Jack."

"Good."

Kuster tilted his mug and drained his coffee. "I don't like the way this thing is shaping up. What it leads to is a confrontation between the U.S.S.R. and the U.S., on a Central American battlefield."

"Not necessarily," Coriolanus cautioned. "But it suggests an increased air war, at minimum. The Sandinistas may get optimistic, or they may begin to overreach."

"In what way?" Colonel Storch asked.

"The fact that the Contras have used Honduras and Costa Rica for staging areas, or that Contra supply has flowed openly through El Salvador, may finally be reaching a point where tolerance has been exceeded. Our people think there's a chance that the Sandinistas may want to prove a point by attacking Honduras, El Salvador, or Costa Rica, looking to cut off support."

"Who's 'our people'?" Kuster asked.

"Harry Downs. He has good instincts."

"I know Harry," Kuster said, "and you're right. Clark still doing the liaison?"

"Yes."

"What does he say?"

"I haven't talked to him in a while. Harry says he's been out of touch, making a tour through the zone."

"You mean checking the drug pipeline?"

Coriolanus bristled at that. "Goddamn it! That's uncalled for, Gene."

"Is it?"

"I know what the fucking innuendos have been, and I don't doubt that some of them are true," Coriolanus admitted. "But we all have our bad apples, don't we, General? Yours happened to be in the White House basement.

It doesn't mean that I condone it, or that I support any activity condemned by the Executive or by Congress.''

"What pisses me off," Kuster said, "is that some of your people got away with it. Or they got fired, then rehired in another job. I'm as much in favor of restoring democracy down there as anyone, but I prefer using democratic principles. The CIA skirts the law too often, Jack.''

"Not when I have anything to do with it," Coriolanus said, and meant.

He knew Kuster had to agree with him on that point, and the general did. "All right. I'll give you that. But I want to be sure nobody in your shop is running some little scam of his own. I don't know what Dilman thinks about that, but DIA will stomp ass if we find out about it.''

Storch fell in line with Kuster. "Admiral Dilman would loan you his boots, General.''

"We can't control the high number of private efforts to help the Contras," Coriolanus said, and you know some of that is going on.''

"Private, shit! Like the CMA?''

The Civilian Military Assistance effort was ostensibly a private support group, but many of its members had been active in the Alabama National Guard and there had been many accusations that CIA and Defense Department materiel had been funneled through the CMA to the Nicaraguan rebels at a time when Congress had strictly forbidden such aid.

Coriolanus did not want to get in a shouting match. "All I'm here for, Gene, is to tell you about something that worries us. Not to go back in the ring.''

Kuster backed off at the same time he stood up, tugging his uniform jacket into place. "Okay. We'll look into it. And we'll keep each other posted.''

"By all means. We're on the same side in this."

"Which means we don't want a war," Kuster said.

"At least, not a war where we're landing Marines on the beach," Coriolanus said.

"We've done that too many times already."


## TEN


**B**ecause of its extensive use during the war in Southeast Asia, and because of the accompanying high-visibility news coverage in that set of hostilities, the Bell UH-1 Iroquois helicopter was probably the silhouette the public most closely associated with military helicopters. Named the Huey as a result of its military designation, various models of the design had been in production since 1959. It was originally designed as a combat-support vehicle, and the "H" model carried fourteen combat-equipped soldiers. In Vietnam, the Pentagon learned how vulnerable the forty-foot fuselage was to ground fire, and some Hueys were armed to act as escorts. Typically, the armament included M-60 machine guns mounted in the side doors and 7.62-millimeter machine guns or 40-millimeter grenade launchers mounted in the nose.

Every man on Bobby Clark's team had logged hundreds of hours in one or another version of a Huey, from UH-1Ds to UH-1Vs, the latter modified from the "H" model for medical evacuation.

Though the Mi-24 Hind had been introduced in 1973 in a role similar to the Huey, later models were altered to increase their ground-assault role. The Hind-D they had in Brooks County, Texas, had the stepped cockpit that located the pilot above and behind the co-pilot/gunner, in addition to an eight-man-capacity cargo compartment. Its fifty-six-foot rotor had five blades compared to the Huey's twin-bladed forty-eight-foot span. While the UH-1H had a single 1,400 shaft horsepower turboshaft, the Mi-24 boasted twin 2,200 shaft horsepower turboshafts. At ninety-nine miles, the Hind had two thirds the combat range of the Huey, but it covered the ground faster, hitting 193 miles per hour, 66 miles per hour faster than the American chopper. And once it covered the ground, the helicopter could tear it up with twin 30-millimeter cannon or a 12.7-millimeter, four-barrel machine gun and, mounted out on its drooping andehedral stub wings, four Swatter antitank missiles and twin rocket pods.

"It's a lethal son of a bitch," Sean McDonough told Hamm over the intercom. His words slurred slightly around the unlit cigar that always accompanied him. He was flying in the pilot's seat while Hamm held the gunner's position.

"Let's go on back there and see if you managed to hit anything."

"Asshole. I always hit whatever I'm shooting at." McDonough canted the craft nearly on its side as he banked hard to the right and shot back toward the deep and wide arroyo they were using as a target range.

Hamm wiped the sweat out of his eyes and worked his shoulders against the web harness. At their altitude of approximately twenty feet, the sage and scrub pine shot by fast. In the low nose cockpit designed for the gunner, Hamm felt exposed, as if he were mounted on the tip of a spear.

The gully ran across their line of flight about a mile ahead. Within seconds, the rim came up, McDonough banked hard to the left around a solitary pine tree, and dropped like a rock into the small canyon. "Hoo-eee!" he yelled exultantly into the intercom.

The small canyon climbed to the west, and McDonough charged ahead, rising with the terrain, but keeping the canyon walls above them. Half a mile later, he slowed abruptly and hovered over the target area. The white cross painted with flour on the dried-mud floor of the arroyo was obliterated. They were going through ten-pound bags of flour steadily.

"See what a Hawkeye McDonough, armed with a Swatter, can do to a bag of flour?"

"Hey, I fired and ran the son of a bitch in," Hamm reminded him. The AT-2 Swatter was radio controlled by the gunner.

"Yeah, but I put you on site."

"All right, Sean, you get an A."

"Shit. No A plus?"

"I'm saving those for finals," Hamm told him. "Let's go home."

McDonough increased pitch and rose out of the canyon to the two hundred feet of altitude that Hamm had set as the maximum for all flights around their training area. The cap on altitude kept them relatively invisible to anyone passing by in the outside world and increased their proficiency in low-level flight.

McDonough headed south at a relatively slow pace,

though there was nothing worth sightseeing. The turbine engines had long before chased away birds and other wild-life. The horizons appeared far away and were undis-tinguished in their ecru monotony. The long and parched brown grass waved lazily in a late-afternoon breeze. For the last three days, they had been faced with mid-afternoon windstorms. When the thirty-mile-per-hour gusts died down, dust hung in the air, giving their world a hazy qual-ity. There had been no rain in three weeks.

The cottonwood stand was visible long before the shrouded figure of the Hercules. The Havoc was on the ground near the tall tail of the transport.

"Our village looks deserted with the Buffalo gone," McDonough said.

"At least I don't have to fly the damned thing again," Hamm said.

At the end of the second week of encampment, Clark had taken the Buffalo back to Miami to exchange their empty fuel drums for full ones. This week, De Veres had flown it back to Florida to return it to whomever he had leased it from. They would no longer need the second transport. De Veres was flying back commercial, and Clark was to meet him in Corpus Christi with the Jeep.

It was Clark's third trip away from the campsite in the Jeep. The first time, the day after their arrival, he had taken their luggage and shipped it to an unrevealed desti-nation. His second jaunt had been a shopping spree, to augment supplies, especially the edible kind. Clark's com-puter had underestimated the appetites of men working hard, long hours. It had especially underestimated the rate of beer consumption, given the humidity, temperature, and Sean McDonough. Iced tea got them through the day, but Anheuser-Busch and Adolph Coors, the evenings.

McDonough approached slowly, losing altitude and speed in coordination, then settled the Hind in next to the Havoc, and Hamm said, "Let her idle, Sean."

"Yo, Chief."

Unbuckling straps, the two of them clambered out of the cockpits, slipped their helmets off, and walked over to where the others loitered around the rear of the Hercules. The engineer, Rick Talbot, was studying an aircraft manual. He had lost nearly twenty pounds in three weeks and his fatigues hung loosely on him.

Hamm squatted at the edge of the group and said, "Peachy, you and Clay load a few bags of flour on the Hind and go set up some targets for tonight."

"Gotcha, Steve."

Four of the others helped load the bags, and after Keen lifted off and shot away, the silence was a relief. Hamm palmed his ears with both hands, trying to relieve a pressure that was not really there. "I'm beginning to think the only sound left in the world is the sound of turbine engines."

"We should write a song," Bellows said. " 'Ballad of the Whino.' That's with a W."

"You don't have to spell it out, Hank. I got it right away," Ketchum said. He had opened up, become less introspective, in the last couple of weeks.

Most of the team, in fact, seemed to feel at ease with one another, though Hamm was not certain that trust levels were yet high enough. A one-shot, three-day-long raid on Nicaragua did not force men to rely on one another as quickly as one-year tours of Vietnam had. Only Pat Canton and Bobby Clark still maintained qualities of aloofness.

Peter de Veres had surprised Hamm. The man was willing to take on any role assigned to him, without bitching about it, and he performed as asked. If Hamm suspected anything about him, it was that he had more talent and ability than he displayed.

Hamm's ears did ring a little. He had been putting in more flight time than the rest of the team, half an hour alone in each aircraft in the mornings, plus his training as a pilot or co-pilot, plus his scheduled check rides with each pilot. As commander, and as evaluator, he had considered it necessary to become more proficient than the others. By the end of the third week, both the Hind and the Havoc felt as familiar to him as three or four models of the Huey once had. His eyes picked out the right instruments automatically, and his mind was comfortable with kilometers per hour and fuel loads rated in kilos.

The wind was coming up, gusting to maybe fifteen miles per hour. The gritty sand rattled against the aluminum of the C-130. Hal Cherry rose and went abroad the Hercules. "I'm closing the ramp, if no one minds. I'm tired of sleeping in the sand."

Hamm moved around to the side of the transport, under the wing, where the fuselage and the hanging camouflage netting offered some protection. The pilots followed and they all settled around the tables, half squatting on the backless camp stools.

"Beer, anyone?" McDonough asked.

Hamm lifted his wrist and checked his watch: 1620 hours. "Only one for Pat, Jerry, Rick, and myself. We've got night runs."

In the last four days, Hamm had begun to schedule night missions, and starting tonight, he had added a strafing sequence to the mission. He rode with each pilot and kept a checklist evaluation. Though he occasionally had to force himself to be objective and to remind himself to delay aircraft commander decisions until the last week, he was already beginning to sense how he would assign each of them to six teams. Some of them were not going to be happy about it.

"Who's cooking tonight?" he asked.

Cherry, standing in the side door of the plane, spoke up. "The chef's right here. I thought a nice leg of lamb, perhaps with a tangy brandy sauce, broccoli in Hollandaise, and butterflake dinner rolls. From the cellar, a bright cabernet sauvignon . . ."

"Which all translates to what?" Keen asked, rubbing the stubble of whiskers he had declared was about to become a beard.

"Meat loaf and french fries."

"All right. While you're showing off at the stove, Hank and Sean will tell me all about the flight characteristics of the Mi-28 and the specification of the Quad 12.7-millimeter machine gun. Pat, you and Harvey roll out some drums and top off the Havoc for tonight."

Ketchum groaned as he struggled off his stool, complaining about muscles from head to foot. Canton did not say anything. His face carried its usual surly reluctance.

Hamm got the manuals and questioned Bellows and McDonough for an hour, until Cherry called mess.

After dinner, they spread blankets or ponchos on the ground and stretched out to relax; it was still too hot inside the Hercules to be comfortable, and the blowing, sandy grit was preferable to the oppressive heat. Cherry finished his cooking chores and went off to fight the flying sand while showering. Those who were allowed to drank beer.

At 9:30, Hamm stood up and stretched. "Let's go for it, Pat."

In the dim light of the dropcord hung from an engine nacelle, Canton's face took on a new glow. He was the happiest man in the valley when he was flying, or about to fly. "Damn tootin'!"

They found their helmets and donned them while walking out to the Havoc. The Mi-28 was probably most comparable to the new McDonnell Douglas Apache, just entering American military service in force. Since he worked for McDonnell Douglas, Bellows had managed to sneak a flight in the Apache. Canton, De Veres, and Hamm had prior experience in the Bell AH-1 HueyCobra, a stepped-cockpit tandem-seater like the Havoc. The Mi-28 was a bigger helicopter and its twin 2,200 shaft horsepower turboshafts could churn out 186 miles per hour, much faster than the Cobra's 141. At 149 miles, its combat radius was about equal to that of the AH-1. The Havoc had not been introduced by the Soviets until 1984, so it was relatively new, and it was not yet in widespread use. U.S. intelligence services did not even have a decent picture of one, and Hamm had been keeping that fact alive in the back of his mind. The one they were training in carried a 30-millimeter cannon turret slung under the fuselage, along with twin rocket packs and four AT-2 missiles out on the stub wings.

Once settled in the cockpit, with the turbine cranked up and whining, Hamm keyed the intercom. "Here's a problem. Let's say, Pat, that your planned approach from the east is blocked by heavy anti-aircraft emplacements. What's your alternative?"

Canton found his RPM setting, and pulled collective. The Havoc leaped from the ground, tilted its chin down, and scooted northward. "I could hit from the south, but I'd only have a half second over target. That canyon isn't that wide at the target area. With the wind from the east, what I'd do is come down the canyon from the west."

"Why?"

"Even though the target lies low behind that hummock in the canyon, and I'll have to slow down by about sixty knots, I've got a better shot at it. The advantage is that I'll be downwind from the enemy, and they won't hear me until the last minute. That gives me the element of surprise. We'll dump some cannon rounds on target, gun it on down the canyon, and if anybody tries a SAM on me, I'll put a couple of radar seekers down their throats."

"Do it."

If Hamm had an edge over Canton in flying ability in the Havoc, it was simply because Hamm had accumulated about twenty more hours in the helicopter. Pat Canton was a natural flyer; the controls and instrumentation simply became extensions of his muscular and nervous systems. When he was forced to fly as gunner, he monitored radar detection and Doppler-type radar without consciously thinking about it. As pilot, the craft might as well have been responding to his thoughts as to his hands. What might appear risky to others was second nature to him.

Canton took the Havoc far to the west, zipping along the terrain at about twenty feet of altitude, crossed the arroyo, and then came back on it. A quarter-moon provided the only light, and the canyon was vaguely defined by silvery reflections from foliage lining the rim on both sides. The canyon depth was indistinguishable, an inky swath cut across the Texas landscape. Canton slowed to 100 kilometers per hour, according to the duplicate airspeed indicator in front of Hamm, then sank into the canyon until the rims were level with the cockpit and about thirty yards to either side.

Almost unexpectedly, the white flour crosses shining in the moonlight appeared. Canton dipped the nose, the crosses flashed into Hamm's viewfinder, and he touched off twelve of the seventy-two cannon rounds in each pod, the rapid fire shivering the airframe.

Canton went to maximum acceleration and pulled up, climbing out of the canyon at the sixty-degree angle.

"Very nice, Pat."

Canton grunted. "We get to do it again?"

"Not now. There are some others that need more practice than you do."

"Shit."

As they headed back for the encampment, Hamm noticed the headlights bouncing across the rugged terrain about the same time that Canton did. They were off to the east, on their left, about three miles away, and the twin beams looked like cat's eyes in the dark. It would be Clark and De Veres returning.

Canton rolled the Havoc hard to the left, lined up quickly on the headlights, and began to close at the helicopter's top speed.

"Break it off, Pat," Hamm ordered.

The younger man ignored Hamm.

The automobile was half a mile away, the headlights bouncing in the night.

Upwind.

They would not hear the approach.

Hamm gripped his duplicate control stick, felt the vibration transmitted along it, and tested the resistance of Canton's grip. "Goddamn it, Canton! Break off!"

"We'll give 'em a little thrill, Hamm."

Hamm had to use both hands to overcome Canton's pressure on the controls. If he had not pulled hard at the last minute, climbing high over the Jeep at about a hundred feet of altitude, he was certain Canton would have made the clearance by less than ten feet.

As it was, Canton hit the landing light switch, and the combination of abrupt, blinding light and sudden, screaming turbine appearing from nowhere in the night scared hell out of whoever was driving.

The Jeep skidded sideways, slowed, and nosed over into a ravine.

Hamm relinquished his grip on the controls, and Canton chuckled deeply over the intercom as he rolled into a tight right bank and shot back toward the cottonwoods. Checking his rearview mirror, Hamm saw the Jeep backing out of the ditch.

As soon as they landed at the camp and the rotors began to slow, Hamm climbed out of his cockpit and waited for a grinning Pat Canton to emerge from his own seat. "Ten bucks says those guys are sitting in wet seats."

Hamm hit him, a short jab with the right that caught him on the side of the jaw, took him backwards, and slammed him into the side of the helicopter.

Stunned, shaking his head, Canton pushed himself off the aircraft with his elbows.

Hamm hit him again, this time with a left, and dropped him on the ground.

"You son of a bitch!" Canton rolled over on his stomach, pulled his knees under him, then a foot, wobbled once, then came up swinging.

Hamm blocked a wild, roundhouse right with his left forearm, then connected with his own right punch, catching him on the cheekbone just under the eye. The solid thud of flesh felt good, the shock traveling up his arm. Canton's head jerked back, his knees weakened and collapsed, and he went down.

"Tomorrow morning, Cherry will get the Jeep, and you get a free ride to Brownsville. From there, you're on your own."

Canton talked to the ground, his voice shaky. "Shit, Hamm! I was just having some fun."

"This is not a fun safari."

Canton rolled back onto his haunches, overtilted, and came to rest against the Havoc's landing gear. "Fuck, man. I'll say I'm sorry."

Hamm stood over him, weighing it. The bastard was a hell of a pilot. He did not need Clark's computer to calculate the odds, and he finally decided the assets outweighed the deficits. "There aren't any more chances, Canton. You aren't commanding. You do exactly as you're told, when you're told to do it."

Canton looked up at him. His eyes were full of hate, but he said, "Got it."

"You fuck up on a mission, and I'll put a few rockets up your ass."

# ELEVEN

**H**amm's leadership style grated on Bobby Clark, though he did not know what it was about it that bothered him. Hamm did not insist upon any kind of discipline; he just gave the appearance of knowing what he was about and issued orders in a level voice that assumed he would be obeyed. And he was.

Hamm did not explain himself to the team members when he set up a series of exercises, and they did not ask for reasons. On several nights, Hamm dropped team members in the target arroyo from the chopper and had them attack the flour crosses on foot, with AK-74 assault rifles—the newest model from Kalashikov. Halfway to the target, they had been required to stop, disassemble, then reassemble the 5.45-millimeter weapon in the darkness. Using compasses, the ground assault team then had to stumble over rough country for five miles, in a black night with a light rain falling, to a rendezvous with Hamm and the Mi-24. They arrived back at the Hercules in the middle of the night, clogged with mud and filth, and never once questioned Hamm's motives, though they actively and loudly bitched about the exercise, of course.

What really irritated Clark was that, though he had not yet detailed any of the three missions to be accomplished

in Central America, two of them *did* involve minimal
ground work for several men and he had not thought to
include it in their training. Hamm had thought about it,
or perhaps about the possibility of having to survive after
a chopper was downed.

It was as if the son of a bitch had clairvoyance, or ESP,
or something, Clark thought as he lay in his hammock.

Sean McDonough interrupted Clark's introspection to
shout, "Louder, Peachy!"

Keen was up in the cockpit of the C-130, tuning one of
the radios to some station out of Brownsville. He fiddled
through some static, then Ricky Nelson's "Garden Party"
thrummed in the hollow bay of the transport.

"Well, now. That's very goddamned appropriate," Jerry
Pickett said.

The third rain of their month in the desert was falling,
heavy drops plunking on the skin of the plane. Out on the
muddy field beyond the lowered ramp, the camouflage-
netted snouts of the two helicopters could be seen in the
circle of light that escaped from the cargo bay. Despite the
rain, it was hot and muggy; Clark's T-shirt clung to his
skin like plastic wrap.

On this, the final night of the training phase, Mc-
Donough was intent upon finishing the last of the beer,
one commodity he hated to see wasted. The stock in the
refrigerator, which had been moved from the Buffalo to
the Hercules, was nearly depleted—or would be, by morning.

Keen descended from the flight deck, humming tune-
lessly along with the radio, and plopped into his hammock. McDonough tossed him a can of Bud.

Hamm sat in the middle of the deck on a crate of re-
packed Kalishnakovs, holding the spiral-bound notebook

in which he had scribbled notes throughout the training cycle. When he spoke, he used enough volume to overcome the rain and Ricky Nelson.

"Okay, listen up. Bobby, bring us up to date on your gaming model."

Clark had spent the morning in the FBI office in Corpus Christi, making a telephoned report to Harry Downs, then using the computer terminal to tap into his operations file. He cleared his throat. "I dug out the data on Moscow's communications with Managua. There are no direct links between defense agencies in the U.S.S.R. and Nicaragua. There is, however, a satellite linkup between Moscow Center and the KGB resident—name: Josef Zhukov—in the Soviet Embassy. It looks as if there *could* be an access to photographic satellite tracking, but there would be a time lag in communications."

"What does that do to your model?" Hamm asked.

"Well, I entered the data, worst-case basis, assuming the Sandinistas figured out who we were and actually wanted to track us and . . ."

"Just the bottom line."

Clark cleared his throat once again. "It dropped the Success Ratio to sixty-one percent."

"Seven-point loss?"

Clark nodded his affirmation. He did not think this was a particularly good time to mention that he had also entered the data for the time on the ground during the first two missions—something that had slipped his mind in his earlier planning sessions on the computer. If he took those into consideration, the overall SR went to 56 percent, and the mortality potential climbed to 21 percent. "Remember, please. That's worst case."

"What's best case?" Cherry asked.

"Sixty-nine percent."

"Sounds like my grades in college English," Keen said. "Not even a C."

"Anybody want to back out? This is the time for second thoughts," Hamm offered.

Sean McDonough drained his beer can, crushed it in his big hand, and got up to head for the refrigerator. "How do you read it, Steve?"

McDonough opened the door, ripped into cardboard cartons, and began throwing cans to those who raised their hands.

"For a bunch of middle-aged, ex-chopper jocks, the training went well. I put that down to both talent and experience. I feel damned good about everyone. I think we know the aircraft well enough to keep them flying. There's a good chance we can pull off something." Hamm threw up a fist and caught a can of Coors as it arced through the air. "If I have a reservation, it's in not knowing the exact targets."

The ex–DIA operative turned his attention toward Clark, but he maintained his position. "Not until we're in the staging area."

"Shit," Hank Bellows said. "Nobody's going to go shooting his mouth off, Bobby."

"No. I'm not taking one chance for a leak. We still have to get everyone down south, and anything could happen."

"Like what?" Harper asked.

"Like you get picked up by Customs, or the FBI, and you want to buy yourself a deal."

For a few minutes, everyone was quiet. Can tabs clicked as Waylon Jennings took over the radio.

Hamm looked around. "Anyone want to settle for the

eighty grand that's supposed to be in your offshore accounts, and go home?''

Canton, though he had been sullen and uncommunicative for the past week, was the first to shake his head negatively. The bruise under his right eye was dark blue and purple. Another few minutes passed before Hamm had eleven negative responses.

"Okay. Give them their passports, Bobby."

Clark walked around the cabin, checking passport pictures and passing out the blue books. Their true passports had gone with their luggage, and these had been produced by a friend of Clark's in the State Department. All the names were false, of course, as well as the home addresses. The passports had been stamped with visas for various travel and looked well used.

Peachy Keen leafed through his. "I'll be damned. I forgot I was in Turkey last year."

Digging into the canvas document case he was now using, Clark found, then handed out, the airline tickets and explained each man's itinerary. Finally, he gave each of them two thousand dollars in travel funds. "Don't get into any trouble before you get to Cruta."

Canton studied his tickets. "This a roundabout way to get where I'm going. Costa Rica?"

"I don't want everyone following the same trail, or traveling in groups."

When he sat down, Hamm made the assignments. "Here it is, troops. Bandito One: McDonough is the aircraft commander. . . ."

"Hot damn!" McDonough yelled, digging in his pocket for a cigar.

". . . and I'm co-pilot."

Clark was surprised Hamm had not given himself a

Havoc. Bandito was the call sign for the Havocs, and the Hinds would be designated by "Vaquero." There were a few other raised eyebrows, too.

"Bandito Three: De Veres is A/C, and Clark is Bandito Four."

Clark was about to object, then figured out Hamm's thinking. The flight commander and the planner did not need to have their hands full flying the aircraft, so they became Banditos Two and Four. Co-pilot/gunners had even numbers and aircraft commanders had odd numbers.

"Bandito Five is Pat Canton, and Bandito Six is Rick Talbot."

Talbot's face fell, but he did not raise an immediate objection.

"Vaquero One and Two: Hank Bellows and Peachy Keen."

Keen looked over to his partner, "You fly that sumbitch into the ground, and I'll shoot you, Hank."

"Vaquero Three and Four are Cherry and Ketchum, and Pickett and Harper are Vaquero Five and Six. Any bitches?"

During the training flights, Clark had ridden with each of the pilots, and they with him. Reviewing each man's flying talents, which were considerable, he could not really disagree with Hamm's choices.

No one else complained, either.

McDonough's bright blue eyes gleamed over the stubble on his cheeks, and he yelled, "Come on, assholes! There's still a few cases to go."

From the cockpit, Peggy Lee torched, "Fever."

After the two helicopters had been de-rotored, winched back aboard the Hercules, and lashed down on the rollered cargo floor, Hal Cherry took the Jeep and drove Canton, Talbot, Picket, and Ketchum down to the airport at Brownsville. By the time Cherry got back, the rest of the team had jammed the C-130's cargo bay with empty fuel drums, the generator, field furniture, and every scrap of cardboard and paper they could find around the campsite. Before they cut down the lister bags hanging in the yellow cottonwoods, Hamm and several others took a last warm shower, then dressed in civilian clothes.

It was another muggy day, overcast, with the clouds disgorging a misty drizzle every now and then. Two or three times during the morning, the sun tried to burn through the haze, but did not succeed.

Cherry got his last set of passengers—Bellows, Keen, and Harper—loaded in the Jeep along with the small valises they had been issued, then waited until Peter de Veres and Sean McDonough, at the controls of the C-130, started each of the four engines, found reverse thrust, and backed the airplane away from the cottonwood stand.

Hamm had raised the ramp halfway to its closed position, and he and Clark stood at the head of it, hanging on to the ropes securing a pallet of depleted fifty-five-gallon drums, and watched as Cherry waved at them, then gunned the Jeep through the grass, headed east. The Jeep would be abandoned at the airport in Corpus Christi.

After a month in grimy fatigues and boots, Hamm felt strange in slacks, a sport shirt, and low-cut loafers. His feet were lighter and felt less protected. He gripped the nylon tie-down firmly as De Veres shoved in power and the Hercules lumbered across the muddy prairie. He could sense the lift increasing, but it was not happening quickly enough. The plane was heavily loaded because Clark had insisted on leaving nothing behind.

Clark's forehead was crinkled in a frown.

Hamm had to yell to be heard above the engines, the rattle, and the wind scream. "Be a shame if we lose it right here, huh, Bobby?"

"We're not losing anything!" Clark yelled back at him, but still looked worried.

The big transport banged and rumbled crossing the uneven ground, the engines screaming at full throttle. The cottonwoods behind them dwindled to shrubbery. They were leaving a deep set of wheel tracks in their wake. Finally, it lurched once into the air, touched down briefly, then De Veres took his time gaining altitude as he circled around to the east. Landing gear clunked up into the bays, and the flaps retracted.

Hamm threaded his way forward, stepping around boxes and crates, ducking under the Hind's tail rotor, and sat in the canvas sling seat beside the port hatch. Next to him was the camp stove. A bungee strap secured his small AWOL bag to the aluminum frame of the seat. Clark followed, took the seat next to him, and they both donned headsets that were hanging from hooks on the fuselage wall.

He listened to McDonough's and De Veres's banter on the intercom and watched Texas unreel behind them. They crossed the coastline at about a thousand feet, two lines of white surf pounding the mainland and Padre Island. The sea was a slate blue under the gray sky. White fishing boats spotted the ocean surface.

An hour and a half later, with seagoing traffic thinned out considerably, Hamm unzipped his AWOL bag and reached inside for his K-Bar. The heft of the combat knife was entirely familiar, though, until the past month, he had not touched one in fifteen years.

Ten minutes later, De Veres spoke: "We're about as lonely as we're going to get, Bobby. We've got six ships in view, but they're a long way off. I'll take it down to around five hundred."

"Good enough, Peter," Clark answered.

McDonough worked his way onto the short ladder, slid down from the flight deck, and joined them. As was his custom, the cigar was unlit in flight. "I sure as hell hate doing this to good aircraft," he yelled.

Hamm stood up and grinned at him, patting the skin of the Mi-24. Shouting over the wind scream, he called, "We could make a stop in Bakersfield. This hummer would make a hell of an aerial sprayer."

McDonough shook his head. "Naw. Scare hell out of the farmers."

Clark and McDonough crossed to the starboard side of the ramp, and Hamm took the left side, his headset cord trailing behind him, working the controls to drop the ramp another couple of feet.

"We've got five hundred. That's it," De Veres said over the intercom.

Hamm reached down with the razor-edged K-Bar and slashed two sets of tie-downs. McDonough cut lines on the other side, waved at him, and Hamm told De Veres, "Let's have a little nose-up, Peter."

The tail dropped slightly and the pallet of fuel drums began to slide backward on the roller surface of the deck, moving easily. The drums were pocked with bullet holes, the results of AK-74 rounds, but they would still take a while to sink.

The pallet disappeared over the lip of the ramp, and Hamm saw it hit the surface of the sea a few seconds later, breaking up, barrels bouncing out of the impact, floating independently. He did not hear the crash.

The three of them worked their way forward, cutting crates and drums loose, and guiding them down the incline, then releasing them for free-fall. As the cargo weight changed, the center of gravity moving forward, De Veres trimmed the Hercules to keep it nose-high.

Hamm slashed the nylon ropes and freed the field stove, which was lying on its back, muscled it away from the fuselage wall, and then gave it a push toward the tail. It slid away into the abyss. He wondered what some scuba diver would think if he ever crossed this trail of evidence on the Caribbean floor.

Clark and McDonough released the big trailer-mounted generator and wheeled it around into the center of the cargo bay, then let go of it.

Then the Havoc. It was loaded tail first, side-by-side on a diagonal with the Hind. They cut the hold-down ropes and it started moving aft on its own, its weight giving it impetus. On the angle, though, it would hit the sidewall and jam. Hamm braced a leg against the C-130's fuselage and pushed the nose of the Mi-28 toward the center. McDonough and Clark guided the tail boom.

Hamm called De Veres on the intercom. "You're about to lose five tons, Peter."

"Let her go."

It was not pallet mounted, and when the main landing-gear wheels dropped off the ramp, the fuselage crunched hard against the ramp edge and it stopped rolling.

"We've got the Havoc hung up," Hamm informed the pilot.

"Hold on."

Peter de Veres increased power and started climbing, increasing the angle.

The Havoc lurched and scraped along its belly, tearing gouges in its skin, then freed itself and dove into the sea. The C-130 jumped with the loss of weight, and the three cargo handlers leaped for handholds.

Hamm did not know what some Angolan minister had thought that particular helicopter was worth, but he estimated that they had just dumped two million dollars into the ocean. A twentieth-century high-tech warbird would find a bed on the bottom, next to an eighteenth-century privateer sporting fifty-pounders and Incan gold.

It took them longer to get the Hind lined up and dropped overboard.

The refrigerator was the next to go, then they tossed the K-Bars out and Hamm closed the ramp. The cargo bay felt cavernous once it was empty of war materiel, and it chattered with the vibrations of the engines.

McDonough climbed back to the cockpit to work the radio as they reentered air-controlled space. They were returning from Monterrey, Mexico.

Hamm and Clark returned to their canvas sling seats and strapped in. Hamm said, "Part One is over, Bobby. How do you feel about it?"

Clark nodded, his eyes focused on the floor, or something below it. "Good. You did it well, Hamm."

"Canton still worries me. We should have dumped him, or given him a ticket to Colombia. Or maybe tied him in the Havoc's cockpit."

Clark looked up, his face carrying the squinch-eyed concern it had shown for the past week. "No. You got that straightened out. We need twelve men."

"Not if one of them is going to get the rest of us killed," Hamm said.

"Goddamn it! I said we need him. You're not on the fucking planning staff."

Hamm let it go.

Sitting in a C-130 headed for a Floridian paradise, Hamm thought maybe there were more than two sides in this escapade. There were the Sandinistas and the several factions within the Contras. The Soviets and the Americans had an interest. Then there was Clark's little group. Then there was Canton.

"We won't know if it's straightened out until it's all over," he told Clark. "But I meant what I said. I'll shoot the son of a bitch before I'll put up with his grandstanding or with his jeopardizing any of the rest of us."

Clark checked Hamm's eyes, then looked away. "Okay by me. And if it comes to that, I'll do it."

They rode in silence for a while, listening to the drone of the engines, then Hamm asked, "You going to give me the targets?"

"I can't do that."

"I only get a week's lead time?"

"That's plenty of time," Clark insisted. "As tactical commander, that's all you need."

"Not if your goddamned computer has missed some vital input, and I've got to adapt."

"It's taken care of."

"Like the Moscow-Managua communications were taken care of?" Hamm asked.

Clark did not respond.

"You holding something back, Bobby?"

"What would I be holding back?" Clark turned his head

to reengage Hamm's eyes, making his own wide and innocent, and therefore suspect.

Hamm thought there was a lie in there somewhere. In fact, he was pretty damned sure of it.

"I want this thing to succeed," Clark told him. "It doesn't do me any good it I skew the data. My ass is on the line, too."

"Who else is in on this thing?"

"What do you mean, who else?"

"You denying there's some Washington, D.C., people with knowledge?"

Clark pondered that, then said, "No. But they're placed where I need information or backup. We'll have influence if we need it."

"Shit. And you're worried about us leaking information? Washington, D.C., and secrets don't mix, Bobby."

"They will this time. There's too much involved and there's very few people."

Hamm was certain that there was a great deal more going on than Bobby Clark was revealing, but he did not know how to get at it. He hated surprises. "By the way, what the hell does your computer call us?"

"The ALECTO Mission."

"One of the Greek Furies. Figures."

"Nobody's going to spill anything, Hamm."

"Sure. That's probably what Colonel North said to Admiral Poindexter."

"It's tight," Clark claimed. "No secretaries, no one in the White House."

"Who?"

"I'm not giving you names. But I have intelligence and defense contacts. We have some good people covering us, if we need it."

"Bullshit! Anything goes wrong, plan on being dumped, Bobby. Ask Eugene Hasenfus."

Despite Bobby Clark's wide-eyed I'm-telling-the-everlasting-truth expression, Hamm was uneasy about the number of people in Washington-based agencies who were involved in this thing. He could not believe that the mission concept had originated with Clark. There was a stubborn set to Clark's lips, so Hamm did not push it further, and they finished the ride into Miami in uneasy silence.

Once on the ground, they left De Veres to return the airplane to its rightful, or unrightful, owners and split up. McDonough was making a quick trip home to Bakersfield, to make sure he still had a business, before he started the journey Clark had devised for him. Hamm took a cab to the closest Holiday Inn and checked in just after six.

It was not his hotel of choice in Miami, but he was eager for a hot shower, a decent meal, and clean sheets. He entered his refrigerated room, immediately forgetting both the Texas and Florida heat, and took the shower first. Dressing in fresh slacks and a clean sport shirt, Hamm went down to the lounge, sat at the bar, laid a fifty on it, and ordered a double Chivas Regal. "Skip the water, and let's see how long a single ice cube lasts," he told the Cuban tending bar.

"Right on, man." The Cuban was of an age where he did not belong to the old order and was not certain of the new. The Spanish accent was Florida bred.

Hamm sipped his drink and studied the darkened lounge in the backbar mirror. A dozen touristy types were scattered about, one couple at the bar and the rest at tables. One tourist, in a light gray vested business suit, studied him back in the mirror.

Just after Hamm ordered his second drink, this time

with two ice cubes, the gray suit rose from his table and walked to the bar, taking the stool next to Hamm.

The Cuban brought Hamm his drink, picked the price out of the change Hamm had left spread on the Formica, and asked the new arrival, "Another bourbon, señor?"

"Yeah. Let's do that." The bartender sidled down to his station, and the man caught Hamm's eye in the mirror and asked, "Hamm?"

He turned to face his accuser. "Sorry, friend. Wrong number."

The man paled visibly and looked away.

Hamm downed the rest of his drink, picked up most of his change, and walked out. He went right out the front doors and crossed the street.

When he saw the gray suit emerge from the motel, looking up and down the street, he rounded the corner and walked leisurely toward the mouth of the alley, then turned into it.

The brick-faced building next to the litter-strewn alley blocked the streetlights and neon. It was like stepping into an inkwell. Hamm did not have time to wait for night vision. He felt for the brick with his hand, then backed up against it and waited.

His pursuer had the same problem. He stepped into the mouth of the alley, his head bent forward, peering into the darkness.

Hamm reached out with one big hand, caught him at the back of the neck, and whipped him forward.

"Hey!" he yelled as he stumbled, then fell onto his hands and knees.

Hamm heard the shoes scraping against broken asphalt as the man rotated, looking for his attacker. He took two steps toward the sound and brought his linked hands swinging down hard. Again he got the back of the neck, though slightly off-center. The man went flat on his belly.

Hamm spun around and dropped a knee into the man's back. He was all hard muscle, but no brains.

"Goddamn!"

"Who are you?"

"Jesus Christ! DIA."

"Not for long. You just blew it, asshole."

The operative struggled under Hamm's knee for a second, and Hamm reached out, found an arm, and levered it upward and back, twisting at the same time.

The struggling stopped. "All right! Let go! Goddamn, man!"

Hamm did not release his grip. "Give me the word."

"Shit. Tango Two."

"At least you got that right!"

# TWELVE

The meeting over at State had been rather intense, and Coriolanus feared that both the Director and the Deputy Director of Operations had sounded off once or twice too often to the sensitive skins that populated the State Department. Coriolanus believed that there was a time for diplomacy and that there was a time for hardheaded action. The career diplomats at State believed there was only time for diplomacy, even if it took ten years to accomplish what the Agency could force in a few months. The meeting, which covered some long-range objectives, had deteriorated quickly. It would take a few phone calls and a few hours to soothe the ruffled minds, to protect the current operations for several projects in Europe, not to mention the budgets for those operations.

Jack Coriolanus was not in the best of moods when he returned to his office after five o'clock, knowing he had to make those calls right away, and knowing he hated playing mediator. Worse, his new assistant, Claude Nolan, was waiting for him.

"So. Is this really important, Claude? I've got some priority calls to make."

Nolan was young, with twelve years' service, but he was loyal and perceptive. "I don't know how important it is, Chief, but I thought you'd like to know. One of our watchers at Miami International spotted Steve Hamm."

"The hell he did! Doing what? Vacationing?" Coriolanus let the sarcasm flow.

"Maybe, except he arrived on a C-130 that apparently originated in Monterrey, Mexico. If he's vacationing, it's a damned cheap package tour. And he was with Bobby Clark and two unidentified Caucasian males. Seemed funny to the watcher, so he reported it."

"With Clark?"

"Yessir."

"This come to you through Harry Downs?"

"No, sir. It goes around Downs—from the team we've had watching the Miami area for Agency operative movements." Nolan consulted his notebook. "The watcher was named Neale. He reported because of Clark."

Coriolanus pondered the unlikely duo of Hamm and Clark for a moment before deciding he did not like it. "Where did they go from the airport?"

"Unknown, sir. The watcher had no instruction on either Clark or Hamm. He just knew Hamm was supposed to be out of any active picture now."

"Yes," Coriolanus said. "That's right. He's supposed to be."

"If you want me to, I can have our people locate him."

"That's easy enough. He'll be in the best hotel in town. Or maybe not, now that he's not on Uncle's expense account. No, I'll make a call first."

As soon as Nolan left, Coriolanus called Harry Downs, but the man had already left his office. It was seven o'clock before he reached Downs at his home in Falls Church.

"Harry, where's Bobby Clark?"

"He's been taking the tour down south, but I don't know exactly where, Jack. Why?"

"He was seen in Miami with Steve Hamm."

"That so?" Downs's voice took on a guarded tone. "I wouldn't know why, except they've known each other for some time."

"You get on the horn to Clark, and you tell him to steer clear of Hamm. I don't know what the fuck Clark's up to, but I don't want him subcontracting anything—anything at all—with Hamm. You got me on that?"

"Well, sure, Jack. Except, you know, Hamm might be a hell of a lot better prospect than some of the damned Contra leaders who are padding their Cayman accounts with our cash."

"You tell Clark that if he's trying to involve Hamm, I'll pull him out of the ring and slap him in the locker room so damned fast he'll . . ."

"Gotcha, Jack."

Coriolanus spent forty minutes calling people who had gotten hot in the meeting, trying to cool them off. He did not like playing diplomat and suspected he was only half-successful. He was about to give up for the day and look for someplace quiet for dinner when the telephone rang.

"Me again, Jack," Downs said. "I finally got hold of Clark."

"And?"

"He says he ran into Hamm purely by accident, when Bobby hitched a ride on somebody's airplane coming up from the south."

"You believe that shit?"

"Yes, Jack. I do."

"What's Hamm up to?"

"Bobby doesn't know. He thought Hamm might be looking for some kind of contract work."

"It's damned fortunate that we don't have any available," Coriolanus said.

"Right. Bobby did pick up an interesting item this trip, Jack."

"What's that?" Coriolanus asked.

"Hot Cuban pilots."

"So? What's so goddamned hot about Cuban pilots?"

"I meant that these Cubans are aces out of the Angola wars. What Bobby hears, they're going to go to work for the Sandinistas."

"Shit. You mean connect them up with these new helicopters?"

"It's only a theory at the moment, Jack. We'll just have to be alert for it."

Coriolanus pulled his magnetic board out of the desk drawer, uncapped a marker, and wrote "Cuban pilots" in the left column. One more damned thing to watch, he thought.

"Where are they now?"

"Bobby's source has them already in Managua."

Lieutenant General Eugene Kuster was reviewing the photographs that had been passed out at the previous day's meeting of the National Security Council when his intercom buzzed. He appreciated the interruption. Photographs bored him silly.

"Phone for you, General. The white line."

"What are you doing here, Clea?" Kuster checked his watch, a gold Rolex that his wife, Claire, had gotten him. Hamm used to say he was hung up on the sound of Claire and Clea. "It's two hours past normal people's quitting time."

His secretary laughed. "I think I'm normal, but I need the overtime."

"You're just out to bankrupt me, that's what. Go home." He picked up the secure line. "General Kuster."

"Merle Nation here, General."

Nation was Air Force assigned to the DIA, and he was based in Miami. "Go ahead, Major."

"I saw Hamm. He's in Miami," the operative said in an aggrieved tone.

Kuster had alerted watchers in all the major airports since he did not know where Hamm might eventually turn up. "Where at in Miami?"

"Airport Holiday. The son of a bitch damned near took my arm off."

"Shit! You didn't contact him?"

"Well, sir, I, uh, yeah, I approached him. . . ."

"What the hell kind of tradecraft are we teaching? You trying to blow his cover, Major?"

"Uh, no sir."

"You're lucky you're able to use a phone."

"Yes, sir."

"He have a message?" Kuster had to make an effort to control his voice.

"He gave me eleven names, but said that all of them are operational types. He said he's sure there are some links to D.C., but hasn't pinned them down yet."

"Give me the names." Kuster wrote them down as Nation read them off. "What else?"

"You won't believe this, General. He says they've been training in Mi-24s and Mi-28s."

"He was putting you on," Kuster said, half-alarmed. It was not anywhere near what he had been expecting.

"No shit. Sir."

Kuster switched his doodling to old freighters. "He share his future plans with you, Major?"

"He's en route to Honduras now, and he wants to know if we blow it open now, or wait."

"We wait, Major, and he's to stick to his original orders. I need those names."

"I'll tell him that, sir."

"Don't go near him again, Nation."

"I won't, General. He's going to call me at a phone booth later."

Kuster lamented the caliber of operative he was getting recently and looked at the picture resting on the blotter in front of him. The silhouette of the ship nearly matched the one he had scribbled. "And tell him he's probably meeting a freighter named the *Southern Merchant*. She's got five Hinds and four Havocs aboard."

# STAGING

# THIRTEEN

Contrary to scientific, computer-driven probability, on either American CIA computers or the Soviet copy of an IBM, Josef Zhukov had absolutely no desire to rotate to Moscow for special officer training as per his new orders.

He did, however, appreciate the broad hint of a promotion to full colonel contained in the orders; such a promotion would be recognition of his capability and his effectiveness.

Zhukov had risen quickly in the fifteen years he had been assigned to the First Directorate, following the completion of his studies at the Moscow Institute at twenty-one years of age. The years did not show in his fair hair and skin, a blondness bequeathed him by a Ukrainian mother.

In all the Committee for State Security, Major Zhukov would have to be considered the most knowledgeable, from firsthand experience, of matters related to the intrigues surrounding Managua. In his five years as the KGB resident in the Managua embassy, he had acquired a passable Spanish language, in addition to his fluent English. He had toured the coast, the jungle, and the mountain areas extensively. He knew and understood the people and culture. The political and administrative problems, and their possible solutions, were second nature to him.

And Moscow now seemed strange to him; he had been too long out of its stream, would not recognize the currents. Besides, it was very cold in the winter, and Zhukov had come to relish the climate of Central America. In Moscow, a certain precautionary evaluation was necessary prior to any step taken. In Managua, his suggestions and advice were taken as orders by his Nicaraguan operatives. He had influence that would evaporate the moment he boarded the Aeroflot Ilyushin for Moscow and home.

Zhukov moved to the window of his hotel suite, overlooking the street by four stories. The sun was low in the west, casting rosy tints on the tree-lined streets and sidewalks. This part of the inner city had been restored since the earthquake. It was reminiscent of Madrid in some way for him, another beautiful city where he had once served a six-month temporary-duty assignment. Of course, in other parts of Managua, the destructive results of the 1972 earthquake were still very much in evidence.

There was a light tapping at his door.

"Enter!"

The door opened upon his aide, Boris Kamorovkin. "Señor Demarco has arrived, Major."

Zhukov was not in the mood for socializing after having

received his orders, but Manuel Demarco's monthly invitation had been long-standing and was not one he could turn down. "Very well, Boris. We shall go."

They took the clanking, open-gridded elevator to the lobby floor and found Demarco waiting in the barren area, all of the framed and gilt treasures of a bygone era having disappeared from the brocaded walls, leaving rectangles of lesser faded paper. It was what happened to grand old hotels requisitioned by the government.

Demarco had his immaculate 1977 Cadillac limousine waiting at the entrance, and the three of them entered it after greetings. The soldier who served as chauffeur closed the door with a solid thump, then went around to get behind the steering wheel.

The man who headed the country's defense and security forces surveyed him with concern. "You appear quite pale, Comrade Zhukov. You are unwell?"

"No, Manuel, the body is fit enough, and I thank you for your concern. It is a matter of the mind, I suppose, that depresses the appearance."

Demarco settled against the soft cushions, appearing uncertain as to whether he should proceed with inquiries about the KGB *rezident*'s mental state.

Zhukov enlightened him. "I have received orders to return to Moscow in August, and I admit to some sorrow at having to leave your fair city."

The Nicaraguan grinned ruefully. "Ah, I understand. A development contrary to my peace of mind also, Comrade. We have worked well together."

Zhukov smiled his appreciation. "So, if I am not up to our usual monthly revels, you will understand?"

"When you see the three young ladies, Major, all most

beautiful, all zesty and amorous, you will certainly be cheered.''

Zhukov sighed. ''For the time being, perhaps.''

Despite Demarco's best efforts to raise his spirits, Zhukov's evening had been a disaster highlighted by his inability to perform as expected for the smiling, though noodle-headed, young woman with whom he had been paired.

The morning brought yet another communication from Moscow.

Josef Pavlovich Zhukov slammed his fist against his desk. The impulsive reaction wrinkled the flimsy sheet of paper that had offended him.

''Comrade Major?'' Boris Kamorovkin asked, alarmed. His superior rarely exhibited emotion.

''I've less than three months before I'm to return to Mother Russia. And look what they send me! If I have to leave, I'd prefer to leave on the graceful note of diplomacy and success that I've achieved in my time. You know what I think, Boris? I think someone at Moscow Center is jealous of my reputation. They would have me soil it.'' Zhukov did not really think that. He really thought that he was getting caught up in something more global, a foreign policy that had gone out of control and could no longer fund itself.

''That is quite possible, Major,'' Boris agreed.

Boris always agreed with his superior, which deprived Zhukov of a reliable sounding board within his own service. He had to go outside the embassy for that.

''Wars cost too much, Boris.''

''I know, Major.''

Zhukov was ordered to use every means at his disposal

to convince the Sandinista government to seek support for their war elsewhere, to increase the burden on city and countryside, on domestic sources. Moscow wished to remain the benevolent, guiding big brother, and therefore, it would be more appropriate for Nicaraguan leaders to determine, on their own, that they were asking for too much.

Behind it all, of course, was the Kremlin's economic miscalculation of decades past. The fiasco in Afghanistan had drained valuable resources in war materiel and men. Agricultural and industrial output planning had never been realistic. The rosy desires of a few men sitting around a table had absolutely no connection in actuality with the goals of those tending the fields or the assembly lines. Zhukov, because he had long been outside the borders of the Soviet Union, and because he had eyes to see, was acutely aware of the standard-of-living differences between the *rodina* and the West.

"To be realistic, Boris, I suppose we must admit that this same directive has been issued to all embassies and consulates."

"Except perhaps in the United States, Major. I do not think they will be asked to reduce their spending by one-third."

"You are perceptive," Zhukov agreed. "No, only where the struggle is greatest, as here in Managua, will we be asked to do more for our allies with fewer rubles and cordobas. And then urged to persuade our friends to accept the decision with charm and a renewed dedication to the cause." He paused as Kamorovkin started to speak, then halted. "Go ahead, Boris."

"I only personally observe, Major, that dedication does not purchase ammunition."

"Exactly!" Zhukov's travels through the country in recent weeks had revealed to him that Nicaragua was becoming a microcosm of the Soviet Union; the lines at the shops were becoming longer. The people were hungrier. The ability of the Sandinista government to divert yet more of its economic resources against the rebels was near an end.

"And yet, Comrade Major, if you were successful, the chairman of the First Chief Directorate might well reward you with an extension of your posting."

Zhukov eyed his aide with some suspicion. Kamorovkin was a small man, only a captain while near his fortieth birthday. He was not filled with the ambition to assume Zhukov's post after his departure, and it was well that he did not have that ambition; he was not bright enough to have come to the attention of Moscow.

"I mean only, Major, that it is possible." Kamorovkin stuttered with some embarrassment.

It was June in Moscow, a time of hope and rebirth, with the smell of awakening spring in the air, and Zhukov could only think of bitter winter. He smiled at his aide. "Yes, Boris, it may well be possible. We have only to come up with a minor miracle."

"But the Americans may be helping us. The more their Congress limits the support of the rebels, the less we must spend also."

"That is true, though it is never easy to take away what has once been given." He must convince the higher-echelon Nicaraguan officers to reduce the amounts they skimmed off the top.

"Well, Boris, would you send the appointments secretary up? I had better make up a schedule, and start talking to the right people. Then, ask Major Prabinovsky and

Colonel Churbanchuk if they could stop by my office this morning.'' The two were the chief Soviet military advisors to the Nicaraguan forces.

Kamorovkin saluted smartly and exited, leaving Zhukov to stare out his open window. It was becoming very hot, very humid.

June in Honduras was not a tropical blessing. Fifteen degrees north of the Equator, the humidity was a warm, wet pillow when Hamm left the Pan Am 727 in Tegucigalpa. He passed through an uncaring customs quickly with his one piece of luggage on his impeccable passport—in the name of Kennedy. Briefly, he wondered how many times he had crossed national borders on improvised passports, but he had lost track.

He ate a lukewarm, cellophane-tasting tortilla with beans, *rosbif*, and wilted tomatoes while he waited for his next flight, sitting in the shadow of a potted palm. The airport terminal was full of transients with callused hands, hard muscles, and harder eyes. Hamm saw three men he knew from earlier days, and he was sure that two of them were current CIA operatives.

It was all reminiscent of Ton Son Nhut Airport, when it was still Ton Son Nhut and Saigon was still the pearl of the Orient. The terminal was overrun with uniforms of various services and intelligence agents representing a dozen cryptic acronyms. When he thought about it, it was almost ludicrous. Passing through Tegucigalpa on errands to or from some headquarters, most of them carried the same odor of arrogance and secrecy. Nonchalantly screening their environment with slowly moving, confident eyes, they pretended not to know one another.

Though Hamm waited behind his potted palm and

amused himself with the game of identifying spooks and spies, he was partially surprised by their numbers. Fifteen years after Vietnam, in the electronic age where spying satellites, bugs and tape recorders, and aircraft-dropped sensors had created the whole field of ELINT—electronic intelligence—it was somehow reassuring to find that HUMINT—human intelligence sources—still had some credence.

Yet, as far as Bobby Clark's enterprise was concerned, Hamm was certain that ELINT would be its more dangerous enemy. It was the area that would require the most awareness on his part.

He was fairly certain that he went unobserved to the next leg of his flight. That was aboard a decrepit DC-3 whose vents gushed warm air. Hank Bellows was on the same flight, but they did not acknowledge each other. The clattering Dakota took him into Cruta by early evening where a mild breeze off the Caribbean at least pushed the humid, moist air around.

A 1960 Ford Galaxie with oxidized red paint and a hand-painted sign reading *"Taximetro"* trundled him in creaking, grating luxury to the Pacifica Hotel, named for the ocean on the other coast. It was a relic of someone's colonialism, facaded with tall columns, sprouting with balconies and slowly revolving ceiling fans. Hamm paid in advance for his room with welcome U.S. dollars, then bought a bottle of gin and one of tonic, and toted them up to his room on the second floor. This was gin-and-tonic weather.

He opened the French doors onto the balcony, poured himself a drink, saluted the Caribbean, and settled into a rattan chair to wait for his contact. His call came at nine-fifteen. Clark did not identify himself, just said, "Mr. Kennedy?"

"That's right."

"Glad you've arrived. I'm afraid, however, that two of our fishing party have missed connections. We're going to be delayed a day."

The DC-9 managed only one flight a day into Cruta. "Oh? Who are we missing?"

"Chuck and Dick. But they are in the capital," Clark told him.

"So we shove off the day after tomorrow?"

"Bright and early. Four A.M."

"You want to get together for dinner later tonight?" Hamm asked.

"I'm going to have to find the captain of the charter boat and explain the problem. Maybe we can have lunch tomorrow, instead."

The telephone line crackled with static after Clark hung up, and Hamm dropped the receiver back in its ancient cradle. He mixed another drink while deciding to skip dinner. It was too hot to be hungry; the sweat rolled off his forehead and into his eyes.

He could imagine Pat Canton missing a plane, but not Hal Cherry. Then again, Latin American flight schedules were adventures in themselves. Airplanes and pilots broke down, all to be fixed first thing *mañana*. The worst aspect of waiting was waiting, and while Hamm was good at that usually, this time he was slightly irked. After the month of intensive training, he was keyed up as he had not been in years, prepared to do . . . something, and irritated at the unexpected delay.

What he really wanted to do was to get Bobby Clark to himself, probe the man some more, and find out what

Clark's D.C. connections were. His orders from Gene Kuster had not changed according to the inept Merle Nation, who had relayed Kuster's message during Hamm's layover in Miami. He was still in deep cover, intent on discovering three names.

Hamm's sham resignation from DIA had been designed to get him inside the ALECTO group, thanks to a whiz kid named Donnie Llewellen.

Llewellen was twenty-two years old. His captivation with electronic brains, however, in combination with his own quick and logical mind, a reverence for study, and an ambition to achieve had gained him both a bachelor's and a master's degree from Fordham University by the time he was twenty. His academic record and his knowledge of computer languages brought him to the attention of corporate and governmental recruiters, and the job offers flowed in like junk mail.

He did not take the highest-paying job; he took the one that offered him the most freedom in design activities along with access to one of the most sophisticated supercomputer systems in the world: systems analyst, in a section called Systems Design and Enhancement, DIA.

Less than two months after he started with DIA, his supervisor sent him upstairs on a special assignment for the Deputy Director. General Kuster wanted an alarm system that would warn him if Defense Department or DIA people got themselves involved in an Iran-Contra situation, and he told Llewellen to create it, using Defense fund account numbers as the basis.

Don loved the assignment. He was moved out of his modular cubicle into a private office, and he devoted long, extra hours to the "challenge," but it still took him nine months to get the prototype up and running. He weeded out thousands of nonessential account lines, like base exchanges, or company unit funds, or ship's store accounts aboard vessels at sea. The general was not looking for fraudulent sales of candy bars. While he did not have the access codes to all classified data, Donnie Llewellen was no dummy. On some days, he sat at the terminal in his office and randomly broke access codes at DIA, at the Pentagon, at Naval Intelligence, or at the Central Intelligence Agency in Langley, Virginia, so his program would have cross-referencing ability in covert funding accounts.

His program, which he called "Sentinel," had been running for two months, and was still under development when the alarm went off.

The machine was traipsing through CIA files, looking for hyphenated numbers that looked like funding-account numbers. It found a bunch of them in one subfile, which was all right.

Except that the account number existed only in that subfile. There was no funding source.

And while there were steady charges against the account numbers, there was absolutely no indication of where the phantom funds had gone, or why.

Llewellen wrote down the number, canceled "Sentinel," and punched in his access code for the CIA computer, following it with the new account number—87–8890–971–56668–3244–2201–3330. What he discovered was a previously unknown file buried behind six access codes in the CIA's massive data bank.

It was called the ALECTO file, and Llewellen printed it, then took it immediately to General Kuster.

Hamm had first been shown the file at a clandestine meeting with Kuster and Llewellen in a Mayflower Hotel suite.

Llewellen bubbled with excitement, and Hamm liked the tousle-haired eager beaver right off, even if he did not understand half of what Llewellen said. The young man spoke in acronyms and hyphenated words that had no relationship with the real world. At least, there was no relationship with Hamm's world.

"What do you think, Steve?" Kuster asked.

"Another Iran-Contra fiasco?" Hamm said. "The Agency trying to run a war at arm's length?"

"That's what I'm afraid of," Kuster said. "I couldn't give a shit whether or not some of those assholes at Langley get caught and fried over this, but damn it, every time something like this happens, it rubs off on Defense, too. Congress and the newspapers dig into everything, good and bad. There's a time and a place for covert action, but not in defiance of the law. Bastards!"

Hamm did not like paper, much less green-striped computer paper. "This is a goddamned maze. Tell me what you have here, Don."

Llewellen seemed to appreciate being called by his first name. His beaming face became even pinker in earnest pleasure. "Sure thing, Colonel. I got into the file by accident, when I was looking for account numbers. The ALECTO file is composed of several subfiles, one of which is a gaming model. Unfortunately, it doesn't tell us much. The targets are code-named. All I can tell you is that there are three targets and the locale is tropical. Beyond that, the aircraft used do not match the specifications of American models. There are twelve personnel involved."

"Which brings us to you," Kuster said.

"Me?"

"ALECTO-slash-three," Llewellen clarified.

"We still talking in English?" Hamm asked.

"That's the subfile for personnel. It has a profile for ideal candidates," Kuster explained.

"And they're still short four people," Llewellen said. "Whenever they hire someone, the file is updated with a code name."

"I fit the profile?" Hamm asked.

"You will," Gene Kuster told him. "They want chopper pilots with combat experience, a special-operations background given preference. They want people with long military service, but who are no longer on active duty."

"But . . ."

"You're going to retire."

"Just what I've always wanted to do," Hamm said. "What else do we know, Don?"

"Besides the profile and gaming files—that one's ALECTO-slash-one, there's an accounting file that started with twenty-one-point-two million dollars—though I haven't connected any transfers from government accounts. There's also a correspondence file."

"All coded, of course," Hamm guessed.

"Of course," the general said. "We can pick out the eight pilots to date, but that damned memo file names some other people. From the gist of it, they're important. Crucial, in fact."

"And you'd like to know who they are?"

"Goddamned right. You're going to tell me, Steve."

"Who am I looking for?"

"Who and what. On the who side, it's Daisy Mae, Li'l Abner, and Pappy. On the what side, it's what twenty million dollars will buy."

And now he sat in the sweltering sauna of Cruta, Honduras, and wondered how he was going to get Bobby Clark to divulge the three key players. And do it before the mission began.

# FOURTEEN

**J**ackson Coriolanus led the way into the hearing room, followed by Harry Downs. The door was shut and locked behind them by a committee staffer.

Coriolanus hated the shabby room. The 1949 restoration was tacked on top of the original mid-nineteenth-century finish, and not very well done. In recent years, when the Senate Select Committee on Intelligence had taken over the room, it was refurbished with padded spectator chairs that would not stay aligned, contributing to the seeming confusion, and a new raised dais for the members of the committee. The blondish wood of the committee bench did not match the rest of the room.

There was one man seated in the spectator section, a veteran Army general named Williams. He was a beefy, hard man, with iron-colored hair and a ruddy complexion, and he and Coriolanus had had previous contacts. The committee members, with one absence, were already in their seats: Senators Conners, Havechuk, Smith, Roebuck, Dawson, Zoelner, Mayfield, and the chairman, Sam Kramer.

"Please have a seat, gentlemen," Chairman Sam Kramer said.

Coriolanus and Downs moved forward and sat at the witness table, setting their attaché cases on top of the table. Coriolanus dialed in the combinations, unlocked his case, then turned to give a questioning look at Williams.

Kramer provided the explanation. "Mr. Coriolanus, I'm sure you know Major General Delmar Williams. As an expert on Central America, and as adjutant for the Army Reserve Training Command, he has requested permission to sit in on this briefing. Do you have an objection?"

Coriolanus turned farther toward the general. "Hello, Del. Any special reason?"

"Only one, Jack. We're currently making plans for a late-summer training exercise for thirty thousand reservists in Honduras. I want to be sure it's a good idea."

Coriolanus turned back to face the chairman. "No objection, Mr. Chairman."

"Very well. We'll get our own exercise under way then. You want to start off by summarizing the current situation?"

"It's slow at the moment, Senator. Mr. Downs will brief."

Harry Downs retrieved his note cards from his briefcase, then spent fifteen minutes giving a concise description of Sandinista and Contra movements and actions in the month since their last report. He provided them with the known quantities of supplies provided to each side. The Sandinista resources were estimated from satellite and SR-71 overflight surveillance of shipments into the country, usually from Cuba. The Contra supplies, beyond U.S.-funded humanitarian aid, were also estimates. He listed each of sixteen skirmishes, along with the estimated number of military and civilian fatalities and casualties.

Senator David Conners of Nevada, a svelte man with longish blond hair, asked, "Civilian casualties seem to be rising, don't they? Which side is knocking off more women and children, Mr. Coriolanus?"

"We're not in there counting bullets, Senator. I couldn't tell you."

"What *are* you doing, then?"

"Just what we're supposed to be doing. Gathering as much information as we can, with limited resources."

"I heard you had a cadre of training people in Costa Rica, working with FDN officers," Senator Harley Havechuk said. From Eugene, Oregon, the senator was an ex-ACLU lawyer with a thick torso and thick-lensed wire-rimmed glasses.

"I'm afraid your information is incorrect, Senator Havechuk. If we had the funds, and the authority, we'd be there. But we don't have either, and we're not." Coriolanus had to work at keeping the hostility he felt toward Havechuk out of his voice.

"I want to know what direct contact the CIA currently is making with FDN leaders," Havechuk said.

"As you are aware, the FDN—the Nicaraguan Democratic Force—is a highly splintered body. There are at least four major factions of the Contra organization, and our current direct contact is aimed chiefly at getting the leadership in each of the factions to work cohesively." Coriolanus managed to hold his temper.

"So you're meeting with them?"

"Yes, sir. Usually in Miami, and primarily with Maldonado, Matamoros, and Calera. Occasionally, our people meet with Enrique Bermudez."

"But not providing weapons or ordnance?" Conners cut in.

"No war materiel of any kind."

"Funds?"

"No, Senator, no funds." Conners wanted to hear Coriolanus's reassurance at every meeting.

"Not even for their Cayman Island accounts? A little addition to the ten or so million the leaders skimmed from the humanitarian aid?"

"Hold on, David!" Senator Jason Roebuck of Ohio interrupted. A four-term Republican, Roebuck was silver haired, silver voiced, and politically savvy. "We don't know anything of the sort, for certain."

"Because the jackasses overseeing those funds don't know crap about accounting," Conners barked back at him. "The last time around, they were spreading greenbacks around the Caribbean like they were free candy for the world's raggedy-assed kids."

Coriolanus sat back in his chair, thinking that he would just as soon play spectator to the infighting on the committee as testify.

Sam Kramer broke it up with one sharp rap from his gavel. "Gentlemen! Debate the issue on your own time, please. We're here simply to learn what's going on, and what's projected. Jack?"

Coriolanus sat up again. "Our intelligence estimates at the moment suggest the Sandinistas will make slow gains in rural areas over the next few months. . . ."

"But nothing decisive?" Roebuck interrupted.

"Nothing decisive, Senator. At current levels of action, the Sandinistas will probably prevail in about three or four years. It will take that long to bring their level of training to suitable levels. If something is not done to provide support for the Contra effort, it will wither and die, and the Communists will reign.'' Coriolanus could ease his tone with Roebuck. The man was a supporter.

"At least there will be some peace in the area,'' Havechuk said.

Coriolanus was not going to reply to that. His response might have resulted in a contempt citation.

Chairman Kramer asked, "And you see nothing that will alter that course?''

Harry Downs fidgeted in the chair next to him, tapping Coriolanus's elbow with his own. Coriolanus said, "There may be a change coming, if our current information proves out. We'll probably know in the next couple of weeks.''

"This have something to do with that merchant ship you people mentioned to the National Security Council?'' Roebuck asked.

"Yes, sir. If, as we are beginning to suspect, the Soviets are going to significantly augment the Sandinistan air forces—with the equivalent of two squadrons, the end for the Contras could come much sooner.''

"You're certain of your data?''

"We know the freighter in question has nine helicopter gunships aboard, and we suspect she has a quantity of small arms. Until she unloads, we won't know the extent of the support materiel.''

"Have they got the competent pilots for increased operations?'' Jason Roebuck wanted to know. "As I remember, we've been told that the existing pilot corps is somewhat ill trained.''

"Well,'' Coriolanus said, "that's the other thing we want to bring up. Harry?''

Downs cleared his throat and turned to his last note

card. "It looks as if they're going to get a unit of experienced helicopter pilots on loan from Cuba.'

"What's your source on that, Downs?" Senator Conners asked.

"Senator, my source is highly placed inside the revolution, very close to Castro, and I'm certainly not giving you his name."

Hamm did not meet Clark until four o'clock in the morning of the first day of staging, and he did not get to meet him alone.

He was standing on the dusty, broken street in front of the hotel, dressed in a knit sport shirt and tan chinos, at four A.M. when Clark and De Veres appeared out of the darkness. If there were streetlights in Cruta, the city fathers were conserving energy. Governmental budget crunches everywhere, Hamm thought.

"Hello, Peter."

"Hamm. You look rested."

"I think *bored* is the word you're searching for."

The three of them began to thread a path through narrow streets beginning to teem with dogs and dark-eyed children and old people seemingly unaware of the early hour. A terrier of some kind greeted the nonexistent dawn with an insistent yap. The closer they got to the waterfront, the more the housing became mud and tin and squalid shacks, separated by equally squalid closed bars that catered to the village's fishermen and probably Contra fighters crossing over from Nicaragua. On the previous day Hamm had noticed quite a few fatigue-clad men who fit that description.

"How did you come in?" Hamm asked De Veres.

"Through Tegoose. I spent one day there and two days here."

"Any Company eyes?"

"I don't think so, though Bobby would know more about that end of it. I checked but didn't find anyone showing exceptional interest in me. Hell, Americans down here are involved in drugs, or arms, or both. No one seems to care."

"Tegoose was full of spook types," Hamm said.

"Just like any war zone," Clark observed.

"Yeah. Like Saigon."

"I try not to think about Saigon," Clark said.

When they reached the waterfront, they stood together on a dirt-packed sidewalk, avoiding the dog excrement, for eight minutes before two shadows emerged warily from the alley behind them. One shadow belonged to a black man, tight and wiry, dressed in well-used and faded tiger camouflage fatigues. He eased up, looked directly at Hamm, then inclined his head toward Bobby.

"It's all right, Blue," Clark said. "Everyone here is on our side."

"Hello, Blue," Hamm said.

"Hamm. Been a while."

Blue Monday had been with the Englishman, Nellie Cameron, in Southeast Asia—all over Southeast Asia, but Hamm had not heard about either of them for years.

"You know each other?" Clark asked. "Yeah, I guess you would."

"Cameron still around?" Hamm asked Monday.

"The man's still around."

"Come on, let's get on with it," Clark urged.

Hamm raised his arms, and Monday's colleague, probably Nicaraguan, patted him down, thoroughly and professionally. He stood back and watched as the same service was performed for Clark and De Veres.

Monday nodded his approval and led them back through several alleys, then down a narrow and twisting street and out onto a wharf. The bay waters lapped gently at the pilings, and the low moon cast a streak on the bay. A forty-eight-foot Hatteras, new but streaked with grime, was tied to the dock. Yellow light spilled through the cabin curtains. Bellows, Ketchum, and Keen slouched against the railing on her stern deck.

"It's just about fucking time the brass showed up," Keen called.

Nelson Cameron emerged from the salon. He was blond, tall and lean, and wore the traditional British field uniform of shorts and epauleted shirt. Thought he never used it, a monocle hung from a braided cord against his belly. "Steve, old chum! So good to see you."

Three fatigue-suited and bearded reprobates lounged about on the flying bridge.

Hamm ignored them and clambered aboard. "You, too, Nellie. I didn't know you were still in the business."

"You know how it is? Once you've heard the call, it is difficult to deny."

"You've been born again in a new hemisphere?"

"My god is profit. Hello! What's this?"

The rest of the team members appeared at the head of the dock, led by Sean McDonough in his slouch hat.

Bobby Clark made a head count and sounded relieved. "That's all of us, Nellie."

"I'd hope so, my dear Chuck. My discount charter did not allow for overages."

"Nellie, you've never discounted shit." Hamm grinned at him.

"Shit, yes. Fishing trips, no." Nelson Cameron smiled broadly.

Sean McDonough was the last man aboard. "Let's go fishing, buckos. You bring the beer, Peachy?"

For some of them, the whole adventure was still a party, Hamm thought.

## FIFTEEN

Some of the men actually fished. Peachy Keen caught a small marlin, and Harvey Ketchum wrestled with a big swordfish for an hour and a half before it got away. There was a poker game under way in the cabin within twenty minutes of departing Cruta's fishing docks.

Nellie Cameron's four silent Latin Americans kept to themselves, except to respond to Cameron's orders or to dish up meals. The sun came up hot and got hotter throughout the day as the big cruiser trolled its way southeastward on a flat blue sea. The Honduras coast disappeared in midmorning, after they had threaded their way through a series of offshore reefs and small islands.

Some of the men in the ALECTO group questioned Clark about the destination. They got no answers.

In the middle of the afternoon, Clark gave up watching the card game and climbed the ladder to the flying bridge. A canvas Bimini top provided shade, and the forward movement of the boat created a tepid breeze. Beside the seat behind the helm, manned by Blue Monday, there was an L-shaped settee running along the left side and the rear of the bridge. Cameron, De Veres, Hamm, Cherry, and McDonough were sprawled along its length, dipping occasionally into an iced chest of beer.

Peter de Veres was shirtless, sweat dripping from the black hair on his chest. He waved Clark to a vacant seat. "Anybody winning down there, Bobby?"

"Keen has unbelievable luck. He's a couple of hundred dollars ahead."

"I gave up playing with him fifteen years ago," McDonough grunted around an unlit cigar, "otherwise he'd own my flying service."

Cameron shed his shirt. The muscles of his arms and smooth, dark chest rippled like those of a man twenty-five, but Clark knew he was in his early fifties. Like Hamm, Clark had met the man in Southeast Asia, where he was transporting some weapons and ammunition to a few Cambodian resistance groups for Clark.

Hamm sat with his elbows resting on his knees and asked, "How long have you been working the Caribbean, Nellie? I thought Asia was your heart and soul."

Cameron pursed his lips, remembering. "June of eighty-one, Steve-o."

"Why'd you change geography?"

"After most of you spooks cut out of Happy Valley, I found I was transporting peashooters and poppy products for people who did not like me very well. Much nastier bunch than the CIA. It got so Blue and I walked around with our backs to each other. Not conducive to the enjoyment of life."

Hal Cherry fanned himself with a Spanish-language

newspaper. "And you picked Central America to enjoy yourself?"

"Actually, old man, I did consider a return to queen and country, but at the last moment, remembered I'd have to pay taxes. And very high ones, at that."

"You picked a side in this *revolución*, Nellie?" Hamm asked.

"A side? Not me, chappie. One does not get involved, one only provides a service. Isn't that right, Bobby?"

"In your case, perhaps," Clark told him. Still, he was always suspicious of people who made extravagant claims of ambivalence.

"In my case, for certain." Cameron swung his head toward Hamm. "I'm running four boats on this side, and two very nice cruisers on the Pacific side. If I remain nonpartisan, I get to keep them."

"So you don't know what you're doing for us? For Clark?" Hamm probed.

"And don't want to know, Steve-o."

Clark felt uneasy with Hamm's queries. The man had a quarter century's experience with operations where need-to-know was the basis of a mission. Why in the hell was he so insistent with his questions? "We're only paying for the service. We're not buying a loyalty."

"Bloody well right on," Cameron said.

Sean McDonough plunged one big hand into the melting ice of the plastic cooler and came up with a bottle of Carta Blanca. He twisted the cap off and tossed it over the side. "I'll halfway buy the neutrality, but you've been around here enough years to get a feeling for what's going on, right? Who you betting on?"

"I don't place wagers," Cameron told him.

"Just as a laid-back, but expert observation, then?" Cherry asked.

Cameron shrugged his muscled shoulders. "As an observation, I often wonder why your country supports losers with such ferocity."

"Losers?" McDonough asked.

"Like Somoza, who kept his subjects groveling while he did as much as he could to emulate the great and legendary Ferdinand Marcos. And when the Sandinistas finally ousted him, the U.S. chose to arm a revolution headed by ex-Somoza people. If I had to guess at it, old man, I'd have to say most of the FDN-Contras are less interested in democratic principles than they are in a return to free handfuls of American foreign aid. Of course, they do quite well as it is, arguing among themselves, and living off of six-figure salaries paid out of your so-called 'private' aid."

Clark did not like the tone of this. Too much time on their hands and they got philosophical. "Sometimes we have to utilize less savory people than we would like, Nelson."

"In the age-old war against communism? Of course, old man."

"These men at least have leadership qualities. The Nicaraguans look up to them."

"The villagers look up to them as they're spraying the village with automatic-weapons fire," Cameron said. "I have not yet seen where your Contras have mounted a solid attack against a true military target. They prefer a war of attrition against civilians and a few Sandinista soldiers, where the risks are minimal."

"No rebels around with the sterling qualities you admire, Nellie?" Hamm grinned.

"You mean both anti-Sandinista and anti-Somoza, Steve-o? Eden Pastora was leading a Contra group out of the south, out of Costa Rica, but look what happened to him."

"What?" Cherry asked.

"He didn't want to play house with the other bully boys, create a unified, Somoza-like command, you know? So his supplies dried up, and he was eased out, almost permanently a couple of times."

"By who?" McDonough wanted to know.

"By somebody important, I suppose. I'd imagine your CIA had a hand in. They always do." Cameron grinned at Clark.

"Not my area," Clark said, raising his hands.

In his third-floor embassy office, Josef Pavlovich Zhukov waited for Churbanchuk and reread Item 14 of the morning intelligence digest provided by Moscow Center:

14. SECOND DEPARTMENT. US SENSELCOMM DISCUS-
SION INDICATES SHIPMENT OF NINE HELICOPTER
GUNSHIPS AND TRANSFER OF CUBAN PILOTS TO UN-
KNOWN DESTINATION IN GEOGRAPHICAL AREA.
(SOURCE: FCD, DIR K, GOOSEDOWN – UR.)

The Second Department of the Foreign Directorate was concerned with Latin America, and the information gathered by the department was therefore of interest to Zhukov. He did not know who "Goosedown" was, but the source operated through the First Chief Directorate's Directorate K, which was responsible for gathering sensitive information from foreign intelligence agencies. The "UR" indicated that the source was usually reliable.

Zhukov set the digest aside and picked up the cable that had come into the communications center on the top floor an hour after the digest:

```
SECRET                              0834061.8-MC

TO:     LINE N, MANSOVEM
FROM:   CHMN, FCD
REF:    ITEM 14, INTELDIG

INFORMATION PROVIDED AN ENIGMA. NO SHIPMENT OF
ARMS CURRENTLY IN PROGRESS OR PLANNED. NO ASSIGN-
MENT CUBAN PILOTS PLANNED. NYC SOURCE, HOWEVER,
NOT NORMALLY DISPUTED. PROBABLE MISINTERPRETA-
TION. INVESTIGATE POSSIBILITY LARGE-SCALE INFUSION
OF AIRCRAFT AND MERCENARY PILOTS IN REBEL SUP-
PORT. REPLY IMMEDIATE.
```

In addition to his duties as resident, Josef Zhukov was also the Line N Officer in Managua, the Illegal Support Officer. In that role, he was chiefly responsible for the flow of information between Moscow Center and the undercover agents who worked for him. His role as an advisor to Nicaraguan leaders was a sideline not actually specified in the organizational chart of the KGB, but it was one that he had personally developed in the past five years. He liked the second role better.

Boris Kamorovkin tapped once on the frame of the open door, then ushered Colonel Ivan Churbanchuk inside. Kamorovkin closed the door as he retreated to the hallway.

"Good morning, Josef Pavlovich."

"And to you, Ivan Ivanovitch. Please, have a chair. And then read these."

Churbanchuk sat and took the papers offered. While he

read, Zhukov studied the man. A colonel in the Red Air Force, Churbanchuk was forty-five years old, with a jowly face, dark eyes, and dark hair. Normally an outgoing man, his nose was traced with the red lines of frequent glasses of vodka and, more recently, tequila. Still, he was a veteran of three tours in Afghanistan and was a competent advisor to the Nicaraguan military. Despite his rank, he was subservient to Zhukov. All Soviet personnel in a foreign country, and frequently within Mother Russia herself, were subservient to the KGB. That line of authority was not on formal organizational charts, however.

The colonel replaced the cables on the desktop. "Interesting, to say the least, Comrade."

"You have heard nothing of new helicopters for the forces you advise?"

"Nothing at all, though they would be welcomed, of course. Especially welcome would be able pilot instructors." Churbanchuk's voice held a trace of hope in it. Privately, within the Soviet advisory group, the colonel frequently complained of the Nicaraguan air arm's incompetence and poor leadership.

Zhukov did not want to get into another discussion about competencies. He had heard it all before—no regard for the maintenance of sophisticated machinery or for following orders, a slap-happy attitude, a reluctance to fly at night or in areas of hostile fire. "And how about the rebel forces? Is there money available to mount an air war against us?"

"Not that any of my sources report," Churbanchuk said. "The latest batch of U.S. dollars is 'humanitarian' only. And the CIA is not delivering the aid, or so we are told. Do we know the kind of helicopter involved? That would tell us something."

"Only what you have read."

"If they were, for example, American Cobra AH-1's, it would require a minimum of a million and a half U.S. dollars for each aircraft, plus a minimum of a half million dollars per year, per aircraft, for maintenance and support. That is eighteen million dollars, Josef Pavlovich, plus an ongoing operational budget. Probably more."

"Let us hypothesize and suppose that the rebels have raised the funds," Zhukov proposed. "What might the expected consequence be?"

"With Cuban pilots trained in the United States? And with new gunships? The result would be devastating, Josef Pavlovich. My advisees would park their Mi-24s and walk away before facing such opposition. They love to fly when the skies are controlled. When they are not . . ."

"Then we must uncover the truth behind this rumor," Zhukov said, tapping the cables with a forefinger.

Churbanchuk stood. "I will see what is to be seen. May I have your permission to contact Moscow for surveillance photographs?"

"Certainly, Comrade Colonel. Whatever is necessary. Report directly to me."

Hamm was on the bridge of the Hatteras with Cameron, Blue Monday, and Bobby Clark at 11:00 P.M. when they rendezvoused with the *Southern Merchant*.

Under the half-moon, the sea was bright, flowing with medium swells, and the freighter appeared as a dark blob against the starlit horizon on the east. She was under way without running lights.

Monday flashed his own running lights once—red and green bleeps diffused by the flare of the bow, and a minute later was rewarded with a similar flash from the freighter.

Two minutes after that, the larger craft began to lose headway, and Monday retarded his throttles, moving in a wide circle toward her.

The Hatteras rocked more noticeably at slow speed. As they neared the other ship, Hamm saw the bob and sway of moving figures on her higher deck. When Monday eased the cruiser against the four tires hanging along the ship's side, Hamm noted the long stains of rust peppering the hull. "You only buy the best, don't you, Bobby?"

"We leased her," Clark replied out of the darkness. "It's cheaper that way."

"Nothing better available?"

"It had to be this one, because of her history and the greed of her owners."

Hamm understood. The *Southern Merchant* would probably have a record of supplying Central American ports and would therefore have a certain invisibility.

As soon as Monday had idled his diesels, two rope ladders snaked downward from the freighter's deck, and the team members began to scramble up them to the freighter's much higher deck. Peter de Veres led the way. It was inky black in the shadow of the ship's hull, and Peachy Keen's voice cut the night, echoing off steel. "Goddamn it! I wasn't supposed to be a Marine!"

McDonough called to him, "Peachy, you forgot to black out your head."

Hamm dropped down the ladder from the flying bridge to the stern deck, followed by Clark and Cameron. Searching the deck, he found his AWOL bag resting against the aft rail, picked it up, and tossed it overboard, thinking, "Bye-bye, Marcus Kennedy."

Clark found his own valise and heaved it right behind Hamm's.

The seas were running medium swells, but the hull of the freighter offered some protection to the smaller boat. Hamm put a foot on the cruiser's railing, waited until the surge rolled away and the gap closed, then grabbed the wet strands of the ladder. He found his footing on the rope rungs quickly and pulled himself upward. The ladder swayed and sagged, leaning away from the hull.

"Cheerio, Steve-o!" Cameron's voice floated on the heavy air after him.

"*Hasta luego,*" Hamm called back, wondering if there would be a "later."

At the top of the ladder, he found a rusty railing and threw a leg over it. He stood for a moment scanning the deck and the dark figures milling about. The deck was greasy, salt infested, and littered with junk, but steadier than the deck of the cruiser. The team members stood around him in momentary confusion, half-mingled with ten or eleven shaggy men from the crew of the ship. Hamm smelled the sooty aroma from the ship's single funnel. It was mixed with the odor of boiled cabbage.

Clark pulled himself over the railing.

A tall black man, wearing an officer's epaulets and cap, emerged from the shadow of the deckhouse, forged a path through the crewmen, and stopped in front of Hamm. "Who's Mr. Larson?"

"That's me, Captain," Clark said from his place at Hamm's side.

Turning to Clark, the captain offered a half salute and said, "It's all yours, Mr. Larson."

"What's left of it," Clark replied.

The ship's captain bobbed his head in a possible acknowledgment, then went over the side. He was immediately followed by the silent scramble of his crewmen.

Two minutes later, the engines of Cameron's cruiser growled and it pulled away, towing an arc of phosphorescence behind it as it picked up speed.

"What in the ever-loving fuck have we got here?" McDonough asked.

Clark's teeth gleamed in the moonlight, his first smile in weeks. "I forget to mention that we also get to run our own freighter?"

# SIXTEEN

**"Y**our staging area floats?" Hamm asked.

"I hope so," Clark said. "Come on, let's find our way to the bridge."

They were standing on the rear deck, next to a huge canvas-sheathed hatch cover. Two cranes were silhouetted against the sky on either side of the deck, aft of the hatch. With Clark leading the way, the group entered the deckhouse, which was lit by dim bulbs in wire cages, found a ladder leading upward, and climbed three levels to the freighter's bridge. The red glow of instrument lights was the only illumination on the bridge. It was cramped with the twelve of them in there, and several men drifted out onto the small port and starboard bridge wings. The wing doors were open, and the windshield glass had been tilted outward, but no breeze took the edge off the heat.

Hamm checked the ancient instruments located under the windshield in front of a hand-worn wooden ship's wheel. The compass heading was slightly to the southwest, but the *Southern Merchant* was dead in the water. The engine-room telegraph handles stood at "All Stop," and would stay there if they could not figure out the engine room.

Clark held up his hand to quell the buzz of conversation. It took a while for his signal to be picked up in the roan-colored darkness. When he finally had silence, Clark cleared his throat and said, "We're now about 190 miles east-northeast of Nicaragua's border with Honduras. What we want to do is continue steaming in that direction at about four or five knots . . ."

"I wouldn't count on it," Bellows interrupted. "That looks like top end for this tub."

". . . in order to give us time to assemble aircraft and load gear. We have until tomorrow night at zero three hundred hours to be ready to launch. That's about twenty-eight hours."

"How come this wasn't on your goddamned training schedule?" Hamm asked.

"Because it's simple enough to do. And it's only for a few hours, Hamm."

"Shit." Hamm was beginning to believe Clark had quite a few more surprises than he had expected from Llewellen's and his own interpretation of the gaming model. "You're the damned planner, and you didn't bother to tell us we wouldn't have a ship's crew? That's pretty fucked up, Clark."

The bridge got very quiet.

Clark finally responded. "We have the talents available

to handle it. That's what I planned on. Remember, Hamm, your only concern is tactics. Leave the strategy to me.''

McDonough got into it. ''Hey, let's not blow it now. We'll work it out.''

''You ever run an engine room, Sean?'' Hamm asked.

''No.''

''Let me take a look at it, Steve,'' Rick Talbot said.

Hamm shook his head in resignation. ''Goddamned desk men.''

''I know boats, though not steam,'' De Veres said. ''It can't be too much different.''

Letting it go for the moment, Hamm said, ''I assume we play this like there's an Eye in the Sky.''

''That's right. During daylight hours, everything on deck has to appear unchanged,'' Clark said. ''We'll be working below.''

''Son of a bitch!'' Keen wailed. ''It's going to be murder down in those holds.''

''There's supposed to be some big fans and flexible tubing stowed aboard somewhere. At least, I paid for them,'' De Veres countered.

Hamm had been evaluating this new development while he argued and listened. Though Clark had told him privately that they would meet the *Southern Merchant* at sea, he sure as hell had not mentioned that they would be crewing it. After Clark finished outlining his version—not necessarily the actual one—of the next couple of days, Hamm spoke up. ''Hal, you're the only Navy we've got.''

''I was afraid you were going to say that. I'm a pilot and a diver, remember? I work over the water or under it. Not on it.''

''Nevertheless, you've got your first surface command. First thing, let's find the running lights and get them back in operation. Despite objectives, we want to look as legal as we can. Talbot, you're an engineer, and now, the first engineer. See if you can figure out the engine-room boilers and running gear, and let's get some steerage on this broken-down tub.''

"I don't even know where the goddamned engine room is," Talbot said, but dropped down the stairway to begin looking for it.

Hamm found De Veres in the gloom. "Peter, the chart room is behind me. I want a course laid out, with time deadlines for task completion.''

"Got it." De Veres worked his way through the group toward the cabin that opened off the back of the bridge. The radio shack was on the other side.

"The rest of us will take a tour." Hamm went back down the companionway, to emerge on the forward deck. Underfoot, the steel plates were an oxidized orange-red where they were not covered with aged, greasy, and flaking gray paint. Two crated helicopters were lashed down, side by side, in the center of the deck. Ahead of them was the large, canvas-covered hatch over the forward hold. Hamm stopped beside the first crate and checked the plank-and-two-by-four construction.

"Harvey, while it's still dark, work over this crating so it'll come apart quickly when we're ready to lose it, and then loosen up one end on each crate so we have access to the choppers."

Ketchum nodded.

Sudden red and green glows off either side of the bow told him Cherry had found the running lights.

Moving forward to the hatch, Hamm squatted to eyeball it. It was simply a square framework of two-by-twelves, reinforced with a wooden grid, with canvas stretched over it, that fitted over the raised lip of the hold. The canvas had been patched many times and still had holes and rents in it. In the center, on the back edge, was a small wooden access hatch.

"Pickett, you and Canton find some kind of shoring—break up crates if you need to—and raise these hatches, this one and the one aft, about two feet off the deck. You'll have to figure out how to use the cranes in order to do it. We want them to appear closed from above, but we want a free flow of air around the sides."

"Yo, Colonel," Jeremy Pickett said. Canton, who had not said five words to him since the incident in Texas, withheld a comment.

Next Hamm pried open the small canvas access door, slipped over the edge, and found steel ladder rungs with his toes. He started down into the darkness, smelling the fetid odor of mildew and rotten bilge water. As his head dropped below deck level, he stopped to feel around blindly on either side of the ladder. On the right, he found an electrical box with a bank of five switches and flipped them all. Perimeter floodlights flashed on, nearly blinding him after the hours of darkness. He lowered himself some forty feet to the floor of the hold.

It was a small ship, and the three big crates took up most of the cargo hold's deck space. He assumed the aft hold contained the last four helicopters. Against the forward bulkhead were stacked multisized boxes of their supplies. The unmoving air was heavy with humidity and heat. As the team gathered around him, Hamm noted the beads of sweat running down the men's foreheads.

"Jesus Christ!" Keen exclaimed. "It's like breathing tomato soup."

"Okay. Jerry and Pat, get the hatches raised. Sean and

Bobby, locate the fans and get them going in both holds.''
Hamm unbuttoned his shirt and tossed it on a crate. Already the sweat was rolling off his back and neck. ''The rest of us find tools and start popping crates. We need to know if Peter's shopping trip was successful.''

''You realize, Chief, that 'the rest of us' is only four?''
McDonough said.

''Sean, I meant to say the *best* of us.''

Bobby Clark took his break at ten o'clock in the morning. Despite two big fans in each hold, drawing outside air through flexible ducting, the heat was so oppressive that Hamm was giving everyone a fifteen-minute break every hour. He was allowing two people at a time to get some sleep in the cramped officer cabins. Clark climbed the long ladder to the deck, saw De Veres atop the forecastle, leaning into the breeze, and made his way forward.

There had not been much pride aboard the old tramp steamer. The decks were littered with pop and beer cans, cigarette butts, sodden cardboard, and paper. Still, the salt-tangy air was a relief after the close, rotting odors of the hold. He wound his way around deck fittings—winches, bollards, unknowns—and climbed the short flight of stairs to the raised foredeck. He could hear the sea parting before the ship's slow forward movement. The vibrations produced by the old engines and drive shaft thrummed through the deck plates and up into the soles of his feet.

De Veres heard the footsteps and looked back. His face seemed pale under the tanned skin, his hair hung in wet locks, and the sweat poured off his forehead. His hands gripped the railing tightly, as if he were afraid they might shake if left on their own. ''You come to bitch about the supply officer, Bobby?''

"No. Looks like we've got almost everything except the flight helmets. But there are enough headsets to make do."

Peter de Veres released one hand from the railing. "That son of a bitch in Angola stiffed me for the AT-6 Spiral missiles. All we have is the Swatters."

"We'll live with them, Peter. They'll do what we want them to do."

"I still don't like getting shafted," he said, looking at his filthy hand. "And, you didn't tell me I'd have to go and get dirty, Bobby."

Clark had long before abandoned his shirt. He looked down at the rips and stains in his Pierre Cardin slacks. "Hell, Peter, you're the one that told me it was time to remember what real work was like."

Moving forward to grasp the bow rail alongside De Veres, Clark leaned against it and pushed his face into the breeze—what there was of it.

"We on schedule?" De Veres asked while squinting at his watch.

"I don't know. I think so, but I'm so damned tired, I lost track."

"Hamm's been handling it well. You did the right thing with him."

"Yeah, I guess so." Clark kept recalling Hamm's incipient questions, little probes of areas where he did not have a need for the answers. Maybe it was just his intelligence training. Maybe it was his distaste for planners. It irritated Clark, and he was about to raise the issue with De Veres when there was a shout from the bridge.

He turned to look back at the deckhouse and saw Hamm waving at them.

"You suppose the commander in chief wants us?" De Veres asked.

"That's as good a guess as any."

"I also didn't plan on a return to basic training and OCS." De Veres grinned. "I'd forgotten how much of a civilian I am when it comes to following orders."

The two of them made their way back to the superstructure, entered the open hatch door, and climbed the long ladders to the bridge. Hamm was in the small chart room, bending over the chart table. As they stepped inside, he said, "Peter, you want to get a fix on our position at noon? I think we're falling off projections some."

"Will do, Steve."

Hamm straightened up, turned toward them, and leaned his hips against the table. "Okay. It looks like Hank and Clay will have the choppers inspected mechanically by eighteen hundred hours. Hank wants Talbot to come up and double-check the hydraulics. Peachy is checking the electronics; he's in the aft hold now. Harvey and Pat are uncrating rotors and preparing them for mounting. By sundown, all of the supplies will be weighed and stowed aboard the Hinds. How's the painting coming?"

Using prepared stencils he had brought with him, Clark was spray-painting Nicaraguan insignia and numbers on the camouflage finish of the aircraft with spray cans of yellow paint. "I've got one more to go in the forward hold, plus the two on deck."

"All right, now you can check me against your computer, Bobby—the part of your game model I didn't get to see."

"What the hell do you mean?" Clark asked him, quickly defensive.

"I knew the aircraft would be arriving by ship. I didn't know we'd have to fly them off. How did your magnificent machine handle that?" Hamm's tone was caustic.

Puzzled, Clark said, "There's nothing elaborate about it. Just take off from the deck."

Hamm unpinned the chart from the table and flipped it over. On the back, he had drawn a scale top-view of the freighter's deckhouse and forward and aft decks. With a compass, he had plotted nine circles overlaying the deck space. Clark saw the problem immediately. The circles overlapped. "Shit."

"So much for computers," Hamm said. "If they don't have the information, they don't think about it, do they? We don't have enough deck space for nine helicopters with fifty-six-foot, five-bladed rotors. Hell, when we get those hatches off and shoved over the side, we don't even have deck."

Clark leaned over the table and peered at the drawing. "If the rotors are positioned right, we can park four on the aft deck and five on the forward deck. We've got twenty-five feet of space on either side of the hatches and sixty feet between the hatches and the deckhouse."

"You can park them, but you can't crank them up," Hamm said.

"Goddamn it! I see that now."

"And once they're on deck, you can't move them around to clear positions. Shit, there's winches, ventilators, and every other damned thing in the way." Hamm used a pencil to point out the deck obstructions he had drawn. "Even if we could get far enough forward, then the loading cranes interfere with the rotors."

"We going to have to leave one or two of them behind?" De Veres asked.

"No!" Clark insisted.

Sean McDonough appeared in the doorway, his shoulders taking up most of it. He was stripped to boxer shorts and held a thick roast-beef sandwich in one hand and a bottle of Corona in the other. "How's a guy supposed to sleep with you SOBs making so much noise?"

"We have a minor problem under discussion," Peter de Veres said, grinning.

"How minor?" McDonough asked.

Hamm waved at the drawing. "Take a look, Sean."

With McDonough in the cabin, it was suddenly very crowded. He took two minutes to study the sketch, then asked, "Your draftsmanship is shitty. What're these?"

"Winches, ventilators. The deck cranes."

"Ah, hell, Steve. That's why the good Lord invented cutting torches."

"You'd level it?" Hamm asked.

"I'd do anything to stay out of those fucking holds. I work best in open spaces."

"We've got to keep in mind," Clark said, pointing upward, "that somebody may be watching us. The deck appearance can't change that much."

"We'll just cut it all loose and leave it in place," McDonough said. "Shove it over after dark."

Hamm stepped to the doorway and called to Cherry, "Hal, what's our weather look like?"

Standing at the helm, Cherry called back, "The last radio report didn't predict any changes until later in the afternoon, Steve. For now, hot and lousy."

"No heavy seas?"

"Cloud buildup in the late afternoon. There may be some swells running."

Turning back toward them, Hamm said, "We'll have to take the chance. But if we start rolling very much, with heavy equipment sliding around, we'll shove it overboard, and to hell with whoever's watching."

That was all right with Clark.

By four o'clock in the afternoon, McDonough, with Pickett's help, had used cutting torches from the ship's maintenance spaces to cut the retaining bolts on heavy winches and fittings on the decks surrounding the hatches. Deck-mounted toolboxes had been freed and heaved over the side. A dozen curved ventilator funnels had their bases all but severed, so that a few quick blows with a sledge-hammer would knock them free. The stanchions for foul-weather lifelines had been demounted and tossed over-board.

High cumulus clouds formed in the southwest during the afternoon, bright silver on top, around twenty thousand feet, and cast-iron gray at the bases. The troughs between waves were closer together by late afternoon and the seas were running three- and four-foot waves. The *Southern Merchant* pitched and rolled with increasing frequency as the sun settled toward the western horizon.

Just before six o'clock, Clark and Bellows completed the installation of the tail rotor blades on the last helicopter, working within the stifling confines of the giant crate on deck. Gaps in the crating allowed in some light, but they had two trouble lights rigged also. Bellows was balanced at the top of a twelve-foot stepladder, tightening bolts with a socket wrench, and Clark was at the base of the ladder, steadying it, when the deck rose under them, then keeled over hard to the left.

Clark braced his feet against the crate's reinforcing planks, but the ladder tilted away.

Bellows yelped and wrapped his arms around the hub of the tail rotor and hung on as the ladder went out from under him.

Somebody on deck yelled.

Metal shrieked against metal.

A seven-ton winch smashed through the side of the crate behind Clark, knocking him aside, and slamming into the Hind's fuselage.

Hamm was on the port bridge wing with a mug of tepid coffee when the ship heaved, then rolled, and the winch started sliding. He yelled a warning, dropped the mug, then headed for the ladder. He reached it just as the heavy winch collided with the crate. Wood cracked. A solid crunch of metal puncturing metal followed.

The outside ladder was difficult to negotiate on a twenty-degree incline to the side. He found the rungs with his feet and started down, sliding most of the way.

Cherry yelled at him through the open doorway to the bridge. "I'm changing course, Hamm! Take the seas head-on!"

The ship righted herself by the time Hamm reached the cargo deck. Three others reached the crate at the same time he did, calling to those inside. Pat Canton peered through the gaping hole in the side of the crate, saying, "Shit, Clark. Can't you take a joke?"

Hamm leaned around the side of the winch and looked inside. Clark lay flat on his back, next to the winch, shaking his head. He sat up. "Son of a bitch!"

"Goddamned motherfucking son-of-a-bitching ship!" A string of curses from above made Hamm look up. Bellows was hanging from the rotor hub.

Keen and Harper ducked and stepped through the hole in the crate, found the remnants of the ladder, and held it in place for Bellows to descend.

"You all right, Bobby?" Hamm called.

"Yeah, I think so." Clark stood up, testing his left leg.

The pant leg was ripped wide open, and the skin of his thigh was blurry with blood. "The bastard caught me sideways."

"Get inside with Clay and have him take a look at it. Pat, you and Peachy man a deck crane, hook onto this damned thing, and drop it over the side. Then, start clearing everything else off the deck. We'll risk the satellite, but no more accidents."

As soon as the winch was out of the way, Hamm, McDonough, and Talbot examined the Hind. There was a foot-deep dent in the lower rear fuselage, with a tear running through the center of it. The floor planks of the crate, now broken and splintered, had slowed the progress of the winch before it could do serious damage.

"Two sections of hydraulic line and about two feet of multiconductor cable, and we'll have her airworthy," Talbot said.

"You don't think there's been any structural damage?" Hamm asked.

"Not that much. I'll bang out the dents in the skin and bolt in a couple of lateral stringers. That should take care of it."

"You're sure?"

"I'll fly it," Talbot told him.

Hamm left them to it and climbed back to the bridge. He found Harper, the ex-Medevac pilot, applying bandages to Clark's leg. Scrapes and cuts, mainly, though Clark said his knee felt a little weak.

"Hit the sack for a little while," Hamm told him.

"No way. We're off schedule as it is."

In the chart room, Hamm pulled a stool up to the table and reviewed the checklist he had compiled. It was a pilot's tool, the checklist, to make sure no minor but important details were left out of the process. Hamm had decided to draft it because twenty years had elapsed since he had had a command. In his job with DIA, he had always been a loner, worrying only about himself and the particular mission. Thinking about it now, he decided he did not like worrying about other men and a few thousand tons of equipment.

At seven o'clock, with a couple of hours of daylight left, he pulled everyone off their jobs and gave them time to eat a cold meal from the ship's galley, to shower for the last time, and to dress in the unmarked camouflage fatigues that were similar to those worn by the Sandinista forces. They were not going to wear flight suits.

Hamm made a final tour while the rest of them finished their break.

In the aft hold, the two Mi-24s and the two Mi-28s were lashed to the rolling deck amidst the debris of their crating. Hamm braced himself against the more pronounced pitching of the ship as he examined each aircraft. The cargo compartments of the Hinds were packed with supplies, several extra fuel drums, and ordnance. The rocket pods were loaded, each with thirty-two 57-millimeter rockets. AT-2 Swatter antitank missiles with one-and-a-half-mile ranges were mounted outboard on the stub wings. Resting in packs of five, the main rotors for each helicopter were wrapped with rope and positioned for the crane to lift to the main deck. There were three extra main rotors available, but they were too ungainly to take with them. Clark had planned to lash them to the sides of the choppers, but Hamm vetoed it. Clark seemed to think in terms of a bivouac lasting a week or two. The more he considered the radar and satellite surveillance, the more Hamm thought of a shortened mission.

The three helicopters in the forward hold were similarly prepared—loaded, armed, and useless without their rotors mounted.

At 9:30 P.M., Hamm assembled the group, less Talbot, who was back in the engine room, on the bridge to give them final instructions. "We have to keep everyone we can on deck until the last minute, to shove helicopters into launch positions. The first five off will carry one pilot only. That will be Banditos One, Three, Five, and Vaqueros One and Three. The rest of us catch rides on the last four choppers. Questions on that?"

There were none. Hamm checked his watch, then said, "In fifteen minutes, we get the cranes, lift the cargo hatches, and drop them over the side. While that's taking place, I want eight men stripping the crates off the two deck-side helicopters. They're to be moved to the starboard side, tails outboard over the sea, and nose wheels positioned on the black tape crosses I measured off this afternoon. Then, we bring the rest of them out of the holds. The Havocs, with tail wheels, get placed nose outboard.

"Aft, we want three choppers parked port side and one starboard. Forward, we set one more on the starboard and two on the port. Lash them down tight, or we'll lose them over the side.

"Next, we hoist the rotor blades out of the holds, then use the cranes to mount them. As soon as the last blade is in place, McDonough and Pickett get the cutting torches and cut down the cranes, and please, guys, push them into the ocean, and not on top of a chopper."

"In these seas, I'm only promising fifty-fifty odds on that," McDonough told him.

From his place at the helm, Cherry asked, "You want all of us, Steve?"

"Yes. There's too much to be done. In fact, you can reduce speed now, just enough to keep us headed into the seas, lock down the wheel, and tell Talbot to come topside." Hamm turned around until he found De Veres. "Peter, at zero three hundred hours, shoot the stars, will you? I want a last position, so we know where we're starting from."

"We've been running more southerly because of the storm," De Veres said, "and we'll be farther off-coast than we originally planned. We'll have maybe seventy miles of water instead of thirty."

"That's still well within our range parameters," Clark said.

"That takes the edge off our fuel margin, though, if we run into coastal radar or gun emplacements," McDonough noted for them.

"Once we crank the first turbine, we won't waste time," Hamm told them. He had them synchronize their watches—all provided by De Veres and of Hungarian manufacture, then went carefully through the last of the schedule details. He announced the radio frequency for communications if they were absolutely necessary. The Soviets, paranoid about having their pilots talking to the free world, did not install aircraft radios that were capable of communicating on international frequencies.

It was a silent and separately introspective group that broke up at 9:45. Hamm thought it was because, for at least fifteen years, none of them had had to think about going into combat again. Now it was upon them, and despite a quarter million dollars of incentive, it weighed heavily, just like the first rookie flights in Vietnam. In the month that he had spent with them, however, he had learned enough about each man to believe he could trust each to do his job. It was, in fact, a minor problem. If he ever figured out the hidden agenda in Bobby Clark's scenario, and found that he could not go along with it, he liked them well enough that killing them off was going to be tough.

Tough, but not impossible.

The time schedule fell way behind, as Hamm had expected that it would. Hoisting the aircraft from the holds was tricky in the heavy chop of the sea and the gusting wind. Despite Clark's plea for the cover of darkness, Hamm had ordered floodlights turned on, and six big lights mounted on the deckhouse bathed the fore and aft decks in milky gloom. With one man operating a deck crane and five men stabilizing the hull of the helicopter with attached ropes as it rose out of the hold, the fuselage would still sway unpredictably in the wind. The size of the cargo hatches did not allow a great deal of tolerance for the fifty-seven-foot length of the fuselages, and they had to be brought out on a diagonal to the hatches in order to clear them.

The third helicopter out of the aft hold, an Mi-24, broke free, spun around in the wind, and bent a tail rotor against the lip of the hold. Before it could be positioned on the side deck, with its tail stuck out over the water, the tail rotor had to be replaced with one of the six spares. That disrupted the timetable.

Forward, one of the Havocs rolled off the now unrailed deck before the chocks and tie-downs were in place. Only the fact that it was still attached to the crane's hoisting cable kept it from going overboard. The fuselage behind the main landing gear was crushed, but Bellows and Talbot both pronounced it fit for service.

Midnight had passed by the time all the helicopters and

their rotor packs were on deck. Hamm moved forward to help mount rotor blades, which was proving difficult. The blades, suspended in air from the crane, bobbed and weaved in the wind. It took longer to align them with the rotor head and collective and bolt them in place than it had taken on a sandy plain in a windless Texas. The deck heaved, and men shouted back and forth from helicopter to crane operator as they struggled to maintain precarious balances on top of the choppers.

It was after two o'clock when Hamm slapped the last three bolts in place on the last rotor of a Havoc, left Ketchum to tighten them in place, and slid down the ladder to the deck. Clark was sitting on the rubber tire of the landing gear looking pale.

"You doing all right, Bobby?"

"Fine."

He did not sound fine. "You lost some blood. I want you to take a break."

Clark jerked to his feet. "The hell with that. How far behind are we?"

"Almost an hour."

"We'll be crossing that damned coast in daylight, at this rate."

"At least we'll be able to see the damned coast," Hamm said. "Take a break."

"No."

"Okay, instead, you go get Engineering Officer Talbot, and the two of you go below and open every seacock you can find."

"Seacocks? You're going to sink her?"

"Hell, yes. What were you going to do with her?" Hamm asked.

"Abandon her."

"Fuck that. Unattended, she's a danger to sea traffic. Go open the seacocks, then make up a big pot of coffee. See if you can't manage some sandwiches."

By three-thirty, half an hour past their launch time, the *Southern Merchant* was already beginning to move sluggishly as her bilges filled with water. Hamm estimated, though, that it would be five or six hours more before she finally went down. It was more than enough time.

By three-thirty also, the fore and aft cranes had been cut free of their moorings and allowed to fall overboard. Bellows and Talbot, the engineers, completed their final inspections of the helicopters and okayed a launch. Keen checked batteries and found most of them low on charge. Everyone had a last mug of coffee and a sandwich.

Talbot went below to shut down the boilers, and within minutes, the freighter lost her steerage and began to wallow in the troughs.

The group split up, heading for their assigned places for the launch. McDonough and De Veres climbed aboard their Havocs, one on the forward deck and one on the aft deck, and both parked in positions to turn rotors without interference.

Hamm stood on the forward deck, watching McDonough through the cockpit canopy as he went through his checklist. When the pilot looked at him, Hamm raised his arm and rotated it.

"The batteries are iffy," Peachy Keen said. "Cross your fingers, Steve, or we'll be stringing jumper cables all over hell."

Hamm crossed his fingers.

The auxiliary power unit hiccoughed, then caught and purred.

Turbines whined in the night, now a quiet one with the

ship's engines shut down. McDonough's Mi-28 failed to catch, and he hit the ignition again. Finally, rotors turned and exhaust ports flared. McDonough threw a thumb's-up, and Hamm and Cherry instinctively ducked as they moved in under the rotors and released the tie-downs.

The deck bucked and rolled sluggishly to Hamm's left as they ran clear.

McDonough let it warm for a full minute more before easing in throttle and pitch and lifting off.

"Bandito One away!" Bellows yelled.

The remaining men unlashed the Hind nudged closest to the deckhouse, then turned it and pushed it into the spot vacated by McDonough, as Hank Bellows climbed the side of the fuselage, slid open the hatch, and crawled into the cockpit. They had to work with the sway of the ship, attempting to hold the helicopter in place on the back roll, then move it forward as the bow plunged down.

Since it was free to roll about on deck, they dropped their handmade chocks against the wheels and held it in place while Bellows started the engine. Four minutes later, Vaquero One lifted off.

Shortly after, the next helicopter rose off the aft deck. Now, there were four menacing gunships circling the slowly foundering freighter.

Moving to the starboard side, Hamm and his remaining shipboard crew released a Havoc and pushed it across to the port side. Bandito Five, with a grinning Pat Canton at the controls, took off.

While they still had enough men aboard to manhandle the heavy aircraft, they repositioned the last two Hinds on the forward deck so that they had rotor clearance, then chocked the wheels.

Vaquero Five rose abruptly from the deck, Jerry Pickett

smiling broadly from the cockpit in the backwash of light from the deckhouse floodlights.

The spare Hind, then the spare Havoc, clawed into the sky from the aft deck.

Hal Cherry got the last helicopter turning after a couple of false starts, and Hamm stood in the wash of the rotors and waited for Peachy Keen, who had climbed to the bridge. The floodlights died, and three minutes later, Keen dashed from the deckhouse to the Hind and clambered into the rear compartment. Hamm took a last look around, then pulled himself into the compartment.

The chocks were slipping and the Mi-24 was rolling inward toward the open cargo hatch as Hamm hurriedly clamped a headset over his ears. He spoke into the intercom. "Hit it, Hal."

Cherry increased pitch and throttle in practiced coordination, and the Hind lumbered upward under her heavy load. The *Southern Merchant*'s rusty decks dropped away, and five minutes later, her silhouette, already low in the water, disappeared in the dark.

The nine helicopters, running without lights, but visible at close range because of their exhausts, formed into a ragged line with Cherry leading the way. Hamm looked back at them, wary for anyone lagging too far behind and alert to the very real possibility of engine malfunction. They were observing radio silence between aircraft, but Cherry used the intercom to tell Hamm, "I've got one-six-zero knots, heading two-eight-two, altitude two hundred feet, give or take fifty."

"Go get 'em, tiger," Hamm told him.

Unfolding his chart and pulling a penlight from his shirt pocket, Hamm rested with his back against the bulkhead and studied the course Peter de Veres had calculated and drawn on the chart. The floor bucked lightly with the crosswind. On the left horizon, seen through the open doorway, jagged bolts of lightning flared impotently. The last forecast, picked up on the ship's radio, had said the storm would pass them by.

Peachy Keen slid over next to him, looking at the chart himself, and spoke over the intercom. "I always wondered what it was like, sitting back here. I was always up in the office before."

Hamm looked up at him in the darkness. "And what do you think, Peachy?"

"I don't like it a fucking bit."

On the Caribbean side, Nicaragua had almost three hundred miles of coastline, but they did not have the full length of the coast to play with. Clark wanted them in the northern part of the country, and his first "X" was located ten miles south of the Honduras border and about thirty miles inland. It was still in a heavily jungled region. Crossing the country to the west, they would find jungle, then mahogany forests, then high plains surrounded by mountain peaks. With the fuel range of the Havocs, Hamm did not have time or fuel to play around. Supposedly, there was a radar installation at Sandy Bay, so they would cut the coast south of it, staying below detection parameters, then follow the Rio Wawa for a while, searching for a tiny clearing in the middle of five hundred square miles of jungle.

Hamm studied the dark sea for fifteen minutes. The whitecapping became more sporadic as the winds fell behind them.

Cherry's voice came over the intercom. "Zero-four-four-nine hours. Hostile zone coming up."

Hamm leaned out the open doorway to peer ahead. A few dim lights on the right oblique identified the coastal town of Sandy Bay for him. The sun rising in the east, behind them, cast a pink hue across the jungle canopy inland from the coast. It appeared peaceful enough, but he understood Cherry's comment. It looked too much like another landscape, a couple of decades earlier.

He used the intercom. "All right, Hal. You can put it on the deck."

Cherry bled off altitude until the wave tops were less than thirty feet below. Looking back, Hamm saw the other helicopters follow their lead. There were still eight of them back there.

They crossed the coast passing over the mouth of a bay south of Sandy Bay. The crews of a dozen run-down fishing boats putting out to sea jerked their heads up in astonishment as the roar of turbines caught them. Some of them waved, as if it was expected.

"I don't see the goddamned river we're looking for," Cherry complained.

"Bear to your right," Hamm told him. "Almost due north."

They traversed the elongated bay in seconds, turning northward, and the earth below turned green as the jungle thickened.

Peachy Keen pointed out the right door. "Over there, Steve?"

Hamm saw the indentation of the bay and checked his chart. "That's a creek, I think, Peachy."

"Up ahead!" Cherry called.

Easing his head out into the 160-knot windstream, Hamm squinted his eyes. A dark stream, half a mile wide, cut through the jungle. "Follow it, Hal."

The Hind trailed the river northward for a few miles, then swung left as the stream turned inland again. The water looked dirty, and jungle canopy hid the shoreline. An occasional hut flashed by. The faces in early-morning canoes and small boats gaped upward as they shot overhead. Again, they were saluted with halfhearted waves.

"This is it," Hamm said. "In about ten miles, Hal, go to bearing three-three-zero to avoid the village of Cuyo Tigni. Then let's start looking for our international airport."

"You think customs is going to be ready for us?" Cherry asked.

"Shit!" Peachy Keen called out. "We don't have anything to declare."

"That right?" Cherry asked him. "Here I thought we were declaring war."

# SEVENTEEN

The National Photographic Interpretation Center was utilized by a large number of intelligence services, primarily military, and those services contributed their experts to the staff, but it was operated under CIA supervision. Jack Coriolanus experienced no problem in getting an appointment with the duty officer at seven o'clock in the morning.

After skimpily outlining his interest, Coriolanus was taken down a long corridor to the Central American section, passing through a rabbit warren of cubicles whose inhabitants engaged in deciphering strategic movements of military units or single ships and aircraft. The optical photographs and infrared pictures, or images on special film, taken by satellites or the SR-71 reconnaissance planes, the Blackbirds, could be brought up instantly on dozens of computer terminals. The magic of electronics could also link the Pentagon, the small Situation Room in the White House basement, or the more elaborate, high-tech situation room, called the Electronic Situation Room, in the Old Executive Office Building.

When they reached the section chief's office, the duty officer introduced him to a secretary and to an Army major. "Anything Mr. Coriolanus wants, Major Whaley, you see he gets it."

"Yes, sir."

The major and the petite redheaded secretary would both be wondering just what was the interest of the special assistant in their particular section that early in the morning. They would also wonder why he was there in person, why he had not sent some minion on this particular errand. Coriolanus declined to explain it for them. "Major Whaley, show me the terminal used by visitors."

"Right this way, sir." Whaley led him to a small office containing only beige linoleum, a computer terminal, a chair, and a printer. "This is where authorized visitors may use the system."

"I want to see the past six months' log on that terminal," Coriolanus told him.

"Yes, sir," Whaley said, looking to the redhead. "Marilyn, if you would?"

Marilyn turned away from the door and trotted off somewhere.

Coriolanus entered the office, sat at the terminal, and had Whaley explain how to use it. He did not know *what* he was looking for, but he knew *how* he was going to go about it. In the last couple of days, he had become very uneasy about Harry Downs and Bobby Clark, probably because Hamm's name had come up.

Whaley completed his instructions in about ten minutes, then said, "Miss Vernon should be back from the computer center with the logs shortly."

"Thank you, Major."

"Coffee, sir?"

"If you've got it."

Miss Vernon brought in the terminal log at seven-twenty. Coriolanus thanked her, then began to flip through the pages. The logging of terminal usage was automatically accomplished by the central computer and was useful in backtracking reports or research and in billing each department or section for its actual computer usage. While an entire department's terminals were billed as a unit, the machine could still select and analyze one terminal. The log for this particular terminal started on January 1:

* * * * * * * * * * * * * * * * * * * * * * * * * * * * * * * *

```
NPIC COMPUTER BILLING SYSTEM        TERMINAL ANALYSIS
REPORT DATE; 06/21              TERMINAL: P501-94066
```

* * * * * * * * * * * * * * * * * * * * * * * * * * * * * * * *

| DATE | LOG-ON | LOG-OFF | ACCESS | FILE NO | FILE NAME/DESCRIP |
|------|--------|---------|--------|---------|-------------------|
| 0101 | 0835 | 0847 | MINX | JDC-041 | CENAM AERIAL SEQ QVRFLT 0101 |
| 0101 | 2217 | 2231 | CAPO | DKJ-009 | SOAFR SAT SEQ 1227 |
| 0101 | 1029 | 1055 | MINX | SLT-965 | INDOCH SAT SEQ 0101 |

The information went on and on. The stack of computer paper analyzing the terminal located behind him was seventeen inches high. Jack Coriolanus sighed, ripped off the January section, and started running his fingertip down each of the columns, looking for anything out of the ordinary.

Harry Downs's access code of MINX—which was only the primary code, secondary codes remaining secret—was in frequent use at this particular terminal, and that item was suspicious in itself. Just as for Coriolanus, a man in Downs's position would not normally handle this kind of drudge work himself.

There was also an access code linked to many of the file numbers, preventing unauthorized personnel from delving too deeply into secured files. Any terminal user could create his own files, too, and secure them with his or her own code. At this point, Coriolanus had no intention of trying to get into Downs's locked files, for that would require bringing in the computer experts and devoting time to cracking the codes.

By eight o'clock, Coriolanus had worked through the whole log, checking every entry where Downs had logged on to the machine. His assistant, Claude Nolan, arrived at ten minutes after eight. "Sorry I'm late, sir. I didn't get your message until I arrived at the office."

"Go get a chair from somewhere and bring it in here, Claude."

Nolan went after a chair and sat next to Coriolanus as the special assistant began calling up the files, one after another, that had interested Harry Downs.

"What are we doing, sir?"

"What we're doing is trying to figure out what Harry Downs is doing."

"Oh."

Coriolanus stopped tapping keys for a moment. "Something's funny."

"In what way, sir?"

"For six weeks, Harry's been emphasizing this *Southern Merchant* thing."

"That's all?" Nolan asked.

Coriolanus gave him a sardonic grin. "No, that's not all. Out of the blue, I learn there's a bunch of Cuban pilots showing up in Managua. Source: Bobby Clark through Harry Downs."

"Did he get a snapshot or anything?"

"No, and in Senate Select Committee, when that asshole Conners pressed him on a source, Harry lied to him. He implied that there was someone in Castro's camp. And that's bullshit."

"Did you ask Downs about it, sir?"

"Hell, yes, but he just said he was pissed at Conners."

In the next half hour, Coriolanus and Nolan looked at each of the photo files Downs had accessed. Each sequence of photographs had either the *Southern Merchant* or the *Riga Star,* the ship that the *Merchant* may have met in the Arabian Sea, as focal points. In the last few weeks, the photos also included shots of the Nicaraguan/Honduran border, with some blowups of Sandinista and Contra strongholds. Some of the Contra camps in Honduras showed cargo aircraft unloading materiel.

"We know all this stuff," Nolan observed.

"Yeah, but we don't know why Harry was doing his own work on this. Or why these are the only ships he's personally interested in. Major Whaley!"

After a minute, the major appeared in the doorway. "Yes, sir?"

"How do I get the latest shots of this area?"

Whaley came over, checked the map coordinates printed in the upper right-hand corner, then reached around Coriolanus and pecked out keys on the keyboard, working through a series of menus and indexes. A new picture appeared on the screen, heavy with white clouds in the lower corner. Coriolanus, because he had been watching similar photos all morning, took only a moment to find the freighter, one of hundreds of watercraft shown on the screen. It looked to be a couple of hundred miles offshore. The Central American coast dominated the left side of the screen.

"This is from twenty-seven thousand feet, taken on June twentieth," Whaley explained.

"Can we zoom in on this?" Coriolanus asked, pointing out the freighter with his fingertip.

"Not with this particular shot, sir. What I can do is print it off and have it enlarged."

"No. What's the latest?"

Whaley went back to an index. "There was a satellite pass at seven-fifteen this morning, Mr. Coriolanus. Let me see what I can find."

Two minutes later, they had a new picture.

But no *Southern Merchant*.

All three of them crouched before the screen, scanning for a familiar shape—an ancient freighter with two large crates on the forward deck.

It was not there.

"This is strange," Major Whaley said.

"Get a bunch of your people, Major, and check every photo you can find over the last three days. I want to know what happened to that ship. Come on, Claude."

Coriolanus and Nolan went outside and climbed into the backseat of Coriolanus's limousine.

"Where to, Mr. Coriolanus?"

"Langley, Dean." Coriolanus ran up the window between front and back.

"Sounds like you suspect something," Nolan said.

"I don't know," Coriolanus admitted. "I just don't like being half-aware of what's going on."

"What would Harry be up to?"

"Shit. I have no idea. Maybe it's not Harry. When we get back to the office, you find Bobby Clark and tell him I want to talk to him. Clark could be feeding Harry a line, for all I know."

"Or maybe it's Hamm?" Nolan suggested. "Remember Hamm and Clark were seen together in Miami? With a couple of others?"

That was the scenario that made more sense to Coriolanus. Whenever Hamm was connected to something, the regulations got bent all to hell. And a Hamm not tied to any regulations since his retirement could really screw things up. "That has promise, Claude. Find Hamm, too. And call Miami and see if they can backtrack some and identify the two men who were with Hamm and Clark."

"Apparently, the four of them flew in from Monterrey, Mexico, together."

"Then get somebody down to Monterrey. In fact, Claude, get a message off to every chief of station in Mexico and Central America. We want to know if Clark or Hamm, anyone they know, or anyone interesting at all, has been passing through their domains."

"Technically," Nolan pointed out, "this should go through Harry."

"Hell, no!" Coriolanus could bend a rule now and then himself.

\* \* \*

Camp Rogers was sited two and a half miles north of the Coco de Sogovia River, the natural border between Honduras and Nicaragua to the south. It was seventy-five miles inland, still caught in the mahogany forest, but on the edge of rising terrain that eventually climbed into high plains country to the west.

It was humid and hot most of the time. In the rainy season, the soil underfoot was transformed from baked clay to ooze that sucked at footwear.

The camp's primary feature was a short landing strip hacked out of the forest and roughly smoothed by a D-9 Cat that now sat rusting behind Warehouse One, one plate of its left tread split across the middle. The runway was not long enough to handle anything much bigger than old C-47s or twin-engined Providers, and it served as the division point between the storage facilities on the higher side, to the north, and the collection of living huts, sheds, and tents to the south.

Built primarily as a resupply point, the camp still occasionally housed and fed FDN-Contra fighters who appeared out of the jungle and hung around for the simple fare provided in the mess tent and the collapsible cot and dirty blanket allotted in one of the bunk tents. At any one time, there might be fifty or sixty transients in residence, in addition to the fifteen permanent staff who manned the administrative and technical functions of the camp.

Except for three R&R junkets to Tegoose, Norman Jessup had spent the last sixteen months at Camp Rogers. Originally from New Orleans, Jessup had lived in L.A., Memphis, St. Louis, and Detroit since his return from Vietnam, anywhere he could find a job. The Army had trained him as a supply clerk, and he had been a supply clerk ever since, his best job landing him with Ford Motor Company in Detroit. Until that job was cut back in a massive layoff.

Jessup was six foot four inches tall, and his arms and shoulders looked like the front quarters of a water buffalo—the muscles rippled and his ebony skin glowed in the sunlight. In the heat of Camp Rogers, he rarely wore a shirt with his cut-off fatigue pants and high-laced jungle boots. He also wore a Western-styled gunbelt adorned with a Colt .45 Peacemaker, a row of heavy .45 cartridges, and a sheathed K-Bar, though it was unnecessary. His stature alone cowed his bunkmates and took what aggression there was out of the small-boned Contra fighters.

He took his job—tending the inventories of the six tin-roofed, tin-sided warehouses—seriously for two reasons. He was making $3,000 a month, the most he had ever made, and the most welcome after he had been unemployed for a year. He was not paying taxes on it, but he was sending $2,500 a month to Marlene, the mother of his three children, two, three, and four years old, back in Detroit.

After a breakfast of refried beans, tortillas, and overcooked pork, Jessup got a can of Pepsi from the washtub near the mess-tent entrance and wandered down to the end of the airstrip. Kip Dennis had the cowling off the left engine of a battered Cessna 310, looking for a vaporization problem. Jessup talked with him a while, then crossed the strip and made one of his frequent circuits of the warehouses.

The buildings were backed in under the edge of the jungle canopy, giving them some partial protection from aerial observation, and the rear of the structures was always in shadow. As he neared the back corner of Number Six, he heard the screech of tearing metal.

Jessup slowed for long enough to bend over and set his Pepsi can on the ground and slip the thong from the hammer of the Colt. He eased his way to the corner, leaned his shoulder against the hot tin, and peered around the back. Two Nicaraguans in filthy jungle fatigues were on their knees at the back of Warehouse Five—which housed weapons—trying to peel the corrugated tin from the studs.

It was difficult enough dealing with the noncoms and Contra leaders who tried to rip off M-16s to sell on the black market. But with the average jungle fighter, he had less patience. He let these two work a while longer, bending back a sheet of tin and disappearing inside, then he walked over and stood next to the fresh entrance.

The first man exited on hands and knees, clutching seven assault rifles to his chest as he crawled through the hole. Jessup let him get to his knees before he extended his Colt at the man's head.

The thief went rigid and his eyes widened in fright, his eyeballs trying to peer sideways at his captor.

The second man scrambled out of the torn wall, and Jessup kicked him in the face, the steel toe of the jungle boot nearly taking his nose off.

That man screamed loudly enough to bring the camp residents running.

Twenty Contra fighters rounded the warehouse to find one of their own facedown in the dirt, trapped by a 13-EEE jungle boot in the middle of his back, and another sprawled in front of Jessup.

Jessup stood in front of the man, speaking his barely passable Spanish with a Louisiana accent. ''My man, you got to know when you rip me off, you taking the food out of my kiddies' mouths. You hungry for lead, all you got to do is ask.''

The camp manager broke up the fun after a while, banishing the two Contras back into the jungle, and Jessup went back to his room.

He did not live in one of the Camp Rogers bunk tents. Instead, he had moved a cot into his small office in the front of Warehouse One. The office was twelve feet by twelve feet, with canvas interior walls, and housed his cot, desk, chair, four filing cabinets, an old Remington typewriter, and a propane refrigerator.

In midmorning, he wandered over to the mess tent to get three bacon-and-fried-egg tortilla sandwiches, and walked back to his office to prepare inventory sheets for the incoming flight. The airplane, a Dornier Skyservant wearing the logo of Carib AirFreight, landed an hour after he had finished his snack, raising a cloud of dust that would hang in the windless air for hours. Jessup went over and located fifteen unwilling volunteers among the transient Contras to unload it.

The airplane was carrying humanitarian supplies, including uniforms, first-aid kits, toilet paper, sheets, blankets, morphine, quinine tablets, penicillin, M-79 grenade launchers, five M-60 machine guns, eleven crates of fragmentation grenades, and twenty-one boxes of variously sized ammunition. The supplies paid for by U.S. aid were interspersed with arms that had begun to show up unexpectedly a week before. Jessup never asked where it came from, just listed it on his inventory sheets and took care of it.

The unloading process was half-complete when an M-151 Jeep that looked as if it had been rolled two and a half times came speeding down the twin ruts that passed for a road into the camp. The driver of the Jeep brought it to a sliding stop alongside the airplane, and Diego Contrarez popped out of the passenger seat.

Contrarez was immaculately dressed in pressed fatigues. He wore a sidearm in a flap holster on a web belt and carried an M-16. Four concussion grenades dangled from the belt. A lock of curly black hair hung on his forehead from beneath the bill of his olive-drab baseball cap. Contrarez was an aide to one of the central FDN leaders—Jessup never remembered which one—and was also rumored to be on the CIA payroll. That rumor gave him extra protection.

Contrarez strode directly toward the stack of materiel building on the ground outside the airplane and started pointing out boxes and crates he wanted in the back of his Jeep, issuing orders to Jessup's unloading detail.

Jessup intercepted him with a clipboard. "Sign here, Contrarez. You take what you need, and I'll fill in the blanks."

The Contra commander had to gaze up a full foot in order to look Jessup in the eyes. He said, "I ain't signing a fucking thing."

"Then you ain't taking a fucking thing." Jessup took a step forward, so Contrarez was staring directly into his bare chest.

Contrarez took a step back, which he never liked to do in front of subordinates, in order to see Jessup better. "Listen, asshole. I'm running a goddamned war. I'll take what I need."

"And you're going to sign for what you're going to take, my man, so when those M-60s end up in San Salvador, your bosses are going to know who got the money for sending them there."

"What I can do, *my man,* I can shoot your black ass."
Contrarez started to raise the muzzle of the M-16.

Jessup let his eyes get hard. "I figure I can take five,
six rounds from that peashooter before I die. In the mean-
time, I'll take your balls off by hand. You going to have
to walk funny among your friends."

"Gimme the goddamned clipboard."

All nine aircraft were refueled from the drums they had
brought with them by eight o'clock. It was strenuous work,
lifting the heavy drums out of the Mi-24s, spinning the
handles on the manual pumps, and rolling the depleted
containers off into the jungle surrounding the clearing. The
temperature and moisture trapped on the jungle floor did
not help. Humidity seemed to drip from the rubbery leaves
of the trees as well as from armpits.

From the air, the clearing had been difficult to find,
even though Hamm had been working from satellite photos provided by Clark. It was smaller than he had expected, with the triple-canopied jungle hanging out over
the open space. The choppers had had to lose altitude to
almost ground level, then slideslip into a landing. The
nine helicopters, resting in a circle, pretty well took up
the available space. Hamm was glad he had competent
pilots. The cramped quarters were suitable for accidental
collisions.

The odor of fuel overlaid that of mildew and crumbling
earth by the time Hamm and McDonough finished fueling
their Mi-28. Hamm rolled the barrel to the side and stowed
the pump in the cockpit while McDonough performed a
more thorough inspection of the helicopter than he had
accomplished in the early-morning darkness. When he was
finished, the two of them walked across the clearing to

where the team was gathering around Clark and De Veres's Havoc. The ground was soft and squishy underfoot.

Rick Talbot and Hank Bellows, the group's able maintenance officers, were questioning the pilots about the morning's flight and taking notes. Besides the complaints about the way the Soviet aircraft handled—despite their superior speed, the choppers felt clumsy—there were a few specific bitches.

Jerry Pickett said, "You want to take a look at Vaquero Five, Rick? She likes to dance."

"Samba or hard rock?" Bellows asked.

"More like the Twist. Rear rotor control is sensitive as hell. The tail takes unexpected jumps to port."

"She's the one that connected with the winch," Bellows said.

"I'll bet we've still got a crimp in a hydraulic line, fouling the flow," Talbot said, scribbling in his notebook. "We'd better take a look at it. Anyone else got heavy problems?"

Pat Canton, lolled back against the hub of the Havoc's landing gear, said, "Bandito Five. There's a radar glitch."

"That's my field and my problem," Peachy Keen said. "What's she doing?"

"When I went to active, there was nothing. I couldn't even read the rest of you guys."

"What in the hell did you go active for?" Hamm asked, angry. "You had strict instructions to leave the goddamned thing alone."

Defensive radar in the region would more easily pick them up if anyone utilized the radar, sending out electronic signals. Canton raised his chin a little, to glare more directly at Hamm. "I wouldn't know I had a problem if I hadn't checked it out, would I?"

Hamm held the gaze. "Canton, you can stop worrying about the Sandinistas and start worrying about me. Step out of line again, and I'll have your ass."

"Shit."

"I couldn't care less whether you endanger yourself, but you're not going to make the rest of us targets. That won't happen again."

Canton straightened up. "Listen . . ."

Rick Talbot, who was riding gunner in Canton's Havoc from this point on, broke it up, tapping the butt of the nine-millimeter Walther riding on his hip. "Tell you what, Steve. He blows it again, I'll turn around and put a slug in his gut. That way, I can fly the bird. We do it your way, with cannon rounds, I get to be one of Bobby's statistics."

"Deal," Hamm said.

After a moment's silence, Canton started to study the ground.

Bellows asked, "Anybody else with bugs?"

A few more minor problems were listed for the engineers, then Clark spread a chart on the ground. Hamm walked over to the Hind parked behind him and dug around for a canteen. The water was lukewarm. He carried the canteen back to the group and passed it around.

Clark pointed out the X on the chart. "This is our present position. We've got one more short hop to make by three o'clock."

He marked the next X about sixty miles due west and twenty miles south of the Honduras border. The countryside there was more mountainous, though still sprinkled with forest. The chart showed no villages or hamlets in the vicinity; it was an inhospitable region.

"I still think we should be operating from the Honduras

side,'' Clay Harper said. ''Just being in Nicaragua with all of this hardware makes my spine itch.''

''Both sides have to think we're based in Nicaragua, a new air unit,'' Clark answered.

''One that's based in a hell of a remote area,'' Mc-Donough noted, working on the wrapper of a fresh cigar. He struck a kitchen match and lit it.

''You'd rather have us based in Leon or Managua, Sean?'' De Veres asked.

''They have cold beer?'' he asked back.

Hamm went over and squatted next to Clark. He dug into Clark's canvas document bag and brought out the aerial photos. Leafing through them, he asked, ''Your new place going to be as hard to find as this clearing was?''

''I've been there three times,'' Clark said.

''That's not what I asked.''

''Well, yeah. It might be tough.''

A major problem in the Contra resupply effort was simply finding designated drop zones. Coordinates marked on a map did not translate easily to a pilot's viewpoint when the whole landscape was a green blanket. And aircraft flying clandestine cargo did not like to pinpoint coordinates by making their positions known to available air controllers in the capital cities of Central America.

Hamm checked his watch. ''All right. It's zero nine zero five hours. Banditos One, Two, Three, and Four will take off in ten minutes and go find the site. The rest of you get hot on repairing aircraft. You take off at eleven hundred hours and follow a two-seven-zero heading. At eleven fifteen hours, and every five minutes after that, we'll give you three blips on the Tactical Two frequency. You should be able to home on that.''

The men scattered to their tasks, and twenty minutes

later, McDonough's and De Veres's Havocs were skimming the jungle top at 180 miles per hour. In his seat in the nose of the Mi-28, Hamm felt as if he were the point of the arrow. The world flashed below him at dizzying speed.

"Love it!" McDonough told him over the intercom. "Pretty good-looking country."

"Until they start launching SAMs at us."

"That's why you've got ECM," McDonough said.

The electronics aboard were sophisticated. There were on-board computers and terrain display screens—useless since they were not programmed for the area. The Electronic Countermeasures equipment could jam radio and radar frequencies. With the press of a button, he could scatter shredded bits of aluminum, meant to confuse radar-guided missiles.

Hamm studied his chart and the scan of the radar scope. In the passive mode, the scope did not show every object in the area distinctly. In this deserted region, however, he did not think he was missing anything important. Bandito Three was clearly shown, right alongside them. He looked over at Clark in the forward cockpit, and Clark waved toward the right.

"Bear to starboard a little, Sean."

"Righto. Jesus. Now I'm starting to talk like your buddy Cameron."

Two minutes later, they passed over a twin-rutted trail. A topless Jeep with a mounted machine gun and two men in it was struggling up a steep slope. The men waved at them as they passed over, and Hamm waved back at them.

"Sandinistas?" McDonough asked.

"Must be. They think we're theirs."

"Should we take a two-minute break and blow them up?"

"I don't think one Jeep is Bobby's idea of a mission," Hamm said.

The terrain began to rise steeply. Mountain peaks poked out of the jungle growth, their tops shining in the sun. For all of the individuality of each peak, the earth below had a mesmerizing sameness to it. As they climbed higher, the foliage thinned out, becoming mahogany forest, leaving big blank spots. In some areas, Hamm could see where the natives had struggled to grow corn and maybe some cotton. There were very few people visible. He saw a man and a boy herding a five-member herd of emaciated cattle.

Clark waved, then gave him a thumb's-up from the other helicopter.

"Slow it down some, Sean."

McDonough backed off to 100 miles per hour, and the two Havocs separated, peeling off in different directions, searching for Clark's idea of the ideal Sandinista air base. Heading southwest, McDonough and Hamm scanned the ground, but nothing resembled the aerial photograph Hamm had taped to his control panel. After a fruitless ten minutes, McDonough banked to the right, flew several miles in that direction, then headed back to the northeast.

Hamm reported fuel status. "We're down to a three-quarter load."

"Bobby better find his goddamned camp soon. At the rate we're going, we'll have to walk in."

Far off to the west, Hamm saw three helicopters. "Check your seven o'clock, Sean."

"Goddamn, Steve. You may be getting old, but your eyes are all right. They look like Hinds."

"They are."

"I hope they don't come over and want to be friendly," McDonough said.

Hamm guessed that the Nicaraguans had not even seen them. Four minutes later, the three aircraft disappeared behind a mountaintop.

At 10:12 A.M., Hamm heard three clicks in his headphones. He scanned the mountains ahead and saw the sun's reflection glancing off rotors five miles ahead, and below them. "Petal to the metal, Sean. Bearing zero-three-five."

Peter de Veres waited until they were within a half mile, then slowly sank out of sight below the faded green velvet top of the forest. McDonough came in low, spotted the other Havoc, and settled to the ground alongside it, then killed the turbine. Hamm and McDonough tumbled out of their cockpits.

At this altitude, around twelve hundred feet, the air was a little drier, but not much. The temperature was close to a hundred. It was quiet except for the low sigh of a breeze in the forest and the residual ringing of the turbine in Hamm's ears. The ground was harder, with reddish soil peeking through an overgrowth of weeds and wild grass. Yellow and white wildflowers spotted the clearing.

"Paradise," McDonough proclaimed it.

Peter de Veres grinned at him. "Sean, baby, I've yet to find a paradise from which women were excluded."

"Details, details," McDonough said.

Using an extended finger, Clark pointed around the space. "We'll park aircraft along this side, but we don't want any sort of formation. Back under the trees, over there, is where we'll put the tents. Dig the latrine twenty yards farther back."

McDonough clambered back up to his cockpit and came

down with two entrenching tools. "I'll get started on the latrine. I've got to take a leak pretty bad."

"Give me one of those shovels," Hamm said, "and I'll help you."

By twelve o'clock, all nine of the Soviet helicopters were on the ground and sheathed from the sun and prying eyes by camouflage netting. Clark's planning had taken into account the red, brown, and olive colors of the region, and the netting matched. After a short break for a C-ration lunch, they would set up eight tents, six for sleeping, one for an orderly room—complete with field desk and files of forged orders written in Spanish—and one for supply. It was more than they needed, of course, but Bobby Clark wanted the camp to look well utilized. He had even shipped in four large boxes of refuse, so they could scatter the camp with candy wrappers, pop and beer cans, tortilla chip sacks, chicken bones, empty bean cans, and Spanish-language pornographic novels.

"Just like any well-organized Sandinista operation," Clark said.

"I thought we were supposed to be well-organized Cubans," Hamm told him.

"Well, same thing," Clark responded.

Will Hunt and J.P. Conover arrived at Corrosion Corner just after noon. Hunt had survived five tours of Vietnam—four as a civilian—Angola, Uganda, El Salvador, Iran, and other specialized missions. Conover's resumé was just as varied, though not quite as long.

They walked across the lot to Operations, checked in, and found that the paperwork had been taken care of, as promised. Conover filed a flight plan and checked on the weather while Hunt went out to inspect the aircraft. He had completed the external checks by the time Conover caught up with him.

"Beat-up son of a bitch, isn't it?" Conover asked.

Climbing through the side hatch, Hunt said, "Looks all right to me."

The C-130's cargo deck was littered with sand. It scraped underfoot as they inspected the pallets and parachutes.

Conover toed a small mound of sand caught in the corner of a fuselage rib. "Jesus. I'll bet this honey's been sitting in Saudi Arabia."

Hunt did not reply, but climbed to the flight deck. Conover followed him and dropped into the right seat.

By one o'clock, they were climbing to twenty thousand feet, headed west-southwest, to clear Cuba off its western tip. The target was three hours away, four o'clock Miami time.

Conover spread a chart over his lap and pulled the map light close. "So where's this drop zone?"

"Called Camp Ramirez."

"I don't see it on the chart."

"That's because they didn't build it until this morning," Hunt told him.

# EIGHTEEN

In Washington, it was three-thirty by the time Claude Nolan tapped on Coriolanus's door frame and entered the special assistant's big office.

Coriolanus did not invite Nolan to have a seat. He just looked up and gruffly asked, "What do you have?"

Nolan stood in front of the desk, leafing through a thick stack of telexes. "Quite a few things. May I sit down, sir?"

Coriolanus waved a hand indifferently, and Nolan took one of the stiff-backed visitor chairs.

"Come on," Coriolanus urged.

"First, there's not much new on the *Southern Merchant*. We found some shots from a satellite pass around midnight last night, and they were a bit strange—looked like light emitting from the edges of the cargo hatches, both fore and aft. But no activity on deck. And then, this morning, the damned ship's disappeared."

"I phoned Downs and asked for an update on it," Coriolanus said. "When he called me back about eleven, he sounded puzzled himself. Said he'd do some more checking, but didn't think I should yet write it off as no threat. I don't think Harry knows what the hell's going on."

"That's interesting," Nolan told him, but his face said he did not quite know why it was interesting.

"Yes. What else?"

"As far as I can find out, that C-130 Hamm was on was never in Monterrey."

"You didn't think that it would have been, did you, Claude?"

"I guess not, sir. Anyway, the two on board the plane with Hamm and Clark were Peter de Veres and Sean McDonough. Our watcher shot a couple of photos, fortunately."

"Who the hell are they?"

Nolan picked through his telexes. "McDonough runs a flight service in Bakersfield, California. He's ex-military, and he served a couple of tours in Vietnam with Hamm, back when Hamm was flying combat."

"Ah."

"And De Veres is a playboy type out of Miami, an old pal of Clark's. He's also an ex–chopper pilot."

"I don't think I like the way this is being carded," Coriolanus said. "All these old war buddies getting together."

"But didn't you warn Clark away from Hamm?"

"I gave Harry the message, and it damned well better have taken hold."

"Yes, sir."

"Where are all these hotshots now?" Coriolanus asked.

"Nowhere we can find them. De Veres lives on some big boat in Biscayne Bay, but it's shut up tight. Hamm's not answering his telephone, so I sent someone down to check his house. The woman answering the phone at the flight service says McDonough's taken a vacation somewhere in Mexico. Clark is on a tour of operations."

Coriolanus leaned back in his chair, his elbows on the padded arms of the chair, and pressed his fingertips together. "You know, Claude, every time I've asked Harry about Clark lately, he's been on a tour of operations. He's never where he can be easily reached. Let's find out how long all of these guys have been out of touch."

"Yes, sir." Nolan made a note. "Now, our other list. I've asked the affected COSs to go back and check on all Americans who've arrived in San Salvador, Tegucigalpa, Guatemala, or San José in the past week. Those are the major airports, and about the only ones we can easily check. There were three hundred and sixty-four people carrying U.S. passports. We're currently checking on whether or not they went on to hotels, but as of ten o'clock, we can't find one hundred forty-six of them."

"That's going to end up not telling us shit. Half of them will disappear into the countryside."

"It's all we can do, sir."

Coriolanus kept pressing his fingertips together, feeling the tension pulse in his biceps and watching the veins pop up on the backs of his hands.

"How about the shots of the military camps, Claude?"

Nolan leafed through his notebook. "On those, I went back four weeks and compared activity and population as best I could. On the Nicaraguan side, the Sandinista camps seem to be maintaining the same level of both activity and population. On both the Nicaraguan and Honduran sides of the border, the Contra camps appear to be filling up with materiel and with people coming out of the jungle."

"Why is that?"

"I'd have thought, sir, that it was because the Contra patrols are running short of food and ammunition, pulling back to the bases for rest and recuperation. Using up the soft supplies that AID is sending in. But then I ran a comparison of supply flights.'' Nolan fingered his sheaf of photographs. ''I don't have a constant picture, of course, but the supply runs appear to have been stepped up in the last couple of weeks. This week, for example, there were sixteen percent more flights than last week. I should really check it out over a six-month period, to be more accurate.''

Coriolanus mused over that information. ''We may not have time for that. Maybe there's been an infusion of philanthropic dollars this week?''

''Maybe, sir. I could run a check of appropriate CIA funding accounts, to see if there's been a corresponding set of expenses.''

''No. They'll be blocked. I'll ask the DDO to check on those, Claude. But there'd damned well better not be any unexplained disbursements from anybody's contingency funds.''

''Yes, sir. What next?''

''Who've we got in Miami?''

''Ben Neale's the team leader.''

''Okay. Get him to start checking on equipment, fuel, and other shipments that have gone south in the past month.''

''That's going to be a hell of a lot of checking, Mr. Coriolanus.''

''So, make it easy. Have him start with the flights where the Agency arranged for customs to skip an inspection.''

''Yes, sir. Anything else?''

''Tomorrow at ten, the DDO and I are meeting with the director, and I'll have to tell him what we know. What's your opinion, Claude?''

Nolan was taken aback. He had never been asked such

a question before. "I haven't given it much consideration, sir. Being tied up with details and all."

"Give it a try."

Nolan took a full minute to organize. "Well, on one hand we have indications that the Soviets may be escalating the war in Nicaragua, shipping in sophisticated aircraft and the pilots to fly them. This information directly conflicts with the new trend in Soviet policy."

"Yes, that's what makes me suspicious of the whole thing, Claude. But then, we could be wrong," Coriolanus admitted. "A wind-down in Afghanistan, where they know they'll lose, in favor of increased resources for the Sandinista government, where they figure they'll win. What else?"

"On the other hand, you also seem suspicious of Harry Downs. Or maybe the information Harry has been providing. And Harry Downs's information involves Bobby Clark in the field."

"And the people Bobby has been playing with?"

"Clark might be planning an extracurricular raid. Defying congressional edicts."

"He's been down there a long time. I've known him for long enough to know that he believes in what he's doing," Coriolanus said, then conjectured, "It isn't too tough to raise some outside dollars. For the sake of argument, let's say Bobby raised a few bucks, got the FDN-Contras to pull their people in for regrouping, and is going to mount a couple of operations on his own. Maybe send a big Contra group at a large Sandinista outpost. A major offensive."

"It would be the first time," Nolan said. "Full-scale attacks on military targets are rare."

"I know that irks Bobby. So, let's say that's what he has in mind. What happens?"

Nolan knew that answer right away. "He runs smack into this new Air Force unit—assuming it hasn't been sunk at sea, and gets cut to ribbons. And the CIA gets blamed for overstepping its charter again."

"Find out what Clark has been doing for the last couple of months," Coriolanus ordered. "Keep Downs out of it, and use the Bureau if you have to."

"Yes, sir." Nolan gathered his paper, rose from his chair, and went out.

Fifteen minutes after his assistant left, Harry Downs called.

"What did you find out, Harry?"

"I don't know yet about the ship, Jack. They may have sunk it. What I do know, from eyewitness reports out of Sandy Bay and Puerto Cabezas, is that nine Soviet-built military helicopters crossed the coast early this morning south of Sandy Bay and headed inland along the Wawa River. Four of the choppers had new silhouettes, and they were all carrying Nicaraguan markings. My guess is that the Cubans met the ship at sea and flew the choppers in." Downs paused, then added, "One more thing. The Soviets have a small task force steaming in the area."

"How small?" Coriolanus asked.

"A show-of-force thing. Ships normally playing around the Atlantic. There's a Sverdlov class cruiser, the *Zhdanov*, two Kotlin Sam class destroyers, the *Bravy* and the *Skrytny*, and the carrier *Baku*."

"That's the naval group that was visiting Fidel? All of them?"

"That's right. But they left port sometime after midnight last night."

"Shit. I want some hard data on that fast, Harry. On that task force. And you find out where those helicopters were headed."

"Will do, Jack." Downs hung up.

Coriolanus replaced the receiver. Then, deciding he could not wait until ten in the morning, he called the DDO.

"Topic?" his boss asked.

"Nicaragua."

"Go."

"I've got a major unit of Soviet-built helicopters now in the country. I have a suspicion that the Contras may be planning a big push of some sort—nothing hard on that except for a buildup of troops in rear supply areas, but we're looking into it."

"A major confrontation, then?"

"Possibly. If so, it could be disastrous in two ways— one for the Contras and one for us because Clark may be personally involved."

"How?"

"Either he's got some private money all of a sudden, or he's convinced the Contra money people to build up a reserve. Wherever the money is coming from, I'd bet on Bobby devising a time schedule where an infusion of supplies coincides with a Contra realignment of their troops and their tactics."

"Nothing wrong with that that I can see," the DDO said. "Be about time we saw some direct, and strong, action out of the rebels. Who cares if Clark gives them some planning aid?"

"Not me, unless the Contras cross the border and get decimated. We also need to pin down the locations of the other Sandinista air units."

"Recommendation?"

"I think the director should take it to the NSC. I think we need twenty-four-hour surveillance of the Honduran and Nicaraguan areas. Also, we especially want to watch a Soviet task force that's just departed Cuba."

"How do you want that covered?"

"By moving a satellite into geo-stationary orbit," Coriolanus said.

"That would, of course, come to the attention of the Soviets."

"I don't think we have a choice. We have to know what's going on, and right now, I feel I'm not getting everything I need to know."

"I don't know the current configuration for our own satellites. We might have to ask DOD for the use of one of theirs."

"Then that's what we should do," Coriolanus said. "And goddamned fast."

The DDO considered that for a moment. "I'll talk to the Director, Jack. And I suppose he'll have to talk to some people on the oversight committees."

"Jesus. I don't want to make this a fucking party," Coriolanus said.

"But that's what you'll get."

"An Oh-two, I think," Conover said.

Nicaragua operated Summit Aviation–modified versions of the Cessna Skymaster, primarily as reconnaissance aircraft. The one Conover had spotted was about four thousand feet above them and three miles to the south. It was flying westward, just inside the border.

"And not a cloud to hide in," Will Hunt complained. He eased back the throttles and let the Hercules dip even lower toward the mountainous terrain, taking on a slight right turn.

"We're still over Honduras. He's just patrolling the border."

"We're not even supposed to be in Honduras, J.P."

"Do a nice big three-six-zero. Give him some time, Will."

Hunt maintained his right turn, completing a full circle that covered ten square miles. By the time they approached the border again, identified by the Rio Coco de Segovia, the Cessna was a tiny dot far to the west. He lined up the gyro compass on 260, which would drift them toward, and over, the Nicaraguan border as they continued inland. At 2,500 feet on the altimeter, they were about 1,300 feet above the forest. Some of the mountain peaks to the south and west rose a thousand feet above them. Seventy miles ahead of them, Cerro Mocoton was visible at 6,900 feet, a halo of heat haze around its tip. Hunt checked the temperature and manifold pressure on each of the four engines again. In an emergency, there was no place to put the beast down.

Conover spread open the chart, refolded it, and laid it lightly against his control yoke. Peering forward through the windscreen, he said, "The Montañas de Colon coming up on the right."

They were approaching the northern thrust of the border, where Nicaragua bulged into Honduras as it followed the river. The mountain range ran east to west along the north side of the river. "Going to one-nine-five," Hunt said.

Conover pulled his headset firmly over his ears and dialed the radio to 160.20, the frequency of the homing signal they were supposed to find. "I've got one-five-one-one hours, local time. We're a little off the pace."

"Nobody in Central America is ever on time," Hunt told him. "Why should we be different?"

"How about if we want to collect our paychecks?" J.P. Conover suggested.

Hunt turned right to bypass a rising hunk of terrain, then settled back on course. He began to bleed off altitude, getting down to where he could hug the terrain. Neither man spoke for five minutes.

"Got it!" Hunt yelled. "Go to one-eight-six."

Hunt banked left, picked up the new heading, and concentrated on staying with it.

The patchwork of forest and smeary, eroded hillsides below gave no evidence of life. Hunt scanned ahead, but saw nothing that moved. "This guy De Veres picked the asshole of the world to live in," he said.

"Starting to flutter," Conover said.

A quick glance at the Omni Bearing Indicator confirmed that the needle was shaking.

"I'll watch the OBI. Go on back," Hunt said.

Conover scrambled out of his seat and slid down the ladder to the cargo bay.

Hunt nearly missed it. Pulling the nose up to clear a hillock, the plane climbed to two hundred feet above the forest top as the landscape dropped abruptly away. The forest broadened quickly, several miles wide all of a sudden, appearing impenetrable to ground travel. The OBI needle went crazy as the plane passed over the top of its signal source, and Hunt glanced down through his side window. The clearing was several hundred yards to his left, a one-hundred-foot swath cut in the mahogany forest.

At this distance, he could see the irregular shapes of the camouflaged aircraft parked along the eastern perimeter.

He signaled Conover with the horn and with two flashes of the red light in the cargo bay, flew on by for a half mile, then made a tight turn and came back at slower speed, lining up with the clearing, and climbing another five hundred feet. The forest did not allow a zero-foot drop.

Hunt figured it would take three passes to drop the six pallets in the small clearing. He was eager to get it done, get back to Miami, and figure out how he was going to spend his new bucks.

As soon as the clearing disappeared under the nose, he counted to three, then signaled Conover with the green light. Five seconds later, he saw the first drogue chute pop, then the first main parachute bloomed in his rearview mirror. Automatically, he trimmed controls for the loss of weight.

Boris Kamorovkin woke him from a very deep nap at four-thirty in the afternoon. Zhukov sat up groggily, shaking his aide's hand from his shoulder. "Boris? What is it?"

"An urgent message, Comrade Major," Kamorovkin told him, waving the flimsy at him.

Rubbing his eyes with his forefingers, Zhukov asked, "What is the message?"

"There is to be a major frontal assault by the rebels against border installations."

"What!"

"That is what it says."

"Who says it?" Zhukov demanded.

Kamorovkin read the heading of the message. "It is from Moscow Center and cites a Washington source. You are directed to obtain further information and to squash the attempt.''

Zhukov snatched the paper from his assistant, tearing off one corner. "And what else?"

"That is all there is, Comrade Major."

Zhukov sat immobile for many moments, oblivious of Boris's staring. He was to prevent some kind of stupid invasion with absolutely no clues at all. "Boris, get Manuel Demarco on the telephone. Then, a message to Moscow Center. I want copies of all the latest satellite photography for our area."

Hamm sat on a camp stool in the shade of raised tent flaps and watched the sun setting in flashy reds. He reassembled the Kalashnikov AK-74 he had just cleaned. He thought it was a better weapon than the old AK-47s.

It had taken all afternoon to retrieve the fuel barrels. One pallet had missed the clearing entirely, smashing into treetops thirty yards back in the forest. The twin parachutes had ripped apart in the trees, the steel bands securing the drums to the pallet had parted, and drums had scattered over a seventy-foot area. Rolling the damned things through the thick underbrush and between the crusty boles of trees, stopping to lift one end of a drum and flip it over, had been backbreaking, sweaty labor.

Like most of the others, Hamm had removed his fatigue shirt. The sweat poured off him, running in filthy rivulets down his back and chest. The legs of his pants were sopping and stuck to his thighs and calves. The lister bag shower of Texas now looked like a luxury. Here, they did not have water to waste.

Despite the fact that Clark wanted this camp to look lived in, they were not firing up any camp stoves, creating

a signal that might be spotted by hostile forces. Mc-
Donough had devoured two boxes of C-rations, plus
Hamm's beans and franks. Wearing the slouch hat that
Clark complained was not part of their disguise, he leaned
back against the bole of a tree and said, "Damn, I could
use a beer."

"Amen to that," Peachy Keen added. He was with a
group of four men playing five-card stud on a crate, holding their cards five inches in front of their eyes in order to
read them in the dim light. Everyone was dog tired after
the hours of shifting fuel drums, topping off tanks, examining ordnance loads, checking and rechecking mechanical and electronic systems. Talbot and Bellows and
a shaded flashlight were over on top of a Hind, checking
a rotor-locking mechanism.

Clark and De Veres sat inside the orderly tent at the
field desk, going over the computer printouts from Clark's
canvas document case.

Hamm was tired of waiting. It was too bureaucratically
military. "Goddamn it, Bobby. Let's get on with it," he
called out loud.

"Fucking-A!" several men said in agreement.

Clark raised his head, scanned the men watching him,
then stood up. He ducked his head and slipped through
the tent doorway to assume a position in the middle of the
group. He called out to Talbot and Bellows, and when they
came over, said, "All right, then. I'll brief you on the
first of the three missions."

"I want to hear about all of them," Pat Canton said.
"Let's quit fucking around."

"One at a time," Clark insisted. "The first is scheduled
for ten o'clock in the morning."

Knowing a timeline subdued them. Now it was 'Nam all over again.

"Why so late in the day?" Bellows wanted to know. "Why give them an easy shot at us?"

"So we'll be seen. Being seen is the major objective."

"That's stupid," Canton said.

"What's the target?" Hamm asked.

Clark studied them hard in the waning light. "Camp Rogers."

There was a moment's stunned silence, then Sean McDonough said, "Hey, asshole! That's one of ours. They're friendlies."

Clark smiled at him. "I know."

# MISSION

# NINETEEN

"**W**hy in the fuck would we attack the Contras?" Bellows asked.

"Think about it, Hank," Clark told him. "If we have a success against some Sandinista installation, what would that do for our Congress?"

Peter de Veres came out in his support, but then Peter had known the true intent from the beginning. "Let me answer that for you, Bellows. They would only think that the Contras are finally able to handle this on their own. There wouldn't be additional funds forthcoming."

"We want to get the Contras some U.S. funding that they can count on," Clark said. "From the beginning, I said this was a public relations effort, didn't I? Well, this is how it's done. Make it look like the Soviets are using a bigger hand, that the Contras are overwhelmed.''

"Attacks on friendlies produce tax support, not attacks on the enemy,'' De Veres added.

Clark turned to Hamm, sitting on a camp stool, working the bolt of an AK-74 with a series of quick snicks. "What do you think, Steve?''

Hamm offered a grin, barely visible in the gathering darkness. "I'll admit you've pulled a one-eighty on me, Bobby, but I suppose I should have expected it. So far, I don't like it a damned bit.''

"But you know it'll work?''

"I know we're getting deeper in shit. I know we don't need this kind of surprise.''

"Damn it! It *will* work!''

"Your Contra buddies know about any of this crap?'' Hamm asked him.

"No. I didn't chance any leaks at all, Hamm.''

"Tell me, then, which one of your cute friends in Washington came up with this circus?''

Clark did not answer. Hamm was digging again.

Sean McDonough was disconcerted enough that he had let his cigar go out. He said, "Jesus ever-loving Christ! Now I do need a beer. Anybody mind if I take the car down to the supermarket?''

"No goddamned wonder you kept this to yourself until now,'' Keen said. "Everybody in favor of cranking up and going home, raise your hands.''

Clark saw half a dozen pale hands raised. The last sunlight in the west suddenly died away, and the stars became brighter. Well, he thought, I knew this was going to be the tough part.

Peter de Veres asked Hamm, "You really think it's a

circus, Steve? You think Bobby hasn't worked it out to the nth degree?''

"We missed a couple of degrees along the way."

"But the concept is valid," Clark insisted.

"I do see your point," Hamm said. "And now I see the real reason for the Mils. Hell, we go shoot up a few grubby Sandinistas, we might be helping the FDN in the short term, but that's not going to convince any senators on the appropriations committee. But if a flight of nine Soviet-supplied gunships attacks a couple of Contra bases in Honduras, it's a different story. The war is escalating out of control. Invasion of a friendly country. The Soviets have jumped into bed. Shit, that's why you've even got a legend prepared for the pilot cadre."

"Of course. That's the reason we're Cubans," Clark admitted. "And on the first mission, we're only using seven birds."

Hamm's voice became disembodied, rising on its own from the dark. "Let me guess. We leave one behind at the scene?"

"Right again. Like it's been shot down."

"Food for some reporter's thought. Let the media outrage the Western world."

Clark went on to explain that a number of reporters had been primed with leaked, background-only information, and should already be spread all over the area, eager to write that Pulitzer Prize winner.

"There's got to be somebody feeding this shit to the intelligence communities," Hamm said. "Harry Downs?"

"You know Harry, right?"

"I didn't think he'd buy into something like this."

"Harry passed on what I gave him," Clark said.

Every once in a while, Clark heard the click of the oiled

bolt in the Kalashnikov's receiver. His distrust of Hamm was increasing, but he had no alternatives now. He needed Hamm because whichever way Hamm went, most of the others would follow. He did not want to sound like he was begging, but after the silence lasted three minutes, he gave in. "Hamm?"

"I'm still digesting your fiction."

Hal Cherry said, "This has all the earmarks of a fiasco."

"Not the way it's planned," Clark insisted. "We've got the contingencies covered."

"Your goddamned computer has already proven itself senile," Cherry told him.

"Fuck it, let's get out of here," Harper said.

"I'm with you, Clay."

Clark was dismayed that McDonough, an advocate throughout, was turning traitor.

"It's a long walk to the coast," De Veres told him.

"If I think I'm big enough to take one of those Hinds away from you, Peter, then I am," McDonough promised.

"Ah, hell," Canton broke in, "what the fuck difference does it make? These greasers all look alike, anyway. Who gives a shit what side they're on? Just think of it as a quarter-million bucks, Sean."

"Don't get carried away, damn it!" Clark shouted. "First of all, no one is going to kill anyone. It's all a facade."

"You've got to be kidding," Cherry said. "We're sitting on enough ordnance to start World War Three, and you think that, in the heat of battle, someone won't launch a missile in the wrong direction? Hell, Bobby, are you going to vouch for the accuracy of those Russian Swatters?"

"I'll put my quarter of a million on the line," Peachy Keen said. "Even odds that two out of three of those Swatters miss the barn entirely, no matter who's guiding them. Any takers?"

"Not me," Jerry Pickett said.

"Now, wait!" Clark tried to regain control. "Can you all just listen to the operational program before you make judgments? For Christ's sake! I thought we were all pretty savvy combat pilots, but you're ready to condemn the mission before you even know what it's about."

"I'll listen," Canton said.

The other men nodded.

"Let's go in the orderly tent," Clark suggested, leading the way and stumbling over a log someone had dragged in to serve as a chair.

Inside the tent, De Veres lit a kerosene lantern. It was unlikely to be seen by any passing aircraft. Clark went through his document case, then passed out twelve enlarged photographs of the supply base called Camp Rogers in honor of its American benefactor. The pictures were clearly detailed and labeled, identifying huts and tents in a residential and social area on one side of the short landing strip and aircraft maintenance facilities and the large, tin-roofed sheds serving as warehouses on the other side. They were dated two weeks before and there was an old C-47 sitting at the end of the strip.

Pulling the computer scenario close in front of him, under the yellow light spilling from the lantern, Clark spent fifty-five minutes fully detailing the operation. He covered every flight maneuver, every minute in the air or on the ground, the position of each member of the team, and every planned detonation.

When he was finished, Hamm said, "Bobby, this takes

into account everything but human reaction. You're making assumptions about how the Camp Rogers cadre will respond, where they will run. Me, I've learned to predict only the humans who are already dead.''

''Hamm, I'll agree with you. But what's been done here is to provide the computer with all the possible reactions, given the proximity to cover. The machine selected the most likely outcome.''

They debated the subject for another hour, then Clark, sensing he had an edge, asked, ''How about a vote?''

They grumbled, but following Hamm's lead, agreed to go along with him on the first mission, at least, and evaluate the next operation afterwards.

Hamm said, ''I'm going with it, Bobby, but I want to think about the seat assignments before we take off. I may have some changes in the morning.''

''What morning?'' Keen asked. ''It's damned near here.''

When Clark finally flopped on his cot, he was exhausted, but he did not sleep the rest of the night. He was too keyed up. He thought that Major General Robert Clark would have approved of the operation wholeheartedly. And he had been a damned hard man to please.

Josef Zhukov spent the night on a folding cot brought to his office in the embassy, so he was close by when Boris awakened him before dawn. ''The photograph interpreter believes he has something, Comrade Major.''

Zhukov sat up and pulled on his suit trousers, then slipped into his shirt. He carried his shoes and socks and walked barefoot and buttoning across the hallway to the operations room and stood behind the analyst. The floor was cold, and there was a slight chill in the air.

The satellite photos were in color, transcribed from
Moscow Center, but were blurry from their five thousand-
mile journey over the as-yet-imperfect microwave relay
system. Zhukov saw a brownish-red haze, with white lines
superimposed to designate the national borders north and
south of Nicaragua.

"Interpret, Corporal."

The technician pointed to a stack of photographs.
"These were all taken from the pass of satellites in the
last three days, Comrade Major, and we have received
them from Moscow at two o'clock this morning. I have
placed them in two sequences, and this is the first sequence."

The white lettering in the upper left-hand corner noted
the time the picture was taken in Greenwich Mean Time.
The corporal had handwritten the corresponding local time
below the lettering. The technician placed a dirty finger-
nail on a long, wide, fuzzy streak. "This suggests the
passage of a large aircraft, probably with four engines. It
is moving to the west, south of the Montañas de Colon. I
have checked with Señor Demarco's air control people,
and they say it is not one of theirs."

He picked up the next picture. "Here, this fishhook. It
is the aircraft turning to the north, leaving Nicaraguan
airspace. It is thirty minutes later."

"It is simply another of their airplane supply operations, no doubt."

"Assuredly, Comrade Major. And here, in the first photograph? This airplane to the west is a Nicaraguan border
patrol aircraft. They missed seeing the intruder by less
than five minutes."

"Typical," Zhukov said, thinking that, so often, his

Latin American friends were just one step out of synchronization with the world around them.

"What is typical, Major Zhukov?" Manuel Demarco appeared in the doorway.

Zhukov turned around and smiled grimly at the visitor. "Come in, Manuel. We are lamenting yet another missed opportunity."

The defense minister walked across the room and bent over the table behind the technician. His was a practiced eye, and he read the photographs easily. "Do we know where the drop was made, Corporal?"

"Unfortunately, Señor Demarco, no. In time of need, this satellite can take pictures every one-half second. In routine surveillance, as this was, the time sequence is every half hour."

"All it suggests," Zhukov said, "is that there is a hostile force somewhere in the north, on this side of the border. As in the past, it is probably not a large group."

"This is contrary to what my own intelligence arm has been telling me," the Nicaraguan said, his face becoming darker with his anger. "I have been told that the region is clear of rebels."

The technician went swiftly through the small stack of photographs, selecting another sequence. "This one was taken early yesterday morning, Major Zhukov, as the satellite moved out of our sector, and the film is infrared. Down here, at the bottom, it has barely captured the northeast seacoast. This blue line is the Rio Wawa. You can see there are nine red pinpricks of heat sources from exhaust."

The corporal selected another photograph and pointed to the same nine blips, this time in the upper left corner. "This is an earlier picture. The unidentified aircraft are above the ocean. Judging the speed from the coordinates and times of each photo, I would suggest that they are helicopters. Fast helicopters.''

"And they were moving inland," Demarco noted.

"Yes, Comrade."

"Are there more, Corporal?" Zhukov asked.

The technician indicated several small mounds of photos with a gesture of his hand. "Many more, Major, but only these show unidentified aircraft."

"How about rebel troop movements?" Demarco asked. "Have you examined those yet?"

Spreading several pictures on the tabletop, the corporal began to point out a number of encampments. "Here is another sequence I have assembled, spread over three weeks. There are only the encampments of which we are already aware. But the pictures do suggest that more of the rebels have retreated to rear areas. The camps appear to be more highly populated than normal, and resupply has increased."

Demarco offered a slight, sideways shrug of his head. "I do not like the presence of unidentified helicopters in my country."

"The earlier reports we have received from Moscow Center suggested that Cuban pilots and new gunships would be entering Nicaragua."

"A fabrication, you told me."

"Yes, based upon what I knew at the time. But there is another possibility."

"I suspect that I may not care for what you are hinting," Demarco said.

"We cannot hide from the alternatives, no matter how distasteful."

Manuel Demarco nodded. "There are those, within the

government, who think that we do not pursue the war against the rebels with sufficient aggression. It *is* possible that some secret faction inside the government has acquired its own army. Or air force, in this instance.''

''It cannot be overlooked,'' Zhukov said.

''None of this is well documented, Josef.''

''So, we should ignore it?''

''No. I will talk with some selected members of the secret police, and see if they can ferret out any dissensions among my compatriots. We will examine the fund sources for leakage—this would be a very expensive proposition. And I will mount an extensive search of the northern provinces. The helicopters and the large aircraft seem to have been aimed in that direction. A rendezvous seems likely.''

''We should involve my co-advisors,'' Zhukov said. ''GRU Major Prabinovski, advisor to military ground forces, along with Colonel Churbanchuk, advisor to the air forces, should both be present. Perhaps they will have other perspectives.''

''Of course.'' Demarco pointed a thumb at the technician. ''It would be useful to get more satellite photographs.''

''I will see to it.''

# TWENTY

Jack Coriolanus and Claude Nolan presented their credentials to the Marine sergeant manning the entrance to the Old Executive Office Building and then followed another Marine down a long, echoing hallway to the Electronic Situation Room.

Coriolanus was furious. He had personally briefed the Director of Central Intelligence, suggesting that not only was his current information flimsy—though probable—but that the DCI should inform other members of the Security Council of the theory so as not to present surprises later. And so as not to attract large numbers of sightseers if he had to make some sudden moves soon.

The DCI had declined, preferring to keep everything in-house for the time being.

But Coriolanus had spent a restless night, tossing motives and possibilities from one side of his head to the other. By morning, he was convinced that Bobby Clark, and possibly Harry Downs, were up to something that would backfire.

In the morning, when Coriolanus told the DDO and the DCI that he needed the greater speed and capability of the CIA's Mission Room, he was turned down. The DCI felt that the military would have to be involved, along with some of the civilians, and he did not want them in the Mission Room. He called the White House and received permission to use the Electronic Situation Room. The request had amazed unprepared council members from Treasury to Defense.

Now he had to enter the Crisis Control Center, past yet more Marines, to the sullen faces of generals, an admiral, and representatives of civilian intelligence agencies and oversight committees. No one wanted to be left out. The President's national security advisor was also present and in a foul mood. The mix was not only of intelligence people, but also of Defense Department personnel from the Joint Chiefs. General Delmar Williams, who Coriolanus thought should not even be there, smiled at him and said good morning.

"Still thinking about those reservist exercises, Del?" Coriolanus asked.

"Still worried about them, Jack. And about what's going on in Central America. Admiral Dilman asked me to attend. What's up?"

"I'll brief in a moment."

General Aaron Messenbaum, Air Force chief of staff, greeted him with a half-sneering smile. "Good morning, Jack. Nice to see you again."

The contrary was true, of course. "Hello, Aaron." Coriolanus always ignored the military rank if he could get away with it.

The national security advisor scowled. "Your boss coming, Coriolanus?"

"No. He has another appointment, and I'm here in his place."

"Figures."

The Navy chief of staff, Admiral Joshua Simpson, was

just as abrupt. "I understand you've got yourself a little problem, huh, Jack?"

Coriolanus turned the corners of his lips down and spread his hand to encompass everyone in the room. "It may belong to all of us."

Continuing to look around the room, he spotted an unknown face and confronted it. "Who are you, and what the hell are you doing here?"

Startled, the young man pushed a hand self-consciously through a brush of sandy hair, hiding behind the hand from all the experience surrounding him. "I'm Bret Davis, Mr. Coriolanus. I'm the intelligence aide to Senator Roebuck. He couldn't be here."

"Shit. This isn't a crisis control committee. It's a fucking circus."

Bret Davis quickly scooted away and found a chair at the side of the room.

Nolan went to stand at the side of the brightly lit room and sat down.

Military technicians had focused one of the giant electronic displays down to the immediate area of Nicaragua and Honduras, with Caribbean and Pacific regions also shown. It was a clear representation, villages and military installations noted. It was also a dynamic representation. The computer drew upon all incoming data from all available sources, and instead of displaying one picture after another, continually changed the display. The infrared emanations from towns, hamlets, factories, and the like were electronically edited out. The tracks shown on the screen were those of moving aircraft, coastal shipping, and a few miles off both shorelines, bands of moving blips in the Pacific and Caribbean commercial shipping lanes.

At the big walnut table in front of the display, Messenbaum, Simpson, and Army Brigadier General Damon Carter, representing Army Intelligence, were ensconced in the soft leather conference chairs. Coriolanus wondered why Kuster was not present. Later, he would tell Nolan to call him. Standing around the room were the NSA and Evans and Fulton, from State Department and FBI. Carey Rung, the intelligence advisor for the Treasury Department, nodded to him. The straight-backed chairs at the back of the room and along one wall were 60 percent occupied by staffers.

Aaron Messenbaum raised a hand and brought the murmuring to an end. "This morning, gentlemen, I'm standing in for the chairman of the Joint Chiefs. I don't guess this is a formal meeting, but Mr. Coriolanus requested several items early this morning, including use of this room and the movement of a HALO—that's a High Altitude Low Observable—satellite into geo-stationary orbit over Central America. I guess the word got out."

The Air Force chief looked around the room, shrugged, and said, "Okay, Jack. It's your show."

Coriolanus moved to the head of the table. "Gentlemen, we all have a problem. One of my people may be involved, but I didn't create it. I just inherited it. And unfortunately, it may have escalated to the point where it could affect not the national security so much as the national image."

"That translate to the CIA image?" Admiral Simpson asked. His disenchantment with the CIA's handling of naval intelligence was long-standing.

"That's only the way the media plays it, Josh. But all of us here know just who's involved in intelligence matters, don't we?" Coriolanus briefed them on both the facts and the inferences in fifteen minutes.

Senator Harley Havechuk, having entered the room just after Coriolanus began to speak, could not remain silent, as usual. "Mr. Coriolanus, we've known about these Soviet helicopters for some time. What evidence do you have on Clark? Something you haven't told us?"

"All circumstantial, Senator."

"You say it's likely he's preparing some operation against the Sandinistas without CIA approval or funding?"

"The Agency only makes recommendations to the FDN-Contras, and a quick audit of expenditures shows that our accounting is in balance," Coriolanus insisted.

Marine General Mike Parch said, "Damn, you have to admire guts like that. It's about time those good old boys down there did something. You sure you didn't organize all this, Jack?"

"No, general. I didn't send him."

The national security advisor remained silent, and sat down. He pulled the red phone out of a drawer in front of him and placed it on the table. He would be keeping the President apprised.

"Clark's gathered some people around him that increase my suspicions," he said. "None of these people can be located at their residences in the States at the moment, and we have indications that they may be in Central America under assumed names."

Claude Nolan stood up and read from his notebook. "Peter de Veres, Sean McDonough, and Steven Hamm all disappeared from their normal routines for a month, beginning in mid-May. They were seen in the company of Clark. On June eighteenth, in a bar in San José, Costa Rica, there was a brawl involving an American traveling under the name of Joe Treller. He was out on bail, and had skipped the country, by the time he was identified as Patrick Roger Canton. The FBI backtracked him and discovered that he, too, was missing in May and June. Currently, the chiefs of station in the area are unable to account for twenty-seven Americans who have passed through the major airports.''

General Delmar Williams stood up and raised his hand at the side of the room, and Coriolanus recognized him. "Del."

"I don't want to butt in here, Jack, but you're suggesting that Maldonado, Calera, Matamoros, and maybe a couple more of the Contra leaders are going to coordinate their efforts?''

"Yes. That's what I'm suggesting.''

"Never happen,'' Williams asserted, then slumped back into his chair.

"I grant you your expertise in the area, Del,'' Coriolanus said, "but what if Clark put together a staff-assistance team and a war plan that looked very good? It's something Clark could do.''

"There'd have to be more sweetener than that,'' Williams insisted.

"We're getting photos together that show a dramatic increase in supplies. We'll put them on the screen for you shortly.''

"Well,'' Williams conceded, "maybe.''

Messenbaum turned to the Army's Carter. "Hamm just retired from DIA, didn't he?''

"I believe that's right, yes.''

Messenbaum directed a question to Coriolanus. "Five men take vacations at the same time. That all they have in common, Jack?''

"No. They're all pilots and Vietnam veterans. In one

way or another, they know one another from combat operations. We're trying to trace the other twenty-seven unknowns, but most of them appear to be under false
documentation.''

"Central America is full of pilots. It's a haven for down-
and-outers who will fly any cargo for big bucks,'' the national security advisor said.

"Seems to me,'' Simpson said, "that our facts are pretty
slim right now. Anybody here know of recent FDN-
Contra stirrings in the hostility department?''

"No. And that outfit couldn't keep a secret past the first
set of ears it came to.''

Bret Davis raised his courage and his hand. He asked,
"What's the significance of the new Soviet aircraft in Nicaragua?''

"There may be none,'' Coriolanus responded. "They
add significantly to the Nicaraguan firepower. With competent pilots, they turn the war drastically in favor of the
Sandinistas.''

"Devastatingly so,'' Aaron Messenbaum said. "Hinds
and Havocs carry heavy ordnance.''

"What's our position, gentlemen?'' The President's security advisor was impatient. "How much supposition are
we to rely on in this?''

Coriolanus took a deep breath. "I don't want to jump
off any deep ends until we have more evidence. But I don't
want to get caught flatfooted, either. I'd like to see round-
the-clock satellite coverage of the area.''

Messenbaum looked to the other generals.

The Air Force chief of staff nodded. "I'll talk to the
SecDef. What else, Jack?''

"Whether this thing follows my scenario or not, I think
we ought to prepare for necessary responses.''

"What in hell does that mean?" the national security advisor demanded.

"It means," Admiral Simpson replied, "that if we look up there on that display board, and see gunships streaking toward Managua, we should be ready to take them out."

"What are you suggesting?" the advisor asked. "You'd shoot down American pilots?"

"I guess not, if you want to claim them. After the press gets through with them."

The national security advisor did not like the direction the tone was taking. He looked around as if counting military and civilian heads, looking for the way a vote might go.

"Let's ease up here a little, gentlemen. I've got to advise the President in a few moments, and he will, of course, make the final decision. Would you all agree with Mr. Coriolanus's recommendation?"

There was tentative, preliminary agreement, led by the military side of the table.

"Any alternatives?"

"You ought to recall Clark, Jack," Messenbaum said.

"I'll do that."

The advisor put his hand on the red phone. "We may have to initiate discussions with the Soviet foreign ambassador and others. You'd better get State involved, Aaron."

"Yes, sir."

"How about tactics?"

Admiral Simpson turned to the console operator. "Let's have capital ships and carriers."

The display board flickered and green dots appeared, each carrying a cryptic logo. There was one extra-large green dot. Simpson assimilated it quickly, and spoke, "Not much in immediate range, gentlemen. The cruiser *Virginia* is closest to the area, near Grenada. She'll have six or seven support ships with her. Northwest of San Diego, we've got the carrier *Eisenhower* and the two cruisers, *Long Beach* and *Seattle*. There'll be several destroyers and a couple of frigates in that group. I want to see Soviet surface vessels,'' he told the console operator.

A group of red dots appeared, about a hundred miles south of Cuba.

''We'll want to know of any course changes in that task force,'' Coriolanus said.

''Those are pretty ships, Josh, but we'll need air support more,'' Messenbaum said.

''Very well. Let's order CINCPAC to move the *Eisenhower* south and see if we can get her into a better position. Then, we've got an AWACS at Guantanamo. We can get that airborne right away.''

The security advisor waited, his hand fidgeting with the phone.

''How about the Air Force, Aaron?'' General Carter asked.

''We've got a squadron of Eagles visiting Palmerola Air Base near Tegucigalpa. It's a demonstration team, and I'm not sure what kind of armament they have. We can put them on alert. Also, there's some F-4s in Mexico City, training pilots. Then, of course, we can go to Homestead in Florida or Bergstrom in Texas for tactical aircraft. In the south, we have several squadrons at Howard Air Force Base in Panama. For the time being, I'd leave them in place since getting them to Honduras in a hurry means overflying Nicaraguan air space. We can go around it if we have to.''

''Will these aircraft be able to move quickly enough to

intercept the helicopters?'' the natinal security advisor asked.

''The squadron at Palmerola could. We're not even certain where the choppers are,'' Messenbaum said, ''but we can do the job. Whatever the job turns out to be.''

''And if we can't reach them in time?''

''Then we do it anyway, after the fact, and as quickly as we can,'' Simpson told him.

''Why?''

''So we don't leave incriminating evidence lying around, Mr. Advisor.''

''Gentlemen?'' Messenbaum asked.

They all agreed.

Messenbaum turned to the security advisor. ''I'll bring State in on this as soon as I can reach someone.''

''Yes. I'll tell the President.''

Coriolanus spoke up. ''The orders for the air crews will have to be very clearly stated.''

''Under no circumstances will they engage aircraft of Soviet or Nicaraguan origin,'' Messenbaum offered. ''The final authority must come from this room, and they will attack only aircraft designated here. If any of this goes public, the Soviets and the Nicaraguans will have difficulty complaining that we've shot down our own people. If they can even identify the remains.''

The national security advisor picked up his receiver.

# TWENTY-ONE

At six in the morning, Peachy Keen told Clark to go to hell, and fired up a propane stove for a hot breakfast. It was not very good, but it was warm. Bellows and Mc-Donough searched a few dozen boxes of C-rations for beans, tomato soup, and stew. Hot dogs served as sausage.

After they ate, Hamm said, "I've got some changes to make."

Clark looked up from his cup of beef stew and thought, Here we go, the bastard's going to screw up all of the planning. "There aren't going to be any changes, Hamm. It's locked in."

Hamm was standing, leaning against the fuselage of a Hind. He rattled the pages of the mission plan in his hand and said, "The only thing locked in is your mind, Bobby. This thing's designed like a B-52 strike on Hanoi. It didn't work there, and it won't work here."

"Nevertheless, that's the way it comes off." Clark let his resolve show in his voice.

"Shit. You've got us at four hundred feet, popping AT-2s at some warehouses."

"That way, nobody gets hurt," Clark told him.

"And I've got to assume you're hoping for some photographer to get a front-page shot of us?"

"That, plus the bird we leave behind. That's all the evidence they'll need."

"It'll look like a half-assed, overly cautious strike to any veteran chopper pilot," Hamm said, "and you're going to have a hell of a lot of veterans in the Pentagon analyzing it."

"Exactly what we want," Clark told him.

"Why?"

"Because that's the way the Sandinistas operate, goddamn it! We're playing a role, Hamm. Try to remember that, will you?"

"You don't write a very convincing script, Bobby. I thought we were Cubans."

"We are, damn it!"

"Then we're going to fly it like we've had Angola time. And like I'm the goddamned tactical commander." Hamm was standing straight up now, as if he were ready to take the argument to blows.

"I don't want the results changed."

The ex–DIA operative did not answer him, but moved to the center of the eating men, squatted, and spread papers and pictures on the ground. Hamm ran his finger over the photo of the target area and said, "I want two attack groups, instead of the massed formation. And we'll be right on the deck, as if we know what we're doing. We want to scare hell out of them, and let the guys with the Brownies get good pictures.

"Group one will be the Havocs, Bandito One on point. Sean, you'll be alone. As soon as you make your pass, you set down here, a half mile beyond the runway. Banditos Three and Five will be your wingmen, Canton on the right. After the pass, Three and Five fly cover for Sean while he's on the ground.

"The second group will hit one minute later and will be composed of Vaqueros One, Three, and Five. I'll fly the spare Hind at the back of that diamond, and crash-land it after my pass. Sean, if I happen to crash it right, I'd appreciate a ride back."

McDonough's cigar was unlit in preparation for flying. He grinned at Hamm. "While you're on the ground there, Steve, see if you can't pick up a six-pack or two, huh?"

"Here's another change. Canton, you'll be flying alone. I want Talbot to ride with Vaqueros Five and Six. Rick, as soon as your pass is made, take a half-loop around the end of the runway and drop a couple dozen smoke bombs. Throw some tear-gas grenades. We want to create as much confusion as we can."

Talbot said, "Got it."

"Next thing, we come in from the east, rather than the west. When we pop out of the jungle, I want the sun at my back and in their eyes."

"Did your goddamned computer miss that, Bobby?" Peachy Keen asked.

Clark clenched his teeth. Fucking Hamm was changing everything. "It means a farther swing to the east, and more time in the air. I was going for the quickest route."

"This way, we have the quick route home," Bellows said. "I like that."

"We aren't coming home," Hamm said. "At least, not back here."

"What the hell?" De Veres asked. "We spent a lot of time setting up this fake base camp."

"Fine. We leave it as evidence in the end, which was the idea, but we don't come back right away, or they'll tag it," Hamm said.

"Who will?" De Veres asked.

"One side or the other. It doesn't matter which, but we don't want to give away our fuel supply just yet. In these mountains, the land-based and airborne radar won't affect us much. However, if anyone spotted us coming in, we may have satellite or look-down radar now active. You can be damned sure that, as soon as we hit Rogers, there's going to be a lot of confused people who would like to meet us."

Hamm pulled a chart from under the photograph and pointed to a new X he had drawn.

"This clearing is two miles this side of the border. As soon as the Hinds complete their pass, they head here. The Havocs, after stopping to pick me up, will bring up the rear. We're going to settle in here and wait for nightfall before making the final jump back to this base. If we've got satellite or aerial reconnaissance taking place, I don't want to pinpoint our center of operations just yet."

"All right. That looks good to me," Peter de Veres agreed.

Clark thought Peter was being entirely too agreeable. Attempting to keep his anger in control, he said, "I might point out, Hamm, that that particular clearing was a Sandinista outpost less than three weeks ago. One of the advantages of having intelligence at one's fingertips."

"How old is this photo?"

"Six days."

"You think they might be back, then?"

"There's no guarantee they won't be. I wouldn't give you one," Clark told him.

"How many were on the post when it was manned?" Hamm asked.

"Four men and a vehicle."

"Shit," McDonough said, "if they've come back, it's four dead men and a vehicle. Let's go for it."

"One thing. It's going to be a bitch finding our way back here at night," Bellows said.

"I think Peachy's got that covered," Hamm said. "We had a little discussion last night."

"You discussed, and I worked my ass off half the damned night," Keen said, holding up a walkie-talkie. "What I did was take a pair of these things and rig up a remote control. I press this transmit button on our return flight, the signal activates a relay hooked into the transmitter on the spare Havoc we're leaving behind, and it will send out a homing signal. That should get us back to here."

Clark thought it over. He did not like Hamm's making all these last-minute changes, but decided to say nothing. Grudgingly, he admitted to himself that they were good ideas. Then, too, watching how the others hung on to Hamm's words, he knew he had lost anyway. He could not control this bunch.

"Last thing," Hamm said. "When we jump out of the jungle on those people, there's going to be panic. The computer says they'll run for jungle cover, but let's not rely on the computer. We go right down the middle of the runway, and no deviations. Blow the hell out of it. We want lots of craters. After the initial shock wears off, we're going to get some ground fire, but I don't think it's going to be more than rifles. Anybody fires on the tent side of that airstrip, I'll hold a quick little court-martial. That's one of the reasons I'm going to be the last one through, to assess the damages.

"Now, then, Bobby says the fifth warehouse in line is

the armory. You wingmen on that side of the runway are to put missiles into it only if you don't see people around."

"What about the rest of the warehouses?" Canton asked.

"Again, only if there is no personnel activity around them. We want this to look good, but we're not out to slaughter our own. Questions?"

There were none.

"Let's mount up."

Clark and De Veres walked out to their Havoc together, climbed into their respective cockpits, and donned headsets.

"Well, Bobby, here we go." Peter de Veres did not sound nervous at all. Clark thought he sounded eager.

Clark's own stomach was knotted. It was not only Hamm's modifications. There was always the chance of a stray bullet.

"You doing okay, Bobby?"

"Just thinking. We're going to turn this son of a bitching civil war around."

Norman Jessup was feeling a little uneasy that morning. First of all, there were nearly eighty Contra fighters in camp, more than ever before, which made his patrolling of his warehouses more frequent—the little bastards would steal anything not nailed down. He had loaded out packs for seven horses after breakfast, and the camp manager had given him another list for another packhorse shipment for the afternoon. It felt like something was shaping up. Sometime late in the evening, there was supposed to be an aircraft load of something or other coming in. They never really knew what they would get until they got it.

Second, in the morning of the day before, a CBS camera team and two newspaper reporters had shown up and asked the camp manager for space in a tent. No one knew what they wanted. They just walked around shooting pictures of everybody and everything and asking ten thousand stupid questions.

After the furor over Eugene Hasenfus, Norman Jessup did not want his picture in the papers. None of the other eleven Americans working at Camp Rogers did, either.

Just before ten o'clock, the aircraft mechanic, Kip Dennis, came over to his office in the warehouse, got a Pepsi out of the propane refrigerator, and the two of them moved a couple of chairs out in front of the building. There was no wind there, either, and they sweated, bitched about the weather to each other, and drank their Pepsi-Colas.

Across the airstrip, the Contra fighters were lolling about in the shade of tent flaps, being interviewed by the American reporters. The Nicaraguans liked to talk about their bravery in battle which, as far as Jessup knew, was very little.

"You hear those guys talking to that blonde from the TV?" Kip asked.

"Uh-huh."

"Talking about re-fucking-instituting democracy in the homeland?"

"Shit," Jessup said, "what the hell they going to know about democracy?"

"Everything. The way that little guy with one eye, Enriquez, told her, a ballot box and a Ferrari got it covered. He's going to race Formula I cars, soon as he gets the war won. Shit, with one eye!"

Jessup laughed. "You set him straight, my man?"

"Shit, no. I thought he had it right."

They both laughed at that, but the laughter died away

as they became aware of the *thrup-thrup* of rotors drifting over the jungle top.

"Fuck's that?" Jessup asked.

"Choppers," the mechanic told him. "A big damned bunch of them."

The Contras had a few helicopters, old Bell JetRangers and some Hughes Osage and Cayuse models, but they had rarely come into Camp Rogers.

The high jungle surrounding them did not allow them much horizon, and Jessup did not see the helicopters until they suddenly shot over the eastern end of the runway.

Turbine scream.

High speed. Bastards were flat moving out.

"Jesus Christ!" he shouted, jumping up and kicking over his chair.

"Son of a bitch!" Kip Dennis yelled. "Those fuckers are Sandinistas!"

Despite his year in Vietnam, amidst all kinds of Huey and Cobra gunships, Norman Jessup had never seen anything like these. Coming out of the sun, the three helicopters were difficult to see, but they bristled with weaponry.

And they opened fire.

Rockets and missiles lanced out at them from the stub wings. The air abruptly filled with the horrendous cacophony of machine guns and shrieking missiles.

Streaks of flame and smoke.

Plumes of dirt and gravel began erupting for the length of the runway.

"Oh, my God!" Dennis yelled, diving through the doorway into the warehouse.

"You bastards!" Jessup yelled, drawing his Colt Peacemaker and firing off six quick rounds at a chopper that was streaking down his side of the airstrip.

The helicopter immediately veered toward him, firing a missile that flashed into a warehouse to his east and erupted in an ear-stunning detonation. A stuttering line of machine-gun bullets walked across the ground toward him, leaving puffy dust balls behind.

Jessup ran for the corner of the warehouse.

Too late.

The heavy slugs took both of his legs off at the knees, and one bullet that slammed into his meaty shoulder knocked him spinning fifteen feet down the strip. Jessup landed on his back and lay there in the dirt, spurting blood from the stumps of his legs.

Up there in the leaves, he saw Marlene's face.

Hamm's Hind was the one that had been damaged by the sliding winch, and Jerry Pickett was right. The tail boom was itchy as hell, constantly trying to scoot to port. With sensitive pressure on the rudder pedals, he fought it all the way to the target, nerve-wracking at treetop levels.

Ahead of him, he had Hank Bellows's Hind for a guide. Cherry and Pickett were out on the flanks. Rick Talbot hung in the open cargo doorway of Pickett's chopper, looking ahead. The smoke bombs and tear-gas grenades were in a cardboard box strapped to the floor behind him.

Hamm could not see the target for the layer of jungle canopy below. The sun, now at his back, highlighted the green waves. A minute later, he saw a white wisp of smoke, probably from a kitchen fire. And an instant after that, the Havocs pounced.

A mile ahead of them, the Havocs had disappeared, followed immediately by streaks of red-orange flame and oily smoke. It was a silent movie.

In his headset, Bellows spoke in Spanish: *"¡Andando, vaqueros! ¡Andando!"*

Vaquero One surged ahead, followed by his wingmen, and Hamm let them widen the gap. He would come in late, and last, more of a target if anyone on the ground had recovered from the shock. He relaxed, then tightened his grips on the control column and the collective pitch stick in his left hand.

The Mi-24 raced forward at 150 miles per hour, falling behind. Thirty seconds later, the Hinds ahead suddenly dove into the jungle.

The camp suddenly appeared in the rim of the jungle. Hamm armed his weapons systems, then eased throttle and pitch, and nosed down.

A quick scan left to right gave him jangled images he would have to sort out later: green-clad bodies rushing for the jungle from the tent city on his left, some who had recovered from the shock aiming upward with assault rifles, four warehouses on the right gushing flame and smoke, Vaquero Three dancing sideways and letting off four Swatters—two of which arced into the first warehouse in line.

Over the turbine roar, he heard the pinging of small-arms fire peppering the armor of the Hind. A bullet bounced off the port-side armored cockpit window.

Then he was at ground level, streaking through a swarming haze of dust and smoke that hampered his vision. He saw the camp through gauze.

He touched off a dozen rockets, watched them explode like a giant's footsteps in the already obliterated earth of the airstrip.

A TV camera turned with him, racing him to the end of the strip. Clark's media was in place.

And there!

On his right.

A legless corpse off on the side of the strip. Pickett's chopper stopped firing as it shot over the body.

Hamm fired the rest of his rockets before reaching the end of the runway, pulled up as the jungle reappeared, and began looking for his crash site.

Bearing slightly left, he saw the two Havocs hovering over the designated clearing. It took him twelve seconds to reach them. Looking back, he saw Vaquero Five making his circle to drop smoke bombs. He lost forward momentum as he came in, spotted McDonough on the ground, then lowered the pitch lever and set the Hind down thirty yards away from Bandito One.

Reaching up for the twin throttle levers on the overhead console, Hamm reset them for ground idle, but ignored the rotor brake and left the rotors turning. He popped the hatch open and slid out, shoving his toes into the inset steps in the fuselage as he descended to the ground. The heat was suddenly oppressive. He paused long enough to switch on the timer for the pack of *plastique* strapped to the left outboard AT-2 missile, hoping Bellows had rigged it correctly, then ran like hell for McDonough's helicopter.

With his hatch open, McDonough signaled wildly.

Tripping in the thick weeds, Hamm charged the Havoc, slid to a stop alongside it, braking his rush with his hands, and then began climbing for the gunner's cockpit.

He did not have the hatch closed, or his harness in place, as McDonough lifted off.

The three Havocs streaked toward the south, bare feet above the jungle. Hamm looked back in time to see the tremendous explosion. Orange flared out of the jungle. A black-and-blue fireball spewed upward when the fuel tanks and the rest of the ordnance went in a secondary explosion.

McDonough laughed and said, "They won't even find body parts in that one."

"I've already seen enough body parts for the day," Hamm told him.

"What are you talking about?"

"I got a body count of one. Right side of the airstrip, big black guy, and from the Group One pass. Pickett did his best to avoid adding to it."

"Fucking Canton," McDonough said.


# TWENTY-TWO

General Juan Cerone, head of the Sandinistan air defense forces, had been stumbling between pride and anger all morning. He was extremely proud that the Soviet advisors chose his sophisticated command center at the Managua airport as their battle headquarters. However, he was put out they hadn't informed him earlier of the unknown helicopter intruders.

Technicians and military aides littered the large, air-conditioned room, and Army General Ricardo Suarez paced the room with nervous energy, like a hungry ocelot. Additionally, Army advisor Major Prabinovski, Air Force advisor Colonel Ivan Ivanovitch Churbanchuk, and Manuel Demarco fidgeted, moving between chairs and windows. Prabinovski simply sat and waited.

Zhukov spent a lot of time at the window himself, watching the activity outside that seemed to have a purpose, very much unlike the activity in this room. Heat haze wavered over the hot pavement of the runways, and commercial aircraft occasionally whisked by, their jet trailing kerosene vapors.

Boris Kamorovkin huddled with the Soviet corporal interpreting photographs coming in from Moscow. The microwave linkup had been shifted from the embassy, but there was still a lag time of approximately twenty minutes from the moment a satellite transmitted information to Moscow on its downlink, then the picture was transmitted to Managua via a teleprinter. Zhukov assumed that someone in Moscow felt it necessary to view each photograph before forwarding it.

The current run of pictures appeared the same as their predecessors and provided no new information, just as all their efforts during the morning had been fruitless.

Cerone pointed to the initial sequence of photographs, pinned to the wall in a row. "Perhaps there was a malfunction in the equipment, Comrade. Perhaps there were no invading helicopters."

"I think not," Josef Zhukov said. "They are here in the country. Somewhere."

"We have followed your advice, Major Zhukov," General Suarez added. "We have dispatched search units to the north. To no avail. It is my feeling that this is a waste of time. Far better, I think, for General Cerone and myself to return to what we are supposed to do: defend our country. Especially in light of what appears to be a rebel buildup of forces on the Honduran side. If there were alien helicopters present, we would have found them by now.''

The Soviet resident was relatively certain that Cerone's air-search teams would have trouble locating a whore in a brothel, but he did not say as much.

Manuel Demarco did not want to appear completely on the side of the Soviet advisors in front of his subordinates, of course, but ventured to ask, ''You are certain that Moscow believes the opposite, Major Zhukov?''

''Absolutely. To them, and to me, the photographic evidence is clear.''

''Then how is it that we cannot find them?'' General Cerone asked.

''Perhaps because your country has many square kilometers of difficult terrain.''

Boris Kamorovkin suddenly blurted in Russian, ''There! Look at that!''

The Nicaraguans, none of whom spoke Russian, looked over at him, puzzled.

Zhukov spun away from the cloudy window, where he had been studying a trio of taxiing MiGs, and strode across the room. ''What is it you see, Boris?''

''It is your helicopters, my colonel. Some of them, anyway.''

The Nicaraguans and their Soviet advisors all grouped around the table as Kamorovkin indicated the obvious on the latest photo. This time it was not infrared, and the camera had captured clear images of two groups of helicopters in flight, just passing out of Nicaragua, over the Rio Coco a Segovia.

''There are only seven,'' Cerone counted.

Colonel Churbanchuk took the big magnifying glass from the photographic interpreter and leaned over the picture, studying the small images intently. "They are Mi-28s, Comrade Major. Impossible."

"All of them?" Zhukov asked.

"Just the three in the lead formation. The others are Mi-24s."

Cerone asked, "The Mi-28s? Like the photograph you showed us? The assault craft we have been promised?"

"Like the photograph," Churbanchuk acknowledged, ignoring the promise and shaking his head in disbelief. "I do not understand this."

"You had better check with Red Army headquarters," Zhukov said.

"Immediately." Churbanchuk turned away, searching for a technician with a teletypewriter.

"What do you suppose they are doing?" a confused Demarco asked. "Are they leaving the country?"

"It appears so," Zhukov told him.

"Unfortunately," Boris Kamorovkin said, checking his watch, "we will not know for another seventeen minutes, until the next photographs arrive."

"In seventeen minutes, a world war could have been completed," Demarco said acidly.

They were long minutes. And when the picture began to appear on the printer, the black-and-white image stunned them.

The angle was different. The satellite was in another, more northern, position, beginning to move out of the area. It took several moments for the men clustered around the printer to orient themselves.

"There! Six of them now, flying south," Suarez said. "And look! The flames! The smoke!"

"That is the camp the rebels call Rogers," General

Cerone said, peering with the magnifying glass. "It appears to be mostly destroyed."

A cheer went up in the room. The technicians and aides were elated.

Zhukov was not.

"This becomes ever more puzzling," Demarco said. "I do not like it."

"A victory for our forces is puzzling?" Cerone asked, ignoring all the basics of political consequences and confirming Zhukov's assessment of the man as a simpleton.

"Can you tell me exactly what unit you have utilized here, General?"

Cerone went silent.

"Worse," Zhukov said, "Honduras has been invaded, and it has been invaded by our aircraft. The Americans will not be as confused as the people in this room."

"The attack lasted less than ten minutes," Juan Cerone argued.

"It is more than enough time to upset the United States. Does anyone in this room doubt the reaction of the American president?"

Manuel Demarco said, "I will notify the ruling council and then initiate a call to the Honduran president, denying everything."

"And we had better locate that rogue helicopter squadron quickly," Zhukov added.

"We will increase our search tenfold," Suarez offered immediately.

Zhukov could imagine that Suarez and Cerone would like to do this on their own and capture personal rewards for their valor and administration.

"What would you propose, General Suarez?"

"Intensive ground and air search of the region south of

the border. We will devise a grid immediately. And we need more of your satellite coverage.''

"We will have them pinned down within six hours," General Cerone estimated.

"You will do this on your own?" the Air Force advisor asked.

"Naturally, Comrade, I am thinking in terms of cooperation with the training squadrons of our Soviet friends. There are MiG-23 fighter and Mi-24 gunship squadrons that could be usefully deployed."

Zhukov eyed his advisor colleagues. "Comrades? Do you have comments?"

"It will be difficult in those mountains, I think," Churbanchuk said. "Even look-down radar will be confused by ground clutter."

Prabinovski nodded in agreement.

"I believe there may be a great deal more to this puzzle than we yet understand. Without going into the reasoning just yet, I would gamble that our mysterious squadron will yet again help us by attacking rebel positions in Honduras. Do you follow me, Comrades?"

A few halfhearted nods encouraged him to continue.

"A search for the intruders may be a waste of resources. Rather, it would be more prudent to block them, to entrap them when they make their next move."

"Are you suggesting a blockade at the border?" Suarez asked, again pacing nervously.

"Perhaps a few squadrons of well-sited gunships, lying in wait."

"The better course is to put every aircraft we have to the search," Cerone said, not wanting to be upstaged by the Navy. "Confront this ghost unit and cut it down."

"We still do not know the makeup of the ghost unit, as

you call it, General,'' Zhukov said. "If it is indeed piloted
by Cubans, in a dubious support of the Sandinista effort,
how do you think your own Cuban pilots will react to
shooting down their brothers?''

"We will not use Cuban or Soviet pilots, Comrade Major.''

"Ambush. That is the way," Churbanchuk insisted.

The leaders in the room agreed.


General Eugene Kuster arrived at the Electronic Situation
Room just after noon. The first thing he detected was the
strong undercurrent of nervous tension. Of the many people he thought should not be there, most of them were in
shirtsleeves, and most of them were sweating.

Delmar Williams greeted him. Williams had often been
helpful to the DIA on Latin American problems.

A Navy lieutenant was on a phone, apparently calling
National Security Council members. An Air Force major
who looked completely unperturbed was manning the main
console. Several enlisted personnel were huddled over
telex machines and other consoles at the side of the room.
Officers of less than field grade gave them instructions in
loud voices, looking for attention from the general officers. The chatter level was high.

Jack Coriolanus was talking to Aaron Messenbaum and
the national security advisor in one corner of the room,
so Kuster wandered over to the electronic map of Central
America for a closer look. Just north of the Honduran/
Nicaraguan border, a dot on the map labeled "Camp Rogers" had a cryptic note next to it: "2 fat/16 cas/.5 destr.''

Kuster turned back to the room. Jason Roebuck and
some blond kid were in conference at the side wall. Roe-

buck's aristocratic face seemed to be in control, but his hands fluttered in either eagerness or anxiety. The liberal from Oregon, Havechuk, marched through the door with an aide, wearing matching scowls. Colonel Winfield Storch and his boss, the chairman of the Joint Chiefs, were in a huddle with Josh Simpson, the Navy chief of staff.

Mike Parch came across the room and offered him a grim smile and a hand. Kuster returned the firm grip of the hand. "How are the Marines taking this, Mike?"

"Hell, Gene, we're ready to go, soon as the C-in-C gives us the word. They used the Eighty-second Airborne last time, so I figure it's our turn."

"What are the details?"

"How much do you know?" Parch asked.

"Only that there's been an incursion into Honduras. An attack on Camp Rogers that must have been brief. I see on the map that we've got two dead, sixteen wounded, and half the camp destroyed."

"The dead are both Americans."

"Shit."

"And so is one of the wounded, a reporter from San Francisco."

"What's the President's reaction?" Kuster asked.

"Not much he can say about the Americans. They were there on their own. But he and the Honduran president have been on the phone for the last hour. I expect we'll send in some troops as a show of force." Parch sounded hopeful.

The secretary of defense arrived, flanked by six or seven assistants, and joined the chief of staff, Admiral Joseph Dilman. Lately, since Hamm's apparent retirement, Dilman and Kuster had been getting along a little better, though their relationship was still like that of two hungry lions sharing one antelope.

The phone rang shrilly, and the room went silent except for the hum of electronics.

The national security advisor walked over to the walnut table, opened a drawer, and picked up the receiver. No one said a word as he spoke quietly for several minutes, then handed the phone to the Secretary of Defense. That conversation was a short one, then the secretary hung up and nodded to the national security advisor.

"Gentlemen," the advisor said and waited until he had everyone's attention. "The State Department is now delivering a note of protest to the Nicaraguan government."

There were a number of notes of protest raised in the Electronic Situation Room, some of which bordered on the obscene.

"The Secretary of State is flying to Tegucigalpa in one hour. While the Hondurans have not yet requested assistance, Admiral Dilman, the President would like to have you place two battalions of the Eighty-second Airborne on alert, along with the Delta Force."

"Yes, sir," Dilman said.

Marine General Parch's face darkened with anger. "The pricks!"

The advisor turned to Messenbaum: "The Air Force should prepare transport for those troops. About sixty planes, I'd guess."

Messenbaum shook his head in agreement, looked to the SecDef for confirmation, then signaled an aide.

"The measures that we discussed earlier this morning?" the advisor reminded them. "We are to scramble the AWACS at Guantanamo Bay, and put the *Eisenhower*'s Tomcats and the Eagles at Tegucigalpa on twenty-four-

hour alert status. General Messenbaum, you should see
that the Eagles have armament shipped to them.''

''Do we have permission from the Hondurans?'' Messenbaum asked.

''Yes, of course.''

''Good, because it went out by C-5A to Palmerola Air
Base this morning.''

That startled the national security advisor for a moment. ''Just what did you send that required a Galaxy?''

''Support staff, vehicles, and maintenance equipment, in
addition to the ordnance.''

The national security advisor gave a reluctant nod.
''Any questions at this time, gentlemen?''

Joe Dilman eyed Messenbaum speculatively, probably
unhappy about the Air Force's precipitate action.

Senator Jason Roebuck said, ''What about the goddamned Russkies? They're behind this.''

''I wouldn't be so sure of that, Jason,'' Senator Harley
Havechuk intervened.

The secretary of defense responded, ''The President
has sent for the Soviet ambassador, and they will be meeting in the next half hour. The President will ask for restraint.''

''Restraint, my ass! The Communists have just attacked
a sovereign power, a friend, and we're asking for restraint?''

The Secretary of Defense worked his jaws silently and
threw his palms up in frustration.

With no more questions of the national security advisor, the room erupted with simultaneous conversations.

''Once again, Gene, it's going to be too damned little,
too damned late,'' Parch said.

Kuster looked back at the map. ''That's rough territory—jungle and mountains, Mike. Rogers is three miles in from the border. A lot of ground-pounding for the Sandinistas. Surprises me a little.''

''Ground attack? Hell no, Gene. Rogers got hit by seven gunships. Havocs and Hinds.''

Kuster's chest tightened the moment he heard ''Havocs.'' ''Mil Mi-28s?'' he asked, to cover his shock. ''You're certain?''

''Too damned right. They've got three Havocs on videotape, and they shot down a Hind.''

''They get the crew?'' Kuster asked, alarmed and thinking, That goddamned Hamm's gone way beyond orders yet again.

''No sign of the crew. They may have been picked up. The Soviets have gone too far this time.''

And so have I, Kuster thought, trying to quickly evaluate his position. He had information that others in this room should have, but he had it sub rosa. He might even lose his job over it, he decided, but better the job than involve the country in a war. ''Excuse me, Mike. I've got to corner Coriolanus.''

''We'll get together for a drink later.''

''That's looking like a better idea all the time,'' Kuster agreed.

''Goddamn! Can you believe the luck of the Eighty-second Airborne?''

Kuster drifted across the room, around the group in which Coriolanus was engaged in animated dialogue, and waited until the CIA's special assistant looked up. Kuster caught his eye and gestured with a shake of his head.

Coriolanus muttered an excuse to the others and walked over to him. ''Hello, Gene.''

Kuster flipped a thumb at the map and said, "Tell me what you know, and tell me all of it."

The CIA man's nostrils flared momentarily, but he finally related his theory about Clark's intentions on the Contra side—with the buildup of fighters and supplies—and what he knew about the Soviet helicopters and the Cuban pilots on the Sandinista side. "Your good old buddy Hamm's in on this, too, Gene. I don't know where or why, but he's down there with Clark. I think they're trying to build up the Contra air capability."

Kuster heard him out, evaluating. "We've got a bit of a fuck-up here, Jack."

"Don't I know it!"

"Actually, you don't," Kuster told him. "The real problem is, Clark's bunch of pilots and your Cuban pilots are one and the same."

After Corialanus grasped the import, his face went pale. "Jesus Christ! You're sure?"

"I can give you the name of each pilot. Not one of them is Spanish."

Diego Contrarez and his chief, Esteban Maldonado, had spent most of the day in meetings with other Contra leaders at Palmerola Air Base, the presence of foreign rebels in a Honduran military conference room overlooked by their hosts. A variety of CIA representatives sat in on the meeting, but did not offer much in the way of encouragement. They did tell the leadership to complete the coordinated attack planned for the morning, although they seemed to have no knowledge of the detailed plans that Bobby Clark had provided a month earlier. Even more queer, they did not know about the influx of supplies that had been coming in for two weeks. The display of ignorance was not new to Contrarez. The CIA criticized FDN coordination, but frequently appeared to be confused by their own operations.

The FDN leaders had the information about the attack on Camp Rogers by radio at ten-forty-five, and immediately changed the topic of the meeting. As was usual, the bickering prevailed and nothing substantial was accomplished by three o'clock, when Contrarez and Maldonado left to return to their camp.

The Cessna 0-2, once the property of the New York Air National Guard before it had been declared surplus during the Boland Amendment era, put them down at Camp Castenada just before four o'clock. By then, the radio and the early newspapers in Tegucigalpa were shouting about the deaths of Americans in the morning raid on Honduran soil. Of diminished importance was the fact that the Contras had been able to shoot down one of the attacking helicopters. The shattered remains were undoubtedly those of a Soviet Mil Mi-24, like those in Sandinista inventories.

"This may be the turning point, Diego," Maldonado said.

"The Americans will be fighting mad. I hope they don't take our war away from us."

The pilot parked the Cessna off the runway, in line with eight other aircraft on the apron, and the two leaders deplaned.

Castenada was a large base, fifteen miles north of the border. Its two landing strips were composed of linked steel planks—a U.S. gift, avoiding shutdowns during excessively wet weather—and the runways would accept larger aircraft, such as C-130s and DC-6s. Part of the complex was made up of steel buildings and Quonsets for the storage of military supplies. Many of the warehouses, almost empty in recent months, were now crammed with the goods Bobby Clark had promised in May. Five large storage tanks were again filled with aviation fuel for the airplanes and with gasoline for vehicles.

A Contra fighter in a camouflage-painted Jeep was waiting for them, and they crawled into it, Contrarez in the back. The driver pulled away from the airstrip and headed toward Maldonado's combination living quarters/headquarters.

Located a quarter mile from the runways, it was surrounded by sparse trees and the tents of his men. On any day, there might be as many as six hundred fighters encamped at Castenada, scrounging for food and waiting for orders.

There was a strong American presence at the camp as well. Some 120 mercenaries, CIA agents, Army and Marine advisors, air freight people, medical personnel, and civilians were housed in a separate section of the camp. In the last week, Western news teams had inundated the camp, always busy with their questions and their cameras.

Half a dozen people were hanging around the outer office of Maldonado's headquarters when they arrived. The colonel took some time to bring them up to date on the raid at Camp Rogers, then led Contrarez back into his private office. It was a stark and spartan place with a rough wooden floor, one beat-up desk, and four chairs. There were no other decorations, and nothing there provided an indication that its occupant was a millionaire in his own right.

Maldonado went behind his desk and dropped into his chair. "Well, Diego?"

"You're asking me about the attacks scheduled for tomorrow morning?"

The colonel looked to the map stretched on an easel, with Sandinista military outposts highlighted with a yellow marker. There were eleven such targets for Maldonado's troops alone, and it was estimated in Bobby Clark's tactical summary that the Contras would outnumber the Sandinistas in each of the attacks by at least three to one. Of course, Bobby Clark had been wrong in the past.

"Yes, that is what I am asking."

"We may be in for some trouble, if there are to be enemy squadrons along the border," Contrarez said. "Before we left Palmerola, the Hondurans were reporting highly increased Sandinista air patrols, possibly in support of this morning's raid. Clark's plans did not consider such increased air activity."

"Let's say that half of our units encountered enemy gunships and took fifty percent casualties. We could stand to lose four or five hundred men, my colonel."

"And yet, if we do not go forward?"

Contrarez spoke of the priority concern. "Bobby Clark does not make a half million dollars in deposits to our accounts. Plus, Esteban, we will be out of pocket the hundred fifty thousand dollars that we have contributed in . . . presents to our compatriots."

"For their cooperation."

"For their cooperation," Contrarez agreed.

"At this point, Major Contrarez, I do not see that we have any choice but to move ahead, as planned. And, too, we must remember that hope is rekindled. The American Congress must be highly enraged by the death of Americans at the hands of the Soviet-backed invaders of our friends. We must do our part."

"That is true," Major Contrarez said. "I will pass the

word to the field commanders that we must be in position by zero three hundred hours.''

# TWENTY-THREE

**W**ill Hunt spent the afternoon washing Melodee's white BMW convertible, then his silver-blue Stingray. When he was done, he ran them both in the garage, shut the door against the sun, and began to wax the Corvette under the fluorescent lights he had installed. From time to time, he slipped into the kitchen to retrieve a beer from the refrigerator.

At six o'clock, when most of the body panels had been buffed to a high luster, Melodee opened the door from the house and stood there in the string bikini she wore every afternoon. Hunt looked up. ''Dinner, babe?''

''Will, there's a man at the door wants to see you.''

Frowning, Hunt went into the house, patting his wife on the bottom as he sidled past her. In the tiled entryway at the front door stood a blocky man in a wrinkled light gray suit. As Hunt approached, the man held up a plastic credential folder. ''Willard Hunt? I'm Ben Neale with the Central Intelligence Agency.''

''Yeah, I'm Hunt.''

''I need to ask you some questions.''

''What about?''

"About a C-130 you just piloted on a seven-hour round trip out of Miami."

"Once again, in the leading story of the day, the President has ordered all Honduran defensive forces in the country to full alert and has notified the Nicaraguan government that further intrusions on Honduran territory are tantamount to an act of war. . . ."

Peachy Keen clicked off his portable radio, and Hank Bellows was forced to stop translating from the Spanish. "We've heard the rest of it."

They had been listening to the Spanish broadcasts, via Bellows's interpretation, out of Managua and Tegucigalpa all day while they rested in the humid shade of the camouflage netting covering the aircraft. Hamm thought most of the tension had been relieved. These men had once again proved to themselves that they were invincible in combat. Rick Talbot, in checking over the helicopters, had counted only sixteen minor hits, all inflicted on the Hinds in the second strike group. The surprise at Camp Rogers had been total.

Bobby Clark had worn a half-assed, smirky, self-satisfied grin all day. It was developing just as his computer said it would. He was elated that the press, especially a TV cameraman, had been present. "The six o'clock news will spread that footage all over the world."

Hamm was angry, but he let it seethe inside, and he waited for what was next. He liked his role of mole even less than he liked his role of commander, but Kuster's orders had been clear enough—get the names. Do what you have to do to get the goddamn names. Pretty damned soon, he thought, he would be exceeding his orders in some way. Maybe he could start by shooting Bobby Clark? He patted the flap of the holster on his hip.

McDonough pointed up at the dark sky. "Check it out. Two o'clock high."

Everyone looked up. There were two jet aircraft at about ten thousand feet. Their navigation lights looked like odd-colored stars.

Canton laughed. "We've got them scared off. They're not going to see much from that altitude."

"Ten to one, they think whoever they're looking for has a few surface-to-air missiles waiting for them," Keen said.

"Bet they're Soviet or Cuban advisors," McDonough said. "Maybe MiGs. I don't think the Nicaraguans do much night flying."

"You're right there, Sean," Clark confirmed for him.

"In fact," Hal Cherry said, "we've seen more Honduran aircraft this afternoon than we have Sandinistan. I'm beginning to think something's haywire."

Hamm had been thinking about that, too. "And both sides are keeping well clear of the border, avoiding incidents. They're leery of each other."

"We may be doing something your computer forgot to think about, Bobby," McDonough said.

"What's that?" Clark's voice was skeptical and fearful at the same time. "We're supposed to be causing confusion."

"We may damned well be starting a war between Nicaragua and Honduras. Which would bring U.S. troops into it. Hell, we could end up with another 'Nam, instead of increased aid to the Contras."

"No way," Clark insisted. "Everybody will back off, just as they have before."

"Let's get back to immediate problems," Hamm said.

"This little sortie of ours, on the surface, has pretty clear intentions as far as the Contras, the Hondurans, and the boys back in the Pentagon are concerned. The only ones really puzzled by it will be the Sandinistas. They don't know what the hell's going on."

"So? Keep them guessing," De Veres said.

"If I put myself in their boots, I have to tell myself that what's happening is not good for me, or for my country. All sorts of shit could start raining down. I don't know what unit is operating, or what its purpose is. Hell, maybe I'd start to worry about a revolt within my own ranks."

"That's all right," Clark told him. "If they think they've got a mutinous commander in their own backyard, it'll add to the confusion."

"Maybe," Hamm said. "We studied the profiles of Demarco, Suarez, and Cerone while we were training in Texas. I'd give Demarco points for intelligence, but I guess I wouldn't worry much about the leadership of Ricardo Suarez or Juan Cerone."

"That's exactly the way I played it," Clark said in rare agreement. "They have more concern for 'face' than they have knowledge of tactics."

"You didn't say anything about the Soviet expertise hanging around, Bobby. Other than the KGB resident."

Clark had the information in his head. "The KGB biggie is Josef Zhukov, a major. The Company's intelligence says he's about to rotate back to Moscow, after being in-country for five years or so."

"What's the profile?"

"Intelligent, tactful, likes the country and the culture. He's got good credentials and a good record."

"Anyone else?" Hamm asked.

"Advisor to the Army is a Major Prabinovski, and the

air force advisor is Colonel Churbanchuk. Both long-term veterans, fairly sharp.''

"And these advisors went into your computer?'' Hal Cherry asked.

"Of course,'' Clark said.

Hamm knew he was lying. It was another oversight in the planning. "Okay. Back to where I'm standing in someone else's boots. I've got a rogue air unit threatening to pull me into a major confrontation that I don't want just yet. I know, or I suspect, that they're sitting on Nicaraguan soil, waiting to make another hit I don't want, so I'd like to neutralize them. The problem is, they're in rugged country and difficult to locate because I haven't pinpointed an operational base. What do I do about it?''

"I'm reading you,'' Cherry said.

"Me, too,'' McDonough echoed. "If I'm a hip commander, playing my units on a chess board, I don't go running around with my pants down around my ankles.''

"What the hell are you trying to get at?'' Peter de Veres asked.

"Ambush. I deploy all my gunships along the border and wait,'' Hamm said.

"No,'' Clark said. "First of all, Demarco isn't going to destroy some fifteen million dollars' worth of aircraft. He'll want to capture it. Second, he'll want to make sure he hasn't got a coup under way. You're giving them too many points for reaction time.''

"If it was just Demarco, I might go along with you,'' Hamm said. "However, with a sharp KGB resident and military advisors with battle experience in Afghanistan, I boost the response time. We're targets of both sides now.''

Clark's lips went into their stubborn mold, but he shut up.

The group sat in silence for a while, except for the frequent slap of palms against mosquitoes. There was a new tension in the air. Jungle boots shifted uneasily, bodies rocked on their buttocks, seeking comfort on hard earth.

"What'll we do about it, Steve? You have an idea?" Cherry finally asked.

"Give me about an hour to think about it, Hal. I can tell you that I suspect this is the point where we abandon the goddamn computer."

"Now, wait a minute!" Clark yelped.

"From here on out, I'm going to balance survival against battle plans, Bobby. First things first, we can't make the coast on the fuel we have, so we have to get back to our supply. If we rely on the data you have, it's unlikely the Nicaraguans have the technology to spot us immediately on a ten-minute night hop. Moscow might know right away, as will the Pentagon, but I'm guessing we have at least a ten-minute lead time."

"At least," Clark said.

"Electronic warfare left me behind a long time ago. What the hell are you talking about?" Ketchum asked.

"Satellite coverage," Hamm said. "By now, Demarco's people will be hooked in with Moscow, and they'll be getting delayed instant replay. We'll use that supposition, anyway, given Zhukov's intelligence. With a jerry-rigged system, they may still have gaps. Our major disadvantage may be the Pentagon."

"How so?" Bellows asked.

"I'd bet they're watching this area like a hawk via satellite. The greatest deficiency of the Mi-24 Hind is that big, undisguised exhaust on the side of the fuselage. It leaves an infrared signature that can be read like a comic book. The minute we fire up, the generals back home will know where we are and where we end up."

"The question is not that they know where we are, but what they want to do about it," De Veres responded.

"That's right, Peter. I know a few of the people who will be watching the action, probably in the Electronic Situation Room. . . ."

"So do I," Clark interrupted. "I can judge the reactions as well as you can, Hamm."

". . . and while they're all mad about the two Americans killed, I'd suspect most of the civilians will be pushing for cautious responses while some of the military will be spoiling for a fight."

"Not all the civilians," Clark said. "We've got supporters on the oversight committees."

"Nobody with enough support to hold back on a total war in Central America," Hamm said. "We *have* to have enough strength in that room to keep the U.S. out of it while we play out our role, then drop out of sight."

"That's been the idea," De Veres said, "though, listening to you, I'm beginning to worry."

Clark did not like seeing De Veres back down. "Bullshit! I'd give odds that Jason Roebuck will be behind us all the way. And he's persuasive enough to swing a lot of votes the way they need to go, Hamm."

Hamm shrugged. "Maybe."

"Damned right! He'll hold the line right where we want it held. And he's not alone in there."

Bingo. Hamm wondered if Roebuck was "Daisy Mae," "Li'l Abner," or "Pappy." He continued, "Working the worst-case scenario, let's say the Pentagon knows exactly where we are in an hour from now. What are their options?"

"Number one," De Veres said, "they say nothing. They wait for the next strike, to see if public and congressional pressure builds enough support for the Contras. After all, they don't know that we're not Sandinistas."

"You can safely bet that the President's been conferring with Capitol Hill leadership all day, as well as with the Soviets and the Hondurans," Clark said.

"Okay, that's possible," Hamm agreed. "Number two, the Defense Department identifies our location for the Hondurans, and the Hondurans send about eight of their Mystere-Falcons in on us. One pass would be sufficient, if we're caught on the ground. And if we're airborne, I don't think we're here to engage the Hondurans. Certainly not in a one-sided air battle."

"But if the Hondurans cross the border, that increases the chance for war between Nicaragua and Honduras," McDonough countered. He lit his cigar for the fifth or sixth time, and the red glow gave him a position in the dark.

"True, Sean. Except the Sandinistas might be grateful that their rogue squadron has been taken out of the action."

"Maybe the U.S. will just hop in with some carrier planes and do it up right?" Cherry said.

"Shit!" McDonough said. "We've got the U.S., the Contras, the Hondurans, *and* the Nicaraguans after us, and we've only had one sortie."

Hamm was still considering the actions and reactions. "Okay, Bobby, get your paper and lay out the next target for us."

The stars were brighter that night, and Hamm could see enough of Clark's face to tell that he was not yet ready to divulge Mission Two, but he gave in and said, "Camp

Castenada. It's fifteen miles inside the border, in plateau country, a bigger base than Rogers. Two steel-mat landing strips.''

The target was not a surprise to anyone this time. "Why that one?''

"It is a larger base. We want to suggest the increasing threat to American interests.''

"How many Americans did we have at Rogers?'' Hal Cherry asked.

"Eleven. Plus I don't know how many reporters.''

"And we got two of them? How many do we get this time? Your computer tell you that?''

"We don't kill anyone. That's always been the objective,'' Clark insisted. "At Castenada, the storage facilities are farther removed from the camp itself, again on the opposite side of the runway. We have a lot more tolerance. And we have five fuel-storage tanks on the list of targets.''

"Those will go up nice,'' Canton said.

"What's the third target?'' Hamm said.

"Not yet.''

"We may skip number two, and go right to three.''

"No, damn it. We've got to build to three. Give the international press time to get into the action. Hell, by now, every newspaper and network in the free world will have booked all the commercial flights.''

"Fuck.'' Hamm thought it over. "Break down Castenada for us. Then we'll decide.''

They opened the side doors of a Hind and climbed inside. The oppressive humidity made the compartment feel smaller. Clark turned on an overhead red light, unzipped his document case, got out his photographs and maps, and spent an hour detailing the attack.

While he narrated, stopping to answer questions, Hamm thought over his own options. He had one of the names, possibly, and two to go. He had already decided he was not going to get hard evidence. With the names, though, the FBI could play search-and-destroy, look for connections that would convince a grand jury. He would go for the other two names.

When Clark was done, Hamm said, "The site looks better this time. Less chance for casualities, unless there's a heavy guard component around the storage area."

"There isn't," Clark said, pointing out details on the photograph. "The warehouses are fenced off and have two guards. The fuel depot normally has one guard."

"And you chose zero nine hundred hours for purposes of visibility, again?"

"Right. We've got to be seen."

"What do you guys feel about it?" Hamm asked.

"Our chances get slimmer by the minute," Cherry said. "Especially in daylight."

"I agree. As it stands, Bobby's mortality rate is a damned low guess," McDonough said.

"I think you're right," Hamm told them. "And as far as visibility goes, we've already set the tone. The media will hazard a guess, even if they don't see the aircraft insignia. For damned sure, Washington will know exactly."

"Maybe we've already accomplished all we need to accomplish," Rick Talbot said.

"We're close to the end, and two more days will wrap it up," Clark argued. "We've come this far, and we can't turn back now."

"Problem is, this thing has been set up by the book," Hamm said. "Zip out and shoot up the enemy, then rush back to base. It's a sample of classic air operations, and with the technology working against us, we no longer have two days.''

"You've got logistics problems to deal with, Hamm. Minor things like fuel and ordnance." Peter de Veres came up with the obvious.

"I think, if we want to complete this thing, we'll change tactics. We've got . . .''

"You're getting a quarter million dollars to complete it,'' Clark said.

". . . we've got to turn ourselves into a guerrilla air squadron.''

"I want to hear this," Keen declared.

"We have to use hit-and-run tactics. Never stay in the same place. Change the timetable, and screw Bobby's computer design.''

"Hold on, goddamn it!" Clark said.

"You want this done, or not?" Hamm asked him.

"How do we overcome the logistics problems?" De Veres asked. "You don't get much hit-and-run on one load of fuel.''

"Conservation, for one. We reload weapons only one more time, unless we end up with a little extra weight allowance, and we use half the ordnance load on the second target, and hold the rest for the last target. We take as much extra fuel with us as the Hinds' payload will allow. We stay on the run, ready for an interception at any time. We also remain ready to abandon targets and run for the coast if necessary. We dump choppers if we need to do that.''

"It's sounding better," McDonough said.

"Tell me, Bobby. Is the third target to the west?" Hamm asked him.

Reluctantly, Clark said, "Yes."

"Good. Every move we make is toward the west, closer to the coast, saving fuel."

"I don't know about the rest of you," Harvey Ketchum said, "but I'm still in this to jerk Congress back into line. If there's a possibility of completing the missions, I'll go for it."

"How are you changing the timetable?" Clark wanted to know.

"Our time for free movement is running out. We need to use every minute we've got to meet the objective. It's twenty-one forty-five hours now. If we go with this, we take off from here now, put down to load up as much as we can, and immediately hit Castenada."

"In the middle of the night?"

"In the middle of the night. Then we settle in somewhere for an hour to regroup and refuel, and then go right after your third target. Then we get the hell out. If we stay on the move, we've got a chance."

"Can't do it," Clark said. "There's other things at work that you don't know about."

"Like what?"

"Like at zero three hundred hours in the morning, five hours from now, the Contras are launching a major offensive against twenty-seven Sandinista bases. This is supposed to be coordinated with the diversion for the Sandinistas and the fact that Camp Castenada will be almost uninhabited, to cause confusion."

"Shit, I'm already confused," Keen said. "Let's get the hell under way before my nerves deteriorate further."

"Coordination is gone, if you want us to complete this, Bobby," Hamm said. "Otherwise, I'm in favor of shifting fuel right now, loading everyone on two of the Hinds, and making a run for the Pacific.''

Clark sat silent in the red light, his face suggesting a changing set of reactions. Finally, he said, ''I guess we'll have to do it your way.''

''Any dissent?'' Hamm asked.

There was none, and he spent twenty minutes outlining a plan of action. When he was done, he asked the group, ''Questions?''

There were no questions.

''Okay, light 'em up.''


''Hot fucking damn!'' Major General Mike Parch of the U.S. Marine Corps was ecstatic. ''Here we go!''

Coriolanus jerked his head up at his place at the table, dropping his doughnut and almost spilling his coffee.

The major at the console extended a collapsible pointer and used it to focus attention on the activities demonstrated by the crimson streaks that had suddenly appeared on the electronic map. ''We have six aircraft, gentlemen. We're reading them in infrared, and the ID computer classifies three of them as Mil Mi-24 Hind helicopters. The other three signatures are weaker, and there is no identification as yet, but we believe they may be Mil Mi-28s. Heading is west-southwest.''

Aaron Messenbaum, who was sitting opposite Coriolanus, turned around in his chair to see the map. ''They're staying in-country?''

''Looks that way, sir,'' said the major.

''Why no identification on the others?'' Jason Roebuck asked from the side of the room.

''Our computers have never gotten a decent base reading on the Havoc, Senator,'' Eugene Kuster told him. ''We may have one now.''

Coriolanus was almost afraid of catching Kuster's eye. The DIA director had not given him much time to double-check the data Kuster had collected. A quick search of Langley's computers had revealed that there was a god-damned ALECTO file. There were twelve goddamned pilots and three goddamned undefined code names. Beyond that, there was nothing but circumstantial guesswork to put Clark and his bunch in Nicaragua. Coriolanus resisted giving in to Kuster.

The men in the room looked a trifle fatigued from the long wait. Coriolanus had sent Nolan back to his office for a fresh shirt at seven o'clock.

The National Security Advisor eyed the screen, then turned to Admiral Dilman. ''Do you have some kind of action in mind, Admiral?''

''Not just yet, I think. They're staying in Nicaragua, and I believe we'll just watch for a while.''

''Despite the fact that the Nicaraguans have moved more air units to the border?'' The advisor referred to the earlier shifting of eight Mi-24 helicopters into positions at Bocay and Cerro Kilambe.

''It's threatening, yes, sir,'' Dilman said, ''but no action has been taken.''

Jack Coriolanus noted the baleful looks on the faces of the civilians. General Aaron Messenbaum's gray, hard eyes were bright and alive. ''At the least, we had better alert our people.''

''Minimally, Aaron,'' the chairman of the Joint Chiefs told him while looking to the President's advisor.

The national security advisor nodded his approval after

a moment's consideration and picked up his nearby telephone receiver to call the White House.

Admiral Josh Simpson turned to the operations officer: "Any radio traffic, Major?"

"None in that group, sir. Not on anything powerful enough for us to intercept it, anyway. There has not been any chatter between Managua and Bocay or Cerro Kilambe, either."

Dilman chewed his lip, then asked Messenbaum, "What do you think, Aaron?"

"Let's get the Eagles airborne, Joe, and keep them at about forty thousand feet. Josh, can the *Eisenhower* reach the area with Tomcats?"

Simpson studied the blue circle representing the carrier on the map. "We can get them there, but we can't hold on location for very long. They'd have to land at Tegoose or Palmerola for refueling."

"We'll wait on them, then." Turning to the operations officer, he asked, "Where's the AWACS?"

The major consulted his console. "Flying figure-eights at thirty-six thousand feet, eleven minutes away from the area, General. We're now using their data to help feed the display board."

"Good." Messenbaum swung his short-cropped head to look at Coriolanus. "Okay, Jack?"

Coriolanus nodded, but he was not happy. He looked down the table to Kuster, who was eyeing him strangely, waiting, his reflection in the gleam of the walnut top stern. Coriolanus thought that Kuster would not wait much longer.

Abruptly, the streaks on the map began to slow, then to blink out one after another.

"They're landing, gentlemen," the major said. "And they're still in Nicaragua."

"Hold up on the Eagles and lock in on those coordinates," Admiral Dilman ordered. "We may want to just zip a missile or two in there."

Kuster looked up from the memo pad he was doodling on and watched the infrared sources shut down sequentially, like minutes blinking off a timer, and felt he had given Coriolanus enough time. He got up and walked along the table. "Come on, Jack."

Coriolanus looked up. "Now?"

"Now. You check it out?"

"Yes. Your man Llewellen knows what he's doing. It's shitty, Gene, your tagging after us."

"Can't help that now. Let's go."

The CIA man slid back his castered chair and got up to follow Kuster around the table. Kuster tapped Dilman on the shoulder and, when he turned his head around, said, "Admiral, I'd like to speak to you for a couple of minutes. Across the hall."

"What's this about, Gene?"

"We'll find an empty office."

The chairman's aide, Winfield Storch, appeared immediately at his boss's elbow.

"We won't need you, Winnie," Kuster told him.

The national security advisor appeared even more anxious than was normal for him when Kuster asked him to accompany the group.

Last, he interrupted a conversation between the Secretary of Defense and one of his assistants. "Mr. Secretary, would you join us for a moment?"

Coriolanus led the way out of the room and a short way

down the hall until he found a vacant office. Kuster ushered his august group inside, then shut the door. He had their attention, whether he wanted it or not.

"Mr. Secretary, gentlemen, this starts very simply, but becomes somewhat more complicated. I've been spying on the CIA."

# TWENTY-FOUR

The latest satellite photograph, now utilizing infrared, showed the six helicopters streaking toward a new destination within the country. In fact, the pessimists in General Juan Cerone's headquarters were quick to project the flight path as intercepting the capital and were eager to go on the public radio and alert the populace of Managua of an impending attack. The only disagreement lay in the identity of the attacking force. Were they capitalist-supported marauders or Sandinista mutineers? Josef Zhukov stepped out of his role as advisor by strongly urging Manuel Demarco to wait for the next photograph.

When it came rolling out on the photostat machine eighteen minutes later, there were no tracks at all on it. The ghost helicopters had disappeared yet once again.

Ricardo Suarez said, "Juan, get one of your technicians to calculate the speed and distance. We can narrow this search down to a much smaller area."

Zhukov turned to his assistant. "Boris, will you try to reach Moscow Center for me?"

"Of course, Comrade Major." Kamorovkin went to find a free telephone.

Cerone crossed over to the regional map mounted on the wall where Suarez was standing. Using a marker on the cellophane overlay, he noted the last position of the helicopters on the map, then drew a dotted line along the indicated flight path, following up by drawing a rough pie-shape angled to either side of the flight path. "At one hundred fifty miles per hour, the fugitives could cover up to forty-five miles in a time span of up to eighteen minutes. If they altered course by forty-five degrees south or north, this would suggest the search area. It is about two hundred fifty square miles."

"That much?" Suarez asked.

"That much. In mountainous country where ground clutter all but invalidates our radar readings. And at night. What were your thoughts?"

Suarez pointed to two border locations. "I have mobile ground units, with armored cars, here and here. We could move them south."

"An impossible task in that country," Cerone argued. "Better if we use the Third Air Assault Squadron, which we have positioned at Bocay. There are four Mi-24s."

Zhukov thought that the commander of the 3rd Air Assault Squadron would walk across the border to Honduras and join Bermudez's forces before he would fly an offensive operation at night, much less against six hostile aircraft. Looking to Pavel Prabinovski and Ivan Churbanchuk, Zhukov saw similar thoughts in their eyes.

Churbanchuk went to the map, saying, "The odds are

against you, General Suarez. Why not wait for daylight, wait for the fugitives to show themselves again, then close in on them with the Third Air Assault, and with the Fifth, ready at Cerro Kilambe. You would have an advantage of two helicopters, eight against six.''

"Or," Cerone suggested, "a squadron of MiG-23s could put them out of action in seconds.''

"If we knew the exact position where the helicopters landed, and if your pilots were willing to make the attempt . . .'' Churbanchuk countered.

"I am not speaking of now, Comrade Colonel. Rather, I was suggesting adding the MiGs to the gunships.''

"Ah. That would be helpful, if your pilots are ready for such a mission.''

"I was thinking," Cerone said, "perhaps, of the training squadron pilots. . . .''

Zhukov spoke to Demarco. "Soviet pilots? That would require the permission of Red Army Headquarters, which I do not believe would be forthcoming.''

"And unnecessary," Demarco agreed. "We will follow Comrade Colonel Churbanchuk's suggestion, waiting for daylight, and using the two helicopter units.''

Boris Kamorovkin was beckoning to him, holding a telephone receiver high in his left hand. Zhukov walked across to him in the corner of the big room and took the telephone, covering the mouthpiece with his hand. "Who am I talking to, Boris?''

"The chairman!" Kamorovkin blurted out.

"I see." Zhukov took a deep breath, then uncovered the telephone. "Comrade Chairman, this is Major Zhukov.''

"I am glad you called, Josef Mikhailovich. There are developments.''

"Yes, Chairman, developments about which I wished to make a request."

"And that is?"

"The time lapse of our satellite information is . . . inadequate, Chairman. Would it be possible to place the surveillance satellite in stationary orbit, and set up a direct link with this headquarters? It may very soon be of the utmost importance."

"An unnecessary expense, Comrade Major. And anyway, you do not have the proper ground equipment for direct communication with the satellite. I am in residence at the general staff headquarters at Stavka, since we seem to have the military involved with your little fiasco. However, we have all of the appropriate military and Politburo leadership available for decisions, and we see everything quite clearly."

"That is a relief, Chairman," Zhukov said, trying to believe it.

"We will maintain an open telephone line and notify you directly if the helicopters move again."

"It is appreciated."

"There is more," the chairman of the KGB told him. "Our sources along the Honduran border have indicated that the rebels are massing on a front some two hundred miles long. The strategists here expect that coordinated attacks against Nicaraguan positions will come with the dawn."

Zhukov felt as if his residency in Managua would end in flames. Flames that would increase in intensity upon his return to the motherland. "That is distressing, Chairman."

"And more. The United States has issued alert orders, to air and naval units in the region, to include arming their aircraft. That comes from an extremely reliable source within one of their intelligence oversight committees."

"I see," Zhukov said. "Will they become involved, do you believe?"

"There is no consensus among the staff here, as yet. But we are, of course, driven to alert our own forces. The *Baku* has been ordered to put its Yak-38 and Ka-25 helicopters aloft on a rotation patrol basis. They will be available on the east coast, if we find it necessary. You will note that authority to utilize the *Baku*'s aircraft remains here, Major."

It was as if Josef Zhukov were destined to be in the center of a war between the motherland and the U.S., the battle played out on his beautiful, adopted country. "Of course, Comrade Chairman. It is the correct strategy."

"I am glad you approve, Josef Mikhailovich," the chairman snapped. "I suspect that the strength of our resolve will convince the Americans to reverse course."

His superior hung up abruptly, leaving Zhukov with the task of informing his colleagues of the news that they were now confronted with not only a spectral helicopter unit, but also assaults from the Hondurans, the rebels, and the Americans. However, twelve Yak-38 naval fighters and eighteen Kamov Ka-25s would save them.

The national security advisor and the secretary of defense had left the Old Executive Office Building to cross the street to meet with the President personally. Until either of them came back, or called, no one was to say or do anything.

The mini-meeting in the vacant office had broken up in a set of different rages, Coriolanus thought. Kuster was half a hero for uncovering a dastardly CIA plot. The director of central intelligence had been sent for, meant as a slap on the hand for Coriolanus. Everyone was pissed off at Bobby Clark, and Coriolanus might feel the back-splash.

In the Electronic Situation Room, not much had changed on the map. A dot cruising in large circles 18,000 feet above the Nicaraguan mountains had been identified as a Tupolev Tu-114, a fifteen-year-old Soviet version of the American E-3A Sentry. Its AWACS capability was considered unsophisticated, but Kuster's information said that this one had been possibly upgraded for look-down radar. Still, that would be useless against Clark if he kept his assault group well down in the canyons. Infrared and, in daylight, direct-camera photography were still the best bets, and currently, the AWACS out of Guantanamo and the HALO satellite were providing combined infrared coverage.

Coriolanus and Kuster sat at the table, drinking what Coriolanus thought must be his second gallon of coffee in the last twenty-four hours. It was strange, he thought, to be allied with Kuster. Normally, he and the general were at odds over methodology or jurisdictional areas between the CIA and the DIA. Coriolanus was still angry over the fact that Kuster had been running an operation against the Agency.

Coriolanus could tell that the chairman of the JCS, Joe Dilman, was seething inside also, wanting to confide in his chiefs of staff, but unable to do so at the express order of the secretary of defense. Dilman, too, had come close to blowing his top when he learned that Hamm's retirement had been faked.

General Delmar Williams, the military expert on Central America, had shed his three-starred uniform jacket and gone into a huddle with Simpson and Parch. Coriolanus overheard only heated negatives as the three discussed possible actions and reactions by a wide variety of Latin American groups. Mike Parch was arguing for a Marine intervention.

Harley Havechuk and his assistant were in animated dialogue, oblivious of the people around them. Senator James Roebuck and his sandy-haired aide, Bret Davis, sauntered from the row of chairs at the side of the room and sat, uninvited, at the walnut table across from Coriolanus and Kuster. Roebuck said, "These things seem to go on forever."

Gene Kuster grinned at him. "Senator, these things are going on all the time, but more subtly. This cold war just has a hot spot in it."

Roebuck leaned forward conspiratorially. "Is there something else going on here?"

"Like what?" Coriolanus asked, trying to keep the defensiveness out of his tone.

"Like the intelligence people are withholding something from my committee, in defiance of the law." Roebuck's threats had never been abstract.

Bret Davis obviously enjoyed his employer's power. He grinned hugely.

Coriolanus thought the best defense in the current circumstances was silence, and he maintained his.

Kuster stepped in. "Maybe it's the tension of the coming Contra attack, Senator? They're scheduled to jump off at zero four hundred, our time, and it's zero one thirty already."

"You actually think Matamoros, Calera, and Maldonado will work together on this?"

"We'll have to keep an eye on Ripley's 'Believe It Or Not,' " Kuster said. He pointed at the map wall.

The senator leaned back, unconvinced. "What about the helicopter unit, though?"

"We may not see more of them until morning, Senator, if they follow yesterday's drill. You might want to go home and get some rest."

The senator pushed his chair back and got up, disgusted, and went to intrude on another group. Bret Davis followed him.

Kuster opened the drawer in front of him, selected one of the telephones, and dialed.

"Who you calling?" Coriolanus asked.

"National Security Agency. Checking my Tango Two code."

Kuster got a negative response from the duty officer he talked to and hung up. "Nothing."

A phone rang at the side of the room, and Coriolanus watched while the FBI representative answered it and then passed the receiver to Claude Nolan. He talked for a moment, slapped the receiver back in its cradle, and marched over to squat between Coriolanus's and Kuster's chairs. "That was Ben Neale in Miami."

"And?"

"They've got two pilots on ice. Free-lancers named Hunt and Conover."

"So?" Coriolanus demanded.

"They're talkative," Nolan said. "They made a fuel drop from a C-130 for Clark's buddy, Peter de Veres."

"Where?" Kuster asked.

Nolan turned puzzled eyes to the DIA man. "The Nicaraguan side."

"Shit!" Coriolanus exclaimed.

"You need any more confirmation than that, Jack?" Kuster asked.

Coriolanus told Nolan, "You get hold of Harry Downs and tell him to shag his ass over here. I want him standing by in the hall."

"Yes, sir." Nolan stood upright and drifted away.

"Goddamn it, Gene! Why did they think they'd get away with it?"

"Who knows? Some people are closer to God than I am. I still think you may be in the clear. No government bucks involved."

"Shit. But there's some of my people."

"And there's some others, too. I want to know who they are," Kuster claimed.

"Gentlemen!" The lieutenant colonel who had replaced the major at the console silenced the room. "The *Baku* has just launched aircraft."

With everyone else, Coriolanus spun toward the map. Four dots, in appropriate red, had been isolated on the east coast of Nicaragua. The White House chief of staff got on the telephone, reported briefly, then hung up.

Inside of ten minutes, it became apparent that the Soviet aircraft, computer-identified as Yak-38 Forger-As, were only patrolling the coast, but four more airplanes had been launched from the Soviet carrier, and joined them.

And two minutes later, at 1:42, the lieutenant colonel cleared his throat and said once again, "Gentlemen, if you'd look at the map?"

Heads rotated in unison.

"We have eight helicopters departing the target position. Heading three fifty-five degrees, speed one-four-zero knots. They're eight minutes from the border."

Admiral Joseph Dilman turned to the secretary of defense. "You'd better call the White House."

He was already on the red phone.

* * *

Zhukov was as surprised by the boldness as anyone in the war planning room.

General Juan Cerone, standing behind the radar scope and the infrared scanner linked into, and monitoring, the radar and scanner aboard the Tu-114 reconnaisance aircraft, exclaimed, *"¡Madre de Dios!"*

Commanders and advisors rushed toward the technician's console, elbowing each other for space. A sergeant said, "We are tracking on both radar images and IR sources via the Tupolev."

Zhukov saw the eight bright green blips caught in the rotating sweep. In his mind, he could not transpose them from the scope to a mental map. "Where are they?"

"Fifteen kilometers southwest of Bocay," Suarez said.

"Eight of them now. And at altitude," Cerone added. "As if they are unafraid of being seen."

"Or as if they want to be seen," Demarco clarified.

Kamorovkin called Zhukov to the open telephone line to Moscow, and an analyst there told him, "The helicopters have taken off, Major."

"I know that," Zhukov said, disgusted.

Zhukov gave the phone back to Boris and returned to the mini-conference in the middle of the room.

Cerone and Suarez looked to their defense minister, Cerone asking, "Señor Demarco?"

"There is no other help," Zhukov said. "You will have to do it on your own."

Demarco did not hesitate. "You had better send the air units from Bocay and Cerro Kilambe. They are to intercept and destroy."

"At night, Manuel?" Zhukov asked.

"Do I have a choice? What of the MiG-23s now on patrol?"

"The pilots are Soviet. I would have to ask Moscow again, and I already know the answer."

"Then I do not have a choice. Send the helicopters immediately, Juan."

The border was twenty miles away, and they reached it at 12:51 A.M., streaking above a ground mist that had begun to form around eleven o'clock. Hamm had decided to take no chances, and had ordered the three attack groups to fly at a thousand feet above indicated land altitudes. The mountain range to the north of the Rio Coco de Segovia was unfamiliar territory, not to be negotiated at speed in fog. Ahead and above the mist, Hamm could see stars. The mild light made the high plains gleam where they were visible through the haze. The fog was breaking up the farther north they traveled.

They had spent almost two hours on the ground at Ramirez, reloading rocket pods and machine-gun magazines, cramming C-rations into cockpits, and rolling fuel drums aboard the Hinds. Except for the one he was flying, the Mi-24s were at maximum payload.

Hamm was flying point in the first group, alone in a Hind, and Pat Canton had a Havoc out on his right flank. He wanted Canton where he could keep an eye on him since the man was again flying solo. The second group, all Havocs, was led by Peter de Veres, and the third group, headed by McDonough, was composed of the remaining Hinds. Hamm had switched McDonough to an Mi-24 because he wanted him to be the one picking up Canton and himself after they crashlanded the helicopters to be left behind as evidence. And in this case, Canton's Havoc was to suffer only minor damage. Clark wanted the U.S. military to acquire a complete airframe for analysis.

The Rio Coco de Segovia flashed under him, and Hamm gained altitude for the crossing of the Montañas de Colon. He looked at the tactical screen in front of him, showing a dim, forward TV picture of the fog and the stars. He longed to switch to the radar, to know where his enemies were. He felt vulnerable, despite the sophisticated electronics of the Hind. The panel was lit in rows of amber, blue, green, and red LEDs signaling the status of everything from landing-gear retraction to Electronic Countermeasures availability. The "Heads Up Display" cast the digital readouts of important instruments—altimeter, compass, attitude, engine monitoring—at canopy level so that he did not have continually to look down to the panels.

Tired of the TV picture from the camera in the nose, he switched the tactical display to IR. All that gave him was the exhaust readings from the eight helicopters, and he already knew where they should be.

"Click-click-click. Click-click." The mike-button signal sounded in his earphones, and he immediately searched the skies above. Peachy Keen, in the second group, had been given permission to utilize radar for thirty seconds every four minutes, and he had engaged a radar signal he did not like.

Hamm found them to his right, swiftly moving dark blobs blotting out the stars, running without lights.

There were four of them coming up the Rio Coco, Mi-24s judging by the side exhaust. He gauged the distance at something over a mile. "The hell with it! They already see us," he said to himself and flicked on the radar. The four blips showed up immediately. They were targeting toward the center of his screen.

Hamm went to the radio. *"Cinco Bandito. ¡Asalta-mos!"*

The order to attack was sweet for Canton. The Havoc shot forward, leading with its greater speed and agility, and Hamm fell in behind him. Rolling to the right and climbing, they sought the enemy head-on.

Their Swatter antitank missiles were not going to be effective in a dogfight, and Hamm did not bother arming his. He flicked the toggles for the rocket pods and the machine-gun turret, which was locked in a forward position—he had no gunner to traverse it. Canton's configuration was the same, set for a solo pilot.

According to Clark's sources, the Sandinistan helicopters were normally armed with AS-8 air-to-surface missiles, also not particularly useful in air combat.

The oncoming Hinds were in tentative hands. Way too early, they launched missiles. Canton jumped up and right, and Hamm followed, hitting the button to scatter chaff behind him. Three streaks went by, wide to the left, chasing the false radar signals they picked up from the aluminized chaff, and Hamm suspected they were indeed air-to-surface missiles.

Hamm rolled back, now to Canton's left, and a hundred yards behind him.

The Nicaraguan V formation loomed larger, becoming clear in the starshine, and even clearer on the radar screen.

The communist nerve evaporated when the squadron was still a half mile away, and the formation broke up after firing two more ineffective missiles and a stream of rockets. Two of the Hinds peeled off, diving away toward the south, and two banked away to the north.

Hamm and Canton went after the north-bounders, simultaneously pulling increased pitch with their left hands and ducking nose-down with the control sticks in their right hands. Hamm reluctantly admitted to himself that he and Canton would have made a great team in Vietnam. They thought the same way in the air.

Peter de Veres and his group pounced on the other two.

The target Hamm selected was afraid of tight turns. By the time his quarry had completed a ninety-degree turn to the north, Hamm had cut inside him and closed to less than four hundred yards. He fired a burst of rockets. The target dove, and ten rockets whished above him.

Hamm shoved the nose down and coaxed more speed out of the Hind.

In his peripheral vision, Hamm saw Canton's target change its mind and turn back to defend itself.

Too late.

Canton never gave way. Head-on, at almost point-blank range, Canton sidestepped a stream of machine-gun tracers, then poured a half dozen rockets into the enemy cockpits.

Hamm missed seeing the explosion and flames as he fired six more rockets at his own quarry. The Nicaraguan slithered to the right, his tail boom yawing too far to the left in his panic, costing him speed, and Hamm rolled with him, locking down the machine-gun button under his thumb.

The tracers passed under the target. Hamm pulled the nose up.

The tail rotor shattered at the same time 12.7-millimeter slugs flooded the turboshaft engines. One turbine engine exploded. The Mi-24 ahead of him started shuddering and breaking up in midair as it spun to the earth.

Hamm recovered quickly, climbing to avoid a small, treeless peak that appeared out of nowhere.

He hit the radio button. *"Tres Bandito. ¿Que paso?"*

Clark called him back. *"De nada."*

Well, Hamm thought, that's four fewer Hinds to harass the Contras.

In the Electronic Situation Room, Admiral Josh Simpson had yelled, "Jesus Christ Almighty! They're fighting among themselves."

Coriolanus had seen that the Nicaraguan aircraft, twelve of them identified as orange dots, had scattered, mixing it up with one another, flying all over the damned place.

Aaron Messenbaum had ordered the console operator to color the eight original aircraft blue, to clarify the action.

As he did so, the lieutenant colonel intoned the action. "Of the squadron out of Bocay . . . we've got one down . . . now two. Two escaping south. Engagement. Three down . . . and four."

Coriolanus had to shake his head to catch up. It had taken less than two minutes.

An enlisted man at a subconsole went, "All riiiight!" then lapsed into embarrassed silence when no one joined his cheering section.

The orange blips disappeared from the map, and the blue dots reformed into three groups of two, three, and three. They resumed their original northwesterly heading. Four more orange dots, originating from Cerro Kilambe, were homing on the area, but were obviously flying at slow speed and were going to be too late to intercept. The high-flying Tu-114 continued its circular patrol.

Looking around, Coriolanus saw that the civilian decision-makers had not yet returned.

The raiders were across the border now. Messenbaum

again spoke to the console operator. "Let me have possible ground targets."

"Yes, sir." The lieutenant colonel pressed buttons and scattered yellow squares appeared in a jagged row along the border, just inside Honduras. "Those are Contra supply and rest camps, General."

The chairman of the Joint Chiefs spoke to the Air Force chief. "Goddamn it. What do you think, Aaron?"

"I think we're going to lose a yellow square."

"Shit!"

"We ought to warn the Contras, even though we're probably too late."

"Do it," Admiral Joseph Dilman ordered.

Clearing the mountain pass, Hamm cut off the radar and dropped to two hundred feet above the plain and turned to a more westerly heading of 285 degrees. On this side of the mountains, the fog was only scattered clumps clinging tentatively to the earth that split and roiled as the thundering helicopters sped through the night.

It was desolate country, west of the mahogany forests, composed mostly of treeless plains ringed with mountains. Flipping on the red-tinted map light for a moment, Hamm checked his position on the chart clipped to his right thigh. If they had had the right map cassettes, the tactical display could also be used as a map readout, with computer enhancements of strategic areas. De Veres had been unable to locate Central American map cassettes in Angola.

Castenada was about seven miles away. They would hit it from the southwest, crossing the airstrips on an oblique that ignored the troop quarters set a quarter mile to the left.

The targets were tethered aircraft, warehouses, and especially, the fuel-storage tanks.

Hamm checked his right flank and found Canton in position. In the rearview mirror, he saw the shaded exhaust
of the Havocs a mile behind.

He wished he had use of the radar scope. It might tell
him what was happening at Castenada. Somebody somewhere had seen the skirmish at the border, and alerts had
possibly been issued. He tuned in the IR scan.

Two miles away, he saw the yellowish lights of the camp
slightly to the right of his line of flight. He corrected
course, and Canton moved with him. The heat sources
showed up dully on the tactical screen.

The camp lights flickered out suddenly, but he was already locked in.

A half mile out, Hamm flicked on his running lights for
ten seconds—his signal to the others, then extinguished
them and dove to fifty feet above the grassy plain.

Ahead, he saw a four-engined aircraft taking off. The
camp had been alerted and was trying to save airplanes.
That was all right with him.

A second plane got off the ground before Hamm's Hind
reached the airstrip.

The steel-plank runway gleamed in his gunsight. Small-
arms fire picked at him from the left. Hamm ignored a
Beechcraft taxiing to the end of the runway, armed his
Swatters, and let all four of them go into the center of the
airstrip.

The missiles whooshed from the stub wings, causing
the Hind to buck erratically, then arced downward and
exploded in cherry-orange flames. Steel planks erupted
into the air, and Hamm dodged to the left so as not to

collide with either the debris or with Canton. That would change the Beechcraft's mind.

Canton effectively disabled the parallel runway with his own AT-2s.

Almost instantly, Hamm was faced with warehouses, and he triggered off twenty rockets, peppering the tin structures. The rockets detonated out of his sight, but the image of tin walls inflating like balloons caught in his mind. He cleared the roof peaks by fifteen feet, and explosions and fire flared behind him. The Hind bobbled in the turbulence.

Banking slightly to the left, he found the fuel tanks where they were supposed to be and let the last of his rockets go, simultaneously triggering the quad guns of the 12.7-millimeter turret.

The rockets all missed, chewing up earth in futile explosions.

The green slices of his machine-gun tracers danced toward one tank, and he followed them, urging them in the right direction with delicate adjustments of the stick.

The fuel-storage tank detonated with a concussion that overcame the scream of the turboshaft engines and with a white-yellow flash that nearly blinded him. The Hind flipped abruptly over onto its left side, threatening to cartwheel its rotor along the ground.

Hamm fought the controls, finally righted the chopper, and immediately began to look for his landing site. Anywhere appeared to be all right. There was plenty of nearly level ground.

He rotated as he set down a mile northwest of the camp. He saw Canton angling in five hundred yards away, and he saw the Havocs making their pass into a Camp Castenada that was already aglow with burning storage buildings and one yellow-and-orange flare over a fuel tank. The destruction reflected off the rotor disks in strobic flashes.

The residential area on the south was dark except for muzzle flashes and the tracer streams from two heavy machine guns.

None of the choppers approached the area, and it looked as if it were going just right.

By 0100 hours, Castenada had been nearly deserted except for thirty administrative and support cadre, the Americans, and some fifteen *Yanqui* reporters. Under field commanders, the freedom fighters had moved out, headed for their assigned targets, many of which were a long way away by foot. Contrarez and Maldonado, along with six associates, had gathered in the headquarters building to monitor and direct the attacks by radio.

When the alarm about a possible air assault came in from Palmerola Air Base, Maldonado had immediately ordered the generators shut down, all lights extinguished, and the aircraft—with pilots on alert status for the morning raids already aboard—evacuated as soon as possible.

Contrarez had stepped outside to watch for attacking gunships, his vision slow to adjust to the night. Then, over the babble coming in on the radios, he heard the helicopters approaching. He waited, unsure of which way to run. Airplanes at the field taxied about in seeming confusion. One took off.

The night smelled suddenly sweet, dust tinted with honey, as if it were to be his last aroma. He looked for a place to hide and saw a two-and-a-half-ton truck parked a short distance away.

Another airplane took off.

The first two helicopters screamed across the runways,

leaving a trail of fire and thunder behind them. Contrarez could not remember seeing so much destruction occur all at once.

Flames and eruptions among the warehouses. All of those new supplies!

One of the fuel tanks exploded, and the concussion rolled across the ground, jolting him.

Three more helicopters swarmed in, missiles and rockets lancing out in seemingly endless, racketing noise.

Contrarez stood fast, as if he were growing roots. He was afraid to move.

And then they were gone, but the encampment on the far side of the runways was an inferno. Behind him in the hut, Maldonado and his subordinates had taken to the floor, but Contrarez stood his ground.

When the next three helicopters appeared out of the dark, Diego Contrarez thought about the two hundred thousand dollars that Bobby Clark was going to pay him on July first.

And the three hundred thousand dollars that Clark would pay to Esteban Maldonado.

He looked up at the next three helicopters just opening up with their missiles, then he unhooked two of his concussion grenades, pulled the pins with his teeth, and tossed them back into the headquarters hut.

Diego Contrarez ran twenty yards and dove beneath the deuce-and-a-half.

# TWENTY-FIVE

**A** mile away from Camp Castenada, Hamm could hear the cooling exhaust port ticking as he clung to the side of the fuselage, his toe inserted in an inset step, and slapped the plastic explosive against the metal skin just below the turbine intake. He inserted the blasting cap, twisted the timer, and then dropped back to the ground and picked up his AK-74.

As he stood upright, three shots crashed out of the dark, and three slugs slammed into the side of the Hind. The impacts rang and echoed.

Hamm hit the ground, rolled beneath the chopper, and slithered his way behind a landing wheel, searching for the point of attack. The hard earth still held the previous day's heat. Hot dust filled his nostrils.

Another three coughs, three muzzle flashes, and three bullets kicking dirt in his face located his attackers. They were below the crest of the rise, hidden behind a small copse of stunted shrub. The starlit plain behind silhouetted the shrubs, but did not identify the inept marksmen. Honduran military? Contra patrol?

"Shit," Hamm said to himself. He did not want to engage in a firefight with, much less kill, anyone from either group. He clicked the Kalashnikov's safety off and snicked the bolt lever back to load a round.

He had two minutes to decide. In three minutes, his protective cover of downed helicopter was going to take off in about a hundred directions simultaneously. Flipping the firing selector of the AK-74 to semiautomatic, Hamm fired four times, aiming ten feet above his targets.

The three Havocs shot overhead with turbines screaming in high throttle, peeling off to the north.

Hamm fired another four spaced shots, again aiming high over the copse to buy him time to run.

Another series of bullets peppered the Hind's armor. The tire on the other side poofed, went flat, and the chopper settled on a tilt.

He could not hear the timer, but he felt it.

Three hundred yards away, between Canton's semi-crashed Havoc and himself, and out of the blast range, an Mi-24 swept in, punched its landing light for a second, yawned abruptly, and then lowered erratically to the ground, bouncing off the hard soil a couple of times. That would be McDonough.

Immediately, two of the riflemen swung toward Mc-Donough's chopper and opened fire.

Hamm fired another four shots above their heads. "Run, you assholes!"

The return volley was closer to its target this time. One slug whanged off the oleo strut above his head. He heard the drip of hydraulic fluid.

Hamm looked for somewhere to run, scanning the ground in a full circle, but the best cover seemed to be the shrubbery his attackers had already selected.

An AK-74 on full automatic rattled for fifteen seconds,

and he heard a grunt and a high-pitched scream. Then Canton yelled at him, "Come on, Hamm! Let's roll!"

Canton rose out of the darkness, climbing to the rise behind the stunted pines. Hamm saw the silhouette against the plain, the assault rifle held at port arms. He levered himself out from under the Hind and dashed toward Canton, jogging through the ankle-high grass and weeds.

As he passed the copse of pine, he saw the bodies of the three riflemen, fatigue clad, sprawled with arms outstretched. One pair of wide, dead eyes reflected starshine back at him. The mouth was frozen open. Canton ran up beside him, and the two of them trotted toward where McDonough had landed.

"You have to blow them away?" Hamm asked.

"They were holding up Bobby's schedule," Canton panted. "Your schedule now. Shit, I thought you were a better shot, Hamm."

As they neared the idling Hind, Hamm sensed that something was wrong. Thirty yards from the helicopter, when the backlit earth reflected through the cockpit canopy, he saw that McDonough was slumped forward in the cockpit, leaning against the restraint of his harness.

Behind them, the abandoned Mi-24 exploded. A split second after the blast, the concussion pressure tapped him in the back. Glancing over his shoulder, Hamm saw crimson-yellow flames spreading over the airframe. Two of the five rotor blades drooped to the ground.

He had reached the rescue chopper, ducking instinctively as he went under the rotating rotors. Dropping his assault rifle as he banged into the side of the fuselage, he twisted the handle on the cockpit hatch, slid it out of the way, and scrambled up beside the pilot. Over the muffled thrum of the turbine engines, he yelled, "Sean?"

McDonough, hunched forward with his eyes squinched tight in pain, rolled his head toward Hamm. He grunted deep in his throat, then said, "Took . . . some . . . ground fire . . . Steve."

"Let's get you out of there." Hamm eased him back in the seat, found the harness releases, and popped them. "Where?"

"Right . . . side."

McDonough's right shoulder and side were coated with blood. Blood specks were spattered against the seat and side of the cockpit. It gleamed a shiny black in the multi-hued lights of the instrument panel. The Plexiglas on the right side of the cockpit was shattered, and a five-inch hole gaped.

With effort, McDonough raised himself off the seat and rolled his big torso over the coaming. Hamm wrapped his arms around McDonough's shoulders, feeling the hot blood on his hands, helped him get his legs out, got a grip on his belt, and lowered him down to Canton.

In the burning Hind, machine-gun ammo started exploding, an occasional tracer arcing out of the bonfire.

Hamm saw another Hind landing half a mile away and wondered who was putting down.

"What'd you go and do that for?" Canton called to McDonough.

Grimacing, McDonough managed to say, "Keeping up with . . . Bobby's . . . computer."

Shoving back the side door of the main compartment, Hamm crawled into the cargo bay, which was crammed with fuel drums and other stores. Canton eased McDonough into position against the floor sill, Hamm took his shoulders, and the two of them levered the big man up onto the floor.

Canton said, "I'll take it."

"You stay with Sean. I know where I'm going." Hamm stepped across McDonough's body and dropped to the earth. He scrambled up into the pilot's cockpit and buckled in, feeling the moist wetness of McDonough's blood on the back of the seat seeping into his fatigue shirt. Wiping the blood from his hands on the legs of his fatigue trousers, he clamped the headset in place, scanned the panel for indications of damage to major systems, then reached up and advanced the throttles from ground idle through flight idle to the high setting for flight. The turboshafts thrummed, the Hind trembled, rolling forward until he applied brakes. The rotor disk turned silver above him and he gripped the controls.

He pulled in pitch and the heavily loaded Hind struggled off the ground, rotated to the left as he touched rudder, and dipped her nose to the south. He looked for the other Hind he had seen landing and found it taking off again.

Climbing to four hundred feet above the earth, he picked up speed to 140 miles per hour. The other helicopters materialized out of the night, formed on him, and he switched the tactical screen to IR scan and counted exhausts. The count was right.

Camp Castenada was in flames behind him, on his left. As far as he could tell from this distance, the residential area was intact.

He searched the sky, saw what was probably the two cargo planes that had taken off just before the attack. They stayed away, circling to the north. There were no other aircraft in sight. Hamm thought that was amazing. Where in hell were the Hondurans?

Clark's voice came over his earphones. *"¿Uno Bandito?"*

Hamm triggered the mike button on the control stick. *"Es Dos Bandito."*

Clark shut up when he learned McDonough was not in control of the bird, and Hamm concentrated on his flying, climbing gradually as they approached the Montañas de Colon range. The wind shrieked at the hole in the right side of the canopy. He was conscious of the bloody dampness on the back of his right shoulder. He checked his watch against the chronometer readout showing on the Heads Up Display. Both agreed that it was 0114 hours. The attack on Castenada had taken three minutes. Hamm and Canton had been on the ground for seven minutes, four minutes more than planned. The computer would have choked on that, he thought.

Now, more than after the first raid, reactions were going to be important, and he wondered what responses were taking place. The U.S. had declined to enter the melee, so far. Otherwise, he had no doubt that there would have been American night fighters all over them. Certainly, the squadrons at Howard Air Base in Panama had been alerted. No Honduran attack craft had appeared, either. The alarm probably had been sounded in the camp just prior to the attack, and that meant that the Pentagon was monitoring them.

Somebody in the War Room, or maybe the Situation Room, was arguing in their favor, holding off an American response. Pappy, or Daisy Mae, or Li'l Abner? Or maybe it was just indecision? Hamm was certain that Roebuck carried one of the code names, but there were two to go. He was also certain he was running out of time to uncover them. Clark's third attack would be met with a counter-force.

The Rio Coco de Segovia passed below, and Hamm started losing altitude.

He scanned the skies above, and at first saw no evidence of hostile aircraft. No, wait. High to the southwest was a multiengined aircraft, flying with navigation lights. The Nicaraguan AWACS? Far to the west, emerging from behind a mountain peak, was another set of navigation lights. Possibly a commercial jetliner.

He switched on the radar for a count of fifteen, then cut it off, remembering the image. Far out on the edge of the 150-mile scan, toward Tegucigalpa, there were two blips in formation twenty miles to his west.

Taking the Hind down, Hamm found a long valley and scooted along its northern side, hiding from radar. In his mirrors, he saw the others follow his lead.

As long as it was dark, Hamm felt fairly secure in Nicaraguan territory. With the dawn, however, they would have to have crossed the border northward for the last time.

Turning on the map light, he found the chart stuck behind an electrical conduit, its corners flapping in the gusts from the hole in the canopy. He pulled it out, and held it against his thigh. They were now seventy miles west of the fake Camp Ramirez and about six miles south of the border. They had been steadily zigzagging across the border, always moving toward the west. The Pacific coast was 150 miles dead ahead. Tegucigalpa was 125 miles to his right oblique. With the fuel expended on the attack at Camp Castenada, he could not now make a run for the coast without refueling.

"This place is as good as any other place," he decided aloud and to himself. He was beginning to get tired. Fatigued physically, and tired of the whole charade. His arms ached.

There was very little cover for six helicopters in this part of Nicaragua, and anyway, they had abandoned the camouflage netting to save weight. The terrain of the shallow valley was mostly caught by engulfing mountain ranges and wide grassy plains. Hamm dropped to skim the immediate surface, followed by the rest of the choppers and, two minutes later, spotted a stand of trees that jumped out of the night at him.

Cutting off forward speed, he hovered for a moment while he evaluated the area, and then he circled the mini-forest, listening to the rotor thump echo, finally settling down as close to a big mahogany tree as he could get without risking the rotors. He killed the turbines, popped the hatch, and slid out.

The rest of the helicopters landed, one after the other, in a tight semicircle against the trees. As the turbine roar died away, Hamm crawled into the cargo compartment. Canton was sitting on the floor with his back to the bulkhead and his boots lodged against a fuel drum. He had stripped McDonough's shirt away, bandaged his arm, shoulder, and side heavily, and now had his right arm in a sling.

Hamm turned on the red overhead light. "How you doing, hoss?"

McDonough's face looked haggard and sickly in the red tinge of the light. He grinned, though, and the short rest seemed to have revived him somewhat. "I'm tired of Bobby's game. I think I'll take my gun and go home."

"Pat?"

"I think he took two slugs. Either that, or pieces of a heavy slug that fractured. One chunk passed front-to-back through his side, but missed the lung. Otherwise, he'd be coughing blood. The other must have shattered on the armor. His bicep is peppered with fragments. Did some damage to the meat and muscle.''

''Doc says you'll live to regret all of this,'' Hamm said, looking back to McDonough.

''I want a second opinion. And a beer.'' McDonough used his left hand to pull a cigar out of his left breast pocket.

Hamm looked at the fuel drums. ''Don't light that son of a bitch.''

''Nah,'' he said, sticking it in his mouth.

Hamm thought he could hear the whisper of a breeze, but was not sure with the turbine aftermath buzz in his ears. The air smelled of dust and wildflowers.

The rest of the team appeared in the hatchway, Harper babbling something.

''Hey, Clay! Ease up. What's wrong?''

''Jeremy! He got hit!'' Harper's face was grim, and he looked strung out.

Hamm rose off his knees and started out of the compartment. ''How bad?''

''As bad as it gets.''

Hamm sank back to his knees. ''Fuck.''

The silence that followed suggested they were all thinking about Clark's mortality rate.

Peter de Veres finally noticed McDonough and said, ''Damn, Sean. What happened?''

''Earned my hostile-fire pay.''

Hamm brought them up on McDonough's condition, then searched for Cherry's face, ''Hal, you were the last man through. Damages?''

''Three fuel tanks burning, Steve. Seventy-five percent

of the warehouse area was on fire, and the runways were beat to hell. None of the aircraft on the ground were hit that I could see, and I'm hoping that was because everyone saw that they were manned and trying to get off.''

There was a murmur of morbid assent. The adrenaline high of combat was draining off.

"I saw one fire in the personnel area," Hamm said.

"I missed that, Steve."

Bellows said, "And Jeremy. Damn it, I liked Jeremy."

"We knew it could happen," Clark said. "It was part of the deal."

"Your goddamned money better be in those offshore accounts," Keen said. "Jerry's family had better be covered."

"It's there," Clark promised.

Hamm said, "Hal, I want to talk to you in a bit. Right now, let's assess our own damages. Rick, we've got a battle wound on the right side of this bird to check out. Maybe just stick some duct tape on it. The rest of you find a body bag for Pickett, then top off tanks and discard any fuel left over. Rearm with whatever twelve-point-seven and rockets we have left. Spread it among the birds as evenly as you can. Eat something. I want to be off the ground within the hour."

"Sooner, if they find us," Peachy Keen said.

"Hell," Hamm said, "everybody in the hemisphere has to know where we're at by now, or damned close to it. Who's holding them off, Bobby?"

Standing on the ground outside the aircraft, Clark was forced to look up at him. "Friends."

"Besides Roebuck?"

"We have lots of friends, Hamm."

Shit. "What's Target Number Three, Bobby?"

Clark grinned at him. "The American Embassy in Tegucigalpa."

The yellow and red and green and blue blips were clearer now when they appeared on the giant screen. In addition to the information provided by the AWACS out of Guantanamo Bay, the computer had added to the infrared satellite input the data gathered by the radar of the *Eisenhower*'s E-2 Hawkeye early-warning aircraft, now 170 miles from the action, and the cruiser *Virginia*, 135 miles from the Nicaraguan coast in the Caribbean.

The cheering of the military men in the room had been raucous with the apparent downing of two of the attacking helicopters. It had stopped with the scowl of the national security advisor, who had returned midway through the attack.

The lieutenant colonel at the console reported to the JCS chairman. "Admiral, we had two more radio transmissions, but they were brief. Coded IDs in Spanish. They were on HF, in Soviet bands."

A Marine sergeant approached the table, stopping to speak to selected men, then to Kuster and Coriolanus. "General, Mr. Coriolanus, the SecDef would like to see you across the hall."

They left the Situation Room, followed by the suspicious glares of the military chiefs and civilian onlookers.

The small office they crowded into now held the President's chief of staff and the director of central intelligence, in addition to the secretary of defense. Kuster noted that the DCI gave Coriolanus a seering glance that had demotion and perhaps ouster written all over it. Coriolanus was in big trouble.

The President's chief of staff said, "We raised hell with the Soviets."

The advisor asked, "And?"

"They raised hell right back. Accused us of escalating the war. Demanded that we take our forces off alert and get the F-15s out of Honduras. We made the same demands regarding the *Baku*'s aircraft, and we're currently at stalemate. They're not going to back down, gentlemen."

"Any other Soviet alerts?" Kuster asked.

The DCI said, "Nothing overt, but leaves have been canceled for Strategic Rocket Forces, Red Army, and Red Banner Fleet personnel. It doesn't look good, Gene."

"What's the foreign ambassador's attitude?"

"Irate," the chief of staff said. "He insists that this flight of helicopters is an American ruse."

"He knows they're Mils?"

"He knows, and accuses us of the theft of Soviet aircraft. It's still a U.S. stunt intended to escalate the war."

"General Kuster, you're absolutely certain that there were no public dollars involved in this?" the secretary of defense asked.

"Not that my computer man could uncover, sir," Kuster replied. "The accounting in the ALECTO file had no linkages to other CIA or defense funding sources."

"How much?"

"Twenty million."

"So it's private funds, a few mercenaries, and one wayward CIA agent?"

"That's what it looks like to us," the DCI said. "Twelve men."

"That's men on the scene, and I don't want anyone here to count my agent," Kuster said.

"But he's going along with this crap."

"My orders," Kuster said, "and I'll take the responsibility. We've still got three names to uncover, and that's why he's there."

"You're certain of that? Three conspirators?" the secretary of defense asked.

"Yes, sir. The code names are in the file."

"I might get you one of them, Mr. Secretary," Coriolanus said. He stepped to the door and looked out into the hall. "Nolan, get Downs in here."

Two minutes passed, then Harry Downs appeared in the doorway. Coriolanus put a hand on his shoulder, pulled him in, and shut the door.

Kuster thought Downs looked a bit pale around the gills. Downs stood beside the door and felt the heat of the people staring him down. A flush rose along his throat and into his cheeks.

Coriolanus asked, "Harry, are you Daisy Mae?"

Downs's head went back, his lips parted slightly, and his spine stiffened. "What are you talking about, Jack?"

"You heard the question. We've got all of Bobby's ALECTO file."

Downs's lips tightened, his hands curled into fists, and he did not respond.

"Harry, it's now or it's later. You're better off if it's now," Coriolanus told him.

The weight of so many heavy, malevolent eyes finally convinced Downs.

"It's working, isn't it?" The left side of his lips rose in a half smile, and he looked around at the faces that did not smile back. "I don't know what's going on in there, but the right people are excited about it."

"What's working, Harry, is that U.S. and U.S.S.R. forces are on alert. Are you Daisy Mae?"

Downs's eyes went wide, and his lips thinned and tightened over his teeth. "No. I'm Li'l Abner."

"Who are the others?" the national security advisor demanded.

"I don't know. Beyond Bobby."

Kuster believed him. He kept his voice soft, though he felt like shouting. "What was your role in all of this, Harry?"

"Just passing on the data to Jack. Making sure it got where it was supposed to go."

"The pictures and the Cubans?"

"Yes. That's all. The photos were accurate."

Kuster looked at Jack Coriolanus, whose face was clamped in tight planes of anger. "And you made up the Cuban pilots?"

"Bobby made up the Cubans."

"You do any of the fund-raising? Buy any of the ordnance or materiel?"

"No. I told you what I did."

"And I believe you, Harry," Kuster told him.

So did the DCI. "You're under suspension, Downs. Get him out of here, Jack."

Coriolanus opened the door and shoved Downs outside, then closed the door again. His anger was evident in the taut way he held his upper body. His shoulders tended to move with his head.

"You have any suspects, Gene?" Joe Dilman asked.

"Sure, quite a few of them, but none I'm going to mention until I have proof or word from Hamm."

"No matter where we stand on a conspiracy, we still have an immediate problem," the secretary of defense said. "I have to get back to the President with a recommendation on how to handle the Soviets."

"A very immediate problem," the security advisor echoed. "Clark's group is back in Nicaragua, on the ground. Camp Castenada was hit hard. First reports, not yet confirmed, have nine killed in the raid. Esteban Maldonado was one of them."

"Maybe not a loss to the Contra leadership," Dilman evaluated, and Kuster silently agreed.

"I don't have to tell you, I suppose, that one of the options discussed was just to let it ride," the White House chief of staff said. "In his discussions with congressional majority leaders, the President found a lot of outrage. The feeling among White House staff is that these attacks will result in renewed funding for the Contras. On the other hand, the Soviet foreign ambassador has suggested to the President that they feel compelled to defend their ally if we escalate in any way."

"Shit," Dilman said. "They've got to be as addled about this as the Sandinistas must be. They can't know what's going on!"

"Not yet, anyway. Not until the media gets it teeth into it. If any of this leaks to the press, the Soviets will jump on the excuse," the chief of staff said. "I could see retaliatory attacks by MiGs and Forgers against every Contra camp."

"Do we tell the Soviets the real story, and say we'll take care of it?" the SecDef asked.

"Hell, no!" Dilman said. "We use Clark's cover, and tell them we're pissed that Moscow is providing hardware and personnel in support of the Sandinistas. I'd even have the President go to DefCon Three to show our resolve."

"No alerts. But stay tough with the foreign ambassador. After all, we haven't crossed any borders," the NSA said.

"I agree," the DCI said. "The General Secretary isn't looking for a confrontation. It's just the reactionaries in the Politburo and Army that he's saddled with."

"I'll tell the President that," the chief of staff said.

"So we brief everyone across the hall on the actual situation?" the secretary of defense asked.

"That's going to alert Daisy Mae and Pappy," Kuster said.

"Tough," the chief of staff told him. "But, yes, we bring everyone up to date. We can't have our own people working in the dark. And we issue orders to those F-15s that Messenbaum's got in Tegucigalpa. As soon as Clark's raiders cross the line again, we down them. No evidence left behind."

"But I've got Hamm with them!" Kuster blurted out.

"That's tough, too, General."

Josef Zhukov held the phone to his ear and waited for whoever had answered it to fetch the chairman. Zhukov was tired.

The command center was unnaturally silent, the lights dimmed for some reason. Outside, the runway lights seemed brighter. A commercial jetliner taxied into position at the far end. Normal life seemed to go on no matter what intrigues were being played out behind closed doors.

Colonel Ivan Churbanchuk sat at one of the desks, his hands clasped in front of him, his head down, staring at the green blotter.

"Josef Mikhailovich?" The chairman's voice was soothing. Oily.

"Yes, Comrade Chairman."

"So. It has not gone well?"

He very well know exactly how it had gone. "Not well, Chairman."

"And there is a reason for this? A lack of resolve, perhaps?"

"Perhaps." Zhukov could not openly argue. The others in the room did not look at him, but their ears were trained in his direction. "I should have control of our night fighters, Chairman, if I am to reverse the tide."

He was ignored. "Have you ferreted out the identification of this rogue unit, Josef Mikhailovich?"

Zhukov had not even considered such an investigation, did not realize until just then that he had been expected to take on the role of detective. He had been too busy with more pressing matters. "Not as yet, Chairman."

"The helicopters are missing from inventory in Angola. It is not difficult to trace Mi-28 helicopters."

"But how. . . ?"

"A deputy minister of defense will have to be chastised," the chairman told him. "As soon as he provides names and the number of his Swiss bank account."

"I understand, Chairman."

"Failures of character do not advance the cause."

Zhukov wondered just what failures in his own character were being prepared for him. It made him feel weak, and he did not come up with a response before the chairman continued.

"On more pressing matters, I assume from your statement that you wish to use Soviet pilots?"

"The MiG-23 training squadron, Chairman. They are all veterans of Afghanistan. It is imperative that we not allow this ghost squadron again to attack a target in Honduran territory. Already, the radio in Tegucigalpa is inciting the populace, bewailing the death of Esteban Maldonado.'' The words spilled out in a rush as Zhukov found the gap in which to insert them.

''And you do not foresee the Nicaraguan helicopter forces having the ability to contain them?''

''No, Chairman. Intelligence reports arrive by the minute, confirming an alarming buildup of rebel foot soldiers along the border. Minister Demarco feels he must align his forces to repel the attack.''

The KGB chairman sighed deeply. ''Just as alarming is the minister's inability to wage battles on two fronts. Especially when one front is a handful of helicopters.''

''I agree, Chairman. Perhaps if they were not such advanced Soviet aircraft . . . ?''

''Do not attempt to placate me, Major Zhukov. Hold.''

The chairman came back on the line. ''If your phantom helicopters take to the air again, we will order the MiGs to take off. However, Comrade Major, the generals here in this room will give the orders and maintain control of the aircraft. Is that clear?''

''Very clear, Chairman.'' Josef Mikhailovich Zhukov had responsibility for conducting this chess game, but he could not control the pieces.

The aftermath of Bobby Clark's target announcement had taken most of the time. When he identified the American Embassy, after a shocked silence, Peachy Keen had said, ''You're out of your fucking mind, Clark!''

''Not at all,'' Clark responded. ''Can you think of anything—any place—that would more quickly draw intense media and congressional attention? Hell, Peachy, they'll be tripping over themselves to pour millions of dollars into the Contra bucket!''

"What they'll pour into that leaky bucket is American troops," Hal Cherry said.

"Seems to me that some of your wild-eyed operatives tried the shit on the Costa Rican Embassy a while back," Hamm remembered.

"Those guys were jerks with no sense of careful planning," Clark said.

Hamm swung around to face De Veres. In the red light from overhead, De Veres's face seemed contorted. "You've known this from the beginning?"

"Yes."

"And you go along with it?"

"It'll do the job, Hamm. That's the reason I'm here. Let's not fuck up Nicaragua like we did Vietnam."

Hank Bellows spoke up. "We've already had accidents, people dying who weren't supposed to die, according to your goddamned computer."

And maybe not so accidental, Hamm thought, looking at Canton and thinking about the three Contras who had pinned him down.

Canton saw him looking, and grinned back at him.

"The embassy will be evacuated, completely deserted," Clark said. "We'll be going in on an empty target."

"Now, how in the hell do you accomplish that?" Hamm asked, not believing him in the least.

"A coded message on a prearranged frequency, half an hour before we go in."

"And everybody scoots out on your say-so?"

"It's arranged, Hamm."

"Who arranged it?" Hamm asked.

"You don't have a need to know."

Hamm sat back on his haunches in the cramped compartment and eyed Clark. "I'm going to have the name, rank, and serial number, right now, or we saddle up and see if we can't find a Pacific Ocean."

Clark glared at him for a long time, then changed his mind and came up with a general's name.

"Well, hell! That's the man that could do it," Cherry said.

And it was true. Hamm knew him. Now he had a second name.

"Anyone have a comment?" Hamm asked.

There was nothing specific.

"How about you, Sean?"

"Hell, it's on the way. Let's stop in for a drink."

"All right, then. Gas 'em up."

As he had done with all of Clark's tactical plans, Hamm went through it carefully, checking charts, timing, chopper positions. He made his changes, and then he walked around and covered the changes with each team member. He put Canton alone in a Havoc and moved Canton's co-pilot, Talbot, into Pickett's seat in a Hind. He figured that, without a gunner, Canton might do less damage.

Hamm took off first, with an insistent Sean McDonough in the gunner's cockpit of his Havoc. When Hamm had suggested that McDonough might be more comfortable riding in the back of a Hind, he had clinched his big left fist, then raised one thick forefinger out of the fist. "This's all I need to punch a fucking trigger!"

It had taken longer than an hour to refuel and lay out the mission, but they had not seen any hostiles, Nicaraguan or Honduran. While the team members pumped fuel with the hand pumps and examined airframes for damage, Hamm went around to each team, making new aircraft assignments, changing codes, and evaluating each man for signs of fatigue or lack of concentration.

Talbot and Bellows had located more battle damage than had been apparent. Nicks in rotors that were not serious. A radar dome pierced with shrapnel, and the radar shot out on Vaquero Five. Small-arms fire had dented, pitted, and dinged the fuselage skins of all of the helicopters, but necessary wiring, hydraulic lines, and controls were all in operation.

They were off the ground at five minutes after three, moving fast on a heading for Palmerola Air Base. The bearing was intended to be deceptive on any radar scanners that picked them up. At the last moment, they would veer off toward Tegucigalpa.

"How you doing up there, Sean?" Hamm asked over the intercom.

There was pain in the tone when McDonough replied. "I know I've got an arm. It's a bigger arm than I thought it was."

"Take a pain pill."

"No. I want to be alert for this. Shit, Steve, I've been in worse condition."

"Don't be a damned hero."

"Just can't help myself, babe. You know I've always been a hero."

Hamm reached out and dialed in a new frequency on the radio, then hit the mike button. "Tango Two."

On the intercom, McDonough said, "Who you calling?"

"Old girl friend." He hit the button again. "Tango Two."

# TWENTY-SIX

A lieutenant at a telephone console called to him. "General Kuster. You have a call on line six."

Kuster pulled opened the drawer in front of his chair, punched the button on one of the two phones, and picked up. "Kuster."

"Eddie Constantine, General. NSA, Supervisor, Southern Hemisphere."

"Go ahead."

"I have standing orders to call you if I get a certain message on a certain Soviet-only frequency."

"That's correct."

"I have the message. It's just two names."

"That's all I need, Eddie."

Kuster got the Tango Two message at 0215 hours, Washington time. He was half-surprised by its contents, but wrote the two names down on a memo pad.

Sliding the pad sideways, he showed the names to Coriolanus.

The special assistant, who had been watching him in some trepidation, said, "No shit?"

"No shit."

"From Hamm?"

"That's right."

He checked the electronic map. Clark's helicopters had crossed the border once again and were on a course for Palmerola. It was a tough target, but a logical one for media impact, which was the way Clark seemed to be thinking. He asked the lieutenant colonel, "What's the ETA at Palmerola?"

The lieutenant colonel tapped calculator buttons. "Indicated airspeed is one eighty-five knots. About forty-two minutes, General. Zero two five seven hours."

The whole atmosphere in the room had changed once the national security advisor had identified Clark's mercenary pilots as the strike force out of Nicaragua.

"What's the goddamned purpose?" Senator Harley Havechuk had shouted.

"I imagine, Senator, to change public opinion."

General Delmar Williams, in a chair at the side of the room, spoke up, "We can't go shooting down our own people. No matter their motives. Hell, as far as that goes, the motives are all right."

"Well, shit!" Josh Simpson put in. "We can't let the Soviets shoot them down, either."

The Marine commandant agreed. "Let 'em ride on through. The outcomes will be okay. Maybe the damned Soviets will listen up."

For once, Jason Roebuck had nothing to say.

Havechuk and his aide conferred a moment, then started for the door.

The room was unnaturally quiet and Aaron Messenbaum's voice louder as a result. "Are you leaving the building, Senator Havechuk?"

"Yes."

"Then, I'll send a couple of Marines with you."

"The hell you will!"

"As a matter of national security, I have those orders from the President."

The senator looked around, but saw only the chairman of the Joint Chiefs nod in agreement.

Havechuk sat down, angry and red-faced. He would not get to chat with his favorite reporters.

Now the map showed that the fighters out of Managua, identified as MiG-23s, were five minutes from the border. Kuster wondered if the border would stop them.

The Eagles had departed Palmerola. "Intercept time for the F-15s?" he asked.

"Eleven minutes, sir."

"Come on, Jack." Kuster tapped Coriolanus on the shoulder, and the two of them went around the table to interrupt a conversation between the national security advisor and the secretary of defense. He set the notepad on the table between them.

"You're certain?" the secretary asked.

"Absolutely."

Glancing up at the map, the secretary said, "How much time do we have?"

"Eleven minutes. Less than that, sir."

Opening the drawer in front of him, the secretary of defense grabbed a red phone. It was a short conversation, and when he hung up, he conferred briefly with the chairman of the Joint Chiefs, then surveyed the crowd in the room, all of whom were glued to the map.

Spotting Roebuck's intelligence aide, the secretary of defense said, "Mr. Davis?"

The aide looked up. "Sir?"

"You are to leave the room immediately."

"Sir!"

"Right now, Davis," the national security advisor affirmed.

Jason Roebuck took exception. "Now, just a goddamned minute. . . . "

"Senator Roebuck, the President would like to see you in his office as soon as you can get there. Sergeant Evans will accompany you." The advisor tilted his head toward the Marine at the door.

Roebuck started to argue, his face darkening with menace, took another look at the map, and strode out of the room. The door was opened for him by Evans, and his assistant trundled after him.

Everyone else in the Situation Room now sported raised eyebrows.

General Delmar Williams looked as puzzled as anyone there, Kuster thought.

The secretary of defense said, "General Parch, will you come with us?"

Kuster followed the small but powerful group out into the hall. He was beginning to believe that more crises were being handled in the hallway than in the Crisis Center. The SecDef did not bother crossing to the vacant office. He stopped in the middle of the corridor and, as soon as the Marine sergeant who had replaced Evans shut the door, turned on Parch. "I want to know Clark's target, General, and I want to know it now."

Parch let wonder cross his rugged face, but it was patently false wonder and a sudden muscle tic appeared below his left eye.

Admiral Dilman spoke. "As of this minute, Mike, I have to place you under house arrest."

"What the fuck's going on?" Parch asked.

"The target!" the SecDef insisted.

"You've got to call off those Eagles," Parch said, abandoning pretense. "Let the choppers through."

"Nothing is changing unless you tell me the target."

Parch's proud shoulders slumped. "Tegoose. The American Embassy."

"Jesus Christ, Mike!" the JCS chairman shouted. "What in the hell were you thinking about?"

"Let 'em through, Joe. It's all planned out."

"How?" The national security advisor demanded.

"The embassy will be all but vacated by the time they get there, and the choppers will only do minimal damage. I've got two squads of Marines standing by at Tegoose, with twenty Stinger SAMs. Every one of those helicopters is going down. There won't be shit left of them. But after the headlines are made, damn it!"

"You bastard!" Kuster lost his temper. "Clark doesn't know what you have waiting, does he?"

Parch did not reply.

"Return to your quarters, Mike, and await further instructions," Dilman ordered.

Parch came to stiff attention, saluted, turned on his heel, and marched away down the hall. Once again, his shoulders were stiff in pride.

"Time to intercept?" The secretary of defense asked.

Kuster checked his watch. "Five-point-five minutes."

"The President has told the General Secretary that we will shoot down his MiGs if they cross the border. Admiral, you be ready for that. What are the other alternatives?"

Kuster jumped at the chance. "Let the Hondurans know what's going on, hold off the Eagles for now, and make sure the embassy is evacuated."

"Why?"

"To give Hamm a chance to act."

"What makes you think he'll do anything?" Dilman asked.

"Because he got me those names, and because he's never failed to act in the past. You know that, Joe."

"And what do you think he can do?" the national security advisor wanted to know.

"Hell, I don't know."

The secretary of defense turned to Coriolanus. "What's the CIA's position?"

"I don't like Hamm much, but I'd give him a shot at it," Coriolanus said.

"I'll agree," the director of central intelligence said. "Until the last three minutes."

"Christ. I can't make a decision without knowing outcomes! I've got to clear it with the President." The SecDef did not look well.

"That's all right," Kuster said. "The President has gone with Hamm before."


The radar link with the air control and command plane was showing the MiG fighters just crossing the border into Honduras. "Two minutes to contact with the helicopters," Churbanchuk estimated.

Zhukov was more interested in the American interceptors. "The F-15s have broken off!" The intercept course was now against the Soviet jet aircraft.

"They're coming after our airplanes!" Demarco said.

"Go!" Colonel Churbanchuk shouted. "Our pilots will rip them apart!"

As they had in Syria and Libya, Zhukov recalled. Of course, those planes had not been piloted by Soviet personnel. He felt a sense of whirling chaos enter his mind.

He had no control. His beloved Nicaragua was about to erupt in a major war.

As Zhukov watched, the blips representing the MiGs abruptly swung left, then circled back toward the border at speed. The F-15s trailed them for a minute, then turned off at the border. Moscow Center had called them off.

Demarco sighed.

"You are disappointed, Manuel?"

"I am very relieved."

"Until the helicopters reach a target," Zhukov pointed out. "Then will come the blame. And the retaliation."

Telephones began to ring.

After the first few were answered, it was apparent that some six or seven Nicaraguan outposts were under heavy fire by ground troops.

General Suarez took over. "This is my area. You experts of the air may have lost many battles for us, but I will win the war."

Major Pavel Prabinovski stepped forward. "I will be happy to assist you, General."

Suarez waved him away, "You have been too much help already, Comrade Major."

McDonough used the intercom to relay his reading of the radar scope. "Break off! Break off! They've turned away, Hamm. They had to be MiGs."

"Where they headed, Sean?"

"Back home, tails between their legs. Those Hondurans out of Palmerola are chasing them."

"Keep an eye on the Hondurans. They may come back on us."

"Roger that."

Hamm took a deep breath. It might only be a momen-

tary respite. Once their final course toward Tegucigalpa
was identified by the Hondurans, there would be more
than four planes flying against them. He had to keep the
threat, as it appeared on Palmerola radar screens, balanced. Or hope that Parch and Roebuck were arguing in
Clark's favor. Shit, maybe he had sent the message to Kuster too early?

"The Hondurans are riding the border now," Mc-
Donough reported.

"Good. How's the arm?"

"What arm? Can I stay with the radar now?"

"Hell, yes. Everyone in our world knows where we are,
anyway." Hamm turned on his own tactical screen and
cut in the radar. Blips were showing up everywhere.

After several minutes, McDonough came back. "I've
got another six aircraft taking off from Palmerola."

"The future looks dimmer, Sean."

Hamm concentrated on his flying for a while, frequently
checking his radar scope and his mirrors for the other
helicopters. Everyone was staying in formation, relying on
the leader.

Off to the east, the first streamers of dawn were poking
around the mountain peaks. Streaks of light shot across
the plain below.

"What the hell would we have done if the MiGs had
jumped us?" McDonough asked.

"Put these hummers on the ground and run like hell."

"That's still a damned good option," McDonough said.
"I'll throw up my good arm and play prisoner of war."

"And one we may still have to use. I'm surprised that
Bobby Clark's buddy in the Pentagon has been able to hold
off an intercept."

"He's a goddamned chief of staff. Can you believe it?"

"Position?"

McDonough checked his chart. "See those few lights ahead on your left? That's Danli. We're seventeen minutes out of Tegoose at a hundred eighty knots. Right now, you'd need a bearing of two-seven-two."

"The coast?"

"Thirty-six minutes for the Hinds, putting the pedal down. Heading two-two-eight."

Hamm rolled left until his gyrocompass readout centered on 272. Checking, he found that the others had followed him. He waited four minutes, then broke the radio silence he had himself imposed. "Vaqueros. Jaguar."

With the code word, Cherry, Bellows, and Talbot broke out of the formation and took up the new heading, their speed climbing to 190 miles per hour.

As soon as he saw them slide off, Hamm slowed his forward speed and quickly climbed a hundred feet. Both De Veres and Canton shot by below him, pulling into the lead with their Havocs.

Hamm moved in behind Canton.

McDonough said, "I've got my Quad TV sights on Canton."

Back on the ground, Hamm and McDonough had agreed that Canton was the most dangerous.

Clark was so flabbergasted by the sudden shifts, he used English on the radio. "What the hell's going on?"

Bobby Clark sat in the nose of the Havoc, spinning his head left and right. Canton was on the right. The Hinds were nearly out of sight already. In a moment of unreasonable panic, he snapped the transmit button down. "Come back here! You bastards! Come back!"

There was no response.

Clark keyed the mike again. "Bandito Two! What's going on?"

Hamm came back to him in the earphones. "Time to go home. You can read the radar. We've got ten speedy aircraft that don't like us. Go to two-two-nine, Bandito Three. Bandito Five conform. I'll follow you."

The son of a bitch was ruining everything. Just when he had it all in hand. Minutes from being over.

Canton's voice came in. "Bandito Four here. Your choice, man."

The sun was much brighter, peeping over the mountains, and throwing bas-relief shadows that mesmerized him whenever Bobby looked down.

Tegucigalpa was a scattering of morning lights dead ahead. It looked very far away.

Peter de Veres spoke to him on the intercom. "He's probably right, Bobby. Those UFOs are bound to be Honduran F-4s. It's not likely we're going to cross the city limits. There's been too much forewarning."

"But this is the big one! The one that kicks 'em all in the balls."

"What's it going to be?" Hamm asked them.

Clark weighed the possibilities. "Hamm might be right. We might not make it."

Peter de Veres laughed, tinny in the headphones. "Somebody has to fulfill the predictions, right? That doesn't matter, either."

"You all right?"

"Hell, I was behind you from the beginning, and I'm behind you now. I feel good, Bobby. We going, or not?"

"Let's go!" Clark told him. Major General Robert Clark would never have given up at this point.

And Peter de Veres got down to business. He hit the mike button. "Bandito Five. Take out Bandito Two."

In a flash, Canton's Havoc disappeared, trailing ineffective tracers from McDonough.

Canton did not ever bother to reply to Peter de Veres.

Hamm rolled right, trying to stay on Canton's tail. The 12.7-millimeter Quad chukkered, shaking the airframe, as McDonough traversed the turret, chasing the Havoc with green tracers and the low-light TV lens.

Abruptly, Canton hauled his Havoc back, climbing almost straight up.

Hamm shot by underneath him.

Canton suddenly cut pitch and dropped like a stone, and then he was behind them, in hot pursuit. Hamm's earphones blared, "Hamm, you asshole! I've been waiting for this!"

Hamm barrel-rolled the Mi-28 Havoc, wondering if it had ever been done before. As they rolled over the top, McDonough shouted, "Motherfucker!"

Two Swatters slashed by, trailing spits of flame. These were apparently on infrared-seeking, and having missed their IR source, they arced toward the earth, chasing an unfortunate stakebed truck that was out too early in the morning.

Hamm banked tightly to the right and felt the G-forces build, pushing him down in the seat.

Canton went by on the left, outmaneuvered by their unexpected roll to the left.

"Fucker!" McDonough yelled. "He hit a truck!"

Hamm swung in behind him, diving when Canton dove. "Rockets, Sean!"

A dozen rockets spewed out of the pods, converging on the diving Havoc, but too high, Hamm thought.

Canton misjudged the ballistics. He pulled out of the dive, to allow the rockets to pass under, but rose directly into their path.

Four of the rockets ripped into the Havoc. One passed through the fuselage skin from above and slammed into the under-floor fuel cell.

The Havoc exploded in a bright orange ball.

Hamm nearly went into another roll, this one inadvertent, as he tried to avoid the debris, and when he righted the chopper, he had lost track of De Veres and Clark.

"Give me a target, Sean!"

"Jesus Christ! Hold on! I'm still drying out my seat. Radar says go to two-seven-one."

Hamm followed the gyrocompass around, glancing down to his own radar scan.

"They've got two miles on us, Chief. I think they're climbing."

Hamm began to climb. "ETA the embassy?"

"Eight minutes. We're over Tegoose in five."

"Weapons status?" Hamm spotted the Havoc ahead, its rotor shining silver in the low morning sun.

"Two thousand rounds of twelve-point-seven. Sixteen rockets. Two AT-2s."

Hamm was using all the power he had available, but so was De Veres, and the gap did not close.

"No way we're going to catch 'em, Steve. We've got the same machine."

"But they're climbing," Hamm said.

He put the nose down and entered a shallow dive at full power, finding more airspeed than the climbing Havoc would be capable of.

The Havoc's top end speed was supposed to be 186 miles per hour. The airspeed indicator showed him 195.

"We have a mile of separation," McDonough told him seconds later.

"Now seven hundred yards."

"Use the radio," Hamm ordered. The AT-2 Swatter had both infrared homing and radio control.

"Roger."

Hamm pulled the nose up, and McDonough launched one missile, guiding it by radio. Hamm watched, almost in slow motion, as the Swatter streaked upward, climbed too high, corrected, then whooshed into the Havoc.

A brilliant red-orange-silver drowned the dawn as the helicopter detonated.

"You're now an ace," Hamm told his gunner.

"For about fifteen seconds," McDonough called back. "We have company."

Hamm looked left and found an F-15 Eagle almost foundering, trying to match his speed.

The pilot stared at him.

Hamm waved, then lost speed, and the Eagle had to throttle up to avoid a stall.

Another F-15 went by fast enough to rock them in its turbulent wake, and Hamm turned off to a southerly heading, away from the capital city, terminating the threat.

"Those are goddamned U.S. birds," McDonough said.

"Maybe we were closer to it than we thought," Hamm said.

"You want to just get us to the closest bar?"

"I'm looking," Hamm said.

He bypassed Tegucigalpa by fifteen miles and headed for the sea. The F-15s were joined by Honduran F-4s, but they all left him alone, escorting the chopper with large, lazy circles. Somebody, somewhere, was greasing the rails. Still, Hamm did not feel entirely reprieved until he passed over the surf and began looking for his rendezvous.

Five miles out to sea, the fighters abandoned them.

McDonough was looking for the yacht, too, and seven minutes later, told him, "Got 'em on radio direction. Come to three-five-one."

Six minutes later, they spotted the yacht, waiting dead in the water. A two-million-dollar Hind was just sinking off its port quarter. A dinghy with an outboard motor was racing around the mother ship, collecting swimmers.

"Get out of your harness, Sean." Hamm unclipped his own seat and shoulder straps.

"Done, Chief!"

"Hatches," he called as he settled the Havoc toward the water. There was a two-foot chop to the sea, a minor whitecapping. He unlatched his own cockpit hatch.

"Done. Kill her."

When the wheels touched the surface, Hamm reached up and shut down the turbine throttles, then killed everything electric.

The Havoc lowered into the sea, perched for a moment, then let hell break loose. She canted sideways, the rotors caught the waves, and everything jumped sideways, rotors shattering.

Hamm was thrown against the right side, stunning him. He shook his head as the cockpit began to fill with water, then grabbed the coaming and pulled himself out into the warm green water.

Within a minute, he was looking up at an extended hand. "Right here, Hamm."

"Hello, Blue."

# DEBRIEFING

# TWENTY-SEVEN

At the Managua airport, Josef Zhukov watched while his luggage was trundled out to the Aeroflot Ilyushin. He wore a light gray suit, he perspired freely, and he knew he was going to miss it. The heat of Moscow was not the same as the heat of Managua.

Manuel Demarco stood next to him at the chain-link fence. He smiled hugely. "You could always defect, Josef."

Unthinkable. One did not defect from the KGB. "I trust that is a joke."

"Of course, a joke."

An embassy car pulled up behind them, and Ivan Churbanchuk and Pavel Prabinovski got out. The driver also got out to open the trunk and unload their suitcases.

"It will become more difficult for you, Manuel."

"I suspect as much."

"Moscow is not happy with the way things have turned out. The U.S. Congress is discussing renewed assistance—though that will be couched in humanitarian terms."

"Yes," Demarco said, "and at the same time, our aid from the U.S.S.R. will dwindle."

"Disunity always makes the Politburo uneasy. They cannot understand lack of control."

"What disunity? We have insisted that there was never a rebellious faction within our own ranks."

"But that is what they believe," Zhukov said. "Someone in Nicaragua purchased helicopters and defied your authority, threatening everything you have built up here. They could well have turned on you and mounted a coup if they had survived."

"It is nonsense!"

"Certainly. But I and your other advisors are being recalled."

"Completely circumstantial!" Demarco insisted.

"There is reliable information from Washington. That is what I have been told."

"And why is Washington always more reliable than Managua?"

Perhaps because you have been caught in so many lies, Josef Zhukov thought, but did not say it. "The airplane is ready. I must go."

They embraced, and Zhukov slipped through the gate to join Churbanchuk and Prabinovski. As they walked toward the airliner, he hoped that the "just reward" mentioned in his recall was not a desk on the Kamchatka Peninsula.

\* \* \*

After some consideration, they had buried Jerry Pickett at sea, with Nelson Cameron presiding, reading from a rarely opened Bible.

They had also buried every last vestige of Bobby Clark's adventure at sea, from fatigues to K-Bars and sidearms, though Cameron had been very interested in acquiring the small weapons. Hamm liked having his own clothes and his own passport back.

The team members took a lot of saltwater showers aboard the seventy-foot yacht, fished away the daylight hours, and pokered through the nights for six days on the northward journey.

Blue Monday was a self-taught battle surgeon. He spent three hours with a pair of tweezers, picking pieces of the shattered bullet out of McDonough's arm and shoulder, using lots of purple iodine. He pronounced the bullet track through McDonough's side clean, and McDonough believed him.

Of course, McDonough believed the world was good as long as there was an endless supply of Corona, as there seemed to be.

They arrived in Mazatlan on a bright, sunny morning, and departed the yacht to obtain tourist visas. As a matter of first priority, most of them crowded the telephone banks in the marina office and called their Cayman Island banks to verify that Clark had actually made the promised deposits.

He had.

"That's a relief," Peachy Keen said, his pate gleaming under a sheen of sweat. "That means Jerry's family's taken care of."

"I'm getting a cab for the airport. Anyone want to ride with me?" Hank Bellows said.

Except for Hamm, they were all going, and they flagged three cabs immediately. The good-byes were tenuous. They had seen combat together, and they had survived. They promised reunions that would not happen.

"You need the Navy again, Hamm, give me a call," Hal Cherry said.

McDonough was the last to get in. "Hey, Steve. It's been more or less grand."

"More or less," Hamm agreed. "Take care, Sean, and don't spend that money where they can see it."

"No. Some cash gifts to my boy, to keep him in college. Work some of it into the business. You ever get out my way?"

"Bakersfield? Who goes to Bakersfield?" Hamm grinned.

"Try San Francisco, and then give me a call."

"Sure."

They shook hands, McDonough dropped into his seat, and the cabbie swore at the traffic, then leaped and lurched away from the curb.

Hamm found another taxi, tossed his case on the backseat, and crawled in. He had never been to Mazatlan before, and took a guess, "You know where the best beachfront hotel is?"

*"Si, señor."*

"Let's find it."

Crossing the wide lobby, Hamm checked in with a demand for a seaside, extra-large accommodation. It was granted quickly, and he took the elevator to the seventh floor and opened his door. Looking around the gold-and-blue room, with its king-size bed, he decided he could stay for a while.

Room service delivered a bucket of ice and a bottle of Chivas Regal. He carried the bucket and bottle out onto the lanai. The cushioned chair next to the phone looked comfortable. The sea was an azure blue, with fluffy cumulus clouds low and white on the horizon. Directly below him was the swimming pool, enclosed by a sea of tanned flesh and tiny pastel bikinis. He poured three fingers and sipped it while leaning on the railing and trying to identify which were the secretaries and elementary school teachers taking advantage of low summer rates in Mexico, finally deciding that all of them were.

After necessary reconnaisance, he sat down and called the Consolidated Bank of the Cayman Islands, identifying himself by his account number. He was switched around until he found the vice-president he wanted. "Yes, sir?"

"I need a couple of transactions taken care of."

"Of course."

"First, charge my account a hundred thousand dollars and wire the amount to Amnesty International. The gift is to be anonymous."

"Yes, sir. It will be done."

"Second. There was a man killed in Honduras a few days ago. The newspapers and radio said he had a wife and two children living in Detroit. The name is Jessup."

"I can get the details for you, sir."

"As soon as you do, send the wife fifty thousand dollars. I want it to look like it's coming from an insurance company, so she doesn't have to pay taxes."

"I know a way," the vice-president assured him.

Hamm hung up, deciding to leave the last $100,000

right where it was. Good field men in any intelligence service always had a few accounts lying around for emergencies. This would be his eleventh account.

Then he called Kuster and caught him in the office.

"Where the hell are you?"

"I'm in retirement, remember?"